THE MONTAGUE TUBES

THE KIDNAPPING ANNA TRILOGY: BOOK 3

A. B. ALVAREZ

BRUSHED STEEL BOOKS, INC

To All The Fathers
Who Did What They Had To Do
And
To All The Daughters
Who Still Loved Them
(Eventually)
But Especially
To Lindley

FREE DOWNLOAD!

Get a free ebook copy of Part Two of the *Kidnapping Anna Trilogy, Kidnapping Anna: ADX Florence*, and a selection of short stories, after downloading the *A. B. Alvarez Reader* by going to https://www.abalvarez.com/free-book-en/!

The Boy and the Nettles

A BOY was stung by a Nettle. He ran home and told his Mother, saying, "Although it hurts me very much, I only touched it gently."

"That was just why it stung you," said his Mother. "The next time you touch a Nettle, grasp it boldly, and it will be soft as silk to your hand, and not in the least hurt you."

Whatever you do, do with all your might.

Aesop's Fables
Translated by George Fyler Townsend (1887).

NEW RIVER TUNNEL OPENED

Whitehall Street-Montague Street Tube "Holed Through."

The north heading of the Whitehall Street-Montague Street subway tunnel under the East River was "holed through" at 10:30 o'clock yesterday morning. The last blast, removing the five feet of Coenties Reef between the Manhattan and Brooklyn headings was fired by Fred Mitchell, foreman of the Flinn-O'Rourke Company, Inc., the contractors. The excellence of the engineering work was proved when it was found that the two headings came exactly together. Immediately after the blast those present walked through the tunnel to the Brooklyn side.

...

The contract for the tube "holed through" yesterday was signed by the Public Service Commission on July 16, 1914. The work is to be completed early next year. The contract price was $5,974,809.

The New York Times
Published: June 3, 1917
Copyright The New York Times

PROLOGUE

October 27, 2012

The Skies above Virginia

After three years as a naval aviator, Lieutenant Commander Theola Cason barely heard the constant high-pitched whine in her cockpit from the twin supersonic jet engines that pushed her through the sky like electricity through wire.

"Avenger, we have a visual."

"Do you have a clear shot?"

"Affirmative. I have a clear shot."

"Do not engage. Repeat: do not engage."

The oxygen mask felt snug against her face and the inbound compressed air kept her nostrils cold and her mouth dry while she kept her bearings on the target in her heads-up display.

Her cockpit gave her everything she needed to do her job. Today her job was to follow and destroy a multi-billion-dollar test plane. She wasn't sure what to make of the F35-C Lighting II VTOL (Vertical Liftoff and Landing) fighter jet that she and her fellow test pilot, Lieutenant Lucien Aguirre, were chasing, but whatever was happening was not good. *Do not engage? When the hell are we supposed to shoot that thing down?*

They were going to be over the continental U.S. soon, and that meant the risk to civilian lives superseded shooting down the rogue aircraft. They had no problem catching up. But when could they bring it down?

"Avenger."

This was the call sign of the USS George H.W. Bush aircraft carrier that Cason and Aguirre had just left off the coast of North Carolina.

"Permission to terminate the target."

Just let me shoot it down.

"Negative, negative. Continue pursuit."

———

The plane before Cason, an F35-C Lighting II, flew across the clear blue afternoon skies of Virginia slower than the Super Hornets, but neither chase plane could take the chance of shooting it down now that it was over a populated area. The F35-C was a new jet meant to replace the aging Harrier fleet of less than three hundred that had been in service since 2003, but its level of lethality was much higher. Once armed, it carried missiles that could obliterate a neighborhood in seconds.

Today the F35-C had no missiles.

Civilian Air Traffic Control at Reagan, Dulles, and BWI had yet to be told of the unauthorized incursion into civilian air space. It didn't matter: the plane was stealth so they wouldn't have seen it anyway.

———

Thirty minutes earlier the Lighting II, parked on the deck of the USS George H.W. Bush, had its surrounding footprint cleared by the ground crew when the plane began moving. The aircraft carrier, over 1000 feet long, could go for twenty years without refueling due to its twin nuclear reactors. The busy asphalt-colored deck had about two hundred people performing everything from flight prepping to trash tossing for the day's tests. When the Lightning II began to taxi, no one had worked on the plane at all.

———

The plane entered the airspace of Ararat, Virginia and circled downward. The Hornets could do nothing but follow. Their biggest disadvantage was that the Lightning could hover like a helicopter while the Hornets had to circle. Like sharks, they had to keep moving or face death. There was no way for them to do anything but shoot it down once they had the go-ahead. The good news was that the area around Ararat was mostly unpopulated. The bad news: No one knew what the plane would do next.

———

The guidance system of the F35-C was the most advanced of its kind, though variations of the Lighting II used the same avionics. The new models would have to go through their own testing and validation, but the pilot didn't care. The heads-up display told them everything they needed to know: proximity to target.

The pilot spotted the house surrounded by all the trees. The plane sank with no thought of the g-forces involved. It turned toward the forest and positioned the house behind it. It fired at the base of the trees and they all fell as if cut by a large knife. The plane was going to need the extra room to position itself properly.

———

"Shots fired. I repeat. Shots fired." Cason was getting frustrated. "Permission to engage."

What the hell were they waiting for?

"Are there casualties?"

"Not at this time, Avenger."

"Do not engage. Do not engage."

———

With the trees down, the F35-C lowered itself closer to the ground and turned 180 degrees toward the house. The pilot engaged the infrared system and swung the plane back and forth to get a full view within the house.

The infrared signature was cold. The house had to be at least 6000 square feet. White vinyl siding. No solar panels on the dark charcoal roof.

No one home.

There were two SUVs parked a distance from the domicile and men ran from them toward the hovering jet. The men fired their handguns at the aircraft with no effect. The pilot felt time running out but didn't really care. As messages went, this one was pretty clear.

Besides, the F35-C had something the security detail didn't: a directed-energy solid state laser that had been in the works since 2003 and used in combat since 2010. The laser, powered by the jet's own engines, needed no external battery or cooling source. The fuel tanks dissipated the generated heat.

The laser turret lowered from under the aircraft and fired two four-second bursts. The security detail outside the house saw nothing except the sudden burst of explosions within the house as gas lines caught fire and the house began exploding first from the north side then the basement.

The fire spread from one end of the house to the other. The Lightning II fired two more laser bursts after waiting the requisite thirty seconds to recharge.

The home began to collapse.

———

The plane came down hard on its landing gear, which had extended just seconds before, and sat on the verdant manicured lawn. The local Ararat police force, all two vehicles, came racing up the road as the security detail of General Malik Palma ran to the plane and climbed onto the wings of the F35-C Lightning II that sat like a hood ornament on the lawn of Palma's second home. The building was engulfed in flames. With his gun at the ready, one of the combat-experienced men assigned to protect the perimeter of the house, ran across the wing up to the cockpit yelling for the pilot to come out with his hands up. The engines spun down.

The cockpit was empty.

———

Anna Wodehouse closed her notebook, severing the remote connection to the aircraft.

That was for you, Dad.

PART I
MARSHALL

1

PRUDENT RAINBOW

September 2005

Marshall Wodehouse washed his hands in the sink of the tiny bathroom of the Del'rio Diner, doing his best not to waste the scalding water. The Del'rio was his favorite since he and Anna had moved to Brooklyn in 2003. The white-tiled, single person room had black edging about two-thirds of the way up the wall, and an unidentifiable color going up the remaining third to what he was sure was a white ceiling. The aroma of industrial cleaners bothered him, but the patina of clean made him happy.

Getting to Kings Highway and West 12 Street was a bit inconvenient from where he and Anna lived, but since it was walking distance from the Kings Highway stop of the N train it never bothered him. It was one of his few guilty pleasures, and he knew he would hear about it later from his rather precocious and protective little girl. They went almost everywhere together and a trip to the diner on his own was unheard of.

Anna had a math contest that evening and she preferred that he not attend. She thought it bad enough that she was going to be in public at all; she didn't need her father there to embarrass her even more. Marshall smiled into the mirror. If he embarrassed Anna, he could imagine how she would have been with Ingrid. If her mother hadn't passed, Anna would have been unable to hold her back at events like that. Ingrid was a shy, unassuming woman, but expecting her to contain her excitement, especially for all things Anna, was like expecting fireworks to sound dull and give off monochromatic droopy flashes.

It was hard not to love their child.

He dried his hands with the rough, brown paper towels from the dispenser on the wall and carefully placed the crumpled tissue in the trash. It was time for breakfast, and he was ready, even though it was 7 pm. The waitresses knew his routine, knew enough to leave him alone even when he was there by himself. Marshall was pleasant enough, but he had a lot on his mind with Anna, and making suffi-cient money to see them through the month.

When he exited the bathroom, he stopped. The air was warmer in the diner than in the men's room. He had rolled up his sleeves as soon as he'd seated himself and walked to the back. The hair on his arms felt clammy. Something had changed. He peered in the dark area toward the back. There had been a lot of people in the diner when he'd journeyed to the men's room. Some at the standalone square tables of the main dining area and a few in the booths toward the back, but now they were all deserted.

His brain ticked off the exits: the front door, and one toward the back that led to the street and the rear of the building. It would take him about ten steps to get to the back exit if the sudden disappear-ance of the general population warranted it.

How long had he been in the men's room? Five minutes?

A voice called out. "Marshall!"

God damn it! Marshall took off to the rear exit. As soon as he pushed opened the door, he found himself face-to-face with two large men. Neither moved and he suspected that his rather small frame would not move them either. In another life, he would have taken them both down, but that was not now. Not this life.

He let the door close as he re-entered the diner. It was dark where he stood. He walked toward the light.

The outline of the man in the chair was unmistakable. Marshall hated that the first thing he had done was run, but his brain was wired to know when to freeze, fight, or take flight. The warm air still had the mixed scent of food and fragrance. Marshall walked around the table and sat down in front of Malik Palma. Both men looked at each other and said nothing. The first thing he noticed was that Palma's hair had receded much more than he remembered. A file folder lay ignored on the table.

"Good evening," Palma said.

Marshall, unblinking, looked him in the eyes. "I'm going to say this once. If you make me repeat it, I will come over this table and your men will have to pull me off you.

"Go away."

Palma crossed his arms and grunted. "You won't have to repeat yourself. This is a conversation between colleagues. I just want to know how you're doing."

"You haven't seen me in fourteen years. You obviously know how I'm doing since you've been stalking me for some period of time leading up to this."

"You were hard to find," Palma said.

"Not hard enough." Marshall leaned forward. "I don't want to repeat myself."

"How are you?" Palma asked.

Marshall's heart raced. If he threatened Anna...

"Are you arresting me?" Marshall asked.

"Of course not. Why are you hiding?"

"Someone tried to kill me."

"When?" Palma asked.

"Fourteen years ago."

"It was a car accident."

Marshall felt his chest tightening. "Someone killed my wife." How could Palma look incredulous? How could that bastard...?

"We want you to come back." It was Palma's turn to lean forward.

"It was an accident. I want you to come back. I'm not here to threaten you, or harm you, or your family."

Marshall jumped and flung himself at the man who had destroyed his life. Who'd taken Ingrid. Both men fell to the floor as Marshall grabbed Palma by the throat. At first Palma tried to get Marshall to let go of his neck but then Marshall felt a blow to his stomach as if a chunk of concrete had hit him. He rolled and tried to stand, but Palma stood first and pushed Marshall away with his foot. Not a kick, more of a shove.

"No one killed your wife," Palma said.

"Why are you here?" The words escaped Marshall's lips. He stood up. His eyes were tearing, but not from the stomach punch. His right shoulder hurt where it had hit the ground. "You try to kill me and my family and now you're here trying to convince me to come back into the fold?" He scanned the abandoned restaurant. How had they emptied the room so fast?

Palma held up his hands, palms out. "No more fighting." He picked up his chair. "Just talking. Except for the men in the back I'm here alone."

Marshall stood and walked behind the stock wooden chair he had occupied moments earlier, and leaned against it. Could he swing it fast enough if he needed to? Probably not.

"I don't know what happened that night," Palma said. Marshall straightened. "Jesus Christ, Marshall! As soon as we heard about the accident we went to extract you and your family, but you'd taken off already. I don't know what the hell happened with you, but we were all worried." He lowered his voice as if there were others around to hear them. "We thought you were snatched by the Russians, or the Iranians. It took us a few days to get access to the hospital security cameras to confirm you had left on your own." The Russians and the Iranians. Marshall has a hazy remembrance of work he had done, but he knew they were just two of the governments who would love to have him arrested. If they only knew it was him who had done them in.

Marshall remembered that night. He would always remember

that night. The night Ingrid died. The night Anna almost died. What bothered him the most, what still kept him up on more nights than he cared to admit, was that he didn't remember anything leading up to it. That night began when he woke up in the hospital and a doctor told him his life was over. Rationally, Marshall knew that things like retrograde amnesia existed, but the thought that he would never be able to remember his final moments with Ingrid ate away at him like a sore he couldn't touch or an insect in his ear canal.

"I didn't know who to trust," Marshall said.

"You don't have to trust us. You can go back to your hermit living conditions hacking into systems for money and living the solitary life. I'm not going to stop you."

"Then why are you here? Afraid I might talk about PRUDENT RAINBOW?"

Palma smiled a small smile. "You remember that. Monahan thought for sure you didn't remember anything."

So Palma knew about the memory loss. Maybe he didn't know. "I remember what I need to know."

"We want you back," Palma said.

"It's been fourteen years. That was a ten-year project. Aren't you guys done yet?"

"PRUDENT RAINBOW was shut down. Back in 2002."

"So you don't need me." Marshall let go of the chair. His grip was sweaty.

"You know how that goes. Congress shuts it down, and we give it a new name. We stopped for a bit and re-started."

"You don't need me. I don't need you."

"We need you. Without you, it could take another ten years. This is all about the information infrastructure."

"Give it a rest. The IT is just a small part," Marshall said.

"A part no one else can do as well as you. Without you, it's another ten years. With you," Palma put his hands on the file folder on the table, "we're looking at another three."

"Another ten years? Are you kidding?"

"Rome wasn't built in a day," Palma said.

"Ten years?"

"We don't have you. We only found you a few weeks ago."

"Why were you still looking?"

"That doesn't matter." Palma sat closer. "Will you wake up? You're bored out of your mind. You're poverty stricken. You're a single parent."

"You killed Ingrid."

"It was an accident! It was a random event just like you were always fond of pointing out about every other damn thing in the world. I can prove it to you."

"You can't. Everything you say or do can be falsified. You live in a world where nothing can be trusted."

"Give us, give me, three years. After that, you never have to see us again. You'll have a real pension that no one can take away, and you and Anna can live the life you want free of interference from anyone."

"You mean you. You've got to do better than that."

Palma tilted the wooden chair back. "You need us. You don't exist. We can make you real again."

"You can also have me arrested." What was he doing? Was he negotiating? Was he about to make a deal with the devil? He sat still. *Pay attention. Listen. You're in a corner. How do you get out?*

"Money and new identities if you really want them. Only this time no one will find you if that's what you want," Palma said.

"No."

"Marshall, if you insist, you can walk out right now and you'll never see me again, but the police..." Palma stopped, let the chair come forward, and pushed the file toward him.

Marshall picked it up. It was a surveillance shot. "What the hell is this?"

"Everyone thinks you kidnapped Anna," Palma said.

"What?" Marshall gut turned into a solid mass. His face went cold.

"You don't know?"

Marshall looked at the photo. A younger him. A him he could just remember. He was in a mix of street clothes and a hospital gown. He was carrying Anna in his arms. That night was a blur, but he knew that he and Anna were in danger. He had to get away.

"Listen," Palma said.

Marshall closed the file folder and tapped it twice with his index finger. He needed a next move.

Palma continued, "Listen to me. Somehow you must have known that you were going to cause a stir because you went into hiding."

Marshall's jaw hurt as he clenched his teeth. Images of that night played through his mind. His mouth was dry. "My family. I was afraid for my family," Marshall said.

Palma stood up and walked over to him, but maintained his distance. "I know. I can help you now. It's been fourteen years, and they're still looking for you. I don't know what possessed you to come back to New York, but I can protect you."

Marshall ran his fingers through his hair. This was one of the nightmare scenarios he had played over and over again in his mind. Why was capture a fixation? What was he in denial over?

"Hey!"

Marshall blinked at the sound of Palma's voice.

"Hey. I said I can help you."

"Make the money available tomorrow so I can move it to wherever I want and put all this in writing. I want a get-out-of-jail-free card and your word." Marshall pointed at Palma, almost poking him in the chest. "Your word that Anna will be safe."

"Christ, Marshall. You're going to go home every night. We're not taking you away from her. We need your holistic view. You ran most of the project for a reason: you understand it from the code to the concrete to the international conflicts this will avoid. If all you did was IT everyone would have forgotten you years ago."

"How am I supposed to trust you?"

"You never had a reason not to, but since the accident your paranoia is a touch high."

"How am I supposed to trust you?"

"I'll have the money and the paperwork ready. Tomorrow," Palma said.

Marshall's breathing was shallow. Was he having a panic attack? He and Anna had to move out tonight. No. Palma would have the house under surveillance. It was what Marshall would have done.

A deal with the devil. Would it be better to rejoin PRUDENT RAINBOW? He didn't remember why he ran, but he knew he had to. With Ingrid dead, it was just him and Anna. He could never, he would never, let anything happen to her.

Three years. Three years to figure out why he ran. Why the project was important enough that they had tried to kill him.

And yet...Palma was here talking about it like he was recruiting him for just another position.

"I know you're having the house surveilled. I won't run," Marshall said.

"If you don't want this, my only recommendation is to move out tonight. If we found you so can someone else. Someone who wants to put you away."

"I didn't," Marshall cut himself short.

"You don't have to convince me. We ran DNA on the girl. We know the truth."

Marshall wasn't sure, but he felt a measure of relief hearing that. Fourteen years. Why was he running?

PRUDENT RAINBOW. His brain was shouting, but he had decided to ignore it. He had gotten out once before. If only he could remember more.

"Okay. I'll come back." Marshall gazed down at the tile floor. He pulled his shoulders down to appear calm, but there was only chaos. His jaw relaxed. *What am I doing?* "But only for three years, and the money and the letter are ready tomorrow."

Palma nodded. "You have my word."

The two men took their leave outside the diner. The streetlights illuminated just enough for the men to see each other, but not much more.

Palma extended his hand, but Marshall turned and began his walk back to the N. Palma was satisfied. The owner of the diner could re-open now that he and Marshall had completed their business.

His certainty did nothing to allay his aversion to risk, but he was certain Marshall would return. Three years! He knew the Marshall would live up to his side of the transaction. Marshall was that kind of man.

Palma had his work cut out for him.

He watched as Marshall walked away. *Returning to hearth and home.* A voice in his ear checked in. Palma nodded to himself at another task he could safely take off his list before heading back to the hotel. He raised his wrist and spoke into the cuff.

"Stand down," Palma said and lowered his arm. The sniper could go home for a well-deserved rest.

2

———

ONE OF THESE THINGS IS NOT LIKE THE OTHER

A Few Weeks Later

HALON

The stale air was dry. Marshall found himself downing throat lozenges in a greater quantity than he thought possible just to swallow without pain. While most of the corridors were dry-walled, it was easy to find entire stretches of bare, or plastered, or semi-painted white walls. The floors were a combination of concrete and partially laid tile. The ceilings exposed conduits for filtration, air-conditioning, and cables. He often thought of it as living in a skeleton that was slowly growing muscles and skin until it would become a complete organism.

HALON. A facility built in plain sight that would allow the government the ability to survive in the case of a horrific event. Thousands of people (eventually). Multiple stories. Offices, medical, even a prison area where personnel would be kept if they were found to be doing something they shouldn't be doing. A project that had received no explicit congressional approval, but whose black budget was nonetheless approved, and codenamed PRUDENT RAINBOW.

At least that is what Palma and the others (including Marshall) were telling anyone who asked. A comforting truth for those who needed comforting.

HALON. Not only was that the new name of PRUDENT RAIN-BOW, but Marshall was sure that the gratuitous use of the same would solve one of their problems. Why did decision makers feel the need to solve problems that smarter people had already figured out?

With his classified managerial title, Marshall ran everything having to do with any data coming into, or leaving from, the facility. Security, medical, meteorological, infrastructure, military, biological. Everything. He wandered the facility with impunity, taking over the occasional terminal when he had to get his people back on track. He had some of the smartest IT and IT infrastructure people the agency could find. In many cases, they were fresh out of MIT, or Caltech, or Cooper Union, which meant they had a low sense of frustration with the system and a high-to-borderline-insane work ethic. The continuous stream of work never seemed to end, but they always seemed to have enough energy to keep going. He was quite proud of them.

When Marshall first arrived, he couldn't understand the direction in which the team was going. No wonder everything was taking so long! These kids were fresh out of school and didn't know what it meant to have their training wheels removed. They would all make great engineers one day, but that day was not today.

The system was complex beyond compare, but he had built crazier systems. He wished that Unix was a little more stable (How many years had people been working on that?), but the alternative operating systems were unthinkable. His team took care of that by putting in their own extensions independent of the kernel and base code so they could still upgrade if they needed to, but an operating system upgrade in an environment like this had a twelve-to-eighteen month turnaround time. The operating system team was independent of them, but Marshall's team still handled their own unit and integration testing.

There were times when he felt like he could really use Anna.

The thought of his daughter brought on a wave of guilt. After a few months at the facility he felt at home, making him feel like he was neglecting the one thing in his life that he cared about the most. To add insult to injury, he started putting in several late nights, and that bothered him even more. This was bigger than anything he had ever done before, but he wanted to keep his time away from her to a minimum. He didn't care about making history. He had almost lost her all those years ago and he had vowed not to let himself forget his lesson. She was at home, or at school, and he was here.

Had he forgotten his vow after fourteen years? Or was he just becoming complacent? Did he need another car accident to force him back to the present?

"So who were those people?" Marshall asked Palma when he found him marching the long, windowless corridors later that day.

"Above your pay grade," Palma said.

Marshall tried to keep up. Palma was in much better shape than Marshall ever would be.

They went from light to dark and back to light.

"Why are you following me?" Palma asked.

"Are they the eventual tenants?"

"If you keep following me instead of doing your job, you'll never get finished. You'll never get to start your new life, and I'll lose my job."

Marshall wanted to shake him but thought better of it. "The security integration is coming together, but I want to talk about the thermobaric again."

"There is nothing to talk about," Palma said. "The failsafe is the failsafe. If something happens and we need to take a shovel to this place then we take a shovel to this place. The thermobaric isn't as good as a good old-fashioned nuke. People smarter than you decided."

"First of all, they probably aren't smarter than me." Marshall turned the corner and had to maneuver around a handful of researchers headed in the opposite direction. Lab coats, glasses, and receding hairlines. Were there no young scientists? Or were they all going into finance?

Palma stopped. "You haven't been here a year and all you do is tell me how many problem there are. Is there nothing we've done right?"

"You brought me on. That counts."

"Great." Palma continued down the corridor.

"Look, the failsafe is nuts. I haven't even told my team that they have to work on the software for that because they're going to think I'm crazy. Why would anyone want to set off a nuclear device to erase the existence of a facility that doesn't exist? HALON is not that important."

"Work with Sandia. They've written a lot of the software controlling these weapons." Sandia National Laboratories, as a major R&D group for the Department of Energy, was responsible for the non-nuclear components of the US contingent of nuclear weapons.

"We can never run a real test and I'm afraid something could go wrong," Marshall said.

"Something could always go wrong." Palma walked faster, his back straighter.

"I don't want to destroy New York Harbor."

"Neither do I. But it is a failsafe."

"Good. That makes two of us." Marshall halted and called after him. "A thermobaric explosive would do the job much better without the rather unwanted side-effects."

Palma faced him with the look of a bull wanting to charge a matador. "The nuke was your recommendation."

"I would never have recommended a nuke," Marshall said.

"Could you just do it?"

"We should use the thermobaric."

"It's no better than a nuke."

"It's cheaper, no radiation, and minimal seismic activity."

"You're not listening," Palma said. "Wire up the nuke. That was decided a long time ago and nothing has changed that would make that decision something to reconsider."

Marshall put his hands on his hips. "I'm not doing it."

Palma did a double take. "What did you say?"

"I said, respectfully, that the use of a thermonuclear device in a facility like this is unnecessary and dangerous. A thermobaric device would accomplish the same goal without the side-effects," Marshall said. "You shouldn't care whether we use a nuke or a firecracker to destroy this place. All you should care about is whether or not it gets wiped clean with little to no harm to the people in the facility and outside the facility." He crossed his arms. "Why do you care?"

Palma took two steps toward him. "A lot of people said I was crazy bringing you back. I did what you wanted and you have been a real asset for the last few months, but this is the wrong thing to take on as a campaign. I need you to do what we've been told to do."

Marshall shook his head. "I can't do that."

"Are you saying you want me to arrest you?" Palma asked.

"Arrest me and the world will find out about this place."

"If you even mention the word HALON, I can put you away where no one will ever find you." Palma turned away.

"Or kill me?"

Palma spun back around. "Are you getting dramatic all of a sudden?"

"That airplane crash was pretty dramatic. Didn't five of the defense execs who started PRUDENT RAINBOW die on that flight?" Marshall shook his shoulders. "Coincidentally, of course."

"That was an accident. However, I can make an exception in your case," Palma said.

"Or Anna?"

"Stop putting words in my mouth. I trust your decisions. Why can't you trust mine? Don't you believe in what we're doing here?"

"A biological warfare research facility no one can see?" Marshall asked.

"Government continuity. Not biological. Not research."

"Whatever. A nuke will send toxins into the air. A thermobaric will simply incinerate everything in its path."

"It would leave an empty facility that could be recovered. We can't allow that."

"Either choice leaves an unusable facility. Everyone in it will still be dead. In one case, we achieve the objective, and in another, we achieve the objective and add a few biblical events. Why is this even a question?"

Marshall felt a knot forming in the back of his head. Was this why Marshall left last time? Was this why Palma tried to kill him? Why couldn't he remember? Had the car accident done more damage to his memory than he was willing to admit?

"Alright," Palma said. "You win. I'll have another team look at this again and make another recommendation. If they go against you then you can quit."

"Am I supposed to thank you?"

3

———————

WEATHER TODAY FINE BUT WITH
HIGH WAVES

HALON

Marshall Wodehouse sat in the tenth-floor rec room playing a game of chess he and Garth Donnell had started two days earlier. While Marshall ran all things IT and security, Donnell was Palma's Chief of Staff. Technically Marshall's boss, Donnell never pretended to manage him. They had a peer-to-peer relationship that both men simply assumed. Marshall had on his usual white button-down and jeans. Donnell, though, wore a gray pullover that must have cost him a fortune to match the expensive dark slacks and imported shoes he wore almost every day. The medium-sized room had a round gray metal table upon which lay a chessboard with the game in mid-play. The air smelled of overcooked coffee, some of which Donnell held hostage in a Styrofoam cup in his right hand.

The coffee was unusually bad, but Marshall always made a carafe knowing his opponent enjoyed it. What better way to put him at a disadvantage than to inflict just a touch of reciprocal guilt?

The room had a single wooden door. There was no security pad so anyone could walk in any time of the day or night to grab a snack or a cup of the unusually bad coffee. Marshall had not stayed late enough to find out, but he had heard that some of the researchers were having midnight trysts in the rec rooms closer to the labs.

No wonder they were still smiling in the morning.

Marshall looked over the board as his hands played with his rolled up shirt-sleeves. He was grateful for the light-colored walls so he could examine the board without worrying about shadows. On occasion, a few people came to watch them, but most of the time they were on their own. Marshall was sure that Donnell was going to beat him (he always thought that), but there was always the chance Donnell would screw up and make a move that made no sense, giving Marshall the game.

Donnell always made a mistake.

"Do you remember the Sea of Japan Naval Battle?" Donnell asked.

"The Battle of Tsushima, you mean?" Marshall wasn't sure what that had to do with their game, but he was always willing to entertain a good talk on strategy and tactics. In fact, he lived for those talks.

Something was on Donnell's mind.

"Yeah. What was the big problem with that victory? The Japanese came in and kicked the ass of the Russian fleet. The entire Russian population was on suicide watch after that. Over four thousand killed and over five thousand prisoners. Right? Absolutely humiliating for 1905." Donnell took a sip of his coffee. "Hell, it would be humiliating today. We didn't lose as many people in 9/11 as the Russians did back then."

Marshall tried to lean his aluminum chair back, but it didn't have the give a real Steelcase office chair had. He felt uncomfortable being unable to tilt himself back. "What was the problem? Was there a problem?" He pushed the chair back then let himself fall forward. "You know, I'd still rather be playing Go."

"Oh, c'mon. You know what the problem was," Donnell said.

Marshall knew. It was a fundamental of human nature. "Hubris," Marshall said.

"It's always hubris." Donnell waved his Styrofoam cup as if it were empty. "The bully gets his ass kicked and the victor becomes the new bully. Then he thinks he can't get his ass kicked until he does and the cycle starts all over again."

Marshall wasn't sure where this was going, but he was grateful that the color temperature of the light didn't hurt his eyes. He had put in a special request for that. Office lighting was always too bright for him. A couple of decades of staring at a computer screen seems to have taken its toll.

"So the Japanese beat the Russians. We beat the Japanese," Marshall said. He looked down at the chessboard. Donnell was kicking his ass. He couldn't allow that; Donnell wasn't that good a player. "Who's going to beat us?"

"Who knows?" Another sip. "The one thing we know is that getting our asses kicked would involve the threat of many more deaths than the Russians suffered in 1905. There wouldn't be a naval battle, or a ground assault, or anything else having to do with a conventional war. No one can beat us at that."

"'Weather today fine but with high waves,'" Marshall quoted.

Donnell burst out laughing. "I can always count on you to remember obscure quotes."

"That was Admiral Togo the morning of the battle. The utter humiliation of the Russians began with a mundane description of the weather."

"And then he took them down," Donnell said. "They didn't know what hit them." He took the last sip of his coffee, crushed the cup, spilling Styrofoam pebbles on the table and floor, and tossed it into a large blue trash bin to his right.

"Oh, they knew what hit them." It was hard not to feel bad for the losers in a battle of that magnitude, but it was war, and worse things were to come.

The thought of worse things made Marshall conscious that he liked Donnell but wasn't sure he could trust him. He remembered him from before the accident, but the man sitting before him was different. Harder. More cynical. What had happened to the Donnell Marshall knew before the accident? They had worked on PRUDENT RAINBOW together until Marshall had had enough. What had happened to Donnell? Why didn't he approach Marshall in the diner instead of Palma?

"How's Chloe?" Marshall asked. Chloe, Donnell's daughter, almost the same age as Anna, didn't see her father half as much as Anna saw Marshall. He knew it bothered Donnell, but he didn't seem to do much about it.

"Don't change the subject," Donnell said.

"You want to rewrite the history of Japanese naval warfare?"

"She's doing fine." Donnell stared over Marshall's shoulder when he asked, "And how's Anna?"

"She's doing fine, thanks." Marshall wasn't sure what she was doing at that moment, but he knew that she had a regular day of school, then home to do her work. Or maybe she went to her Tae Kwon Do lessons. All he knew was that she had better have made her bed. Discipline was going to be the only thing that would save her when she started to work at whatever it she decided to do. At seventeen he was sure she thought the world could never be better. For some reason, she stopped telling him what her career goals were even though he asked her every day. Every day! Why couldn't she just answers questions like everybody else? Was she practicing new methods of torture?

His stomach twisted. He remembered where he was and that Anna thought he was somewhere else. He rubbed his hands on his jeans. His legs felt sore. Was it the change in air pressure?

Then he thought of Ingrid.

Donnell gave him a funny look. Sometimes Marshall didn't know what to make of him. He was sure Donnell was a little jealous that he didn't get to see his daughter as often as Marshall saw Anna. He also suspected that Donnell would be served divorce papers soon. Donnell lived down in Virginia when he wasn't at the facility confirming things were done and vendors got paid. He just didn't go home that often. That must have taken a toll on him and his family. It must. Marshall had never met Chloe, but who she was didn't matter. Marshall knew that Donnell missed his only child.

Fathers and their daughters.

"Are we going to finish this game?" Donnell asked.

They had about twenty minutes left of their official break, but they sometimes took longer. They were both managers so they could decide how long they would work. Besides, sixty-eight hour weeks meant they felt no guilt when a game ran long.

Marshall used to enjoy these games. He had not played since that night in 1991. The night of the accident. Anna was too young to learn enough to defeat him, and he considered playing online an unnecessary risk. Marshall would never have the strength of character of the men who fought the battles of the past.

"Monopoly and chess," Donnell said.

Marshall was confused. Was Donnell bringing the conversation back to the Battle of Tsushima? "Are you saying that wars are really about the economy and better standards of living? Everybody knows that."

"No, you asked who would kick our ass. I don't know who, but I can tell you how."

"Well, spill it. Don't force me to make another pot of coffee," Marshall said.

"How does the mafia do it?"

"Do what?"

"How do they win?" Donnell asked.

"I didn't realize they ever won."

"Of course they do. Not all the time, but there is always a period of time when they hold sway and no one can do anything about it."

"They corrupt the people in power and the powerless are put in compromising positions. Or killed."

"Exactly." Donnell placed his large, beefy hand on the table next to the board. "They make sure everybody owes them and then they squeeze."

"So are you saying that whoever we owe the most to owns us?"

"Isn't that how we did it?"

Marshall thought about the visitors the other day (Chinese or Korean?). He wanted to ask someone about them but hated the reaction he observed. It told him more than the actual answer. "Did you see that group of suits who were with Palma the other day?" Marshall asked.

"No." Donnell looked him in the eye. "Why?"

"It looked like Palma was giving them a tour. What kind of secret facility has tours?"

4

KIDNAPPING ANNA

May 31, 2005

"I think I can help you," Donnell said.

A cold spring breeze penetrated Marshall's white shirt, sending a chill up his spine from the sweat crawling down his back. The day couldn't have looked any happier. A few bright white clouds. The bluest sky he had seen in months (what did he expect being trapped in a windowless environment all day?), and birds. Their chirps cut through his ears, making his head throb.

The snarled traffic on the street perpendicular to them got worse. Car horns blared, Marshall's neck tightened and his already sore shoulders resisted his attempts at stretching. He felt more disconnected than usual. Donnell saw a calm man, in control of his faculties. Marshall knew that the calmer he appeared the more freaked out his mind was.

His jaw hurt and the smell of exhaust from the dozens of immobile cars reminded him of standing in the smoking room of an airport.

Paranoia did not become him, but he also knew that paranoia was his best friend. Being outside, surrounded by a beautiful day, and gridlocked cars, was not a choice lightly made. It was strategic. It was noise. Chaos. Movement.

He and Donnell walked and talked. Donnell wore a tie and a light jacket while Marshall had removed his tie and left his jacket behind at the office that was a front for their work. Donnell was comfortable but would feel the heat later. Marshall was cold, but knew no one in the office would realize he had stepped out.

Donnell lived in the moment while Marshall lived in the future.

In the present, Marshall wasn't sure who to trust. His sense of being an outsider grew worse as he began looking in places he knew he wasn't supposed to. Building a facility for the continuity of government was a great cover story, but he couldn't help himself. The more he investigated, the more he knew that Palma was blowing smoke up his ass.

Why was the sun so damn cheery?

"I need to know everything you found," Donnell said.

"I didn't want to bring this to you because I know how you are, and we both know that misreading any of this could not only screw things up, but could land us both in jail."

Both men stood outside of an office park in Newark, New Jersey. Most of the work done for HALON was off-site, which made it easier to bring in resources who had a high clearance level, but not high enough to know the details of the program.

Marshall Wodehouse and Garth Donnell knew details.

"The facility is not for government continuity," Marshall said.

"That's not possible. We've got construction crews, defense contractor personnel, exemptions with the New York MTA. We have a paper trail a mile wide."

"Yeah, and the same way we hid the construction of missile silos on Long Island we're hiding the construction of this facility."

"How do you know?" Donnell asked.

"I know." Marshall walked up the block in the direction of the Gateway Center. The PATH train was a short stroll through there back into Manhattan and a not-so-quick subway ride back home.

It was on one of his trips home that he'd read something on the train that told him HALON was so secret that even they weren't allowed to know what it was for.

But Malik Palma knew. General George Monahan knew.

And now Marshall knew.

"We've been working with these guys for years. Why would they lie to us, of all people?" Donnell asked. He flexed his fists. Donnell would always be a man of thought who used his fists first.

He must be worried for his family. I know I am. "If this project," Marshall was conscious of where they were and the possibility of being bugged from a distance, so he spoke in couched terms, "is not what it seems then what are we doing and why is it in the middle of a population center?"

"It's not exactly in the middle of a population center."

"Are we going to play legal niceties now?"

"Alright. I get it." Donnell crossed the street and Marshall continued to follow him as the wind enveloped him in its icy embrace.

Marshall regretted leaving his windbreaker behind. He considered tightening his tie, but remembered he had taken it off earlier. It rested in his desk drawer.

"No, I don't think you do," Marshall said. Was it worth telling Donnell more of what he'd found? That he'd already had indirect contact with the FBI?

The NSA could connect the dots, but indirection was still something they were working on. The Bureau agent didn't know who was feeding him information, but what Marshall had sent him, while just enough to keep them both out of hot water, was sufficient to get an investigation started. Distance. By contacting the FBI, and by extension Agent Del Kirby, anonymously, Marshall would get him the distance he needed.

"I think," Marshall walked a little ahead of his colleague, "I think workers are being...terminated." He lowered his voice on the last word.

Marshall found himself walking alone. He found Donnell, a few paces behind, who said nothing.

"There have been a number of accidents unrelated to the work, but involving teams of the people doing the actual work."

"Such as?"

"Falls, heart attacks, robberies gone wrong," he knew Donnell understood where he was going, "car accidents, suicides." Marshall was glad that Donnell was playing the role of the skeptic. He needed to hear his thoughts out loud and Donnell was always a good springboard.

"You said 'accident', but you don't believe that," Donnell said.

"And then there are the Chinese." Marshall saw Donnell tense up.

"The Chinese?"

"We hide money, right?"

Donnell's nod was almost imperceptible.

"I don't usually care where the hell the money comes from because it's all in the family." Meaning from the US government. "I traced funds back to organizations that get their money from the Chinese. And I don't mean legit organizations. I mean the ones that exist to hide that they come from the Chinese government."

"This program is legal," Donnell said.

"I think this program is illegal, but regardless it's very damn dangerous," Marshall said.

"You mean the nuke?" Donnell asked.

"Who cares? If the Chinese government is involved then what does it matter? A nuke. A thermobaric. What the hell?"

"Why are you telling me this now? I think we should go back and just ask Palma." The two men were quickly approaching the entrance to the mall that would lead them to the PATH.

Marshall shook his head. "I need your help." Marshall lightly hugged himself, but didn't feel any warmer.

"Not until we talk with Palma," Donnell said.

"I can't stay. I need you to help me. Someone outside the organization has got to be told about this."

"What about Monahan?" Donnell asked.

Marshall thought about all the reports Palma had been sending from and about HALON. Palma would type them up, print them, then send them by courier. To Monahan.

Marshall had a tap on the printer's hard drive and read everything.

"I think Monahan knows," Marshall said.

"Knows what?"

"That HALON is being built for the Chinese."

———

Damn it! Why was Marshall such a pain in the ass? Why did he always have to do stupid shit like this?

Donnell stood at attention in Palma's empty office looking at the various pictures on the wall. He flexed his biceps. The frames held standard-issue office pictures. Some landscapes, some architecture. All pointless.

He turned as Palma walked in. Palma wore very pressed civilian clothes and carried a laptop in his left hand. The two men looked at each other for a moment. Palma closed the door and asked, "He knows, doesn't he?"

"I was serious when I said you should have killed him when you found him."

———

A few hours had passed. Marshall had just left the confines of the subway on his way home when his cell phone buzzed. Incoming text.

Access terminated.

His chest tightened and he cursed. Marshall, as a matter of prudence, had set up surreptitious alerts on the authorization system he had designed for the project. The lack of a name meant that he had just lost his access to key systems.

At least that was what Palma needed to believe.

Donnell must have gone straight to Palma. Now what? His house was under surveillance, he was sure, and Anna needed to be extracted.

Where was she? He looked at his phone. It was after 2 pm so she would be getting out of school soon.

———

Where was the car?

Marshall had participated in surveillance operations before. They wouldn't have many people watching Anna, but even one was too many, and they would increase her detail within the hour. He had to move or he would lose his chance to get her out.

He would not lose his chance. A flashback of colliding cars and hospital lights punched his adrenaline and he almost ran to the nearest kit location.

Marshall had survival kits located all over the city. Having the kits ready for a day like today had been his highest priority when they'd first moved back. They included various items of disguise, for Anna as well, if it came to that. He felt confident when he approached the school wearing platform shoes, a jacket that changed the proportions of his shoulders, and a different hair color. He did his best to scout for the surveillance vehicle but didn't spot it.

Where the hell is the car?

The cloudy sky muffled much of the sound around the school, but the silence was uncharacteristic. He forced himself to continue so he wouldn't stand out.

His heart sank. The car on permanent assignment to Anna wasn't there because Anna wasn't there. A locked fence enclosed the empty playground behind the school.

What have I done?

He pulled his cell out of his pocket and looked at the calendar that he religiously kept up-to-date with all of Anna's activities. His stomach felt hollow and his head screamed.

THEY HAVE HER. THEY HAVE HER. WHAT AM I GOING TO DO?

They had let out early for another of the interminable school events that drove Marshall crazy. Anna was already home. She was exactly where Palma could get to her.

————

Marshall, minutes from leaving to get Anna, scoped out his extraction plan in a Bronx hotel room. His phone buzzed again. It had been buzzing almost non-stop since he'd received the first text message two hours ago.

A text message from the New York City Police Department. He had been monitoring police communications for years and a text alert was always better than having to manually monitor some frequency, or hack into the dispatch systems (which he had done as well). His shoulders sagged and his heart felt raw against his chest. The pain in his midsection made him fall back against the bed in a sitting position.

He turned on the clock radio. He preferred radio news. They didn't waste words. He recognized the announcer's voice (*good old 1010 WINS*). A wave of anxious pain swept over his shoulders, up his neck, and into his skull.

"And this just in: police announced the rescue of kidnapping victim Carpenter Poole who was found this morning in the Brooklyn home of her kidnapper, Arnold Dashman, with whom she had been living for the last fifteen years under the name Anna Wodehouse..."

He clutched his arms to his tight chest. *BREATHE. BREATHE. YOU'RE NO GOOD TO HER LIKE THIS.*

Squirrel. Oh my God. I have to get over there.

They took his Anna. They took his baby girl. By making Marshall a kidnapper, and Anna a victim, Palma could let the authorities do all the work of bringing him in. Palma could dispose of Marshall when he liked and HALON would eventually become operational with a foreign power at the helm.

Marshall gave the room a quick look. The police might burst in here at any moment.

No, they wouldn't. He had disposed of his phones. He had set up the alerts to go to a burner phone that he could remotely reset.

He started shaking. *THEY HAVE MY LITTLE GIRL.* If they

harmed her in any way, he would find Palma and kill him. If they did anything to her, he would hunt down Palma and kill him.

Anything. If they did *anything*. He would kill Palma.

I HAVE TO GO GET HER! I HAVE TO GO GET HER AND WE HAVE TO RUN. There was no time to lose. Marshall would hide her and they would disappear again like they did back in 1991.

And while they ran he would bring HALON down around Palma's head.

5

———

GRADUATION DAY

May 14, 2012
(Seven years later)

University of Pennsylvania

"Do you have a son or daughter here?"

"Yes," Marshall said, "I do. I know you must be very proud about your child's graduation, as well."

He smiled at the couple that sat next to him in Franklin Field at the University of Pennsylvania. It was such a beautiful day. The plastic seat scorched his light-colored pants and his dark sports jacket was doing a great job doubling as a towel soaking up the sweat on his back.

Would he see Anna? Would she see him? Would she even bother looking? He changed his appearance just enough that anyone who knew him wouldn't recognize him, and even state-of-the-art facial recognition software would fail. Of course, there was always something. It was hard to predict random events.

Even so, he was willing to chance it. That didn't stop him from keeping his eye on the security guards doing the rounds in the stands.

The almost perfect day hurt Marshall's arms and legs. He'd never suffered from headaches before, but the last seven years were a string of head pains he couldn't escape.

Am I really here if Anna doesn't know I'm here?

Mistakes. That was all Marshall was looking for, but soon-to-be General Malik Palma had many more resources available than Marshall. There was only so much he could accomplish on his own in addition to staying alive long enough to retrieve his daughter.

Marshall pulled out his phone and pretended to be checking messages. The hot air in the stands pressed against his torso like a body bag. *How could such a beautiful day suck so much?* He tired of talk. It had been years since he'd last seen his daughter. Years since he had teased her about school and dating and books. Years. How to explain to her that he would come back? No matter what. No. Matter. What.

And yet.

It had been seven years. He had done a background check on the Stoddard's and they were clean. He wasn't sure how they had been conned into thinking Anna was their niece, but that didn't matter. They did a passable job taking care of her and he'd sent money their way on a regular basis by paying off things like their debt. He'd set up a bogus grant for Anna to pay for things like books or clothes so she could get the things she needed even if he wasn't around. The UPenn system was easy enough to enter and even easier to add non-existing grants to disburse funds he'd transferred into the alumni coffers from an anonymous source.

Anna's tuition was a different story. She had gotten scholarship after scholarship on her own. He would never, and could never, claim to have helped her there.

Anna's therapist was another story. His office was easy enough to bug, given that Marshall could use either of their cell phones as microphones and listen in on a few of their sessions. Most of the time Anna had nothing to say that he cared about; she was a normal young woman. But sometimes, sometimes, she would talk about him. Never on a regular basis and never for long.

She hated him. She thought he'd abandoned her. She waited, and thought that maybe he had died.

Finally, she wished that he had.

The ceremony was over. The caps went flying into the air in a blur of blue shards. Marshall stood at attention as everyone began to clap. As quickly as it had appeared, the blue cloud was gone. All the caps had returned to earth on the newly-minted graduates.

If only he could see Anna.

A few seconds later, a single cap flew in the air.

He smiled. He didn't know how he knew, but he knew.

That's my girl.

For a moment (but what a moment!), he thought that maybe this was the time. He could approach her, and pull her away, and they could be a family again.

Then he saw the helicopter.

And the reporters off to the side.

Were they never going to leave her alone?

In a moment of anger, he entered the stadium, deciding to go on the field and give himself up. With every step, he thought more and more about what a new mess her life would become. It was just a few steps. One would take him out onto the field, and a few dozen more would put him close enough to her that he could call out her name. She would come over and slap him and punch him then maybe hug him, or not, but she would know that he came back. That he would always come back.

I will always be there.

One step. And then a few dozen more. He had done more before he'd married, plenty after he'd married, and many more when Anna was just a baby and he comforted her when she couldn't sleep in the middle of the night, or it was too cold, or she was hungry, or she just needed to know someone was there.

That he was there.

If I give myself up, she'll still hate me, and Palma will win. Her hatred may abate, but Palma will still have won.

I can't let him win. When this is all over she can kill me with her bare hands if she wants, but for now...

For now, she is safer without me.

With his right hand up against his face, unable to hold back his tears, Marshall walked away.

————

A Few Months Later

Anna was back in New York.

Anna, who had been in the UK trying to track Marshall down so she could kill him (*would she have gone through with it? She did fire through the window of the safe house*), had returned and had continued to fall for the lie foisted on her by the man she knew as Benson who was really General Malik Palma the current head of the National Security Agency and Marshall's boss. She thought she had somehow found Marshall and was about to find out what really happened seven years ago.

Marshall didn't know what Palma had told her, but it had to be good. So good that Anna had let herself be led into an elaborate set-up where she and faux him would meet and both be killed.

Anna was on the roof about to meet Garth Donnell.

The drone flew toward the building on 86th Street and 1st Avenue, painting everything in infrared. The sniper stood out from his prone position on the floor holding the high-powered rifle he would use to find and take out his target.

It had to hurry to get into position. There were two other snipers, but Marshall had gone through enough drills to know the leader. The others wouldn't know what to do once things went south so they would simply leave rather than wait and be found by the authorities.

The drone, now in range, locked on the target. The unique heat signature guaranteed that even if he stood, the drone would compensate.

Just another second and Marshall would stop this.

The sniper fired.

Marshall's breath caught in his throat.

The sniper paused for a second then stood.

Marshall fired.

And fired.

And fired.

Marshall stood in a field on the New Jersey side of the Hudson holding the remote control for the drone. He knew he was too close to what was going on in the Upper East Side, but any further and he would run into radio range issues. The clear sky he had been grateful for mere minutes earlier was useless to him now.

He had failed to save Anna.

A rage he had never recognized or felt before burned in his chest. His skin blushed from the heat. *Time to go kill Palma. His kids will still have their mom.*

With the shooting done, Marshall programmed in new coordinates. He would let the drone fly out over the Atlantic until it lost radio contact, which would then signal its self-destruct sequence. He had the mission video but doubted he would ever look at it again.

The police band he monitored exploded as officers were told to stand down. No one responded. Marshall was sure that the police snipers didn't have enough time to get into position. The person who had planned the deaths of Anna and Donnell had his people in place exactly when and where he needed them. Marshall had simply put a crimp in their plans.

And now Donnell and Anna were dead. Marshall continued to be late to the party and others continued to pay for his tardiness.

Tardiness was not in the works for Palma, however. Marshall was going to make sure of that.

He walked back to his black Hyundai, rented with a bogus credit card, and driver license to match. He would return it to one of the off-site rental office near Newark Airport, and pay with cash. Surveillance photos of a man paying cash for a rental, while unusual, didn't worry him. He would have to look like himself for that.

Time for one last thing before he left. He forced himself to unlock his iPad to look at the real-time feed from one of the overhead KH-class reconnaissance satellites he had commandeered a few minutes earlier. The preset coordinates aimed the satellite at the building where he knew Donnell was staying.

He was nothing if not complete.

There was the roof. Anna was prone on the ground, a person bending over her. The person put their hands up as police came pouring out of the doorway to join them. Marshall wasn't sure, but he thought he saw blood pooling beneath the larger body.

Donnell. How the hell did he let himself get taken like that? How could he not know Anna was just a decoy? If he had only answered one of Marshall's calls! Marshall could have saved them both.

Maybe exhaustion just kicked in, even for a doer like Donnell. Maybe even for a doer like Anna.

The earphones Marshall had been listening to came alive.

"The shooter is still alive. Repeat: the shooter is still alive. Send Emergency Medical to 85th and York..."

Marshall's eyes opened wide.

She's alive!

Was it something he did? He put his hand on top of the tablet and tried to breathe, but only shallow breaths came.

She's alive.

6

TRUE CONFESSIONS

End of May 2012

Marshall looked left and right at his hands then down at his feet. The comfortable pillow he rested his head on belied his predicament. Handcuffed to the dark wood headboard of his hotel bed, with his feet tied to the foot of the bed, he felt humiliated. Had the water been drugged? The coffee he'd made from the water? How did anyone even know what room he was in? He tried to remember what happened, but focus crawled every way but forward.

His hotel room was a standard, drab, tired room with light brown wallpaper and an underlying mildew smell that permeated everything. After his usual reconnaissance, and he had completed circumnavigating the perimeter of the building, he decided to check up on Anna again. He had gotten ice from the dispenser down the hall, poured himself a cup of water, and took notes.

Yes, he felt humiliated. Even helpless.

But not hopeless.

He looked over at his silver notebook. The locked screen reassured him, but he didn't know why.

"You can stop looking over there."

Marshall looked toward the darkened corner. Chinese or Japanese accent. Close cropped hair. Eyes an even distance apart. Symmetrical face. Gun in his right hand.

The characterless curtain let in light like a sleeping security guard let in intruders. The tall man sat in the corner chair. Even as he sat Marshall could tell that the man would tower over him.

"You did everything right," the man said. "You never developed a consistent routine and you changed rooms on a regular basis. But you like ice in your water."

"Let me go," Marshall said.

"What's your name?" the man asked.

This was not going to go well. "Greg Vasquez," Marshall said.

The man stood.

Great, he's tall. The gun helped. White button-down. No tie. Dark slacks. That shirt would be a blanket for at least two homeless people. Marshall, prone on the bed, wore a plaid cotton shirt and jeans. The man had left Marshall's shoes on; it would be harder to release his bonds that way.

"If your name is Marshall Wodehouse, and you can prove it, I promise not to kill you."

"What an interesting incentive." Marshall pulled his legs up. The metal of the cuffs bit into his wrists and the muscles of his arms ached from being in the same position for so long. His feet felt numb. The ropes held tight. "Like I said, my name is Greg Vasquez, but Marshall Whatever works. Now let me go. I don't know who you are or why you want me. If you release me, and go, I won't press charges."

"Vasquez. Nice try." The man walked back to the chair and dragged it over to the side of the bed. The wooden legs made a sound on the carpet like a body pulled across grass on its way to a shallow grave. If the rugs were as old as Marshall, they might tear before the chair got to the bed.

"You've slept better," the man said.

"I always sleep better without handcuffs," Marshall said.

The man reached into his shirt pocket, pulled out some photos, and dropped them on Marshall's chest. Each showed a bloody mess that used to be a man. They all looked like him, but something was always off.

The man bowed to bring his face closer to Marshall. "Those men were not Marshall Wodehouse."

"I guess it's too late to act like a scared civilian."

"There's time. You're not dead yet." The man had a deliberate walk. His blinks were slow. "But you might not be him. You might have ties to organized crime. You might have been in the military. You might have interesting mistresses." The man fell back and landed on the chair. "I have time and you don't. Are you Marshall Wodehouse?"

"No." Maybe the man would kill him. Maybe the man was bluffing. Why shoot people who weren't him?

"This is your last chance. If you answer in the negative then I will kill your daughter."

"I don't have a daughter," Marshall said.

"True enough, but I'll kill her anyway."

"Okay, I'm him. Leave whoever-that-girl-is alone and let me go." He pulled at his legs again. The loops drew tighter as he struggled.

"Prove to me who you are," the man said. His hands opened and closed on the armrests.

"And how am I supposed to do that?" Marshall asked.

"Tell me the one word that will make me let you go."

"Or will kill me."

"I have been surveilling you for a number of days. The opportunities were plentiful. Yet, here you are. Unharmed."

"If you kill me, you have no reason to kill the girl." Marshall relaxed. The handcuffs pulled at his wrists. He was going to kick the shit out of this guy just for that. Marshall was too old for this.

"Young woman, please. That's very un-PC of you." He put the gun on the night table to Marshall's left. "The word, please. I could torture you, but if you are him then I need you whole."

"How many times do I have to tell you? I am not him. Don't harm the girl." Sweat was building up on his back and his shirt felt cold against his skin. "Look, I'm a father. She's someone's daughter and she doesn't have to be mine for me not to want her dead." His entire body shook as he pulled at his hands and feet. "Kill me or let me go."

"If you are Marshall, I can help you."

"I'm not him."

"If you think that I will not kill you, please look at the photos again. All those men look like you because I have been looking for you for many weeks." The man's demeanor never changed. He seemed to be in constant repose. "They all fit your appearance and all had good backgrounds. By being good at hiding, you killed all of them."

"You killed all those men," Marshall said.

"The word. Please."

"I'm not him!"

The man pursed his lips and shook his head. He stood up, and walked toward the window that hid the existence of the outside world. He pulled a cell phone out of his pocket. "I have been following your daughter for an even longer time than you. She is very resilient. You must be very proud of her." The man turned his head toward Marshall. "I know you've been watching over her. Doing your best to protect her." He dialed a number and put the cell against his ear. "You can't protect her right now. If you do not tell me who you are, and prove it, I will have her killed immediately."

"But if you kill her and I'm not this guy you're looking for then you lose a point of leverage." *Damn it.* His eyes felt hot. *I'm cornered. He has to be bluffing, but...*

"I have many more to choose, but I have to admit that I am running out of patience. I need Marshall Wodehouse and I need him alive. I need him, and I am willing to trade the life of his daughter for his cooperation." The man walked over to Marshall. Every step measured and light.

"I'm the guy you're looking for," Marshall said.

The man turned away. "Can you see her?" he asked into his cell. "Good. On my command, kill her."

"Stop! I told you! I'm the guy you're looking for." Marshall felt a wave of helplessness wash over him. How did he let himself get caught so easily? *I've been running for too long.*

"Is she in range?"

"Stop! Stop!" Damn it! Was he faking it? Was there anyone even on the line?

"Who are you?" the man asked.

"Hang up! My name is Marshall Wodehouse." Were his hands shaking? "There. I told you. Hang up!"

"Do you have her?" the man asked. He looked back at Marshall. "The word?" He turned back. "Stand-by." He looked at the figure straining on the bed.

"Halon."

The man put the phone back in his pocket.

"You didn't have anyone on the line, did you?" Marshall held onto his sigh. He let the breath sit like a rock in his chest.

The man sat back down on the chair. Marshall stopped thinking. Release would get him his revenge unless he was shot where he lay.

"I need your help," the man said.

"You could have asked. The answer is no in any case."

"And that is why I didn't ask."

"Why would a big guy like you need to tie down a little guy like me?"

"I know your background. You're good at what you do, though the only time you've ever killed someone was in combat." The man reached over to the gun on the end table, stood up, and holstered it under his jacket.

"I'm pretty certain I couldn't subdue you."

"You could." He reached into his pants' pocket. "In fact, you're calculating how bad you want to kill me for threatening the life of your daughter and for humiliating you by drugging you and constraining you on this bed." He held up a handcuff key. "Your word. If I let you go, you hear me out. If you don't believe me after that then you can try to kill me with no guarantee of success. If you do believe me then we go out and try to stop Secretary of State George Monahan from handing over Halon to an enemy you cannot possibly defeat alone."

"I work better alone." Hot blood emanated from Marshall's neck and up into his head. He wanted to close his eyes, but that would give away too much. It was time to regroup.

"You wrote an internal paper on the importance of collaboration in the decision-making process."

"That was for the development of software," Marshall said.

"The same principles apply. I need you. You need me." The man held the key up again. "Your word."

"If you let me go, I will kill you."

"You Americans have no sense of subtlety. Del Kirby might have still been alive if you did."

"I killed him," Marshall said.

"I know."

PART II

ANNA

7

FRIDAY, OCTOBER 26, 2012

Somewhere in Central Indiana

Everything was upside down.

Anna Wodehouse, a.k.a. Carpenter Poole, looked around the passenger compartment of the olive-drab 2012 Jeep Rubicon she had been driving just minutes before. Given that everything was relative, she decided that maybe the world had flipped over and not her vehicle, since everything in the passenger compartment seemed normal. Except for her necklace. A bird charm she has received on her way out of prison rested on her nose. The afternoon sun was behind her, lighting up the already well-lit dashboard. She could smell the moist ground filled with rotting leaves, the grass, the generic deciduous trees that lined every highway from here to California.

The birds seemed rather quiet compared to the ear-splitting sound of wind she experienced just before...before what? The silence appeared as if someone had turned off the sounds going into her ears.

She tried to look down at her blue jeans-covered lap, but her head seemed to be fighting gravity. She relaxed her neck and her head flopped back. All the sensory input around her fought for brain time and received none.

However, the ground seemed to be above her head and her blond wig was on the ceiling. She was sure it was late afternoon. Earlier, the bright sunshine and sparse cloud cover had signaled a day of goodness and warmth and puppies. And numbness.

Yet everything was still upside down.

A few minutes earlier, Anna had been driving along Interstate 69 just southwest of Muncie, Indiana when she decided she wasn't going fast enough. The thought hung in her mind for a few seconds, long enough for her to realize the implications of her potential actions, but not really caring. However, she was sure that the lack of feeling in most of her body wasn't because of the cold, or low blood sugar. In the past, she had gotten over the numb feelings in her hands by squeezing her fingers and wrist until she could discern a prickly wave of nerve explosions flowing through her skin. What would the equivalent be for her brain?

All four wide-open windows let in a flood of angry air she calculated would ruin the jeep's MPG numbers. *This is not enough.* She floored the gas pedal.

Not the first time she had decided that recklessness was the better part of valor. Anna had already received a number of speeding tickets in towns that barely existed on the map. She'd even given the slip to one particular law enforcement officer who was probably still waiting for her to return from a nearby rest room. Would they never stop falling for that one?

The Jeep's engine revved up as she saw the speedometer go from an already unreasonable 80 mph to 100 mph. What was the rate of gasoline consumption as her speed increased? Was she approaching the point where the amount of fuel it took her to get from 80 to 100 was equivalent to the amount of fuel she had used to get to 0 to 80? The back of her mind registered the silliness of the question. The real questions was whether or not her use of a seat belt would be enough to keep her from turning into road kill for the turkey vultures flying overhead.

Insects slammed into the windshield, leaving trails of yellow and white. The road was a straightaway, but how long could that last? She was determined to find out.

Where were the other drivers? The road was empty and for that Anna gave thanks. If she was going to cause injury to anyone, she would prefer to keep it to herself.

The road veered to the left. She quickly brought her speed down but felt the left tires leave the ground. The right tires skidded and screamed and the Jeep flipped. Once. Twice. On the third bounce the car came to a halt on its tires, with the driver's side facing the oncoming traffic that wasn't there.

Anna looked down the road.

She looked up the road.

Nothing.

She shook her head in appreciation of the Jeep's roll bar, tapped the ceiling, and started the car again after putting the transmission back in Park.

So that's how the roll bars works. I'll have to try harder next time.

She unbuckled her seat belt, opened the driver's door, and stepped out. Slow steps. Her eyes took in her surroundings (the sun was out, the turkey vultures were still overhead, disappointed, the road was concrete rather than asphalt), but part of her brain didn't register. She sauntered over to the right shoulder. Out in the distance she thought she made out a car. Too far. The steel barrier along the road was about a foot or two from a fifty-foot drop. She picked up two rocks, weighed one in each hand, then let them go letting gravity do its job, imagining what it must have been like when Galileo performed his famous experiment from the Leaning Tower of Pisa to prove that objects fall at the same rate regardless of mass. The rocks hit foliage on the way down, causing them to find the path of least resistance to complete their journey. They never made it to the bottom.

The Galileo story was an urban legend anyway.

Anna wasn't sure how long she stood there gazing down at the drop. *What if I were a stone? How long would it take me to fall?* Should she try to find out? She scanned the distance again. The car was getting closer. Was it going slower or was the rotation of the Earth causing her to go faster? Or vice versa?

Her head started to hurt. She decided to move the Jeep.

Anna had been driving for just a day or so after escaping from the federal Supermax prison down in Florence, Colorado with the help of David Hawking, a man she thought was the prison doctor, but turned out to be someone sent to kill her. He also turned out to be someone sent by a group who wanted her out of prison so she could go to Vancouver to meet with them.

Why? She still hadn't figured it out. It was all a blinding blur of betrayal and fireworks.

All she knew for sure was that the man called Benson, who set her up for the murder of the man she thought was her father, wanted her dead. Benson, whose real name was Malik Palma, was somehow connected to her father. She hadn't figured that out yet either.

Her father. Her alleged father. Did he really kidnap her? Were her parents really the Pooles? Was she actually related to her Aunt Marcie and Uncle Ray of Littleton, PA or was that a sham as well?

The Jeep she drove was rented using money Hawking had left her along with fake ID and a clean set of clothes (jeans that mostly fit, a black pullover, gray hoodie, sweat socks, sneakers, and underwear). How did he know her size? Oh, yeah, the mysterious group that wanted her to go to Canada. Yes, of course. She remembered killing the men in the helicopter. The men who wanted to kill her at the prison. She should go back. And surrender.

Hawking had given her the bird-charm-necklace just before she vanished the night of her escape. *That was sweet of him, I think.*

Anna walked over to the waiting Jeep, straightened out her necklace, counted her steps back to her seat, then closed the door and started the ignition. After straightening out the jeep and pushing against the gas pedal harder and harder, she took off.

The vibration of the gas pedal felt good against her foot. She slowed down and sped up in intervals of fifty seconds and ten seconds. *One Mississippi. Two Mississippi. Three Mississippi...*

Then she blinked and the world was upside down. She didn't remember flipping the Jeep again, but she must have done it because there she was with the world 180 degrees in opposition.

She heard rustling to her left.

"Are you okay?" An upside down, overweight white man with a smudge on his forehead appeared with wide eyes and dirty blue bib overalls. "What happened?"

Anna didn't know how to answer. Her brain was still processing how little it felt.

"I think you should get out of your car. I can help you flip it over," he said.

Anna blinked a few times. Where was she? How did the Jeep turn over? When?

The seat belt held her fast and the roll bar had kept her from being crushed by the weight of the vehicle when she took the turn. The roll bar. *What an appropriate name.* She touched the top of her head. She was bald. When did that happen? *Right, a few weeks ago.* She looked up, or more accurately, down, at her blond wig in a tangled pile on the ground over her head.

I don't like being a blonde anyway.

The smell of moist ground reminded her of her backyard in Pennsylvania.

"Hello?" The man returned. "There's no gas leaks and no smoke so I think you're okay."

Anna nodded in agreement. The jeep had left the road and was in the foliage past the shoulder. She couldn't have been going that fast.

What was she doing? What was she thinking about? Her aunt. Uncle Ray. She missed them. She missed the security of her prison cell. She missed the feel of the sun on her face.

I miss my hair.

"Should I cut your seat belt? You'll have to get it fixed right away if I do," he said.

Anna shook her head twice with the movements of an automaton. She put her hand out and touched the ground. She pushed up, relieving the seat belt of her weight, and with her other hand she released the buckle. She put her other hand out and lowered herself to the ground. She felt disoriented.

The world had won.

The man offered to pull her out and Anna waved him away. She slid out and walked over to the nearest tree. The tree had a pungent smell. She reached out her hand, and a piece of bark, curling out like a dried-out piece of thick, dark brown paper, tore her skin and the pain shot through the palm of her hand. A sound caught in her throat. She balled her hand into a fist and hit the tree with the side of her hand. She hit it and felt nothing so she decided to hit it again. And again. And again.

She screamed at it until she felt the blood dripping down. No sound came out of her mouth, and she sat on the ground and put her face in her hands.

Blink. Breathe. Blink. Breathe.

Anna decided to get up. Her body didn't agree. The numb part of her brain had regained control and pushed her feelings off to the side. It took a few seconds before she saw the man standing close to her.

"Are you going to be alright?" he asked.

She nodded and felt her cheeks blush. She had to get up.

"I can call the police. Or an ambulance. You might have a concussion."

His concerned face tweaked her focus. And the mention of police.

She stood. "No. Please, don't. I'm fine." There were trees behind her lining the shoulder. Their leaves were various dull fall colors and the smell of decomposition was stronger than she remembered back at Aunt Marcie's. She brushed the dirt and dry debris from her baggy jeans. Maybe Hawking *didn't* know her size.

"That's not a problem. We don't want you getting into an accident that could have been avoided with a quick look."

"And who's going to look? You?" She took a few steps toward the man, who retreated as his eyes widened.

"No, no." He put his hands up. "I'm just trying to help."

"Is this man bothering you, miss?" a voice to her left asked. An Indiana State Trooper had pulled up.

How had she not heard his siren? Or the car door opening?

"Officer," the man said, "I found this young lady in the jeep. I saw it flip over as I was coming down the road and wanted to make sure she was okay. If she needed any help."

"Miss, please step away from him." The officer took slow steps toward them. He had his right hand on his holster.

"What kind of gun do you have?" Anna asked.

"Miss, please step away from him."

Anna walked over to him. "I just want to know."

The officer, a young man wearing a dark blue, short-sleeve shirt and light blue pants, put his left hand out. "Miss, don't come any closer."

"I just want to know." She took another step. "And why is your hair so short?"

He flipped his index finger and popped the leather strap keeping his gun in place. "Miss."

Anna took another step and he pulled out his weapon. Anna stopped. "Oh. A Glock 17." She turned and walked back to the car.

"Miss," the officer said. "Please stay where you are."

The jeep was still upside down. She turned back to the two men. "Do you think you can help me turn this over?"

———

Being in the back of a police car was something Anna was beginning to tire of. When she was seventeen and the authorities first "rescued" her. After the murder of Garth Donnell.

So this is what the back of an Indiana State Trooper vehicle looks like. Another life goal accomplished. It smelled of sweat and cigarettes. There was an empty coffee cup on the floor and loose dirt on the black carpeting in the black passenger compartment.

Anna retrieved the blond wig before entering the vehicle at the officer's request. She refused the breathalyzer so now he was taking her to the State Police Post where she would have to take it anyway. She didn't care. He had no right to assume she was drunk just because her Jeep had flipped over. She would show him.

They would take her fingerprints. She closed her eyes and clenched her hands to stop from slapping herself.

"Excuse me. I just realized that I'm going to be really late for an appointment. I think I'll be self-righteous next time. Can we go back and I'll take the test after all?"

"Sorry, miss. It's better if we go to the station."

———

The tow truck had arrived at last. She had convinced Trooper Travis that she was undergoing chemo and sometimes it made her combative. She really did need to get going and she didn't break any laws, did she?

At first, he'd refused to comply, but then he pulled over. The sun was almost down and he made her go through all the sobriety tests, which Anna passed with flying colors. She even showed off by singing the names of all the presidents to Yankee Doodle while she touched her nose with her left and right index fingers. She glanced at the dashboard camera that would record her existence for future use and hoped no one looked at it later.

That was more thinking than she'd had to do in a long time. At least in the last twenty-four-hours.

———

She sat on the guardrail looking at the Jeep, which the tow truck driver had turned over for her. She had been ready to get upset with the man but realized that she was giving overreacting a bad name. Time to pull back before she got arrested for real.

She paid with her bogus credit card, which went through with nary a peep. Hawking had supplied her with a fake AAA card so she even got a discount for righting the vehicle.

The metal of the guardrail was starting to hurt her butt. She sighed, entered the car, and drove to the nearest hotel she found on her cell phone. Vancouver. It was going to be a long trip north.

8

SCANNING…

Anna purposely targeted a motel far from everywhere, where her driver license wouldn't be questioned, and paying cash was welcome. The late afternoon light cast soft shadows everywhere, which made the rundown motel look inviting and cozy. The reality struck her anew when she entered the room. Very yellow light. Dark suspicious carpeting. The smell of cigarettes in a non-smoking room.

A flash of her father mopping the wood floor in their home in Brooklyn. The smell of lemon disinfectant.

Sleep. She really needed to get some sleep.

Anna sat cross-legged on her bare bed with her blond wig to her left. Her head felt itchy, but the slight bagginess of her jeans meant comfort in an otherwise uncomfortable position. *Thanks, Doc! Better than sweat pants.* She had pulled the bed cover off because she had a bad feeling about the hygiene of her room and was afraid she wouldn't be able to see any bugs crawling toward her. Anna turned on her notebook and began to surf. She was drained but needed the stimulation of wandering the Net, and talking to people she wasn't supposed to. The denizens of the Internet who knew the magic it took to do very cool things without worrying about their legality. They were so much more interesting than the people she was used to dealing with.

What a wonderful world that even a motel in the middle of nowhere has WiFi.

IRCPlayer: i thought you were heading to canada?

HarlequinNinja: can we talk about something else?

IRCPlayer: sure. why aren't u going to new york?

So he wanted to play that game. Great.

HarlequinNinja: have you heard from CrapIsKing?

IRCPlayer: he's got some pretty serious charges. What did you do to him?

HarlequinNinja: he shouldn't have been talking to me.

IRCPlayer: why aren't u going to ny?

HarlequinNinja: I think there are friendlier places to go.

IRCPlayer: like texas? Oh, wait, you just left there! :)

Was she going to have to deal with this for the rest of her life? CrapIsKing knew she was in ADX Florence, the only woman in an otherwise all-male institution, but the news reports were all saying that she had escaped from the all-female, maximum- security prison at the Federal Medical Center (FMC) Carswell located in Fort Worth, Texas. They couldn't put a warrant out for her arrest and admit they were holding her in a place in which she would never have been allowed.

So somehow she had escaped from FMC Carswell and the attack at the Florence facility that led to her escape was an unrelated distraction.

HarlequinNinja: I'd rather not talk about it.

IRCPlayer: turns out your dad and general palma were best buds for a while. Also general palma <3 secretary of state monahan

HarlequinNinja: how would you feel about a ddos attack on your isp that leads back to you?

Anna didn't know how to set off a distributed-denial-of-service attack, but the members of the IRC channel didn't know that. She was sure IRCPlayer didn't know.

IRCPlayer: you know what else I heard? your dad was involved in stuxnet.

HarlequinNinja: you're an idiot.

Anna was so tired of conspiracy theories. She lived with a father who was always on high alert, always looking over his shoulder. Stuxnet, the virus that had destroyed the Iraqi centrifuges that were part of their nuclear weapons program, was not something he was capable of. He couldn't even find a simple out of memory bug.

IRCPlayer: and you know, he's probably not your dad.

HarlequinNinja: here I am being friendly and now I have to do you harm

IRCPlayer: listen, i'm just looking out for you. I think maybe the general and your dad are still working together. trying to frame you

HarlequinNinja: stop talking. this channel is giving me a headache and i already had a rough day. want me to send a picture of your junk to your girlfriend? I have gimp, and I'm not afraid to use it.

What she would do for an aspirin. The Budget Inn was exactly what she needed with none of what she wanted. Maybe she should walk across the parking lot to Arby's.

If her dad was trying to frame her, there were so many easier ways of doing it. And so many less showy ways of trying to kill her.

IRCPlayer: i'm just trying to help. you asked about what we found and i'm telling you

HarlequinNinja: okay, stop telling me.

IRCPlayer: what's weird is that the program we found for you has your father all over it

HarlequinNinja: what?

IRCPlayer: i know!

HarlequinNinja: no, I mean what are you talking about? my father never left my sight for my entire waking life.

IRCPlayer: look, the program was almost shut down until he showed up and got it moving again. i've got the docs (the ones I'm not supposed to have)

HarlequinNinja: I want them

IRCPlayer: send me a link and I'll upload them.

Anna cursed. She didn't know what sites were safe. For all she knew Benson and his minion had every last site she had ever visited under surveillance. They might be tracking her right now if they had the Internet Relay Chat (IRC) channels tapped. Of course, this particular one would be difficult to find given how far off the radar screen it was, but she was playing with Benson and the other big boys now.

HarlequinNinja: cut-and-paste the doc into the channel and i'll read it later.

IRCPlayer: as you wish :)

HarlequinNinja: if you're lying to me I'm going to send nude pics of your mom to your gym teacher

IRCPlayer: I think she already did that. don't waste your time :$

Anna smiled. She had never met IRCPlayer in person but as much of an annoyance as he could be he was rather interesting. She was certain that he'd flirted with her on a few occasions. She returned the compliment whenever she realized that he was trying.

HarlequinNinja: are we going to meet in st. petersburg for a coffee?

IRCPlayer: are you going to have me arrested?

HarlequinNinja: hell, yeah.

IRCPlayer: then it's a date.

HarlequinNinja: will I be looking for a teenager or a retiree?

IRCPlayer: I'll never tell. I'll be the one holding the newspaper with a rose in it.

She smiled a Mona Lisa smile. A reference to Einstein. If she was the swooning type, she would have swooned. He certainly knew how to talk to a girl.

HarlequinNinja: my dad is probably dead.

IRCPlayer: if he is then he is doing a terrible job of staying that way. There are intel reports that he's in new york. Involved in terrorist activities

sfsayer has entered the channel

HarlequinNinja: he would never do that. i'm opening up your IP to the Chinese

IRCPlayer: i'll send your lat lon to the nsa so they can drone your hotel

HarlequinNinja: grow up

IRCPlayer: psycho witch

SFSayer: hey guys. get a room

A window opened on her screen. *Port scan in progress.* What the hell?

HarlequinNinja: gotta go

She shut down the secure channel and watched as the security software on the notebook attempted to follow the scan back to its source.

The window vanished. An Ubuntu window opened.

A process has crashed unexpectedly. Would you like to report the incident to Ubuntu?

She closed the notebook. The bugs were worse than she thought.

9

CHOKING

Saturday, October 27, 2012

The Waffle House in Daleville, IN was a thirty-second drive from the hotel. While Anna was reminded of how irrational her fear of bugs was that didn't stop her from laying terrified in her bed for what seemed forever as she tried to get some rest. She had turned the bed cover inside out so that the white material under the dark print would allow her to see anything multi-legged approaching her. While she fell asleep within seconds, her eyes continued to open every few minutes at the slightest sound, including the ones that weren't there.

Maybe what she really needed was breakfast. In the not-so-distant distance, she saw a yellow and black sign that read *WAFFLE HOUSE*. The restaurant, in a standalone building like so many eateries along the highways of the US, reminded her of diner breakfasts in New York. She didn't think twice.

As she walked to the glass door, the sound of the occasional car Doppler shifted behind her. Anna wore the same jeans and shirt from yesterday, only with a sweatshirt thrown over it. She'd resigned herself to wearing the wig since it kept questions to a minimum, gave her a chemo story, and made it easier to scratch her itchy scalp.

There were a handful of people at the counter in various states of informal dress sipping at their coffee like drug addicts disappointed with their high. In one of the booths sat a solitary man, and Anna, rather than waiting for someone to tell her where to sit, took a booth as far away as possible from everyone. She was not going to sit at the counter.

The waitress, who looked as tired as Anna felt, took her order and brought back plates filled with comfort food goodness before Anna realized that she had almost fallen asleep again. *Driving is going to be a problem. I'll sleep on the shoulder or a rest stop. Canada can't be that far, but I'd rather not have to take another sobriety test when all I need is some sleep. What's the hurry anyway? So a bunch of strangers can tell me what happened to Dad?*

Oh, yeah, someone is trying to kill me.

The eggs looked plain, but the bacon was crispy. *This is going to taste awesome.*

A plate fell and the smash sent sharp, painful sounds into Anna's ears. She looked toward the counter where the sound had come from and saw a well-dressed man grab his throat and make choking sounds.

5...4...3...

No one moved. Anna ran over to the man, put her arms around his waist, and squeezed. He tried to take in another breath, but he just wheezed a dull pull of air. She turned him away from the counter and gave him another squeeze, making sure she pushed upward into his sternum. She heard something land on the floor that she was sure must have shot out of his mouth.

She released him and led him to a chair.

"Thank you," he said.

"Are you alright?" she asked.

He nodded. He reached up, squeezed her arm, and shook his head again.

The sound of clapping filled the air. The two waitresses and the handful of patrons applauded. *Great. Now they'll remember me. Exactly what I didn't want.*

Anna went back and grabbed her backpack, threw some money on the table, and walked out of the restaurant.

She unlocked her car when she heard the door of the Waffle House open.

"Wait!" It was the choking man. "Where are you going?"

"I suddenly remembered I was late for my lobotomy. Are you okay?" She opened the driver side door.

"Yes, yes." He reached out as if he was going to shake hands, but she noticed the green edge of money sticking out from under his hand. "I just wanted to say thanks and show my appreciation." White male. Full head of hair. Brown eyes. Forties. "Please, come back in. I," he blinked, "I want to pay for your breakfast." Blink, blink, blink.

"No, really, I have to go," Anna said.

"I would have died in there. By the time an ambulance would have shown up..." His hand was still outstretched. Blink.

"No, really, I do CPR for free, and I wasn't that hungry anyway."

He stepped up and with his left hand he pulled her wrist forward and put her hand in his. He left the money behind. She sighed. He turned away and walked back in the direction of the door. She felt the wind against the generic maroon sweatshirt she had thrown on. *Is this how you repay someone who just saved your life? By embarrassing them with money?*

It might be enough to cover the breakfast she'd just walked away from. She took the black backpack off her shoulder and threw it in the car so it landed on the passenger side seat. She opened the thin crush of paper that was her reward for a job well-done and snapped open what turned out to be a $20 bill.

A piece of paper fell out. She looked over at the man. He hadn't entered the restaurant; he had gotten into his rather dusty, dark blue, mid-size car. Did he just have coffee? What did he choke on? She crouched down and grabbed the paper as the wind started to blow it away.

Go to the Fairmont Pacific Rim hotel at 1038 Canada Place in Vancouver. There is a room reserved for you. Wait for further instructions.

Anna felt the skin on the back of her neck crawl. *Like hell I will.*

The man pulled out of his parking space as Anna raced toward the vehicle. He saw her coming at him and took off in a cloud of loose gravel and dirt. Anna ran back to her car, turned on the ignition, keeping her eye on the blue car through her rearview mirror, and drove after him.

———

Anna typed his license plate into her phone, swerving every so often as she tried to keep her typing accurate. There was no way she was going to let him get away. She felt the Jeep shake as she caught up with him on her right. His eyes went wide as she brought the Jeep closer to him.

He pressed his brakes, sending his car back. Anna shot off ahead of him. *Nice move.* In her rearview, she saw him pull over onto the shoulder. *He thinks he can outrun me?* She pressed her brakes and kept the Jeep straight as it screeched to a stop, leaving black rubber marks on the road. She put the transmission into Reverse, floored the gas pedal, and drove along the shoulder until she almost smashed into the parked sedan.

She popped the seat belt and threw herself out. She saw him running into the forest and took off after him. After a minute or so she had a hard time breathing. *Where is he?* She leaned forward, put her hands on her knees, and gulped some air. *Asthma. I hate asthma.*

———

A branch snapped. She looked up in time to see him come at her from behind a tree, swinging a large branch. She put her left arm up in time to block it, but the pain exploded on impact and she cried out. She turned and ran. The sound of branches and crunchy leaves got closer as she slowed down to let him catch up.

She flexed her fingers. It was too late for him to stop when she swung and connected her fist into his jaw. *For every reaction there is an equal and opposite reaction.* The pain of the punch shot up her arm as the man fell back and collapsed on the ground. Anna snapped her hand up and down, trying to shake off the burning sensation. *Why does that have to hurt so much?*

————

Anna startled herself awake. She was sitting on the bare ground and felt her jeans dampen from the morning dew, the smell of rotting foliage all around her. The sun blinded her from its low-on-the-horizon position. Her sweatshirt did a good job of keeping her warm, but not too warm. The man was still unconscious, but at least now his hands were bound. She had checked his neck for a pulse and found she hadn't killed him. It was still a good day.

Tired of waiting, Anna tapped his cheek a few times. The skin was oily and not shaved well. A little bloody spit dripped down his chin and landed on his otherwise new suit. The tie he had been wearing loose around his neck was now around his wrists.

"Hey," Anna said. She tapped his face a few more times. "Hey!" The woods were empty. The occasional car drove by. The police were probably already on their way if anyone had spotted their two cars stopped on the shoulder.

The man groaned and shook his head as if waking from a nap. His brown eyes looked puzzled then surprised then terrified as he stared up at Anna.

"Oh, no. Let me go," he said.

"Who are you?"

"You have to let me go. I don't know anything. Someone gave me some money and told me to get you that note."

"Who are you?"

"Let me go!" The man struggled against his tie. Anna was proud of her knots. "I don't know anything."

"Who gave you the note?" Anna asked.

"Let me go!"

"Fine. I'll just wait here until the police arrive." Anna shrugged.

The man looked past her and tried to stand.

Anna pushed him back down. "Or you could tell me *who you are.*"

"I was just supposed to give you that note. *Go to Vancouver. Wait for further instructions.* That's all I know." His eyes darted back and forth.

Was anybody home?

Anna picked up the branch he had hit her with just moments earlier and slammed it against the tree. The branch tore in half.

"Okay, I'll wait." She plopped onto the ground, crossed her legs, and folded her hands. "Oh, and I will press charges."

"No, you won't." He blinked and blinked. His eyes wouldn't stop moving. "They'll find out who you are."

"Oh? And who am I?"

He twitched. "You'll be safe in Vancouver. Someone will reach out to you."

"Why Vancouver? Who cares if I live or die?" she asked.

"You'll find out in forty-eight hours. If you hurry. You'll be safe. They'll reach out."

"Do you need meds or something?"

"I'm fine." His shoulder twitched again. "Forty-eight hours and you'll know everything."

"What's in Vancouver?" Anna stood and put her hand against a tree. She was running out of time. The state troopers would see their cars soon. "I can't get into Canada. The whole world is looking for me. I sense that I'm going to end up in someone's trunk, stashed like a spare tire, and smuggled in."

He examined her up and down until he stopped at her face. "Your disguise is fine." Blink. "The entry point at the Ambassador Bridge is fine. The Canadians aren't looking for you. Different story if you come back." He looked away. Twitch. "Don't come back. Especially don't come back to New York."

New York? "Why not?"

"There's a storm coming. You have to stay away." Twitch. Blink. "You promised. They know where you are."

"Who? How do they know where I am?"

"If you don't go to Canada, you will be in a fatal car crash, and the police will be told it's you. It won't matter once you're dead." He looked up. "Don't die."

"I'm going to New York," Anna said.

"No!" The man caught himself. "Just go to Canada. They're waiting for you."

"Or your people will kill me."

"They said they were on your side."

"Very convincing."

10

———

"ANY LANDING YOU CAN WALK
AWAY FROM..."

Teterboro Airport
Teterboro, New Jersey

The white experimental plane was already in final approach to Teterboro airport when Secretary of State George Monahan felt the cell phone vibrate in his pocket. He would have answered if he had been upward of ten thousand feet, but he felt final approach deserved his undivided attention. Whoever was calling would have to wait until he was on the ground and in his SUV.

The rubbery smell of the cockpit, the cold air against his skin, and the constant vibration gave him an adrenaline high in a plane that had cost him a fortune and put his life at risk every time he flew it. His security detail was never happy during these times, but he cared not one bit. Life was about risk, and right now he had life by the gonads.

So, a hurricane was coming. He didn't care. He had seen the weather reports, but Monahan knew it wasn't only luck that allowed him to take off and land in what looked like just another beautiful late October day.

It was destiny.

———

The Ronald H. Brown US Mission to the United Nations Building
799 UN Plaza
New York, NY

The long corridors at the US Mission were easy to navigate once you knew where everything was. The stainless tiled corridors were home to a selection of identical doors with nameplates that appeared affixed with Velcro. It always smelled clean, though today someone thought it was a good idea to turn up the heat. Down at the end of the hallway, a man with a long pole and a rubber ball at its tip erased scuff marks from the floor.

Cordell Plante, Monahan's Deputy Chief of Staff, dressed in his usual navy suit and powder blue tie, juggled as he walked. His steps echoed in the otherwise empty hallway, and no one who walked down the same corridor would have noticed the juggling since it was in his head, but juggle he did just the same. He didn't want to admit it, but the day started to develop cracks about an hour ago. Monahan's delay on his way to the city from Teterboro, the US Mission to the UN locking down its facilities, and the probable cancellation of the Host Country Reception planned for Monday all vied for his attention, and he couldn't take his eyes off any of them. For whatever reason, the Secretary had been on a short fuse for the last few days. Things didn't look like they were going to improve anytime soon.

Plante stopped in the middle of the hall. *Yes, this is aggravating.* He didn't work at the US Mission often enough to remember the floor layout, and always found himself wandering the halls as he struggled to remember the location of his office. Once, about a year ago, he had found it on the first try. No such luck this time.

Plante, who had been working for Monahan since he'd accepted the appointment, knew that Monahan was a reasonable man given reasonable tasks, but in the State Department the reasonable tasks were far and few between. An earlier call had gone unanswered which could only mean that Monahan was minutes from the tarmac.

———

"You can't cancel the Host Country Reception," Monahan said.

He was in his convoy of black SUVs: a car in front, a car behind, and some of New Jersey's finest on motorcycles clearing the way and checking on the behavior of the folks who'd stopped to gawk as his motorcade made its way north.

The call he'd missed was from Plante. Now there was a man who did not use the phone very often, and for that Monahan was grateful. However, whenever Plante did call, Monahan knew there was trouble. Probably some crap or other about the hurricane. The landing, and its almost-failure, was already relegated to a memory. He called Plante back once the motorcade was safely on its way to the city.

He reached over and banged on the back of the driver's seat. "My phone says there's a lot of traffic through the tunnel. Take the bridge," Monahan said to his driver.

Plante said, "I understand, sir. However, you should take into account that Sandy is touching down Monday morning and will make it difficult for the guests to arrive."

Monahan usually enjoyed Plante's dry humor, but today's flight was not as therapeutic as he had hoped.

Plante continued, "Mayor Bloomberg has already started the lockdown of the city and the UN security office has sent out notes asking that all unnecessary events be postponed until after the storm."

"I've seen the radar maps. The storm is overblown." Monahan thought he needed a diversion to help with the handoff, but perhaps not. Maybe the storm would be enough of a diversion. The handoff of HALON was going to happen even if it killed him. Monahan tapped on his window. The bulletproof surface was cold. The sound was comforting.

"David wants you back in Washington," Plante said.

David Burrows was Monahan's Chief of Staff and had known Monahan even before his unexpected appointment as Secretary of State.

"He should have stopped me from getting on the plane," Monahan said.

"No one stops you from getting on that plane."

"He could have tried." The plane was something he had worked toward for years. A Burt Rutan special. Monahan loved flying and that plane, a forward swept wing beauty, was something that he enjoyed on a visceral level. On occasion, he remembered John Denver but didn't let the singer's death in another Rutan experimental plane bother him. Life was something that could be taken from you at a moment's notice, with no warning. He had made peace with that years ago when he thought about the accident in which his sister had died and he had not.

"My recommendation would be to be proactive, and cancel the reception before the media gets wind that you would rather put the lives of UN diplomats at risk rather than cancel a meet-and-greet."

"I don't remember the last time that reception was canceled," Monahan said.

"We should make this one just as forgettable."

Monahan turned around and looked at the amount of traffic that was following them north. This was crazy. Shouldn't everyone be buying emergency supplies and getting ready to hunker down in their homes? Of course they should. Monahan had only come to New York to satisfy his own curiosity. He hadn't been this close to this kind of storm before. This one could be record-breaking.

"Don't cancel the reception," Monahan said. "If we have to cancel, that's fine, but let's not do it yet. I think the folks in New York are made of heartier stuff than this and the international community might enjoy a night of eating and dancing while Mother Nature puts on a show."

———

Monahan stepped out of his black vehicle when the lead security agent had opened his door and gave the all clear. He stood in front of the slate gray building with its glass walls and curved stone entranceway.

As he took his first few steps, the driver from the rear vehicle stepped forward. It was Roberts. "Excuse me, sir."

Monahan stopped.

"We had to notify the local police that a car was following us. We took down the plate and handed it over."

Monahan wasn't sure what to think. Someone or some group was targeting him? He received death threats on a regular basis, but he had never had an actual stalker. He gazed up at the clear blue sky. What a beautiful day. "What did you find?" Monahan asked.

"We submitted a preliminary check. As soon as we know, we'll let your office know."

Roberts wore a dark suit and tie, and was one of the few men who always traveled with Monahan. While he was new, having only been with him for the last two years, Roberts had proven to be one of those men who understood the value of staying at least one step ahead.

"Thank you." Monahan turned away. "Now let's get inside."

"Yes, sir." Roberts spoke into his sleeve. "We are entering the building."

Monahan took a quick look around. Who the hell would be following him?

11

MODEL-DRIVEN DECISIONS

"We need to get the remaining personnel out," Monahan said.

"Doing this in the next day or so was never my idea," Palma said. He wasn't sure why, but Monahan was getting on his nerves. HALON had taken more years than even he had predicted and in the last few years Palma wondered when they would finally handover the finished facility. They were closer than they had ever been. Only now, the closer they moved to the handoff the more Palma bristled.

Palma paced the large room and avoided colliding with the sumptuous furnishings. Damn, the office was warm. If he sat down, he might fall asleep.

"We're here. They want to move in," Monahan said. He wore his usual white and navy striped tie with a white shirt.

Palma knew that Monahan usually wore that combination of shirt and tie whenever he spoke at the UN. What he couldn't figure out was what possessed Monahan to come to New York? Speaking before the UN was out of the question and completing the handoff was going to be a challenge. Like an Olympic skier trying to make sure not to hit anything on the way down.

"How was the response to our saber rattling?" Monahan referred to an earlier incursion into US airspace.

"Just another day. The Russian jets went home, as usual. I'm not sure what they're trying to prove, but one day there will be an accident and we'll have to react."

Monahan leaned toward his right. "The Russians don't know anything, do they?"

"They're not that good," Palma said. "We're supposed to be."

"Doesn't matter." Monahan took a sip of water from a crystal-clear glass. "Chinese Year of the Dragon. They feel the storm is a good sign."

"We shouldn't do this. I still have people there and we can't move them with so much police activity. We have to delay the handoff," Palma said.

"Our guests can handle it. Get your people out."

"Our guests, a misnomer if ever I heard one, don't know what they're doing. They need to be transitioned and that's not happening today or tomorrow since they've made their wishes quite clear," Palma said. "Monday is a bad day."

"It has to be Monday. They've already told me that if not Monday then they can't move on this for weeks." Monahan pursed his lips. "You don't know anything about that, do you?"

"About what? That we've got a B team testing them before we let them take over? The most asinine thing I've heard so far." Palma had considered the use of a B team years ago and disposed of that in record time. The A team was the current crop of workers at HALON. The B team would run the new occupants through their paces to make sure they knew what they were doing after the transition. HALON had facilities very few people knew about. Secrets within secrets.

Palma sat down and felt uncomfortable. "The worst is I haven't found anything either within the chairman's inner circle or without. Do they think the Falon Gong might try something?" Could they seriously believe that? The Falon Gong were harmless in the US.

"Will they?" Monahan asked.

"Sir, my people can't come out until Monday and even then this is just crazy. The protocols are complete for most of the systems, but we're still wrapping them up."

"Protocols," Monahan said. "Great."

"That's not going to make things any easier."

"I don't want easy at this point. I want this off my plate." Monahan stood. "Off our plate. Later causes problems." He extended his hand to Palma.

"Later solves problems," Palma said. They shook hands.

"Are we going to have to do this ourselves?"

"You can't even breathe the wrong way during this. I'm not sure why you're here," Palma said.

"Command performance."

Palma raised an eyebrow. Monahan was arm-twisted? "You can't be seen anywhere near this. I won't even be there."

"Good. I don't want to be around if anything goes wrong." Monahan shook his head and blinked. "This needs to be over. If our guests insist, you're going to have to get your folks out of there."

———

Palma sat alone in one of the US Mission's SCIFs at a polished wood conference table meant for twelve. Microphones sat on the tabletop, each a foot and a half apart. The deep brown plush office chair felt too soft against his legs so he sat at the edge of the seat. The filtered air smelled sweaty. He had already removed his jacket, but the tie felt comforting around his neck. The microphone lights glowed green.

"So, there's no getting out before the storm hits?" Palma asked.

"No, sir." The voice on the other end belonged to Dr. Donald Jenkins. "We decided to try out one of the models on the National Weather Service data and it's worse than they think. Unfortunately, if we leave now, we'll have to stop several boot-up sequences and enable the failsafe which will take at least twenty-four hours to complete in any case. Nothing here can be done with any speed." Palma didn't mind delaying the boot-up sequences, the clean start-up of various systems in some of the more dangerous areas of the facility, since part of the transition could be include them. The failsafe could not. It has to be ready. If anything went wrong...

"I want you to get your people out," Palma said.

"Sir, the police are already making preparations to seal as much of New York as possible. We should have left yesterday."

Palma was silent for a moment. "20-20 hindsight."

"It's the clearest vision I have," Jenkins said.

Palma smiled. Even though Jenkins wasn't former military he enjoyed working with him. A shame the IT side didn't have his equivalent. Or it did until Marshall left. A shame Marshall and Jenkins had never met for more than a passing greeting. Maybe it was for the best. Marshall has a way about him. Too negative. Too positive.

"I want all of you out. I need you to make sure all of your people are safe and ready to go." Palma unbuttoned his shirtsleeves and rolled them up. "If you're going to weather this, everyone is going to have to realize that they might be down there for some time."

"I think the models are wrong," Jenkins said.

The weather models were rarely wrong. They could be wrong about storm strength, but wrong about direction and devastation? Palma wondered if it was worth taking the risk. It didn't matter though, did it? No one was going anywhere. "Your own models say otherwise."

"Won't be the first time they've been wrong," Jenkins said.

So much of this felt wrong. Was there a protocol for an inbound hurricane? There had to be. The project had been in place for over ten years. Innumerable disaster recovery plans existed. Had the storm really caught them by surprise? No, there had to be enough time to get them all out. "Doctor, get your people ready to go. If you can get things shutdown in the next twenty-four hours then I'll find a way to get you all out. If you can't get things shut down, start handing out beer and chips for the next few days and we'll get you out eventually."

"Understood. And General?"

"Yes?" Palma asked.

"We appreciate your candor and concern."

"I'm not leaving any of my people in harm's way. You let them know that. If I can get you out, I will." He had to get them out. If anything happened they would all die.

12

KEEPING APPOINTMENTS

It took the Secretary of State fifteen minutes of phone tag to get the FBI director on the phone. What good was it to be this well-placed in the government and still have to chase people down when you needed them?

Especially if they seemed to be investigating you.

For the last week, before each of his meetings, Monahan had taken a good, long look at his surroundings, whether in DC or New York, and knew that he would miss this life. He felt fulfilled in the military, but at home this close to the President.

Monahan had always enjoyed the trappings of politics and power, and working with other like-minded people made his job worthwhile. Especially if he could get something from them tomorrow for a simple favor today.

The digital picture frame on his desk cycled through the same ten photos of his wife and two sons. Most times he didn't think about them, but today the flashing images reminded him of what he was willing to give up to cement his place in the future. He would miss them. Would losing them be worth it?

The meeting with Palma didn't go well, in Monahan's estimation. Palma had paced and did his protective parent routine that meant he was going to be making decisions based on loyalty to the worker bees instead of history or, more appropriately, to Monahan. His people would be fine. No one would think about them in thirty years. Monahan's short-term concerns overrode his long-term worries.

The end was near. That much he knew. The pieces were in place and his guests were getting antsy. Might as well just hand over the one thing that kept him getting up in the morning.

Holding on the phone, Monahan was concerned but did what he always did: he poked and waited for the other guy to blink.

"Mr. Secretary of State, I am sure I don't know what you're talking about," FBI Director Greg Harlan said.

"Harlan, I've got more things going on here than you can possibly imagine...I take that back. I've seen your schedule. You can imagine it, but what's going on?"

The car that had followed him earlier (and it was still too early in the day for this sort of nonsense) turned out to be a Bureau fleet vehicle. His security detail had not only put in the request but were immediately notified that they were not welcome to root around for the vehicle's whereabouts or current use.

"This can't be making you worried, is it?" Harlan asked. "A fleet vehicle that followed your wagon train?"

In fact, Monahan wasn't worried. For the next few days he knew exactly what he was doing. As usual, his people worried about the day-to-day mundane details, and he just had to make sure he kept the current government out of trouble overseas.

"Greg," Monahan said, "If there is something you want to talk to me about, perhaps you should just come right out and say it, but that was one of your cars."

He had met Harlan on a few occasions at the White House and while they were both pleasant men, Monahan knew that Harlan's focus would always be different than his. Harlan was just a cop. Everything about his background—Monahan learned his background as soon as Harlan was sworn in—pointed to a strong law-and-order leaning. That didn't stop Harlan from arresting demonstrators when the mood hit him, but it was obvious that the man was anal about the law.

Why was an FBI vehicle tailing his convoy?

"There must be some misunderstanding. There's only one reason why we would ever tail a senior member of the cabinet. Mr. Secretary, your office is always notified when we are handling threats made to your office, and we always send over the ones that seem the most worrisome. For some reason, there has been an unusually high number made recently, and our intel suggested a possible event. I'm glad to report that nothing happened, and we will continue to monitor the situation."

What a windbag. "I am happy to report that nothing happened either." *Idiot.* "Mr. Director, I appreciate your fine work. Please keep my office apprised of any goings-on and we will endeavor to help you in any way we can."

"I appreciate that. In the interest of confidentiality, I would also appreciate your continued discretion. My men should not have been spotted, so I will also be sure to look into that."

"You do that." Monahan hung up. He looked at the non-descript phone on his desk and wondered how much longer he would be forced to use something so primitive and brittle.

Harlan knew something. This was something that Monahan had feared, but was unavoidable the closer they got to the handoff. He wondered if perhaps there was too much communications chatter captured by the Intelligence community. Perhaps the FBI was simply wondering what the Chinese might have in mind while parts of the country were buckling down for another storm of the century.

The Chinese. The soon-to-be owners of some prime New York real estate.

"Cordell!" Monahan stood after reaching into his desk and pulling out a secure cell phone. While the US cell phone network was riddled with holes, the Chinese, who manufactured most of the cells for the States, made sure that their technology did not suffer from the same shortcomings. Or if the phones suffered, it would be from additional holes in the software that no one knew about.

He punched in the number he knew by heart. He couldn't wait to forget it.

Cordell Plante stuck his head in the office. Monahan pointed at his with the cell. "Get me Roberts. Have him check the latest list of threats reported by the Bureau. They said we've been notified about some new ones, but I don't remember any going by my..." Someone answered the call. "Go." Monahan waved off Plante.

As soon as the door closed Monahan replied to the voice. "Well, good morning and what the hell is going on?"

"You seem upset."

"We've got things to do."

Upset? Did he get as far as he was by losing his composure? No, but this call might cause him to lose it.

"How can we help?" The voice that always answered, a man of unknown age, was always smooth. Minimal accent. Never upset.

"I think your people are getting sloppy."

"That is always possible, but we are mindful of your position."

"If you were mindful of my position, I wouldn't be here."

"As Secretary of State?"

"In New York," Monahan said.

It was true that the Chinese did exert some pressure to get his nomination passed, but that was part of the cost for what they wanted. When a foreign car manufacturer built an automobile plant in the US, it wasn't due to patriotic leanings or tax advantages; that was simply the cost of a congressman. Over the years Monahan had received help over and above what he thought he could get and managed to pull some incredible touchdowns for the government. He had also figured out a long time ago that they would eventually want reciprocity and that day came over ten years earlier. What they wanted was epic.

They were lucky. Epic was on his bucket list.

"Do not concern yourself with the FBI."

Monahan stopped pacing. Were they tapping the office phone?

"While it's true they were following you, they don't have anything more than a hunch, a guess, as to something going on."

"They know something is going on?" Monahan asked.

"As I have said, nothing to raise concern. Perhaps you need to focus more on finding the girl."

"The girl doesn't matter. That's our concern. Either we find her or she surfaces and then we have her," Monahan said. Why did they care so much about Marshal Wodehouse's daughter? She was a loose thread on an otherwise perfectly tailored outfit.

"When will we take delivery?"

"My best people are saying this is a bad idea. We should wait. There are many things going on. Very few of them good."

"Certainly not the Russians. They play tag with your defense systems every few days."

"I am so glad to hear that you have such an interest in our affairs. Perhaps you can put in a good word and have them stay out of our airspace."

"I'm afraid that we don't yet have that level of influence. However, with your help we expect that to change. Perhaps as early as Monday?"

Monahan walked over to the window facing the main building of the United Nations. "Perhaps. We still have many people completing their jobs."

"They can leave safe in the knowledge that we will complete their work. We have all their records and plenty of personnel who have been assigned to learn their responsibilities. Please, as you say, trust me."

"New York City is going to be a mess."

"We're counting on the hurricane."

Monahan was sure they were. "Please have your people out by the time we get there or we will take care of removing them. They will be safe with us. We will take possession Monday. Is that acceptable?"

"Perfectly."

13

THE BLEEDING CEILING

HALON

Dr. Donald Jenkins, Lead Scientist and Director for the Clinical/Biological Research and Development Unit, walked the long corridor on the thirtieth floor to the main elevator. *If only it were possible to do multiple conflicting goals at the same time. Life would be so much easier for those of use having to deal with the insane. Or bureaucrats. Identical concepts.*

The last few days had been quite interesting, surpassed only by the interesting day he'd had yesterday. Based on the Law of Ever-Increasing Idiocy, surely based on Newton's Second Law of Thermodynamics, Jenkins was sure today would surpass yesterday.

The aggravation he felt as he walked down another darkened hallway spilled into his work and his contact with his fellow scientists. Light sensors that didn't turn lights on. The manual switches that hadn't been connected or, if connected, tested. As the only remaining senior person in the facility, he was on the hook to address all problems, from the trivial to the earth-ending, that needed a resolution before they vacated the building. The General had promised,

(*promised!*) that he would be in this building to keep all that sad crap off his plate.

Palma was a good man, but not as reliable, or as organized as he liked to think.

Jenkins stopped at the intersection of four corridors. Behind him, the corridor was dark. Was the storage area to the right or left? He walked right. The dark corridors spooked him.

He turned when he heard the echo of footsteps behind him. He saw the outline of one of his researchers. No time to talk. They were down to just-over-a-day and completion was an impossibility. Jenkins wasn't sure which research group Palma was sending to take over their work, but that new population was going to be in for quite the surprise unless the hurricane made entering the facility difficult or impossible.

Once inside the storage area Jenkins looked up at the stained ceiling of the single elevator that would lead them in or out. The elevator had been giving them problems the last few days and decided to stop working altogether about an hour ago when Ernie, Ernest to his friends, had decided to climb onto the top of the compartment to fix it.

Someone heard the elevator move then a muted, surprised sound. There was silence for a few moments. The ceiling started to bleed.

Ernie's head, shoulders, and part of his torso were crushed under the main gear. Maybe his shirt had gotten caught or the elevator started on its own. The outcome was the same.

Jenkins pressed his lips together and exhaled. Was the elevator even working? The only way to tell was to send it up and see what happened. The problem was that Ernie's body should be extricated from the gears so an autopsy could be performed, with any luck not by him.

They were already down to a skeleton crew due to the evacuation orders which would explain why Ernie worked by himself. Whatever the problem, it was now too late to do anything about it.

Poor man. His family needed to be notified.

Jenkins stepped into the elevator. The unit had not been locked or shut down. Ernie had the keys with him as none were evident in the control panel. He thought of climbing the ladder and pulling the keys from the dead man's belt, but thought better of it.

———

"You have to send personnel down here. Someone needs to remove the body and fix the elevator." Jenkins had been standing in front of the elevator when he called Palma and started to walk when Palma answered. "There aren't enough of us here," Jenkins said.

"Is he dead?" Palma asked.

Was he kidding? "Of course he's dead. I might not be a GP, but I can tell when someone has ceased breathing because of a crushed chest and head."

The storage room where the elevator sat was one of the smaller rooms in the facility, and it was massive. Being the top floor meant it was constructed with durability in mind. Everyone knew where the elevator was, but its location was a mistake. Part of the construction plans had been read wrong. The elevator should have been part of a corridor leading to the main entrance. Instead, it led into a large storage area that made it convenient for freight, but inconvenient for people to come and go without having to get around stacks and stacks of boxes. Jenkins pushed his way out.

"Then I guess you're staying," Palma said. "Have one of your guys send me his name and PIV number so I can make arrangements and notify his family."

"No one is getting you anything. Did you not hear the part about crushed head and chest? Where do you think he hung his PIV? On his belt?" Jenkins exited the room and brushed some dust from his lab coat. He looked back and, given his tall frame, saw the now useless elevator sitting open in the semi-lit room. "Just send someone. Anyone. Preferably medical. I know it's Saturday. I know the day is going by fast, but you must have someone you can spare." The elevator door closed. "And tell them not to use the elevator."

"Can you lock it down?" Palma asked.

"I'm afraid not. The keys are with him, as well."

"Send one of your guys up there and get his keys. Lock the elevator down. We don't need that man to be in any worse condition than he already is."

"I'll see what I can do. What are you going to do?" Jenkins asked.

"What am I going to do? I'll see if someone is available, but almost everyone has been sent away. Because of the hype we're hearing, this will probably fizzle out right after landfall," Palma said.

"The only other way here is by staircase. Make sure they bring a stretcher. There are certain things we didn't count on when we designed this and a spacious staircase was one of them." Jenkins looked at his cell briefly. Two bars. "And by the way, make sure we don't lose power down here. There aren't a lot of windows to open if you know what I mean."

"Got it. Power. No windows," Palma said.

This had to be one of the worse run projects in which Jenkins had ever participated. Why was he even talking to General Palma? For a project as secret as this he should have been dealing with someone levels away from this man. Palma was high enough up the food chain to barely understand English much less the intricacies of this kind of project.

"Wait a minute. Aren't you off the grid yet?" Palma asked.

"Not for another month. The standalone generators need fuel." Jenkins walked down the white concrete corridor lit by an endless line of fluorescent tubes. "General, this is the kind of thing that points out why no one should be left here for the next few days."

"Dr. Jenkins, we've been through this before. You and your people, the handful still there, have plenty of food and water to wait for a few days. Everything will be fine," Palma said.

"Look, I know there is plenty for them to do, but at some point, this feels like a kidnapping and not everyone is equipped for that sort of isolation. And the inability to leave..."

"I understand. Doctor, I truly understand." Palma's voice took on an edge. "They're going to get combat pay for this. No one is going to hold a gun to their heads and tell them to keep going. But the best thing they can do is what they've been doing. Working on completing the protocols."

"Everyone needs to get out of here. Everyone."

"No one is leaving. That's an order. I'll have someone there soon enough."

"Meaning?" Jenkins asked.

"Tuesday."

This man is insane. "General, you've got to be kidding. We don't have enough people here to do anything safely. If it floods, there won't be anyone left alive for you to get come Tuesday."

"Don't get dramatic."

"You haven't seen the models."

"You were fine an hour ago."

Jenkins turned a corner. The lights were out. "General!" he almost yelled into the cell. "You need to come down here. The systems are registering power losses and shutting down the facility in sections. This isn't like we can open a window and let in some sunlight. When it gets dark..."

"Understood. The software wasn't my responsibility."

How many other corridors would shut down? Would they be in the middle of handling specimens and find themselves in darkness?

Another section of corridor went dark.

14

INVESTIGATIONS

FBI Offices
26 Federal Plaza

Terrell looked at the two Internal Investigation agents sitting at the table with him in the FBI cafeteria. His lunch was ruined. He was unhappy about that, as the first bite of his spicy Buffalo chicken wrap demanded a second bite.

"You guys have nothing better to do today than give me an upset stomach?" Terrell asked.

"Good to see you too, Terrell." Special Agent Darren Davila sat down across from Terrell while his traveling companion sat to Davila's right.

Davila introduced his partner, and he and Terrell shook hands. Terrell forgot the man's name within seconds. He wasn't even sure if he'd heard what Davila said. The plight of the busy.

"Are you here to invite me out drinking tonight?" Terrell asked.

"Listen, buddy, I just wanted to ask you a few unofficial questions and run back to my hole in the ground. Nothing we discuss here is real. I'm not recording this."

Davila's tanned skin was wrinkle-free even though he was older than Terrell. The men smiled at each other, but Davila's companion's eyes didn't join in the levity.

Terrell looked around at the crowded eating area, put his sandwich down, and leaned back. "Is this about me or someone I know? And I know this isn't about me."

"This isn't about you." Davila put his hands up, palms facing Terrell. "I wanted to get some intel on that young girl you were investigating."

"I am not investigating Anna Wodehouse."

Davila's blinked and frowned. "You were in Colorado when the fireworks started raining down on ADX. You're telling me you weren't there for her?"

Terrell's eyes narrowed. "You know she was at ADX?" Was he being goaded or did Davila really know that? Anna's incarceration at the all-male prison was a closely guarded secret as far as he knew. Until someone helped her escape by blowing up the facility.

"I also know you visited Charbrand Construction this morning."

———

Earlier That Morning

Charbrand Construction
Brooklyn, NY

"Agent Terrell, you're asking me to break the law."

"You're a lawyer. You do that every day," Terrell said.

Both men stared at each other for a moment and then chuckled under their breath.

Terrell chose Charbrand Construction as his first easy stop of the day. He would have a friendly chat with one of the division heads, confirm that they were doing work for the Department of Defense through one of the usual defense contractors, and call it a day. The man would not be able to contain himself. He'd give away enough information that Terrell could continue digging into who was authorizing what, then scare him with jail time for being an accessory to illegal domestic spying even if that wasn't quite true. The things Terrell had to do to solve a money laundering case that somehow included Anna on the periphery.

A walk in the park until he arrived at the building with three floors rented out by the construction company. The receptionist looked like someone's mother dressed for a wedding reception. When he asked for the division chief, a man by the name of John Walton, Terrell found himself face-to-face with Charbrand's lawyer instead. Standard dark suit, navy tie, white shirt, perfect teeth. The man introduced himself as Mark C. Hammer.

"Seriously? M.C. Hammer?" Terrell asked.

Hammer shook his head. "Can't touch that. I think my parents have a twisted sense of humor. How can I help you?"

"I think we should start by finding a quiet place to talk." Terrell picked up a thin, brown leather briefcase he had brought in with him.

Hammer led him to the nearest door that opened to a large conference room.

"Nice table. I'm sure you and the other legal staff hold human sacrifices here on a regular basis." Terrell slid his hand on the burnished brown surface. His skin was still darker.

As Hammer sat across the table, Terrell asked, "Are you doing any DOD work here in New York? Because if you are, your entire executive board might be going to jail."

Hammer sat up. "We are not allowed to discuss work done for the Defense Department or for any defense-related contractors or anything that might be related to classified programs that are ongoing, in the past, in the future."

"Well put, Counselor. I just want some textbook answers," Terrell said.

"Ask some textbook questions," Hammer said. He folded his hands on the table.

Terrell had his attention.

"Is it the standard practice for Charbrand Construction to hire illegal workers for classified projects?"

"Everyone we hire is legal and cleared based on the work they are assigned to do as an employee or contractor of the firm."

"Good, good." Terrell opened his briefcase, pulled out a file folder, and showed Hammer the photo of a man who might have been from Peru or Honduras. "This man was found at," Terrell read some notes on the back of the photo, "a work site that I have confirmed is a DOD project, and I have also confirmed that the man is an illegal."

"I'm willing to bet that the site that man is on is not DOD, and I'm also willing to bet that this man is legal."

"I'm glad you feel that way." Terrell pulled another file out of his briefcase. "I have another one."

Hammer stood. "File whatever paperwork you think you need to file. We are done here."

"But I'm not done," Terrell said from his chair. "There's the curious incident of the illegals working on a DOD project at a location that doesn't exist who are also now dead."

———

Later That Morning

FBI Offices
26 Federal Plaza

Hammer was a good lawyer. At least good for his firm. Terrell managed to get absolutely nothing from him and didn't bother threatening him with jail time, because, as a lawyer, he would know that Terrell was bluffing. The executive board of a corporation rarely spent time behind bars and then only in extreme cases, and those happened too seldom for Terrell's taste.

He walked through the doors of the FBI office in New York and saw two agents jogging toward him. *Good, not too fast or I might think you're coming after me.*

"Special Agent Garrison!" The man held out his hand and Terrell shook it. "Great to see you again. We need to talk."

The agent, a full head taller than Terrell, gave the lobby the once over. "The word on the street is you're good friends with General Malik Palma. Let's grab a coffee."

———

Terrell sat in his cube while the other two men pulled chairs from other work areas. They set them down in the narrow walkway, cutting off any chance Terrell might have had of escape. Would he need to escape?

"I've heard you're doing a bang-up job on tracking down money funneling through Piercing Ventures," Morris said. He had introduced himself as Special Agent Steven Morris from Counter Intelligence.

"You know Piercing?"

"If you knew Piercing like I knew Piercing."

They smiled.

This was the breakthrough Terrell had been waiting for.

"We need you to stop your investigation. We need access to all of your files and we need to meet with the Anti-Money Laundering team."

"Whoa." Terrell almost stood up, but there wasn't enough room. "I need you guys to help me with this case. Every time I get down deep enough into the mud, I get stonewalled. I'm pretty certain that guys like General Palma have something to do with it, but it could be any of a number of players in the intel community."

"We know. And we're willing to trade intel on this to get you to stop."

"And all this before lunch." Terrell's chair gave a slight squeak. Terrell smirked.

"Look, the work you've been doing is getting close to tipping off someone we have been investigating for a few years now. Our case is becoming more and more solid with every passing day. This person of interest might be passing state secrets to non-friendly countries in exchange for influence here in the US."

"General Palma?" Terrell asked.

"Secretary of State George Monahan."

Terrell sat stock still in his seven-year-old chair.

Monahan?

Monahan.

"I think you guys are wrong. I haven't seen anything that would give me an indication that Monahan is involved in anything. General Palma, on the other hand, might be."

The two men looked at each other. "Malik Palma? He and Monahan have always had a strong relationship."

"Guys, I don't think there's anything there," Terrell said.

"You have to stop. Whatever you're doing. Stop."

"Okay, I'll stop. When do I join your task force?" Terrell asked.

"You don't. Why don't you go grab some lunch and we'll meet you back here? We really need a full debrief."

"Monahan is not your man," Terrell said.

———

After Lunch

FBI Offices

Terrell sat in a dark conference room with the two men from Internal Investigations and could feel his bile rising. His sandwich lay like a rock in his belly. And the day had started out so well.

"This is a wild goose chase," Terrell said.

"We can hold you in contempt," Davila said.

"No, you can't. This isn't an official investigation yet."

"We have sources that point to you knowing that girl before 2011."

"Now I know you're just fishing. That was Gavin Gillespie. He was in charge of her case when she was found way back when," Terrell said.

"For the record..."

"There is no record."

"We are filing your paperwork for review with the IG's office. You were supposed to be on vacation, or on leave, and instead you were in the middle of an escape."

The Inspector General. That was one step away from suspension.

"This isn't even enough for a non-adverse action." Terrell stood up and walked to the door. He had intel to exchange with the other investigators, and a case to fight for. He didn't have time to waste with an internal investigation of nothing.

"Let me know when you're not just blowing smoke up my ass. I'll be at my desk."

15

CANARY IN THE MINE

The building at 2 Broadway was crushed together like someone in a crowded subway train held up by the surrounding crowd and not themselves. The building would forever look like it was held tight by a corset that would never come loose. The usual density of human beings walked back and forth, some carrying a late lunch, the majority holding a cup of Dunkin Donuts or Starbucks coffee. The suits from Wall Street, the tourists looking for the ferry to the Statue of Liberty, the stunning women who could just as easily be secretaries as hedge fund analysts.

Various food aromas wafted down the street along with Terrell as he made his way to the MTA offices. A cold wind picked up, and his suit jacket lost its appeal as his only coat. He just needed to twist his ankle or have a passerby knock into his injured shoulder to complete the start of the afternoon. One New York Plaza peeked around White-hall Street as he looked south toward the ferry.

Terrell was certain he was going to start getting into fights if this insane interruption of his work continued. He still hadn't agreed to hand over the case to the counter-espionage guys, but he was sure he wasn't going to be given a choice. Piercing Ventures. There were other funnel sources, but there was something about the work paid for by

Piercing to other companies that paid off other companies that somehow made its way to construction projects that sometimes existed and sometimes didn't.

He was about to find out which. His trip to lower Manhattan, specifically 2 Broadway, was to one of the Metropolitan Transportation Authority's offices to meet with one of the supervisors whose name was on a work order authorizing work to be done at a work site that didn't exist.

The young woman who approached him was a touch heavy-set. Civil service walk. Her blue button-down and navy pants were tight, but they looked good. Terrell would remember her when he saw her again. He hoped he would see her again.

"Ms. Gonzalez?" he asked. He extended his hand.

"The one and only." She was shorter than Terrell, but not by much. Thick black hair, olive skin, perfect teeth. "That's a joke. There are a million Gonzalezes around here. I'm not even the only Gonzalez at my management level," she said.

Terrell smiled. If she thought she was having a rough day already, he was about to take her to new lows. He pulled out his ID and handed it over.

She took it and began to read.

"Something wrong?" he asked.

"No. You live in the Bronx. Why would you do that?"

"That's actually my parents' address. They both passed, but I do enough work up here that I just stay there," Terrell said.

"Passed?"

"A few years ago."

"Oh, I'm so sorry."

"I don't want to take up any more of your time than I have to. I sent a list of questions to your office, but I'd prefer to hear and see the answers from you," Terrell said. Since she was one of over a few dozen project managers at the MTA who had signed work-orders on this project-that-didn't-exist his interest was piqued.

"No problem." She looked down at his ID again. "Mr. Garrison."

"Oh, Terrell, please."

She chuckled a little. It was like having a conversation with a Latina version of Mae West.

"Well, then. Marisol." She tilted her head down and gazed up at him with a flirtatious smile. "So, fire away, Terrell."

"Montague Street."

"Brooklyn."

Terrell laughed. "This isn't *Jeopardy*. Besides you didn't answer with a question."

"What street can I find in Brooklyn?"

They laughed again.

My eyes are going to start bleeding if we don't get past this. "Marisol, you signed an order for some work to be done on Montague Street."

"I sign a lot of work orders, honey. Could you be more specific?"

He showed her the work order with her signature.

The smile disappeared. "That's work for the government. You should know that."

"The government?"

"You know. The guys nobody likes talking about and don't like being talked about."

"I'm still not following," Terrell said.

"Well, that's good because this conversation is over. I don't want to go to jail."

"Why would you go to jail?" *Damn it, she's retreating faster than I can pull her back.* His neck started to blush and his dry mouth made it difficult to swallow.

"I don't know where you got that piece of paper, but that work order was supposed to be hush-hush."

"Where was the work done?"

"How would I know, Terrell?" She pronounced his name like it was a bad taste in her mouth.

"Ms. Gonzalez." He looked around at the cloudless sky and decided he needed some visuals. "Marisol. Could you take me to where the work was done?"

"I most certainly will not. I've never seen the inside of a jail cell and I don't intend to let you send me there." She put her hands on her hips. "You got that piece of paper. You find the work site. The guys who visited me a few weeks ago to remind me of my federally-inflated responsibility..."

"You were threatened?"

"They don't have to threaten. The way they were dressed, dark suits and sunglasses, all they had to do was breathe to scare the hell out of me."

Terrell's face felt flush. "What's on Montague Street? I'm sure that's not classified. Which, by the way, I am cleared to hear even if you don't believe it."

"Yeah, they told me who I shouldn't talk to about this and the police was top of the list. FBI was next." She motioned a water level with hand. "This is classified higher than you."

"What's on Montague Street?"

"Are you asking me as a citizen of an officer of the MTA or as a federal cop?"

"Private citizen," he said.

"A venting station for the subway."

Terrell took another look at the work order. "They worked on the venting station for ten years?"

"I don't know what you're talking about," she said.

With that Marisol Gonzalez turned and walked back to the MTA building without a glance back.

———

That went well. Not.

Terrell had one more stop to make then he was going to have to return to Federal Plaza and face the Counter-Intelligence music waiting for him.

But first he had to talk to a widow.

He was losing the day fast and he was tired. The MTA woman was no help, his case taken whether he wanted it to be or not, yet he still felt compelled to question one more person. It was mid-afternoon and after sitting in traffic he arrived at a Jackson Heights address, 40-

19 72 Street, looking for a widow. The widow of a man who, like a number of other construction workers he was tracking, had committed suicide a few months after working on the alleged DOD project funded by Piercing Ventures through a number of construction firms to hide the passing of funds.

The partly cloudy sky lit up the neighborhood, showing off which buildings were cared for, and which maintained a state of inattention. The building he wanted had a clean brick exterior. Only five stories. He looked at her address.

Fifth floor. No elevator.

Walk. Walk. Walk. Walk.

Walk.

Apartment 5F. At the end of the hallway, of course. Terrell had been doing this for so many years that there were days when he wondered what the point was. Today was one of those days. The hallway smelled of groceries and must. Sweat poured down his forehead and his shirt was plastered to his skin. Even in the October cool he couldn't stop sweating.

He knocked.

"Go away!"

"Mrs. Beuda?" He knocked again. "This is Special Agent Terrell Garrison. I called earlier."

"Go away!"

"Ma'am? Please. Let me in," Terrell said.

He heard a thump against the door. "I don't want to talk to anyone."

"Ma'am, I just want to ask you a few questions about your husband." Terrell heard sobbing on the other side of the door. He placed his hand on the spot that bulged out a touch. "Please. Let me in."

The door flattened. He heard the door chain being unlatched. The doorknob turned and the lock tumblers fell into place.

With the door opened a crack Mrs. Bueda looked up and started screaming. "No, please don't kill me!" She slammed the door shut just as Terrell put out his hand.

"I'm not here to kill you." He swung the door open and she stumbled backward over a table and stood up.

"Get away from me!"

Terrell had his ID in his hand and held it out as far as he could. The apartment, filled with outdoor light, looked like his parents'. A clock to one side. Photos of various sizes of children on the wall. "Ma'am, I am with the FBI. I'm not here to harm you. I spoke to your sister who told me she would tell you about this visit."

"They showed me your picture! They said that you would kill me!" She cried out loud. "Please don't kill me!"

"Who showed you my picture? I just wanted to ask a few questions about your husband."

"No!" She ran into the other room.

Terrell heard her opening a window. He ran in just in time to see her climb onto the fire escape. He stuck his head through the window as she screamed and screamed.

"Please, Mrs. Bueda. I swear I am not here to harm you!" He pulled out his cell phone. "I will call the police for you. You must trust them, don't you?"

She closed her eyes and shouted out, "Why did he file that report? Why? Now he's dead!"

"Why did he kill himself?" Terrell asked.

"He didn't kill himself! He didn't! They killed him! They killed him because he filed that stupid police report!" She looked out over the street. It was about a sixty foot drop.

"Ma'am. There was a note. He left a note."

"That wasn't him!" She spat out the words. "He would never have left me alone! Never!" She cried out. "Why did they have to kill him?" She sobbed as she brought her hand up over her face. "I was doing better. I thought..."

"Please, come back inside. I'll call the police."

"No. No! NO! You will not take away what little I have of him." She cried out again. "Oh, oh. I miss you so much. Why were you so stupid? Why didn't you listen to me?"

"I just want to know what he told you about why he filed that paperwork," Terrell said. How did this go from bad to worse?

"No! No more!" She looked at Terrell with an intensity reserved for the desperate. "You have to go."

He put his hand up again, palm out. "Okay, I have to go." He started to pull himself back into the apartment. "I'm going. I'm going to get you help."

"No one can help me. No more visits. I don't want to see those men again."

With that she threw herself off the fire escape.

16

SNACKS AND TOILET PAPER

Detroit, Michigan had seen better days, but Anna couldn't imagine them as she drove through the southeast part of town made up of shuttered buildings, dirty parking lots, and the occasional house of worship. The Jeep, after having done various acrobatics as Anna's chariot, decided the front windows were no longer going to open, though the rear ones seemed content to do as they were told.

The blast of cold coming from the back dropped the temperature to a more acceptable level and her body felt the difference right away. The headache that earlier had threatened to surface decided to hide in the warmth even as Anna unzipped her hoodie more and more.

Almost at the bridge. Time for supplies.

Why did someone want her to go to Vancouver? Were they the ones who helped her to escape from the Supermax? Would she have to speak French when she got there? She saw a gas station to her left and pulled in. *Go in. Come out. Keep going. Vancouver waits for no woman. I have no idea what that bridge is going to be like.*

Anna entered the convenience store at the Sunoco station on West Fort Street a few blocks before the entrance to the Ambassador Bridge. She pulled at the various bits of bulky clothing she wore in an attempt to feel comfortable, if not look comfortable. The day was another day. The sky was blue. The sparse white clouds hung suspended in defiance of gravity. The aroma of coffee reminded her how much she really needed a caffeine hit. Maybe she should pick up some snacks? Her stomach needed attention, as well.

Based on the quantity of snacks and drinks the other customers were buying she thought for sure there must be an unreported famine happening on the Canadian side. She changed her mind. No snacks.

She just wanted toilet paper. Maybe some coffee. That was it. She had been scoping out the areas in Canada. It was a long road to Vancouver. Maybe she should have stayed in the US longer then crossed into Canada? No, she needed to leave the manhunt for her. The only way to do that was to get out.

Her mouth was dry. She needed to pick up water.

Don't sweat it. You just need to live through the next few hours.

"Excuse me, miss."

Anna turned almost too fast for her blond wig. She had practiced turning her head to make sure she didn't send her wig flying off in one direction while she was looking in another, but without some sort of sticky tape her head was just too smooth.

There were two Michigan state troopers standing next to her.

All I want is toilet paper. This can't be that hard.

"Oh! Yes, Officer?" she asked.

"Please, come with us."

"Of course." She scoped out the store. She would have an easier time taking them down in here. Many more points of confusion. Harder for them to take a shot at her. No bullets should be fired at her during this encounter. She had a date in Vancouver and she wasn't going to miss it.

The TV in the corner was blaring something or other. Wait! She saw a face she recognized. Heat built up behind her eyes.

Benson? The bastard who convinced her to go to the UK, break into system after system, and ultimately commit murder in pursuit of a man who was obviously dead?

It was him. Malik somebody-or-other.

Benson.

She almost ran out to her car, but she couldn't move her feet.

"Miss?" There was a voice to her left. "Miss?"

CNN.

"New York is in the middle of its own political storm even as Hurricane Sandy approaches, leaving a trail of devastation in its wake. Secretary of State George Monahan arrived in New York earlier today amid calls from the Russians that the US continues to threaten its planes that are flying in legally recognized international airspace. There was no immediate comment from the State Department."

"Miss?"

"Also scheduled to speak at the Security Council this week is NSA Director General Malik Palma who is also in New York. He and Secretary of State Monahan are scheduled to meet with the various dignitaries even as event after event is being cancelled..."

Those bastards are in New York?

"Miss?"

Anna blinked and realized where she was. She had to get out of here before she did something stupid. Like head over to New York.

She turned to them. "I'm sorry, Officer. Is something wrong?"

"No, miss. I just wanted to have a quick word with you." The shorter of the two troopers winked at her. "If you know what I mean." His close-cropped hair seemed to move up and down as his forehead crinkled with his smile.

Seriously? This was dating in the 21st century? A cop acted like something was wrong and instead of just flirting ran a background check on a potential? Of course, she would have done the same, but she wasn't in his position. She was on the receiving end of his attention, and she wasn't impressed, especially since her mind was on Vancouver, not dating or flirting.

The officer leaned in. "You look familiar to me."

"A lot of people say that about me. I look like everybody's high school girlfriend." Anna smiled and tilted her head. "Or you might have seen my YouTube video. I'm trying to travel around the US and Canada before," she pulled her wig up enough that they saw her bald head, "you know, the chemo stops working." Both men opened their eyes wide.

"I don't like talking about it." She looked at the short one and gave him a long, hard stare. "Sometimes I'm just so lonely traveling around the country. But it's always been my dream to see as much of the world as I can and Detroit was on my bucket list."

"Oh, my. Oh. I am so sorry." The shorter officer looked at his partner then back at Anna. "I am, we are, so sorry." He put his hand on his gun holster. "I thought you looked familiar. It must have been the YouTube video." He leaned toward her again. "Are you doing anything on Kickstarter?"

"Not yet. Maybe as my funding starts to run out." The back of her head tingled. "I really need to go."

"Well, before you go, I need to run a quick check on you."

"No. Really. I have to go. I'm meeting my spiritual advisor on the other side of the bridge."

The officer smiled at her. "I might not let you leave."

Anna made her eyes water. "Oh, please don't. I really do have to go."

The CNN story was still on and they were showing a still of Benson. General Palma. Whoever.

She sniffled. "I want to make my dream come true."

"Yes, but," he gave her a knowing look, "you might be a wanted international criminal."

She laughed out loud with the two officers. *I think my head is going to explode.*

Anna returned to the register and paid for the toilet paper and two bottles of water. The thought of using leaves on the side of the road did not appeal to her at all. She was certain she wouldn't need more than that before entering Canada. "Alright." The officer motioned with his head toward the door.

Anna's stomach twisted in anxiety. If they did a basic identity search of the current Most Wanted, she was sure that her picture would come up first. Not second or tenth. First. She scoped out what she would need to do to knock out the officers without injuring them too much.

They stepped outside. The wind picked up. They did look handsome in their uniforms. Why didn't Terrell wear a uniform? Right. He looked awesome in his suit. Why did she think about him all the time? Bad habit. She had to stop thinking about the people who wanted to put her away.

He doesn't want to put me away. He wants to protect me.
Sure. Go on thinking that.

The officer held out his hand. "Driver's license, please?"

She reached into her pants' pocket and pulled out her wallet. She made a show of extracting the license and handed it over with a flourish. She held on to her smile for as long as she could. The license looked good, but it might not have much behind it.

The officer looked at the license. "Oh, you live in Pennsylvania." He handed the license back without swiping it or entering any of its information into his handheld. "I have friends there. Maybe I can give you a call next time I'm down there."

Anna smiled and repositioned her wig. "There is only one thing that would be funnier than that."

"What's that?"

She pulled out her cell phone and took a selfie with him.

17

CROSSING THE BORDER

The Ambassador Bridge, in operation since 1929, would allow Anna entry into Canada but did nothing to make her trip to Vancouver any easier. Driving through the US would have been faster and would still take almost forty hours of straight driving. The trip through Canada was going to be much worse, but gave Anna something she needed: the ability to get lost in the shuffle. Of all the ways into Canada, none would afford her the chaos and congestion of the Ambassador Bridge.

As one of the busiest entry points between the US and Canada, Anna knew that by the time she got to the customs gate they would be happy to just let her through unscathed. She would be happy to go through unscathed. She had a date in Vancouver. Or was that Sumatra?

Vancouver. Who would she find there? This was certain to be a testament to her motivation to take revenge on the people who had put her in jail, but why did she feel like she was just running?

The TV news story. The old feeling of helplessness squeezed her heart spreading heat up her neck and across her face. There was Benson plain as day. She couldn't help but think of him using the name he had first used when they met. Benson.

I will help you kill your father.

What he meant was: *I will kill you and the man you think is your father and no one will know what happened.* Except she didn't die and numerous attempts to kill her had failed.

Too many guardian angels. Or was that guardian aliens?

Anna heard a short squeal as she slammed on her brakes. She almost rear-ended the car in front of her. She was falling asleep. She took a sip of water. Her tongue felt thick. She was sure she was in a dream state for at least a few seconds. That would get her killed, or worse, holed up in a hospital where the authorities would find her, and send her back to prison. But probably not ADX Florence.

She slammed on her brakes again. Her head snapped back and her eyes blinked open. *This is really not good.* The car in front of her was a large pick-up. She would crash into it, end up under the vehicle, and the driver wouldn't even notice.

The bright sun reflected off everything. The metal of the cars around her, the asphalt, the girders holding up the bridge. Traffic heading into Canada was almost at a standstill. Thankfully, the traffic coming into the US was moving at a brisk pace. There was even the occasional joker who weaved in and out.

Someone honked. Anna looked but couldn't see them. The sound coming through her rear windows threw her off. And worse, while her traffic was stopped, the traffic to her left moved like just another day in paradise.

Two pick-ups coming from a distance to her left caught her attention. They looked like they were drag racing, but they were part of the oncoming traffic. She barely had time to register their make when she saw someone in her lane, much further up, pull out.

The car came out as fast as it could. The driver must have thought they could enter the oncoming traffic and complete a U-turn in record time and in perfect form.

Not so much.

With the sun reflecting in her eyes from the rearview mirror, Anna saw the pick-up furthest from her try to swerve away from the car and hit the railing toward the water instead. It wedged itself between the railing and the car which, with a loud squeal and a crash, caused the left side of the car to lift off the ground as if it were about to turn over. Instead, it veered toward Anna's lane where the second pick-up, which slammed onto its brakes, crashed into the car. It exploded upward into a spin until it tore into the parking lot of cars that was the Canadian inbound traffic. Glass and metal flew into the air as Anna covered her face, and twisted down, waiting for the cars in front to slam into her.

1...2...3...4...5...

An alarm sounded, tires popped, and the ground shook like an earthquake had found her. Nothing happened.

Anna looked up with wide-opened eyes, and saw that the devastation had stopped a few cars short of her. She thought her back hurt for a moment and reached over to her glove compartment. She found a box cutter, grateful the border guards hadn't found it.

With shaking hands, she released her seat belt and got out of her car. There was smoke and wreckage everywhere. The driver of the pick-up in front of her didn't come out. She started banging on the truck's fender. "Hey!"

No reaction. She continued walking to the driver's side door. Traffic stopped on both sides of the bridge. "Hey! Are you going to...?" A chunk of metal was sticking out of the driver side windshield. Adrenaline shot up into her brain lighting up her focus. *Oh no! Oh no!*

She looked back at the pile of crumbled vehicles a few car lengths away and saw that there were multiple overturned vehicles.

Okay. Okay. Breathe. How am I going to get to Vancouver now?

Anna saw the crushed roofs of two cars. She fought not to think of who was in there just a few moments earlier.

She heard a cry. She picked up her pace and jogged toward the sound. She found a crowd of people just standing around.

She used her loudest and most confident voice and said, "Okay, everybody has got to either get back in your cars or away from the wreckage."

A man stepped forward. He was bleeding from his forehead. "Who the hell are you?"

"Who the hell are you?" Anna yelled. "Either help or go away!"

"Hey!"

She turned when she heard a voice behind her. She couldn't see who it was. "We need to get some of these people out of their vehicles. There's gasoline spilling on the roadway."

"Just wait for the cops to get here," another random voice said.

"Help me!"

"I think I'm hurt."

There was too much sound.

The cries for help were starting to overwhelm her tired brain. *I need to get to Vancouver. I need to get to Vancouver. They're going to spot who I am.*

She spun around and headed toward the first voice.

An upside-down minivan was sticking out of its lane into the opposite lane, the roof crushed. A man lay on the road.

Anna saw the outline of a little girl in the back seat through the broken glass. She ran and pointed to two men who were standing around shaking their bleeding heads. "You, and you! We need to get the glass removed and the kid out of the minivan!"

They saw where Anna pointed and they ran toward the minivan, the crackling sound of glass piercing the air, but they were not as pumped as she was.

She reached over to the glass and grabbed it with her bare hands. The glass had a plastic coating over it so there were very few shards to contend with. She thought she felt something bite into her palms.

Anna could see the little girl. Upside down. Black hair, brown eyes that were open and crying. For an instant, she looked familiar. The little girl's seat belt held fast. Anna reached in through the driver side window, which was open, and began to strike the back window with the side of her fist until it came loose. One of the two men finished pulling it off.

Anna got on her back and slid into the minivan where the little girl was restrained in her car seat. Using the box cutter, Anna cut the seat belt with one hand while holding the child up with the other.

She didn't remember sliding out, but she had the girl in her arms when she stood up.

She put the little girl down, but the girl wouldn't let go of Anna's neck. The warmth of the small arms overwhelmed her, the shallow breaths hot against her neck. She pulled at the little arms with as little force as she could muster until she was loose, and she put the girl on the ground.

The man who had been lying on the ground was now standing. He took a step toward the little girl. Something scorched the inside of Anna's brain, snapped like a chunk of a wood beam falling from the ceiling of a burning house. She took the few steps between her and the man and she grabbed him by the throat.

"You leave that little girl alone!" Anna continued pushing the man until they were at the railing over the river. Every inch of the man's face was visible to her. She could hear her breathing and his ragged gulps. "She has her own parents! How dare you try to take her? Why would you do such a thing?"

Anna had the man bent over the railing. He struggled against her grip, but she felt a hot focused glow coming from every pore of her body. Her jaw clenched, and her hands slowly closed as her hands bled on the man's neck. If she pushed just a little harder...

Someone screamed and the sound cut through the dull buzzing in her ear.

Blink.

Anna turned and stopped. It was a woman. The little girl held her hand. For a split second: *Oh, my God. It's Mom.* She let go of the man and stepped away. *It can't be.*

The woman bore a passing resemblance to her mother, but that was all. She looked back at the man. He had looked like her father, but now he was just another man. The little girl was crying.

Anna didn't know what to do. She tried finding something for her hands to do, but they were dangling in front of her like disconnected appendages. There was an eerie silence as she looked around at all the people staring at her. The sound of her heart was a dull thud in her ears.

The sounds of reality came back in a flash.

"I'm sorry," she said to no one in particular and walked back to her car.

No one went after her.

———

Anna carefully pulled out from in between the cars and made a U-turn. She'd gotten caught in a web that still twisted her brain, and her gut. She was tired of it. Her red-hot ears and bleeding hands brought the world into focus and she knew what she had to do.

It was time for another kind of closure. The people waiting for her in Vancouver were going to have a long wait. Plans had changed.

That bastard Benson was in New York and she was going to have a word with him.

PART III

HUNTING BENSON

18

AROMA THERAPY

Anna sat on the toilet at the TA rest stop in Columbia, New Jersey, just off Route 80, hugging her legs as close to her chest as she could, wondering when it would be safe to come out of the stall. While the stench of urine and ammonia stung her nose, the smell that bothered her the most was fear.

I am not ready to pee on myself. That would be unbecoming.

Her clothes felt comfortable, but her skin did not.

Her poor car. The rental company was going to be upset.

She thought that she had already had her moments of paranoia and doubt, but she now reconsidered her position.

A Few Hours Earlier

Anna trembled as she left the relative safety of the Ambassador Bridge. Holding the man by the throat at the edge of the railing was an indication that she needed help.

And she needed to stop soon and take care of her hand.

The more she thought about it, the more uncertain she was when help would come. Heading south on I-75, she had a new sense of focus. Her exhaustion melted away, replaced by a push against the inside of her head drawing her east like a magnet.

Her mother.

She saw her mom in that woman's face.

Anna's eyes teared. She had only seen photos of her mother when Anna was three or four years little and the flat inkjet-printed photos felt light in her small hands. The eyes that peered back at young Anna were haunting. Anna imagined her mother entering her bedroom to kiss her good night. Some evenings, when Marshall kissed her good night, she closed her eyes, imagined it was her mother, and pretended to smell the perfume that her father had told Anna was her mother's favorite.

When Anna was about ten, she saw Marshall throw away the last bottle of her mother's perfume that he had kept for years. He used to spray her tiny wrist and tell her, *This is what your mother smelled like.* Anna would inhale deeply and smile and wonder why her father's eyes were so sad while the rest of his face smiled.

A car honked at her. She swerved and missed hitting it. The young woman who drove the vehicle yelled at Anna and motioned at Anna with her hand. Anna knew she deserved it, motioned an apology, and slowed down. She was falling asleep again. How long had she been on the road? She looked at her cell. Three hours. It was time for a pit stop in Freedom, Ohio.

———

On the south side of Interstate 80 was Brady Leap Service Plaza. Anna wasn't interested. She spied a Starbucks on the north side, and drove around until she crossed the Limeridge Road bridge across the Ohio Turnpike and turned into the Portage Service Plaza. The sun was high in the sky, but the clouds closed most of the available gaps, casting a gray pall on the landscape.

Anna could smell the coffee.

She made a beeline into the service area, found the coffee shop, and purchased a cup of black coffee and five bottles of water. She knew the caffeine would do nothing to keep her awake, but the water would. Keeping her core body temperature from getting too warm was the better solution to her exhaustion, not faking out her brain with a hit of anxiety in a cup.

There weren't that many cars in the parking lot, so she parked as close to the entrance as possible. She might still need to make a hasty exit.

As she got back to her car, she froze. There was a slip of yellow paper under the driver's-side windshield wiper. She placed the bottles on the hood of the car and pulled at the note until it came free.

Go to Vancouver.

She looked around. The parking lot was almost empty. She turned the piece of paper over.

I can see you.

The cup of hot coffee dropped from her hand, splashing scalding liquid against Anna's legs. She swore under her breath and picked up the bottles from the car hood. She tried to pull open the driver's-side door but missed the handle twice. Once the door was open, she sat down with the bottles on her lap, tried to swallow, but her mouth was dry, and threw the bottles on the passenger side floor.

———

Anna's next stop was about two hours later: Brookville, PA, just south of Alaska, PA. After consuming all five bottles of water, she needed to stop, though the note, which was in the cup holder, lay untouched since she'd pulled out of Freedom.

The rest stop, a Travel Centers of America, overflowing with trucks, would suit her purpose. She would run to the bathroom and come out in full view of the various truckers, and cameras, and no one would have touched her car.

The note nagged her. *I can see you.*

As she exited the bathroom, after going for what felt like minutes, she checked her phone. Still another five hours to New York. Five hours to Benson's wake-up call. She had powered through her exhaustion, but...five more hours. She could do it. She would have to.

She sat down in the car and turned the ignition key. The gentle rumble of the engine vibrated against her butt, and sighing, Anna pulled out of the spot.

And stopped.

The note was gone.

It had been in the cup holder. The yellow swatch of color that had poked at her brain for the last few hours had been in the cup holder. It was gone.

———

A few minutes into her trip she hit a bump and the car jumped.

Something rattled in her glove compartment. But when she checked, the glove compartment was empty.

Anna pulled over to the shoulder and got out of the car as fast as she could. She ticked off possibilities. Something had shaken loose. Somehow, one of the water bottles had jumped from the floor, opened the glove compartment, fallen in, and closed the panel.

The car hadn't exploded.

How bad could it be?

The car still hadn't exploded.

She walked over to the car even as her shoulders leaned away from the vehicle. She got on all fours and examined underneath. Felt inside the wheel wells.

Nothing.

She was afraid to open the hood. If the engine decided to blow up, she wouldn't be able to do anything but die, and that was not on her bucket list.

She stepped away from the Jeep again. *I have to look in the glove compartment. I have to look.*

Maybe Vancouver wasn't such a bad idea.

Her hand trembled as she opened the mystery panel. The door fell open. There was a cell phone inside.

She thought about touching it. If she feared the phone then she would have to walk or hitchhike, neither of which appealed to her. Anna extracted the phone, and stared at it.

What could this be for?

A remote detonator.

A cheap listening device.

A GPS to track her.

She pressed the power switch. Locked. She entered a few PIN combinations and none worked. She then noticed the GPS icon was on.

It could still be a remote detonator, or a cheap bug, but it also made it possible for someone to follow her from a distance.

Who was following her? The shadowy Vancouver group? One of Benson's minion? A random stalker?

Anna scanned the area. No one was in the woods or in her backseat. She heard a branch snap and hurt her neck when she twitched at the sound.

She hurled the phone into the woods. If it was a remote detonator then she needed to put distance between it and herself. As she sat in the car, she began to shake.

Stop. STOP.

She gripped the steering wheel, but the shaking was so strong that her shoulders convulsed. *You want a piece of me? Come get it.*

———

TA Rest Stop
Columbia, New Jersey

I am going to New York. I am going to get that bastard, and I am not going to let some group of nobodies change my mind.

I am going to New York.

Anna got up from the toilet where she had been hugging herself until she brought her trembling under control. If someone had followed her into the rest room, she would defend herself. If they had followed her to the rest stop, she would scream and hope the state troopers were around.

The one thing she knew, down in her bones, was that she wouldn't be able to handle whoever was following her by herself. They were at least as determined as she was, and there had to be more than one.

She walked outside as the sun was slowing setting to the west. It was time to hope for the kindness of strangers. Truckers were supposed to be nice guys, right? Anna walked by her car as if she had never seen it before, and headed toward the dozen or so trucks parked in their designated area. She knew the security cameras would show her getting out of her car about fifteen minutes earlier, one or more people approaching her car, her walking out of the building, and her return to the restroom after discovering her car had its tires slashed and the driver side window displaying a hand-drawn Canadian Maple Leaf in black permanent marker.

19

KINDNESS OF STRANGERS

Dottie the trucker had an interesting look. A white woman, maybe in her forties (fifties?), slightly overweight, she wore a sweatshirt with some logo on it, comfortable jeans and sneakers, and a baseball cap with the logo for a feed company on the front. A walking billboard. Did they pay her for the use of her forehead as a mobile billboard or did she do it because she liked wearing baseball caps?

Anna, prone on a thin mattress, tried to get some rest. She was in the back of the cab of a white truck, driven by an older woman who was delivering bread to a variety of that were running out of food. People were loading up on supplies in preparation for the end of the world. At least, that was how Dottie had described it.

"You doin' okay back there?" Dottie asked.

"Yes, thank you," Anna replied. The air smelled of roses and lilac. And coffee.

"Do you think you'll make it in time for your chemo appointment?" Dottie's wrinkled hands gripped the steering wheel with the ease and confidence of a veteran. The light black steering wheel cover had writing on it that Anna couldn't read from her position.

"Yeah. It's early tomorrow morning so I'll be okay. Thanks for asking," Anna said. She was going to have to remember that story. It worked wonders.

Anna was thirsty, and she was tired. Thirst would have to wait.

The mattress in the back of the cab was worn, but clean. Anna fell asleep as soon as her head hit the large fluffy pillow. Her last thought before collapsing was: *This woman knows how to live.*

———

Anna woke up on her side over four hours later as Dottie made her rounds around the Garden State. Her left arm felt a touch sore, but she decided not to move much. The roomy cab was messy yet organized. *A world befitting someone who lived where they worked.* The sun was still up, but behind them. They were still in New Jersey.

Anna folded her hands over her stomach. Her hands, dry on a normal day, felt like sandpaper. If they stopped by any place that sold hand cream...

Did her mother ever wear a cap? Anna could imagine that in a fit of playfulness her mother would go to a baseball game and wear the local team's headgear to bug Marshall. The few photos she saw showed her mother wearing jewelry, and a tasteful top. Sometimes a necklace. Always bangles on her left wrist. Was she left-handed? No, bangles on her left wrist just meant that the right side of her brain, peering through the left eye, enjoyed the sight of the decorations on her arm. Anna was right-handed, but wondered if her mother was different from either her or her father.

She scrutinized the ceiling of the cab but registered nothing. The memory of Ingrid did what it always did in situations like this: she floated into Anna's consciousness until Anna could feel her nearby. When Anna was younger, she could hear her mother talking to her, but as she got older Ingrid spoke less and less, and Anna spoke more and more. She never spoke to Ingrid out loud, but they had many, many conversations.

How do you think Dad is doing?

I know he's probably dead. I mean passed. No, I mean dead. He taught me not to sugar coat things.

Yes, I know. I sugar coat things all the time. But that's only because I feel bad telling people the truth and hurting their feelings.

No one cares about my feelings, but I get that. I don't matter to anyone anymore. Well, Aunt Marcie and Uncle Ray care, but only because they think I'm someone I'm not. They think I'm their niece. That my real parents are dead. Maybe they are. How can I ever be sure?

"How're you doing, young lady?" Dottie asked.

"Fine, ma'am." Anna sat up. "I really appreciate your taking me as far as you can."

"Gotta make this delivery. Things are going to get ugly here real soon."

"How long have you been driving like this? As a trucker?"

"Oh, about twenty years," Dottie said. "My husband died a few years after we married and I just never thought to get involved with anyone again." She turned around for a second and looked at Anna. "Why aren't your parents with you?"

"They died a long time ago. When I was two." *They died. When I was two. In a car accident. At least that's what everyone keeps telling me.* Was she starting to doubt that?

"Well, you are certainly a brave young woman to be handling your treatments all by yourself."

"I suppose. I don't like talking about it." Anna was afraid that the details would screw her up. Innocent conversations like this could take a turn for the worst if she wasn't careful. "Tell me about you. Any children?"

"No," Dottie said. "Just me and my truck."

And this will be the life I live after this. If I don't go to jail I'll go hide in the middle of nowhere doing my best to stay under the radar while the rest of the world changes without my help.

I wanted to change the world. I thought I would make a difference. All those years. Shame on me.

She leaned her head to the side and thought of how her mother's shoulder would feel against her cheek. Anna wore a thick gray cotton sweatshirt and jeans, but she imagined her mother next to her wearing a beautiful dress from one of the photographs. It would be black and glittery. The dress strap felt rough against her cheek.

She smelled her mother's perfume.

I want to go home. I wish I knew where that was.

Aunt Marcie is so nice. She wears perfume too, but not like yours. I know why Daddy kept that last bottle with him. Your choice was so elegant. The perfume was subtle, but so you.

"Any pets?" Dottie asked.

"None to speak of. Too much school work. Never at home," Anna said. *This woman must think I am such a loser. Not even a pet. All I'm missing is an eye twitch.*

Anna leaned back against the wall of the cab. The vibrations massaged her back. "How close are we?"

"Pretty close."

Do you think that one day I might visit you at the cemetery? Since there's no god I know I'll never see you again, but...I don't know. I don't know what I'll feel when I get there.

Did I mention Aunt Marcie? She probably hates me, but she was always so nice. Her and Uncle Ray. Why would they think they were related to me if they weren't? I always remember the day she and Uncle Ray showed up the FBI office when I was 17 and saved me from Agent Gillespie. I know I wasn't grateful that day, but right now I wish I could tell them how much I love them for it. Saving someone they'd never met before.

But you know what, Mom? Sometimes I really could have used you there. I know that you're with me in spirit, Dad always told me you were, but couldn't you have made an appearance once in a while? Even once?

Anyway, we're almost there.

The truck pulled into a rest stop. Anna didn't notice which one, but she recognized the road. I-95. She could almost walk to New York. Almost.

Dottie pulled the truck into the designated parking area for rigs like hers. She turned off the ignition and climbed out. Anna grabbed her bag and climbed out behind her.

"Alright, young lady. This is where you get off."

What?

"While you were sleeping there was a news report about a young woman who escaped from a federal jail down south. Down in Texas, I think." Dottie started to walk toward the service area. "There was a mention that she might be wearing a wig and passing herself off as a chemo patient. No hard feelings, but I don't want any trouble, and you seem to have that glow about you. I hope I'm wrong."

Anna stood stock still. How was she going to get to the city? Perhaps she would have to walk.

"And I'd avoid going to the building for a bit. I saw a couple of police cars out front." Dottie turned around. "Unless you're not that girl. Then it doesn't matter."

20

LIBRARY CARD

Anna had a lump the size of the Gordian knot in her stomach and no sword with which to tear it open.

She tallied the rest stop as a minor blip. If Dottie had called the police, there wasn't anything Anna could do anyway. She had other things to worry about. Like the whereabouts of the people who were following her.

A short hitchhike got her to the nearest New Jersey Transit train station where she bought a one-way ticket to New York Penn Station. Anna tried not to touch her wig too often, but the itch at the top of her head wouldn't let up. She was going to have to read up on the proper way to wear one of these things or she was going to pull it off and toss it into the nearest trash bin. It also wasn't letting off the nicest smell.

A New Jersey State Trooper walked through her compartment. Average height. Dark hair under his hat. Bad acne. He gave her a steady stare for a few seconds before looking off to examine another passenger. Her hands felt cold and clammy. She opened and closed her fists to warm them. Anna had heard the news reports; they were looking for her, but everyone seemed preoccupied about something much more compelling: the hurricane. How bad could Hurricane

Sandy be? She hoped to be in a car driving toward Vancouver in the next day or so if she managed to escape Benson's security detail.

Who was she trying to kid? She would take out his detail before injuring him enough that he would know never to mess with her again. Anna didn't have to worry about them. She just needed to get in some more practice. Her asthma was something that would never go away, but speed was always in her favor. If she could take care of business before anyone knew what was going on, her lungs would survive the sudden onslaught of activity.

The trooper stood by the door. He looked in her direction a few times but continued to scan the crowd. Anna felt her chest constrict. Maybe she shouldn't have changed her itinerary. She argued with herself for a few seconds.

Stop overthinking.

Whatever. In the end, if she could pull off a visit with Benson, that would be enough. If she didn't get away, she didn't care. She tilted her head back against the flat seat cushion and pressed her hands against her face. The coolness of her palms made her eyes feel not-so-hot. She had to survive this. Was she feeling sick or was she depressed? Only one way to find out: she had to take the risk and go talk to her people. The hackers who populated their little corner of the Internet.

———

The New York Public Library's Science, Industry and Business Library, at 188 Madison Avenue, between 34th and 35th Street, had public Internet-enabled computers on the street level, the lower level, and the Job Search Center. Anna was on the street level. The large plate-glass windows were to her right and people walked back and forth around her, stressing her out with every step. While all the computers had Internet access, they varied in levels of virus protection and site-blocking software. Anna didn't intend to compromise the computers or the library's network. That would have been counter-productive and rude, two things Anna despised. She refused to contribute to negative outcomes if she had anything to say about it.

The default browser came up. She rolled her eyes. *Only IE?*

She surfed for a minute or so and found a few sites that gave her secure IRC right from the browser. Anna decided no one was looking over her shoulder and it would be safe to be risky.

She grabbed a clump of her hair and moved her fist back and forth just enough to scratch the top of her head. There was a trash can to her right. She knew she wouldn't throw the wig away, but it was tempting.

HarlequinNinja has entered the room.

IRCPlayer: OMG the prodigal daughter has returned

HarlequinNinja: don't make me regret doing this

Her guilt was palpable. Why did she feel that way talking to IRCPlayer? She heard a door open. She flicked her eyes over then continued typing.

IRCPlayer: you're in new york, aren't you?

HarlequinNinja: can't say

IRCPlayer: your boyfriend the general is probably in town to check on his old program. I'm surprised he bothered showing his face. Better not to be seen having anything to do with prudent rainbow

HarlequinNinja: prudent rainbow?

IRCPlayer: oh, you know, just another secret project ;-)

HarlequinNinja: why are you torturing me?

Anna smiled. Okay, maybe she was depressed, but she was feeling better with every keystroke.

IRCPlayer: torture? You should hear about the things the general did in his heyday.

HarlequinNinja: don't care. Can't confirm or deny nyc

IRCPlayer: did you read the file on your dad?

HarlequinNinja: are you never going to give that up?

IRCPlayer: why? It's so much fun reading your anxiety

HarlequinNinja: about the file: tl;dr. got a summary?

IRCPlayer: what am i? your eyes? your slave? your...

Anna unfocused. What did she hear? She looked out the front window as an NYC police car went by. She looked at the time on her cell. She considered pulling up her hoodie but thought better of it.

No strange or sudden moves. Also, if they couldn't see her face, she couldn't see theirs.

HarlequinNinja: today, pls

IRCPlayer: the general probably killed your father.

Today, Anna didn't care. Another unsubstantiated factoid.

HarlequinNinja: anything worth telling me about? If my dad isn't my dad then I don't care.

IRCPlayer: hey, we found something really cool

HarlequinNinja: whatever. What is the general doing here?

IRCPlayer: I told you

HarlequinNinja: seriously? A canceled program?

IRCPlayer: canceled and with a new name, but I have no clue what it's for. Its secret level must be so high that they don't even write it down. That's pretty serious.

Anna glanced at the plate-glass windows again. A parked police car out front where before there was none. Another one pulled up behind it. She tried to reposition her wig as slowly as she could. The New York City Police had that good a cyber-squad?

HarlequinNinja: i think i have to go. thanks for the memories

IRCPlayer: wait! we found a real cool program. you know how the space shuttle could be launched and landed by remote control? well, there's a whole class of jets that let you do the same.

HarlequinNinja: snore

IRCPlayer: ok, be like that. i won't tell you.

HarlequinNinja: hurry. i have guests arriving

IRCPlayer: we found some of the applications that can control them. they're out there right now

Anna was getting excited. Remote control fighter jets?

HarlequinNinja: snore

IRCPlayer: i know you're lying. you love jets.

HarlequinNinja: maybe i do

IRCPlayer: there is a carrier off the coast that's running some training exercises. I expect they won't be doing anything for the next few days.

HarlequinNinja: let me know where they are. let me know if you show off with them :)

IRCPlayer: we'll see. you know I don't like an audience

Anna rolled her eyes. *Right.*

Another police car pulled up. She disconnected the IRC session, killed the browser, and pushed her hoodie back to let everyone get a good look at her face. Was the show of force a coincidence? Had someone called them? Had Benson set loose the might of US surveillance?

She walked toward the door from an angle as three police officers walked through.

As they passed her she turned her face toward the doors and walked out. She could probably catch a bus by the time they found which computer she was on.

21

DESPERATELY SEEKING

Terrell pulled up to the front of the New York Public Library on Madison Avenue, expecting to find a handful of plainclothes officers blending in with the other library-goers so the police would be able to find Anna without raising too much suspicion. If Anna had been sighted in New Jersey then she must have a Formula One at her disposal to get her into New York fast enough to be perusing the stacks at the library.

What he found instead was the front of the Science, Industry and Business Library surrounded by police cars as if it were a crime scene. Patrons exited one at a time with four officers at the door, giving each of the departing patrons a good look. Not one was holding a paper photo or their cell phones, or anything, which might have contained a digital copy of Anna's likeness. The crowd in front of the building just made it difficult for people to leave. The low temperature on the street made him wish he didn't have to go inside. Too much hot air on the other side of the door.

Terrell waved his ID and entered the building. "Where's the Incident Commander?" he asked another officer who stood a few feet further into the room.

The officer pointed to a woman who stood by one of the plate glass windows. Tall, perfectly manicured. Her police uniform looked tailored.

Terrell approached her, holding his ID card before him. "What's going on?"

She glanced at his ID. "How can I help you, Special Agent?"

"Why is the library under siege?" Terrell asked.

"We're doing what we were told to do: seal off the building and look for Carpenter Poole."

"A little more subtlety would have been nice. You mean Anna Wodehouse," Terrell said.

"The paperwork has her legal name and any aliases. I'm sure that one's listed. What's your point? Again, what can I do for you?"

Terrell looked over his shoulder at the mass of people piled up at the door and returned his gaze to the officer. The afternoon wasn't going to get any brighter and they were losing what little sunlight they had left.

"The questions is, what can I do for you? Because I can tell you that she's not here," he said.

"That's not my concern. We're doing what we were told," she said.

"While you're playing card tricks she's getting further and further away. If you want to find her, start posting officers with photos in the subways and on the buses." This was never going to work. "Did anyone recognize her?"

"What do you mean?"

"You know, see her? Recognize her? A concerned citizen? A fan?" The female officer pointed to Terrell's left.

A young girl, wearing thick black plastic frame glasses, hair dyed half-blue and half-brown, was talking to an officer who then walked away. The girl was maybe eighteen, no older than twenty, wearing a puffy scarf over a green top and jeans. The stack of books she held appeared to be getting heavier by the second.

Terrell walked over to her just as a few of the books started to fall. He caught them in mid-air, saw the girl's shocked face, and smiled at her. Her reaction changed from impatience to relief.

"Hi, there. You doin' okay?" he asked. He took a few more of the books off the mountain in her arms and put them down next to her. "I hate to admit I'm with these guys, but I am."

She put the remaining books on the same shelf where Terrell put the others. He held out his hand and she shook it. Soft, weak grip.

"You know," she said, "I'm a law student and what these guys are doing is illegal."

"You are? No insult, but I thought you were eighteen."

"Twenty-two. Are you talking to me because you're flirting or questioning me without counsel?"

"If you're a law student, you're all the counsel you need." He smiled again.

She puffed a little then returned the smile with her eyes.

"What's going on here? Who are they looking for?"

"You know who we're looking for. You saw her."

The young girl shook her head, as though she were getting ready for her close-up. "Anna Wodehouse. She was here." She leaned into Terrell, her eyes opening wide. "Off the record, it was pretty exciting."

"How do you know it was her?" Terrell asked.

"I've been studying her case almost since it happened. Lots of questions. She was wearing a blond wig."

"You're telling me. How did you know it was a wig?"

"It was uncomfortable. She kept scratching her head and," she motioned over the top of her own head, "the whole thing moved."

Terrell looked out the windows in time to see two squad cars go full lights and sirens, and speed off. Things were happening too fast. Where the hell were they getting their information?

———

"Marley, what are you saying?" Terrell stepped outside to take a call from his cell.

He recognized the number right away: his contact at NSA who was helping him with some wiretaps of questionable legality. The Bureau would just reverse-engineer the evidence if it came to anything. Someday, the courts would catch up on the illegal use of the information, but if Terrell's luck held, he would be retired by then. How else could he ever hope to close all of the cases in his queue? Between Piercing Ventures, Palma, and Anna he barely had time to sleep.

"Special Agent, all I can say is that we're finding some interesting relationships in the groups you're tracking. If I were a betting man, I'd say that part of this is just an internal operation gone bad," Marley said.

"Gone bad?"

"I'm not an analyst, but I've been at this a while. There is a history of legal operations being shut down and illegal ones taking their place. I'm just guessing, so don't let me do your job for you, but Piercing Ventures was originally a legal conduit for the US to funnel money into foreign countries for, shall we say, humanitarian goals."

"It's already been a long day. Tell me what you're telling me. Is Piercing Ventures a legal conduit for the outflow of US intelligence funds or not?"

"Piercing Ventures is an illegal conduit for the inflow of massive amounts of funds into the US. All that money, and we're talking hundreds of millions of dollars, is being used to fund foreign intelligence operations on US soil."

Terrell blew air out of his inflated cheeks. This was going to make him or break him. The deeper he dug the more dirt he found.

"Oh, and about that woman you've been involved with," Marley said.

"I'm involved with a woman?"

"Yes, I've been stalking your latest relationship."

He and Marley had been working together for a few years now, and they were both workaholics.

"You know who I mean. I made a mistake and I had to log it to make sure that the audit trail covers my ass. I'm not losing my job over your love life," Marley said.

"Who are you talking about?"

"I just moonlight for you. When I'm not busy helping the Bureau, I do have a real job."

Terrell knew what Marley was saying. In the course of other surveillance he was performing for the NSA, Marley ran across something about Anna.

"I had cut and pasted your lady friend's name into one screen, where her name belonged, don't ask me why, and then by mistake into one of your screens. Wouldn't you know that her relationship graph displayed some interesting names: Arnold Dashman, I guess that's the guy that kidnapped her, you, and General Malik Palma."

The hits just keep on coming. Terrell remembered seeing her the night of her escape from ADX Florence. Why didn't she believe he could protect her? The more he followed Piercing Ventures and General Palma the more her case seemed to be involved. "I need the full report. I want to find her before New York's finest does."

22

MAKING CONNECTIONS

The remaining squad cars left the front of the library just as Terrell came back around the corner to find out what had happened. A police officer who walked toward him became his new target. The sun was cutting sharp shadows on the walls and sidewalk. There were too many people milling about and it made Terrell anxious.

"I have no idea where they're going," the officer said once he was satisfied with Terrell's ID. "A call came in that the girl might have been spotted in three different places."

"Where's your car?"

"Don't have one. I'm a beat cop."

Terrell cursed under his breath and ran to the corner. There had to be another squad car around here somewhere. He looked up and down the block. In the midst of all the traffic he saw one heading toward him. The usual crush of the city made his job harder. The vibrant feel and never-ending movements normally fed his energy, but today was not a day for crowds. His shoulder was not happy, and his head was not happy. How he was going to get anywhere was beyond him. Terrell pulled out his ID and ran in front of the marked car that slammed to a stop, with a squeal, a few feet from his knees. His left arm throbbed from all the exertion. "FBI! I need to talk to the Incident Commander!"

———

"I'm a little pressed for time so maybe you could give me the *Reader's Digest* version."

Did people even know what that was anymore? Terrell had called Marley back on a secure line after fastening his seat belt and ordering the police officer to catch up with the wolf pack that was after Anna. Terrell was in the back seat surrounded by discarded coffee cups and straws. This was a bad decision.

"There's a lot of history here," Marley said. "I'm also certain I don't have everything you need. At some point, people might show up to take me away for looking at something I shouldn't be looking at."

"I hereby grant you authority to look at everything you need to since we don't have any legal authority to be doing this anyway."

The squad car radio crackled with multiple voices interrupting each other. Terrell leaned forward to catch whatever words he could while listening to Marley.

The suspect was going uptown and shot out the tires of a car that wouldn't stop.

She was spotted in the Wall Street area heading toward the Staten Island Ferry.

She had returned to the library, and was on the Internet again.

Son of a bitch. This twisted game of telephone is going to get her killed.

"Officer?" Terrell pulled himself forward. "Is there any way you can tell dispatch to put a lid on this? The only people who should be on are the ones asking for backup." Why the hell did he sit in the back seat? "Stop this car. Stop, right now."

The officer slammed on the brakes. Terrell flew back into the hard-as-a-rock seat. Terrell jumped out, opened the front passenger door, and jumped back in. "Go. Go. Go!" The officer floored the gas.

"Marley, go on," Terrell said.

"What's going on over there?"

"Nothing. Just another day at the office."

"If you're chasing the girl, be aware. There's been some chatter that she might be armed and carrying an explosive device."

Terrell blinked. That wasn't possible. "Is that confirmed?"

"How do you confirm a rumor in this business? You wait for the target to act; otherwise, you never know," Marley said.

"And if we wait long enough we might also find out it's a lie."

"Or the truth. Both are always a possibility."

The radio, already live with more voices than Terrell wanted to hear, changed tone. "Car 54, this is dispatch. We have reason to believe she is armed and carrying an explosive device. Approach with caution. Be prepared to take action. Bomb Squad is en route."

"Marley, did you just say an explosive device?"

"Roger that," Marley said.

"I just heard the same wording from NYPD. What the hell is going on?"

"I don't know everything," Marley said.

Someone is feeding NYPD information. Or, more to the point, misinformation. Anna wasn't a bomber, though she sure as hell was good with a gun. The situation was changing. Terrell knew he'd be able to talk her in, but now it looked like someone wanted her taken out.

"This is dispatch. We just received confirmation from DHS. Suspect is armed and carrying an explosive device. Approach with caution. Repeat. Suspect is armed and dangerous. Approach with caution."

"Terrell? Terrell?" Marley was almost yelling.

"Yeah?"

"Do you still want the summary? Sounds like you might be busy."

"Go."

"This much you can look up. There was a program called PRUDENT RAINBOW that was shut down years ago. Big to do on Capitol Hill and all sorts of people got canned for their part in it. Guess who started and ran the program for over five years?"

"Malik Palma?"

"Close. He was Darth Vader. George Monahan. He was NSA

director at the time and personally involved in the program. Not sure why that would be, since most directors do their best not to know anything for plausible deniability. They approve programs and only take a peek when Congress wants information they lie about anyway."

"You're not giving me a warm and fuzzy," Terrell said.

"If you want warm and fuzzy, buy a blanket. Anyway, Monahan moved on, Palma was promoted after a comfortable number of years, and PRURAIN disappeared from neglect."

Terrell assumed PRURAIN was the shortened form for PRUDENT RAINBOW. "What can you tell me about that? Anything?"

"It's in your backyard," Marley said.

"Car 54, this is dispatch. Join squad leader at Christopher Street subway station with all due speed."

"No," Terrell said to the officer driving. "Why are we heading there? I need to follow wherever the bomb squad is heading."

"Sorry, but I have to go where I'm told and I've been told to go downtown."

Terrell cursed. "Let me out. Let me out, now."

The squad car pulled over at Madison and 47 Street.

Terrell unfastened his seat belt and jumped out. "I need a car. Have dispatch send someone from the team heading uptown to swing by and pick me up."

"Yes, sir. I'll see what I can do."

Did everyone in New York need to be sarcastic?

"Officer?"

The man turned toward Terrell.

"Be careful. Don't shoot to kill. She's my suspect, but don't do anything stupid."

The officer nodded and took off.

Living like this was going to be the end of him for sure. He looked at the cell in his hand. "Marley, you still there?"

"So far," Marley sighed. "You seem a little distracted."

"If they find her and I'm not there..." He let the implication hang in the air.

Where the hell was the squad car? Oh, screw this. Terrell stepped out into the street and stopped another squad car by holding out his ID. He jumped into the front passenger seat and asked the officer for an update on the chase.

"I don't know any details so far."

The radio blurted out the answer. "Dispatch, this is 327. Send cars to 34th and 8th. Repeat. 34th Street and 8th Avenue. We have a confirmed sighting of the suspect entering the C subway station at 34th and 8th."

23

———

HALL OF MIRRORS

In a spare office at the US Mission to the UN, General Malik Palma hung up the phone and shook his head. The alerts were flying and the timing was bad, but he wasn't going to be overcome by events. The police were going to do the job of finding Anna Wodehouse for him, and he was going to get them the information they needed to do it. He should have let them drop Anna off that bridge back in the UK when they had the chance. He hated reacting. Events were to be guided, not allowed to randomly find their way.

If I wait long enough things will turn in my favor. They always do.

On to the next item on his agenda: HALON and the risk to the handoff. Jenkins, bless his heart, was as tenacious about his work as he was about his people. Jenkins the protector was admirable; Jenkins the prima donna, not so much. The genetics lab was world class, and Jenkins was leaving behind some of the most extraordinary work he had ever done. It had been a chore getting him to join, and it was going to be a chore to get him to leave, but Palma was doing it the way he always did. He created the incentive of a hard-to-resist rewards and reminded the people involved of the hard-to-avoid-and-painful results for not taking it.

None of this mattered. Palma rubbed his eyes and his cheeks. Jenkins would disappear. He would disappear, his people would survive, and life would go on. Jenkins' people were more easily controlled, and none knew the big picture. Palma preferred it that way: eliminate the people who knew everything and leave behind the ones who knew enough pieces to be useful. They would never hear from their fearless leader ever again, and they could be called on again for their expertise.

That last phone call to Jenkins was enough to make Palma regret what had to be done, but he would do it. Jenkins and all of the remaining personnel were Palma's responsibility. Ordering civilians to stay in a potentially dangerous situation meant there was no more time. The handoff would take place and the HALON personnel would leave when it was safe. Palma had been involved from the beginning and he always finished what he started.

Now it was time to battle with Monahan. While the weather was holding up, both he and Monahan should leave New York. Monahan would take some convincing, but it was the best course of action. He had others who would get the remaining personnel out, if at all possible. They would take care of the good doctor.

————

Jenkins would be damned if he was going to let some bureaucrat tell him how to run his operation and take care of his people. Palma was getting under his skin and that was the last place Jenkins wanted him.

He walked down the fully painted corridor to Section C looking for Dr. Sandra Patel. Section C was not only the largest part of the facility, it was also the most dangerous. Power was not just a good idea. It was the only thing that would keep them all alive. Power and good seals on the containers. Patel was the best he could find and she would make sure everything worked, not just as promised, but as it should.

As he reached a T in the corridor, he found that the hallway to his right was in darkness, except for emergency lights, and to his left the normal lighting was on. He had been in worse situations, but it felt like the only thing that could go wrong would. He hated being a realist. He didn't want to be right, he really didn't, but he would be. He hoped there would be enough of them left to fight for credit. As if it would matter if any of the biological agents somehow escaped.

He knocked on the white frosted glass door of one of the dozen labs and slid it open. He had insisted on having regular sliding doors to guarantee access in case of an emergency. He only got them because one of the men who Palma trusted, Jenkins couldn't remember the man's name, but he was sure it was something like Wodehouse, had backed Jenkins up. The doors all had good seals, and they had quarantine rooms aplenty. Manual doors meant they could control things without fighting the security software or a loss of power.

Of course, the fire doors between the sections were automatic and needed codes to open and close in case of an emergency, but that was just common sense for a set-up like this. Things like manual or automatic seals were for people. Diseases could care less about them.

———

Monahan was in the US Mission equivalent of the Situation Room at the White House. The high-res screens gave him a view of the world that twenty years ago would have seemed like magic. What he saw did not make him happy and there was nothing he could do to change it, or his temperament.

Palma walked in, closed the door, and stood by the doorway. "Mr. Secretary."

"General," Monahan said. He tapped the large conference table that took up most of the room. There were microphones built into the surface. "I think the time to has come to make some hard decisions."

"Such as?" Palma asked.

He sighed. "We have to find some way to return to DC. Staying in New York is a bad idea."

Palma remained silent.

"I don't see it your way, so don't gloat. I'm seeing it the way the National Weather Service sees it. A Katrina-level storm that will make it impossible for anyone to do anything."

"I was looking over the structural reports. If everything was done properly..."

"Since when is anything done properly?" Monahan asked.

"If everything was done properly, the remaining personnel can survive there for a few days before they're rescued. There is minimal chance of flooding and we can send a rescue team Tuesday," Palma said.

"Leave them," Monahan said.

"Excuse me?" Palma's face went slack.

"Leave them. We can't afford to have more eyes on this than we already have." Monahan leaned back in his chair. "It will be up to our guests to decide how they want to deal with this."

———

Palma walked up the stairs to his office. *Leave them?* He had never done that in his entire life. The people he involved were never meant to pay that kind of price. He would come up with a workable contingency plan to bring them out, and have it do double-duty as a cover for the death of Jenkins.

This was going to work his way or not at all. He would make sure that Monahan was nowhere to be found in the middle of all this, but Palma would save who he could.

Death in the military was always meant to be strategic and surgical, not random and wasteful.

His secure cell phone buzzed. Another alert. More police being assigned to the manhunt. Could he use that to his advantage? The more police on one end of the city the fewer at another. There would be no one to notice odd events.

Like a rescue.

Palma wasn't sure who was smiling on him, but the best distraction he could have hoped for had made an appearance. The alert was not from any of the intelligence agencies, but from CNN.

Anna Wodehouse, recently escaped from a Texas maximum security facility for women, has been spotted in the New York area.

24

—————

CATCHING A TRAIN

Anna felt a touch of fear, but overall things were under control. She wasn't sure how long that would last, but for now there was a chance she could get to Benson in a controlled way once she could hole up somewhere and formulate a plan.

A plan. That was the one missing piece.

Sweating, Anna knew she needed a shower soon. She had been on her journey for a few days now (How many? She wasn't sure. A lack of nutrients was taking its toll). The walk from Madison Avenue had drained her enough that she stopped and bought a bottle of water from a street vendor who appeared to be even warmer than she. She looked up at the corner lamppost. Thirty-Fourth Street and Eighth Avenue.

A police car flew past. The siren pitch went high, normal, then a low. Doppler shift. As a little girl, she'd loved listening to the sound waves of sirens go through the compression and decompression as they approached then went past her. Waves in action. She turned her face so anyone looking in her direction would just see the back of her head. Another car with full lights and sirens flew by, followed by yet another car displaying lights, but otherwise unmarked. Three walls of sound doing their best to keep up with light and failing. Light would always go faster.

Were they looking for her? Maybe not, but she couldn't risk it. She'd already taken a risk getting some cash from a local ATM; her face was now part of the photographic record of the area. They wouldn't find her picture for a few days at best.

She opened her bottle of water and swallowed. Time to keep walking.

———

On the corner of 34th Street and 9th Avenue she stopped at B&H Photo and Electronics. She had heard so much about them from her dad, who used to go there when he was younger. If this was the original location then her dad had been here. Maybe stood in the same spot where she stood at that very moment. Her dead father. The thought had come unbidden yet had always been there.

My father is dead. Nothing could change that.

He didn't come back because he couldn't. He would never have left her alone to face all the trials and tribulations she had encountered in the previous months. She would never have wanted to kill him. She wouldn't have gone to jail. She wouldn't be looking for revenge. She could have been studying to be a veterinarian or a physicist. An ice-cream truck down the block played a jingle for a few seconds before it stopped in mid-note.

Or she could have opened an ice cream stand. In Central Park. Near the Wollman Rink so she could ice skate when she wanted. Of course, first she would have to learn to skate.

She walked up to the plate glass display case, bumping into the occasional pedestrian. Electronics. So many different kinds. Things that other kids had and she never would. Her father gave her various toys, but they were always adult tools. Fully stacked PCs, cell phones, binoculars, telescopes, wireless video cameras. What would he have thought of her obsession with guns when she went to UPenn? Would she have taken up the sport if he hadn't disappeared?

"Excuse me, young lady?"

Anna jumped. A short, overweight man with ringlets of salt-and-pepper hair on each side of his face appeared beside her. Hassidic?

Pulled out of her reverie, she noticed two things: a monitor displaying her face from a camera somewhere in the display, and another showing a news bulletin with an attractive woman reading the news with Anna's face in a picture bubble next to her.

Anna's eyes opened wide. She caught herself.

"Would you like to come inside and look?" He gave the news report a brief glance.

Did he recognize her? The picture was of Anna in prison orange with her hands manacled together.

He couldn't have recognized her.

Something at the corner caught her eye. Was that someone she knew? The flow of bodies had shifted. Couldn't be.

"Come inside. We can help you find what you're looking for," the man said.

Not sure what to do, Anna ignored him and headed back toward 34th Street.

"Wait. Come back."

Well, wasn't he pushy?

"Somebody stop her! The police are looking for her!"

Anna restrained herself from breaking into a run. She turned the corner east instead of crossing the street west. *If I can make it to Penn Station I can get lost again.*

She felt a hand on her shoulder. She grabbed at the wrist and turned to peer at her attacker. Whoa! The giant of a man stood two heads taller than her. She twisted his arm as hard as she could to spin him around, pinned his arm behind him then yanked up. He yelped from the pain as he fell to his knees.

Anna yelled, "Rape! Rape!"

A crowd of people surrounded the man as he rubbed his shoulder.

Anna pushed through the crowd. *Keep moving. Keep moving. Focus.*

She had to walk with the crowds heading east toward Penn. *Look away from security cameras.*

The subway entrance for the A, C, and E trains was in front of her.

Cross the street. Don't go in the elevator to the subway platform.

She circled around the street-level elevator and navigated to the subway staircase. If she got on the train, she would be fine. While this wasn't the height of rush hour, the number of people coming up the stairs slowed her descent to safety.

She thought she heard yelling come from the direction she had left. She bowed her head and continued to make her way through the commuter and tourist cattle. The stairs had never felt this long before.

She stood before the turnstiles. Damn it! She didn't have a Metrocard. The machines were to her left. She took a deep breath. At the machine, she tapped the touch screen.

New card. Add Value.

She ran her credit card at the proper time. Out came the card. She yanked it out of the machine as she heard a train approach.

There were voices coming from the stairwell. She ran the card through the reader and entered the turnstiles as if nothing was wrong.

Ding ding. The doors of the train were closing.

Two police officers came from around the staircase behind her and called out. She ran toward the platform as the train was leaving. It was the local C.

Out of the corner of her eye, Anna again spotted someone she thought she knew. She couldn't stop to find out. She ran down the platform as the train picked up speed, but she was still able to keep up with it.

The police ran onto the platform and called out. She started to run after the train, which was still in the station, roaring as it went, still at her running speed, but gaining velocity.

The police called out again. The last car of the train was just passing her when she jumped and grabbed the guardrail, holding on as there was no floor under her. She reached over with her feet and pulled herself onto the ledge outside the locked door of the last subway car.

The train screamed as it pulled into the tunnel. Not sure what to hold onto, Anna grabbed the bars on either side of the door and looked back.

Two police officers jumped onto the tracks, took a few steps, and stopped. One of them spoke into a radio.

25

"PLEASE HOLD; YOUR CALL IS IMPORTANT TO US..."

This is not good!

Even in the dark tunnel, Anna could see the metal pillars to her right and left. The railroad ties and steel rails beneath her led into the distant dark, with the shrinking circle of light that was the Penn Station platform. The asthma in her lungs burned. Anna tried to take in a breath and her throat closed a touch more. She had managed not to lose her bag, but it was all she could do to keep from screaming.

Her back was to the door of the subway car and there were people vying to peek at the lunatic who didn't want to miss her train. An older woman wearing glasses tapped on the window and motioned to Anna if she wanted to come in. Anna shook her head. The ride would be over soon. The C was a local and the next step had to be...what? She couldn't think. She just left 34th Street. If the next stop wasn't 42nd Street, it had to be something close to that. Eight blocks. How long could that take?

The train swung back and forth. If the train came to an abrupt stop, she would either be pushed even harder against the car door (*excellent!*) or thrown off the narrow platform (*really bad!*) and would be killed on impact by the railroad ties.

She had to get inside the subway car. She tried the door handle.

Locked. She looked into the car. Someone made their way through the crowd that had assembled around the door to view her in her moment of need.

It was a cop. "Stay where you are!" he yelled.

Well, aren't you a genius?

"Promise! Just don't hit the emergency brakes!" She couldn't stay, but she couldn't get off. She could get into the car and disable the officer. *Right, and* two hundred *people will hold me down while the guys with the cattle prods show up.*

The train jumped up and down. Anna lost her footing and slid off the platform. Still holding onto the left bar, she hung on while searching for footing. She braced herself with her right foot and pulled herself back up.

"Are you okay?" the police officer asked.

Anna nodded about thirty times in the blink of an eye. Her neck hurt, but her arms felt worse.

"Just hold on. We're almost at the next station."

Yes! The next station. What the hell possessed me to do this? The metal smell of the air scraped the inside of her throat and the roaring made it hard to hear anything. She only understood what the officer was telling her by reading his lips. She rubbed her free hand on her jeans. If she fell again, she might not be able to hold on if her hands were sweaty. Anna switched hands and rubbed her other hand on her pants.

So this is it. It's over and I lose. They know where I am, and I'm trapped.

At intervals of equal length, she noticed lights against the walls of the tunnel that displayed the street they were at. They were almost at the next station. 42nd Street or not, her ride was almost over.

"I'll notify the proper parties." The supervisor at MTA central dispatch, holding the handset against his right ear, knew he should have been more surprised, but he couldn't find the energy. They had another crazy kid on the outside of a subway car. How many of these kids had to die before they realized how stupid it was to play superhero on a moving train? "I'll have the conductor slow the train down and stop at the next platform."

He looked up at the routing board that told him where every last train in his segment was. For the most part the system was doing well today. "It's the C?" he asked. He put the phone against his chest. "Hey, Larry, get the conductor for the uptown C that just left Penn." This was going to be one of those days. He spoke into the phone again. "So what do you want me to do? Protocol says slow down and meet the police at the next station." The voice at the other end of the line replied. "What? Are you sure? Well, you make sure you get me the paperwork because I don't want anyone to be hurt, and I want it to be official." He hung up. The landline was part of a subway renovation that never took place.

"What am I doing, Bert?" Larry asked.

The supervisor looked over at him. "That was NYPD. The feds want the train to stop at Cathedral Parkway. Tell the conductor: no stopping and to speed up at the stations so the lunatic can't jump off." He shook his head. "Someone's going to get hurt. They always do."

———

The lights of the station blinded Anna for a few seconds as the train entered Port Authority. She felt the air pressure drop away from her face and chest. Anna looked at the cop at the door and gave him a half-wave. *At least someone cute is arresting me.*

"It'll all be over soon," he said.

Yeah. As soon as I can jump off this thing, I am outta here.

The train continued onward as it picked up speed. She measured her chances as the blue metal pillars went by at a velocity unlike the speed of trees going by while skiing. The expressions of the people on the platform all changed as she passed them and they saw her precarious position.

A few seconds later, she was in the tunnel again. "What's going on?" she asked.

The officer shrugged, and spoke into his radio. Then he vanished into the crowd.

She banged her fist on the glass. "What's going on?" They had to be following some sort of protocol. Only she couldn't fathom what.

The train shook back and forth, and she held onto both bars again. It slowed then jerked forward in a burst of speed. Anna almost lost her grip, but this time she was prepared. Relativity was her friend. The initial slowing and stopping came in a jarring staccato that her body couldn't keep up with initially, but once she did, she was safe. Anna just had to be prepared to be jostled around during those intermediate periods.

The train slowed again. And then sped up. And didn't stop. *I'm going to need help when I get off here.* She reached into her bag and extracted her cell.

The train bounced and the cell left her hand for a split second. She grabbed it and held it close. She shivered and looked at the display. She logged in.

The good news: one bar of signal strength. The bad news: almost no battery power. This was a one-call event. Once in custody, she wouldn't be allowed to talk to anyone.

She felt a wave of helplessness flow through her.

No, not yet.

She looked up a name in the contact list she should not have kept. She selected the name and hit the green phone icon.

26

DROPPED CALL

Terrell was at 42nd Street and 7th Avenue, which was not where he wanted to be. In this neighborhood, though, Tourist Central, he could take a train and get around faster. He ran toward a group of officers who congregated at the corner, but found himself slowed down by an ocean of tourists blocking him from every path he attempted to take. The smell of sweat and urine reminded him why he preferred working in the office.

He pulled out his ID to the officer closest to him. "What's going on, gentlemen?"

A tall, balding officer, sweating while standing still, answered, "There's a woman with a bomb, supposedly, down in the subway system. We're just not sure where."

Terrell was breathing hard. *Damn it.* He couldn't just stop here and people watch. The run to Times Square was more than he'd expected. "Get your supervisor on the horn," Terrell said. He took in deep breaths. "I need a sitrep. Where is she?"

The officer looked at him and did nothing.

"Right now." Terrell motioned with his hand to his face like he was making a call. He felt his cell vibrating in his jacket pocket. Another call? He didn't have time for this.

He reached into his pocket, pulled out the phone, and took a look at the number. Private. As he was about to swipe Decline he hit Accept. He rolled his eyes. If he hung up right away, he wouldn't have to deal with whoever the hell it was.

"Special Agent Terrell Garrison."

"Terrell! You have to stop the train!"

"Anna?" Terrell turned away from the officers. "Where are you?"

"On the C train heading uptown. I'm standing outside the doorway of the last car."

"What the hell are you doing standing...?" *Stupid question.* "You have to give yourself up."

"Details! Stop the train! I'm not sure how much longer I can hold on. If you thought travel was hard in the train, try outside it!" Anna yelled.

He had a hard time hearing her over the background noise of the tunnel.

"Anna, listen to me. The city is out trying to find you."

There was a pause then, "I'd say they found me."

"You have to turn yourself in."

"I promise! Oh, I can't."

"This is not up for negotiation. If the train hasn't stopped, it's because they want to have an overwhelming force available to get at you when the train comes in." Terrell turned west and started running.

He had to get to Eighth Avenue. Thoughts of carjacking a civilian vehicle crossed his mind.

"I'm willing to bet that every station between you and wherever that train is going has a police presence. And there's about twenty thousand police officers in New York."

"Yes, but that's all shifts so most of them are home and a lot of them are on vacation."

Was she serious? Correcting him while she was hanging on for dear life off the back of a train?

"What is wrong with you?" Terrell asked.

"I have to find Benson."

"Who?"

"The man who killed my father. He's here."

Her father? The man who killed him? Someone killed her father? "New York? Let me help you."

"You can't. I can't let you get involved."

"A little late, don't you think?" He looked back and forth. Time to commit a carjacking.

"Why is the train slowing down and speeding up?"

"Welcome to New York. That's why you should have been traveling inside the car."

———

Anna put the phone against her mouth. Even if he wanted to he wouldn't be able to do anything fast enough. This was going to end badly. If she survived this ride she was going away forever.

That wasn't going to happen.

"Who's Benson?" Terrell asked.

"Some guy named Malik Palma."

Anna heard him curse under his breath.

"Hold on. I think you just pulled yourself into my jurisdiction."

———

Palma? She told me the same thing at ADX. You have got to be fucking kidding me. "Did you hear me? Hold on. You're mine now."

"Help!" she said.

Terrell heard the screeching of brakes and a scream. The call dropped.

27

AFTERNOON AT THE MUSEUM

Anna screamed as she let go of the phone to grab hold of the door railing as she swung off the platform to her right. Her waist hit the train guardrail, shooting pain through her hips, stomach, up her ribs, and into her already tense neck. The train continued to jump like a mechanical bull, giving Anna no time to correct the grip of her sweaty palm. She pushed against the guardrail and repositioned herself on the platform before the door. She couldn't keep this up. Terrell couldn't stop the train fast enough and she had to get off.

The train had passed well-lit areas with access ladders to the surface. She wasn't sure if they made it all the way to the street, but she couldn't wait to find out. She switched from her left hand to her right. Again, the train lurched, lifted her off her feet, and tossed her off the train. Anna slid down the bar, felt the train coupling, positioned her feet on it, and felt somewhat secure.

Lurch.

The coupling struck her in the stomach and she gasped from the impact. The train began to brake, pressing her against the metal coupling like a battering ram against an uncooperative door. Sparks flew on either side of her as she felt the air pushed out of her lungs and the train brought to a stop. If she let go, she knew that she would slam into the railroad ties and break every bone in her body. She also knew that wouldn't matter as she would smash her skull and die long before she noticed that.

She started to see sparkles from lack of air. Her grip loosened. *No, No, NO...*

She couldn't keep her hand closed any more.

She let go.

And fell onto a bag of dirt. Her head hurt. She looked up and saw the massive train stopped a few feet away from her. The passengers pressed against the window of the door with shock frozen on their faces. *No time to enjoy the festivities.* She turned onto her side and tried to take in a breath. It hurt. One breath. Two.

Okay, gotta go. Gotta go. Get up.

She tried to move and couldn't. She took another breath. *Okay, now I've gotta go.* She looked down the tunnel and saw one of the illuminated ladders.

Walk toward the light.

She stood up and heard banging behind her. The police officer was trying to get the door opened. She ran, doing her best to jump from tie to tie. A few more steps. Another few. There was the access ladder. The ladder was rusty and dusty, but she grabbed the nearest rung and did her best to push up with her feet rather than pull up with her hands. Her palms were in pain so she used them for stability rather than strength.

Move. He's going to get that door open any second now.

She looked up. Light streamed in through a grating. *New goal.*

Three-quarters of the way she thought she heard someone calling up to her. The grating came closer. *Geez, the C really is far underground.* She pushed upward with her shoulder onto the heavy metal grating.

Was any of this worth it? Maybe she should just stop and let the officer coming up behind her have an easy arrest. Then she remembered Benson, and her anger got the better of her. She shoved the grating up as someone walked by. All she saw was their feet, but they reached down and helped swing the grating out of the way. Her grateful shoulders gave thanks.

It was an Asian man. He was older but strong enough that he could lift the metal frame then help her out. She thanked him, pulled the grating back down, gave him a hug, and positioned him over the opening she had just come through. It would slow down her pursuer by only a few seconds, but that would count toward something.

Her body was in pain, but she had felt worse. She couldn't help but smile; she had done it. In the afternoon light, in front of her she saw a statue of three men. One on horseback flanked by two others in robes. It was Teddy Roosevelt and two Native Americans.

She was at the American Museum of Natural History.

The steps looked a touch daunting, but she needed to lose herself in the crowds again. And a soft seat would be a welcome find.

She didn't remember a lot of those at AMNH.

Sirens blared from up the street. The officer on the train must have told them where she was. She started taking the steps two at a time, but not running. She didn't want to look out of place. Just another neurotic New Yorker fitting in one last trip.

A squad car pulled up then another. She made it to the entrance. She pushed against the revolving door as she heard someone yell, "Stop!"

Where could she hide? She had to get far enough inside that they would have to waste time looking.

She entered the main lobby, the Theodore Roosevelt Rotunda, with its high ceiling, and *Barosaurus* and *Allosaurus* skeleton mounts. There were doorways ahead and to her left and right. Families milled about getting tickets. Upstairs. She had to get upstairs. Downstairs was the food court, but that would have to wait.

It was all she could do to stop herself from looking at the dinosaur skeletons. *What a waste! The first time I'm here in years...*

She walked through the lobby and turned right. She heard two voices from the direction she had just emerged from. Something about locking the doors and not letting anyone out.

Keep walking. Get to the staircase. Walk up as fast as you can.

When the police arrived at the scene of a break-in in progress, they would always find the perp at the highest point of the house. Was she just obeying her ingrained sense of survival? She didn't care.

Move it!

The density of people at the museum was thinner than usual. That was bad. She would stand out and people would be able to point to her. She had gone up one flight of stairs, stopped walking, and looked at one of the signs against the wall with pictures depicting the nearby exhibits and the special events of the week. *Interesting exhibit. Don't I look normal reading this? Sure I do!*

She looked to either side of her. No one was paying attention to her except for a little olive-skinned Indian boy who turned away when he saw a little girl walk by with a balloon.

Next staircase.

She had to keep climbing to get to where she needed to go. It had been a few years, but she knew it was there and that might be her way out.

There. Up the staircase and onto the floor.

There was the door. *Employees Only.* She felt a pang of guilt. She could have been one of them instead of... She scolded herself. *Shut up. You have a job to do. Go do it.*

She went through the heavy wood door and did her best to walk on auto-pilot. The area had high ceilings, dark walls, and shelves everywhere. The smells here were different from the rest of the museum: the powdery scent of old parchments, a little must mixed in with formaldehyde and alcohol. Subdued light came in through the windows.

It had been a long time since she had last been there looking at dinosaur fossils as part of a class trip she had taken with her father. She felt a pang of guilt at the memory and pushed it away. He wasn't here. He was a pain even back then.

"Excuse me. What are you doing here?"

Anna stopped. She slowed her breathing and turned toward the male voice.

"Who are you?" he asked.

She smiled her best normal smile. "Hi."

It was one of the curators. Tall, stately looking. Tired sweater over a striped blue shirt. Wire-framed glasses. Was he the same one from her class trip? That was so long ago. Couldn't be. He looked old.

"Uh, I'm a new docent," she said, "and I thought I would get the lay of the land." She shrugged. "I think I'm lost."

"You look familiar," he said.

"I must look like a lot of people."

"No, I remember you. You were about ten and asked some of the best questions about dinosaurs any child ever asked."

Anna blushed. He remembered her? Because of her questions?

"You had the over-protective parent. Made some comment about old people studying old bones." He reached out and shook her hand. "I'm glad to see you here." He let go of her hand. "Now, get out." He smiled at her. "You don't belong in this part of the museum."

Anna smiled back. "Yes, sir." Her thoughts veered from the present, but just for a moment. "Which way to the freight elevator?"

"Why?"

"I'm supposed to help someone move some boxes and I just want to make sure I can find the way out when I get here."

He scrutinized her for a moment. Anna could read the thoughts on his face. He didn't want to tell her, but she knew she seemed harmless enough.

"That way," he said. He pointed down one of the other halls. "There are signs. I know because I still get lost looking for it." He smiled again. "Now get out or I'll tell the volunteer manager."

What a nice man. "Yes, sir," she said. "Thanks." Anna jogged down the hallway toward the freight elevator.

He called out, "Hey! The exit's the other way!"

———

The freight elevator was an average-sized compartment with quilts against the walls and a slow-moving mechanism. Anna's nerves tightened around her shoulders. *Could we not go a little faster?* Would they have security down there? Would she have to fight them, as well? She wasn't sure she was up to it. She hoped that, unless the police and National Guard surrounded the museum, they would never think of going to the basement to look for her.

She would know as soon as the door opened. At first, she pushed herself into the corner of the compartment beside the door. Her palms, dry after her subway escapade, started to sweat again. She was breathing fast and shallow. She closed her eyes. *Slow down. Take deep breaths.*

The door slid open. The elevator had taken her, unmolested, all the way to the bottom of the museum. She might actually pull this off. All she needed was time to get her plan together and get to Benson before he returned to Washington. What if he'd already departed? Everyone talked about Hurricane Sandy as if it were the end of the world. That just couldn't be right.

The basement was dark, crowded, and dirty. She could see the truck docks off to one side and headed in that direction.

From behind the never-ending landscape of boxes and tarp-draped objects, a door opened. She took a few quick steps and hid behind one of the boxes. Was it the police? Anna shuddered. She wasn't ready yet. A museum employee would be better. She would use the lost docent story again. Or maybe the chemo story. Maybe a lost docent on chemo.

Feet slapped the ground, as though someone was running. Her legs were sore but obeyed her command to stand slowly to peer around the box. Nothing. The sounds had stopped. No rustling of clothes, no slow steps on the dirty concrete floor. Had she imagined the sound of the door?

Another sound came from her left. She turned her head and someone grabbed her from behind. Their large hand wrapped itself around the back of her skull and slammed her face and body against one of the taller wooden boxes.

"Why couldn't you just go to Vancouver?"

28

VANCOUVER REGRETS

Pain shot up Anna's head. A dozen thoughts crowded her mind for attention: Who were these people? Why did they care if she went to Vancouver? How had they found her?

Would she be able to muster enough energy to get away?

The voice behind her said, "I'm going to step back and you are going to put on these handcuffs." He had a slight accent, but Anna couldn't place it.

She wasn't very good with voices and even less so with accents. A British accent might as well be an Australian accent.

"The man at the diner said that I would be killed if I didn't go to Canada," she said.

"And he was right. Keep facing the box."

Anna felt the pressure disappear behind her head. She started to turn and he pushed her face against the crate again, but this time not as roughly. She wondered if her face was marked from striking the box so hard. He let go of her head again.

"Kill me here," she said. "Why take me somewhere else?" She felt a metal bar pressed against her head. A gun barrel.

"I'm going to step away. Do not turn around."

Something metallic struck the ground at her feet.

"Reach down, pick up the handcuffs, and put them on with your hands behind your back."

Anna felt him step away. She looked down and saw the handcuffs. *If those come on I'm done for.*

"Now," he said.

Anna looked at the tall, Asian man in the face. The split second of surprise was all she was waiting for. As he reached for her, she slapped the hand holding the gun, and it flew across the room. She didn't have time to hear it land before she punched him in the stomach, trying to land a few more body blows.

The man recovered and blocked her additional attempts to hit him, finally pushing her away into the make-shift corridor between crates.

Her lungs hurt. She stopped thinking and twirled to find the gun. Not on her right. Or her left. She felt him come at her and she spun as far as she could to one side, but it wasn't enough. He reached down, picked her up by her shirt, and smashed her in a crate marked "Fragile." She kept her head from hitting the hard wall, but her shoulder exploded in pain. She grabbed the arm that was holding her to get a stable position and kicked up between his legs. Her knee connected with something unyielding and she winced both from the surprise and the unexpected pain.

He held her with both hands.

"You have to let me go," she said.

"Why couldn't you listen?" He swung her to the side, hitting another crate. "You just had to go to Vancouver." He swung her to his left and she struck another tall box.

"I have a score to settle," Anna said.

He swung her to his right again, striking a crate, but not as hard as before. "You think no one knows that? Why do you think the police are everywhere?" He swung her to his left and let go as she connected with the box.

"Why aren't you in Vancouver?" Anna asked.

"There were others waiting for you." He looked around the floor, taking his eyes off her for a split second. "Now I have to get you out of here so I can take care of this once and for all."

Anna lunged at him again and toppled a few boxes before they both went crashing to the floor. He pushed her away and jumped to her right. She stood up and was about to jump on him when he spun around and aimed the gun at her.

So that's where it went.

"Handcuffs. Behind your back." He stood up with a grace she had only seen in her dojo, and then only from the advanced students.

Anna looked for the handcuffs. She knelt on the ground—she had almost no energy left to stand—and clicked the heavy metal bracelets into place. "I'll scream for the police."

He reached behind her and helped her get on her feet.

"If I get loose, I will kill you."

The man breathed deeply. She had given him a run for his money. "You won't get the chance."

———

The museum parking lot was empty. The man seemed to know more about the museum than she did.

"How did you find me? There was no way you could have..." she said.

They approached a silver sedan with red, white, and blue plates. The man aimed his hand at the car and the trunk popped open.

"A little birdie told me."

A little birdie? It wasn't until they were standing behind the car that Anna felt her cheeks grow hot. That bastard. She looked down and saw the edge of Hawking's gift. Her necklace. They had tracked her through the necklace. So much for a special keepsake. He opened the trunk as far as it would go and said, "Get in."

———

The trunk was dark, but not completely soundproof. Good suspension. Anna didn't feel the bumpiness of the road as much as she'd expected, but they were just leaving the parking area. The smell of rubber made her nauseous.

The car came to a halt. It was so dark that she saw the exact same thing whether her eyes were opened or closed. Were they at a traffic light or had they been stopped by the cops? There was no way for her to tell. Anna's stomach tightened. She struggled to breathe. He had covered her mouth, bound her legs, then attached her ankles to a hook on the floor so she could barely move.

She was not the first person to occupy its trunk.

When she heard voices, she screamed, but the cloth against her mouth muffled the sound. She wrestled against the restraints to hit something (anything!) but only succeeded in making herself dizzy.

The tall, Asian man, with the clipped speech, somewhat dusty suit, and possessor of a colorful license plate, had talked his way out of the search area with a weapon even the police could not combat: diplomatic immunity.

———

Anna tried to work out which direction they were going in, but the bumps in the road told her nothing. Turn, move, stop, move, stop, move, stop. They were in a traffic jam of some sort. She needed to come up for air. They could be stuck for hours trying to get out of Manhattan.

Was he going to drive her to Vancouver? No, he he'd said he was going to take care of her and that meant only one thing: he was going to kill her.

No revenge, no revenge party, and no revenge after-party. He would probably drive the car into the Hudson and drown her. The hurricane would take the car out into the Atlantic and her disappearance wouldn't be noticed.

Her eyes started to tear. Poor Aunt Marcie and Uncle Ray. They'd never know what happened to her and she would never get a chance to see them again.

Her chest was hollow. She would never know, never really know, what had happened to her father. She shut the thoughts out of her mind. It didn't matter. She'd failed to save him. She'd failed to save herself. Terrell. Oh, she would have wanted to see him one last time as well.

———

The car drove up a slight ramp. Maybe he was going to shoot her first? If she had half a chance, she would fight him again until one of them was dead. She needed fresh air. It was hot, she was sweaty, and her lungs hurt.

The trunk popped open and light streamed in. Anna closed her eyes as someone, it had to be the man, reached in and pulled her ankles off the hook that had kept them down. He lowered the trunk lid but didn't close it. She couldn't talk and she could hardly move. So much for rescuing herself.

The man walked away. She heard someone call out then heard them argue. She was dizzy. The deep breaths she inhaled brought a coolness she could feel pouring into her lungs and chest.

"Get her to Vancouver," the new voice said.

"She's not going. I did everything you wanted."

"If she stays, I'm calling this off."

"She won't go," said the man who'd thrown her in the trunk.

"Get her an escort and get her to Canada."

"You take her."

"You need me. When did you become the expert?" the new voice said.

"Then I'll do us both a favor and just shoot her."

"Where is she?"

"In the trunk."

"You put her in the trunk?" The second man sounded frantic.

"The police almost had her."

The trunk opened and the light blinded her.

"Oh, God, you taped her mouth." He tried to sit her up, but she was still weak and dizzy. "This is going to hurt." He pulled off the tape that was holding the cloth in place in one swift motion. "I'm sorry. I'm so sorry."

Anna couldn't cover her eyes since her hands were still hand-cuffed so she blinked and blinked until an impossible image appeared before her. A single word left her mouth before she could stop it. "Dad?"

"Hello, Squirrel."

SPECIAL DELIVERY

Secretary of State George Monahan looked at the crate delivered to his office, signed for by Plante, and suspected what he would find inside.

The courier who had dropped off the box had gone through the unlocking of the container to allow for easier access and left without looking back.

Monahan had been having a late lunch/early dinner with former colleagues of state when he'd received the call from Cordell Plante requesting his presence back at the State Department offices at UN Plaza.

A diplomatic pouch from Pakistan marked Urgent and FYEO. *For Your Eyes Only.*

Diplomatic pouches, as a delivery device between a diplomatic mission and its home country, or between a diplomatic mission and other governments, represented the ultimate in secure delivery. The couriers couldn't be detained for any reason and the diplomatic pouch could not be opened or examined in any way that would allow the examiner to determine what might be contained inside it. Of course, through the years, when it was convenient to ignore diplomatic protocol, the inviolability of the pouch was subject to interpretation. Through the years, they served as conduits for cigars, drugs, replacement parts for the International Space Station, and temporary holding cells to transport bound and drugged people kidnapped in one country and headed for another.

While the delivery was unexpected, it was not a surprise. Monahan was in the diplomacy business and with that came the regular delivery of communiques, private requests for assistance, and various kinds of electronics not allowed on networked PCs.

The brown box, about two feet tall, two feet deep, and two feet across, had a single latch in the front and two hinges in the back.

Plante stood by the doorway. "Would you like some quiet time with your package or shall I wait in case I need to call the Chief of Staff?"

"You go ahead. I'll let you know what I need," Monahan said.

Plante left the room, pulling the ornate, white door closed with a slight click. Monahan leaned on the front of his desk.

Was this really from Pakistan?

Monahan strode over to the container. The lid swung open and he found another box, gray metal with a keypad, suspended in the middle of the container. He picked it up, turned it in his hand to see if the box had been tampered with in any way, and entered a PIN he had only used three times before.

The smaller box opened, revealing its contents: a memory stick. Monahan took the thumb drive and returned to his desk. There was nothing more insecure than a memory stick. There was nothing that could be done to secure it, yet they were one of the most ubiquitous technologies around. If he plugged it into one of the PCs from State, he would have security knocking on his door within minutes asking him to hand it over to the IT staff. They would examine it under a microscope to determine why the item, smaller than a lighter, was hooked into the US State Department's network.

That would not do. He opened the right hand lower drawer and pulled out a Dell laptop. It would serve his purposes. When tablets became cheap enough and allowed the use of USB memory sticks, he would use one of those, but for now the shining purpose of this machine was to read thumb drives and stay off the network. He used it often for browsing documents that were meant to be seen only by him and were not to be found anywhere on a US network.

This memory stick was different. It wasn't from the Pakistanis.

There was a selection of text files in a single folder. They had a three-letter prefix, a six-digit number starting with 000001, and ending with txt. The three-letter prefix was "FBI."

Monahan opened FBI000001.txt. The document was a dump from an FBI system he wouldn't normally have access to because of the sensitive nature of its holdings. Sensitive because politicians shouldn't have been looking at the case files of investigations of other politicians, or of themselves. In the US, background checks on politicians was the norm to confirm or deny conflicts of interest. Things like income tax deductions. Questionable bank accounts.

Associations with foreign countries.

Monahan looked at his FBI file. The date was seven years earlier. Around the time that Marshall Wodehouse decided to leave HALON. Marshall. The IT wiz with the military intelligence background.

Monahan had been under investigation and Palma had not known. Was Palma also under scrutiny? Had Palma turned on him? Monahan pushed that thought aside. He and Malik Palma were in on this for so many years that arresting them would destroy the reputation of multiple administrations, not to mention congressional committees. The one thing he knew for sure, was so sure that he had bet everything on it, was that he would never be arrested for everything he and Palma and the army of unknowing contractors had been doing for over 2 decades. The operation had gone on for so long, and was of a scale never before seen, that no one would know how to charge them.

Yet, there the charges were in black and white. Espionage. Fraud. Charge after charge.

He read file after file. All the work he had done. All the subterfuges. Things that the Bureau could not possibly have known were there for the taking. And there was only one person, one person other than Malik Palma, who was capable of knowing all of it.

Marshall Wodehouse.

Monahan had warned Palma about Wodehouse when Marshall first worked under him. Marshall was brilliant to be sure, but Monahan had dozens of men and women who were that smart (smarter!), but Palma was insistent. Thoughts flooded Monahan's mind. Nothing would change. They would have the handoff of HALON on Monday and Monahan would disappear forever. Palma could do what he wanted. This was just as much Palma's fault as Marshall's. Everyone said Marshall would be trouble and here, all these years later, they were right.

Monahan pulled the thumb drive out of the laptop. This was an invitation, not just a warning. He would have to leave New York, but not for Washington.

———

Plante sat at this desk and typed out an email. The Secretary of State had received another diplomatic pouch, but Plante was certain it was not from Pakistan. Plante always checked with the embassies who sent the various pouches and, while it had come from the Pakistani Embassy, his contact there confirmed that the sender was not someone who had the responsibility, or the title, to send someone at Monahan's level anything of value.

Plante had not had to notify anyone in over a year. Nothing of note had happened. This was of note. New York in one of the worst storms imaginable. Another package from the Pakistani Embassy. Communiques that Monahan kept from him. If Plante was right, Monahan would want to return to Washington. Plante didn't know what was going on, but his briefing with the FBI two years before did not look good for the man he'd once held in such high regard. The Bureau might be wrong, but it was not looking good for the Secretary of State.

30

DIGGING GRAVES

"And the manhunt continues for escaped fugitive Anna..."

FBI Special Agent Steven Morris ignored the news that droned on in the background, and shook hands with General Malik Palma. The General sat down in a Queen Anne chair in one of the residential apartments of the Towers at the Waldorf Astoria located at 100 East 50 Street. The entrance to the Towers, just off the hotel's Park Avenue entrance, lent the hotel an even more exclusive feel than it already had. Having chosen the meeting place, Morris felt the surroundings would suit the General more. Put him at ease. Morris was dressed in his standard issue FBI uniform of dark suit and dark tie. Palma was in his military garb.

"General, it's a pleasure as usual," Morris said. He sat on the couch opposite Palma and put his briefcase on the polished hardwood floor.

"I hope that my call didn't interrupt anything. I know how busy you are in CoIntel," Palma said. Counter-Intelligence.

"Catch any spies?"

Both men chuckled, but Morris felt his stomach tighten. He hated that question. He hoped that during one of the upcoming meetings he would have better news for Palma, even if it meant the General would be less than pleased. "I'd do better if we could get more intel from your side."

The final rays of sunlight came through the white-framed windows. Palma leaned forward and remained in the shade. "Of course you would." He clasped his hands together. "So what can I do for you?"

"You called me, General. I was hoping you could tell me."

"Anna Wodehouse," Palma said.

Morris did his best to remain silent.

"I understand you almost have her in custody."

"Almost. She's as good as."

"Good." Palma stood. "Can I get you a drink?" Morris waved him off.

Palma went to the drink cart and poured himself two fingers of brandy. "What do you know about her so far?"

"That would be telling."

"Off the record," Palma said.

"From the beginning? She was found in the Brooklyn home of kidnapper Arnold Dashman after missing for fifteen years. Seven years later she kills a member of WitSec, a Mister Garth Donnell, is found guilty of first degree, goes to prison, escapes, and returned to New York where we are going to make sure she never gets anywhere near a doorway."

"Good summary." Palma smiled. "You should have been an analyst."

"Did you know her before?"

"I don't understand," Palma said.

"Anna Wodehouse. Did you ever know her?"

"No. Why?"

"It has come to our attention that Secretary of State Monahan might have known Arnold Dashman," Morris said.

"Who?"

"Arnold Dashman. The man accused of having kidnapped her. Turns out he used to work for the Defense Department only then his name was Marshall Wodehouse."

Morris did his best not to look away. Palma's reaction was important this time.

"Marshall was Arnold Dashman?" Palma sipped his drink.

"I'm afraid he is. Or was since all evidence points to his death sometime in the last few years."

Palma stood and gazed at the wall, as though deep in thought. Morris decided to poke a little more. "He also knew Garth Donnell, though we're still not sure what the connection is. Do you think that Donnell may have killed Wodehouse and Anna killed him out of revenge?"

"That is certainly a new theory, Mr. Morris. I had not heard it before. Perhaps I'll have someone look into it."

"That would be useful, sir," Morris said. "When you called, I had hoped that perhaps you had something related to Anna Wodehouse." Morris contemplated standing by the window as a small distraction, but he decided against it.

"Fire away," Palma said as he returned to his chair. "I know all this is off the record."

"How closely do you monitor the communications of government officials?"

"How closely? We know the kind of toilet paper used in the Kremlin. We know the name of every mistress of every Saudi prince," Palma said. "Did you have a particular government in mind?"

"Yes, sir." It was Morris' turn to lean forward. "I wouldn't ask if I thought there was a way to do this without circumventing certain...legal procedures."

"Understood," Palma said.

"I need to know more about the communications between Secretary of State Monahan and some members of Chinese Intelligence."

Palma blinked. Morris would make a note of that for later. An extra second to respond.

"That would be illegal. We're not allowed to spy on our own people."

"Well," Morris leaned back and spread his arm across the couch, "if we gave you the names of certain known figures in Chinese Intelligence, would you be able to tell us if they had any conversations with Secretary of State Monahan or any of his known associates?"

Palma stood. "Special Agent, I have nothing but the utmost respect for Secretary Monahan. I don't know what you're searching for, but you had better get a warrant for what you're asking for."

Morris waited. And waited. He decided to blink. "Of course, General. I was here just to see if we could get things started prior to a signed warrant, but you're right. I shouldn't have asked before having the actual paperwork with me. I apologize." Morris stood and extended his hand.

Palma shook it.

"I'll be looking for that paperwork, Special Agent. You will have the full cooperation of my agency, but I think you're looking for something that's not there."

"And I expect you to find nothing, sir."

———

Morris walked across Park Avenue and got into the back seat of a black, unmarked FBI vehicle that had a driver and one man in the back. Morris unbuttoned his jacket. "Did you get all that?"

"Yes, sir."

Morris always forgot the names of the techs assigned to him. The work was always more than they could handle, and there was always more work.

"Great audio quality." The driver turned around and pulled off his sunglasses. "Do you think he knows anything?"

Morris pulled at his pant legs to straighten out the fabric. "He has the largest Intelligence organization on the planet. He could have his system send him an alert when the subpoena is signed and have his lawyer respond to us before we deliver it." Morris looked out the passenger window. "But he won't. He might be tight with Monahan, but he's just as much of a political animal. They will abandon each other if there is the slightest whiff of wrongdoing that will affect their careers."

"So he doesn't know?" the driver asked.

"No. He would never have let me in if he knew that we were preparing to arrest Monahan."

31

NAME CALLING

Marshall lifted Anna out of the trunk while the man freed her ankles. She was leaning against the car when she felt someone hug her.

"Anna, Anna," Marshall said.

His voice sounded strange. Was he sad? Upset? Her senses felt overwhelmed like she was underwater, or sinking into a quagmire. Anna felt numb, disconnected. Familiar sights and smells that she had not experienced in years. The details of their location, a garage somewhere, were meaningless. Things hung from the walls and ceiling. Florescent lights washed out all the shadows, leaving her in a flat room with a yellow tinge on everything. Anna closed her eyes.

She was being hugged by a dead man who was no longer dead.

She searched and searched (maybe Google would help?), but there was a vast and unmeasurable emptiness in her. Her feelings for the man who had abandoned her crowded into the back of her head. He couldn't be her father; he would never have done this to her.

Anna leaned into him for a short second then pushed him away with her shoulders. "No," she said. "No."

"Anna?" the man with her father's face asked.

"No." She closed her eyes as tightly as she could and felt the tears squeeze out. "No." She tried to mouth other words.

So many things she had dreamed of telling him. Things she had told him in her make-believe conversations in which the only person there was her. "No." The word was crushed and she said it again and again.

"No." Breath. "No." *You're not dead. You just left me.* "No."

"Anna, please."

"No." Why wasn't she crying? The skin on her face felt like a thousand needles stabbed her all at once. "No. NO!"

Anna pulled at her hands that were still handcuffed behind her back as she slid down the fender of the car that brought her to a place where the dead live and feelings became sounds she didn't understand. They squeezed and tugged at her like demented fans at the rock concert from hell.

"I told you that you should have made her go to Canada," Marshall said.

"It's too late for Plan B or C or Z," the Asian man said. "There's a manhunt out there the likes of which you have never seen. Everyone knows she's here and now we either hide her or..."

Marshall stepped forward until he and the man were a couple of inches apart. "Or what?" Marshall took another step closer. "Or what? If I even see you going near her..."

In the middle of their conversation Anna thought, *This is so idiotic.* She inhaled fractured breaths. "Hey!" Had she just run a marathon? Was it just her asthma? "I'm right here." She tried to stand, tumbled forward, and crashed to her knees.

"Take those handcuffs off her. What's wrong with you?" Marshall asked the tall man who pulled a key out of his pocket and unlocked the metal bracelets.

Exhaustion washed over her. She rubbed her wrists as her shoulders got heavier. It was all a pointless exercise. She looked at the dirty concrete floor and couldn't pull her eyes away. "Get away from me."

She gave both men a swift look and returned her gaze to the dirty, bare floor. She stood up. Marshall tried to hold her arm and help her stand, but she yanked her arm away. "Get away from me." She hugged her arms close. "Get. Away. From. Me."

"I'm sorry, Squirrel."

"Don't call me Squirrel." The words came out so fast they startled her. If she hadn't felt so tired, she would have torn a piece of his face off. *Maybe later.* "I don't know how you imagined this happening, but this," she pulled her arms in closer, "this is not..."

Marshall turned back to his companion. "You have to get her out of here."

"You are not listening," the Asian said.

"No!" Marshall yelled. "You are not listening!"

Anna covered her ears and started screaming again. Her burning lungs pumped cry after cry out of her chest until she bent over, and just tortured whispers scraped their way to the surface.

———

Anna blinked and found herself lying down. The room was dark, but not as dark as the trunk. Marshall sat in a folding chair to her right. Her throat hurt. Her heart was gone.

Marshall held out a plastic cup. She took it with shaky hands and sipped. Room temperature water. She took another slow sip and breathed in a smooth breath. Water had never tasted so good.

"What happened?" Anna asked.

"You started throwing things around. Eight glass containers are no longer with us. We won't be repairing cars any time soon. And I think you scared Liko-san."

"Don't joke with me. The tall guy?"

"Yeah," he said.

Marshall looked at her face as if he'd never seen it before. "I told him you've done that before." He smiled a little. A smile on an older face.

He left me. She handed back the plastic cup. Anna focused her gaze on him. "Why?"

"I can't tell you, but you have to go."

"Like hell I will." She sat up from the bed. The lumpy mattress undulated like a waterbed and she struggled to get up. Marshall did not reach out to her this time.

Hell with you. She walked over to the door, which was open a crack, and entered the garage. The glare from the light hurt her eyes again, but only for a few seconds.

Liko, in a white shirt and dark pants without his jacket and tie, was standing off to one side. He had a holster to his left. She would have thought of him as handsome under different circumstances.

She walked up to him and looked up into his eyes. "I'm going to hurt you one day."

"I will look forward to it."

"Anna. Stop that," Marshall said.

She pointed at Marshall. He was wearing blue jeans and a flannel lumberjack shirt. "Don't you start," she said. "You lost all privileges the day you didn't die." He wasn't as tall as she remembered.

"Stop cursing." He took a few steps into the room. "Go to Vancouver."

"Not until you damn well tell me everything." Her eyes swept over dozens of car parts strewn all over the floor. Jars filled with screws and washers lay in shards on the dirty concrete.

"I changed my mind. Just one question. Who are you? Am I your daughter?"

Liko looked at Marshall and held up two fingers. Marshall shrugged. "Of course you're my daughter." He stepped toward her. "Now go to Vancouver."

"Why did you leave?" The next question caused her voice to crack. "Why did you leave me alone?"

Marshall answered right away. "You were safest without me. Those people they found who said they were your aunt and uncle did a good job of keeping you safe and I made sure you were all taken care of."

"They were more to me than you were. They were there." She crossed her arms. "I'm not leaving. Vancouver, the moon, whatever. I don't care."

"You have to go," Marshall said.

How could he looked concerned? How could he feel he had the right?
"Screw you! Where were you?" She flailed her hands. "Where...why..."

"I'm sorry, Squirrel."

"Don't you dare call me that!" she yelled. "Marshall, or Arnold, or whatever your name is."

"Liko-san, please take her to Vancouver."

"No," Anna said.

Liko pulled out his gun and pointed it at her. "It's too late for Vancouver," he said.

32

FATHER KNOWS BEST

Marshall grabbed a greasy carburetor hood off the messy crowded table, and threw it as hard as he could toward Liko. The tall man reacted instantly: he deflected the item once it was close enough, which caused him to aim the gun away from Anna.

What an idiot. Marshall stormed over to him and stood between Liko and Anna. His daughter stood frozen; Marshall guessed she wasn't used to having a gun pointed at her. He had never seen her react so slowly.

"So, let's get this straight," Marshall said. "When you pull out a gun, it's because I tell you to or you're protecting me or her."

Liko clenched his jaw.

Marshall was sure Liko wanted to take a swing at him, and Marshall could care less; he had taken down bigger men. He wondered if Anna would step in to stop Liko, or if she would let her old man get beat up. Didn't matter. Marshall took another step toward him. "You said you were here to help."

"We can't leave the city," Liko said.

"And pointing a gun at her accomplishes what exactly?" The two men stared each other down. Marshall pursed his lips and tilted his head.

Liko put the gun back in the holster. "Keeping her here is a mistake. Sending her away is a mistake."

"And killing her does what? I would disable you and set fire to your body so you'd know how angry I was. Nothing she does will change what we have to do. She's a null variable. Adding her to the equation changes nothing." Marshall stepped back and felt embarrassed but kept a straight face.

Where did that reaction come from? He had often thought what it might be like to have Anna back, but this was not what he had in mind.

He had a job to do and after all the things he had done to keep her away and safe she was in the thick of it anyway. He would be proud later. She needed to stay alive. He pointed at his daughter. "You have to go."

"No," she said.

The years had not made her any less stubborn than he remembered. What was he going to do? She was twenty-four and an adult. She was just another civilian.

But she was his civilian.

"My friend here is a little nervous, but he understands you're part of this as long as I say you are." He looked at Liko. "And I say she is." Marshall turned back to her. "And you have to go."

Anna leaned in. "No."

Every move she made was new, yet her gestures were all her. Hands on her hips. Fire in her eyes. That pout on her face. He wanted to reach out to her. Hug her. Tell her how much he missed her. Instead, he had to be the parent. Again. *Eat your vegetables. Go to bed. Get out of New York before the one person who can help me kills you.*

Marshall turned in time to see Liko shoot him a look before he shook his head, grabbed his jacket, and walked away. Marshall's stomach tightened as the door slammed shut.

They were alone.

"So those are the kinds of friends you have? No wonder you never introduced them," Anna said.

"You have to leave."

"Why?"

"I can't tell you."

"Then we don't have much to say." She crossed her arms. "Why?"

"I can't tell you." She looked like she was ready to stomp her foot on the floor from impatience. She hadn't changed a bit. "Aliens are landing here. They're causing the hurricane about to hit and you have to go."

"Really?"

"No." He grabbed his forehead. *If I got headaches I would have one right now.* "I can't tell you. If you can live with the alien story then run with it."

Anna leaned on one of the tables and crossed her legs.

Great. Her arms and legs were crossed. Could she be any more closed-minded if she tried?

———

Anna looked at father. *I will be damned if I let him think he won. First chance I get I am leaving and heading to Canada and not telling him. I'll leave him and see how much he likes it.*

"I would have stayed for aliens too. You think I would have missed that?" she asked. "You're losing your touch. Maybe you should have kidnapped another little girl to stay in practice."

———

Rage boiled inside Marshall. "How dare you? I've followed you everywhere you've ever gone." He took a few steps toward her. "I've helped you every time I could. I was always there."

Anna stood up and pursed her lips. "And you've been such a great help, Daddy. Here, let me give you a hug." She scowled and crossed her arms again.

"I couldn't stop them framing you for Donnell's death. I couldn't stop you from going to prison because Palma knew I would do everything possible and he pushed your case as hard and as fast as he could."

"Thanks, Dad. I loved ADX. The skiing was awesome. Maybe you can go there some day."

"You're the one who teamed up with Palma to try to kill me," Marshall said.

"There's that effing name again! The guy who helped me was called Benson and he convinced me to kill you." She looked away. "But it was my idea."

"Well, you certainly got your wish," Marshall said. He couldn't stop the hurt he knew was in his eyes. "Why would you want to kill me?"

He felt the wave of frustration and anger emanating from her as she stood away from the table. "Are you kidding? You left me! I waited and waited for you and you never came! You left me with two people who loved me and I left them." Her eyes glazed and Marshall felt her pain, along with his. "And I humiliated them and I made them the couple who got stuck with that broken kidnapped girl and they still stayed!" She pointed at him and he felt a knife cutting through his heart and his brain.

"Where were you?" She clenched her hands into tight, pale fists. Her eyes got red and glassy from tears she wouldn't release.

Marshall's shoulders sagged enough that he felt the extra weight he always carried. "I was there. You couldn't see me." His eyes teared. "But I swear I was there."

"Then go back to the damn shadows where you belong. Why couldn't you leave me alone?"

His mind refocused. "Because you came back to New York. You can't stay here."

What was it going to take to get her to leave? Was he going to have to sedate her and put her in the trunk again?

"I have one last thing to do," she said.

"Can it wait the weekend?" His arms went up in disgust. *Are you freaking kidding me?*

"No."

She turned away and Marshall saw her signature look, the look he was always happy to see. She figured something out and he could see her eyes focusing on something in the distance. Then she looked right at him. "You're going to help me."

33

TRUTH...

"Yeah, that's not going to happen," Marshall said.

Anna looked at the ground. She reached for a piece of glass and examined it.

Was she going to attack him with it? "Excuse me," she said and entered the room where she'd been resting when she had fainted upon arriving at the garage. When she took the cup of water from him, he thought that perhaps she had released enough anger that they might be able to have a civilized conversation. Well, maybe not civilized, but at least less heated.

"Get some rest. We'll talk later," Marshall said.

She didn't reply. The light went on and she closed the door.

I could never figure out what she was thinking. Just like her mother. He remembered not responding to her comment about kidnapping another little girl. She was crazy. She bought into Palma's cover story of being a kidnapping victim hook, line, and sinker. How was he ever going to prove that he was her father? Really, there was only one way.

Had she gone back to sleep? It didn't matter. Maybe she was on the secure PC in the room. She always had so many online friends. He wished she would waste less time online, but her stellar grades meant he'd cut her the slack she deserved. He hoped she didn't get online. It might give them away and they had taken a long time finding this abandoned garage in the middle of Harlem only to get caught. He had already worked out a few escape routes, but he was tired. No more escapes for the next few hours.

He hoped there was another sleeping bag somewhere; otherwise, he was going to have to sleep in the car.

In a split-second something clicked in his mind. *Damn it!* He ran to the door and threw it open. Anna was cutting herself with the piece of glass she had taken with her into the room. *What is wrong with me? How blind can I fucking be?*

"What are you doing?" he asked as Anna looked up with empty eyes he had never seen before.

He snatched the shard from her right hand and tried to look at her arm, but she pulled away from him.

She was bleeding just enough to be noticeable, but the cuts weren't deep. There were multiple thin scars along her arm just above her wrist. "What do you care? These aren't that bad."

Marshall couldn't find the words. "Anna, please."

"Get out," she said. "That helps me feel."

"Anna, no. I'll tell you part of what happened."

"I don't care anymore."

"No, it matters."

"To you, apparently," she said.

Marshall couldn't believe the look of exhaustion on her face. Her tired eyes reflected disconnection. *Oh, please, don't give up. I need you. I need you to live. What is all this about if not for you?* "I'll tell you part of it. I can't tell you all of it. I can't."

"It's okay, Daddy. You can shut up now. I'll go to Vancouver. You were right." Her face shifted to anger as she thought private thoughts. "You were always right." She looked up at him for a moment. "It was the right thing to leave me."

"I did something terrible and I have to fix it."

"I changed my mind. You can stop. And you didn't have to fix it.

You were right to leave me." She sat unmoving. Her body as still as her voice. Damn it, she was having mood swings. He had to bring her out of it. He couldn't be with her 24/7, but now he wasn't sure what she might do next.

He would be with her 24/7. After this.

"Please, stop," she said.

"I," he began, "I helped to design a terrible place."

"I know. PRUDENT RAINBOW. Please, shut up." Anna sounded listless.

"Stupid name, I know." Then he froze. "Where did you hear that?"

"I have friends who like to torture me with information about you and Benson. They told me you were dead." She took in a series of shallow breaths. "Please. You have to stop talking." Her eyes were pleading. "Why aren't you dead? This was so much easier that way. You couldn't come for me because you couldn't. You were dead." She closed her eyes and a tear fell. "You were dead."

"There were days I wished I was." He sobered up. "What do you know about PRUDENT RAINBOW?"

Anna shrugged, her shoulders hunched in defeat. "Nothing. It has a new name and no one knows it."

If he told her then he would be sacrificing the life she might have if she survived. "You have to forget everything you know about that. And everything about Palma."

"I know. I have to go. To Vancouver. And I don't know why." Her face contorted, but no tears escaped. "I don't want to."

"I'll meet you there."

"You're lying to me."

Of course I am. "No, I'll meet you there."

Anna's breathing was shallow again. "I was so afraid that day." He reached out and she pulled back. "When the police came and told me who you were..."

"Palma was trying to have me arrested. He thought I was a threat." Marshall wanted to be angry, wanted to rail about Palma. Instead, only guilt filled his chest. "He was right. I was on my way to the house to get you and tell the world what we were doing. What we were creating." He blinked. "I was too late. I heard the story about a kidnapping and I almost walked into the police station just so they would let you go." He leaned toward her and she leaned away from him. "But I knew I wouldn't be able to help you if I was in jail. It would have been worse. I did everything I could for you."

"You didn't do anything." How could he explain the Stoddard's mortgage mysteriously paid off? The summer job offers that paid so well?

But not the scholarships. That she had done herself. *I'm so proud of you,* he wanted to say but held back.

"Leave me alone." She turned away. "I lost so many years."

"That's changed now. I have things set up for you."

"In Vancouver?"

Without him. "Yes."

"Did you kidnap me?"

"No."

"My name is Carpenter Poole."

"Your name is Anna Wodehouse."

"My name is Carpenter Poole."

"That's not who you are."

———

Anna looked with despair at the man who had been the largest part of her life. *If I'm not Carpenter Poole, and Anna Wodehouse is dead, then who am I?*

The sides of her head tightened as the back of her head became hot. She climbed off the bed. "I'll be alright," she lied. The words rolled off her tongue and she saw them walking away, taking on a life of their own.

She had to do something. She didn't know what, but her head was going to explode if she didn't do something.She walked into the garage and spotted a door. She entered the room and saw four notebook PCs set up on a long, wooden table fresh out of an office supply store commercial.

Anna knew what she had to do and she would do it without Marshall's help. It was time to make him wish he had never screwed around with her life. She was going to even the score between her and the bastard who destroyed her life.

34

...OR CONSEQUENCES

The yellow pallor from the overhead lights dulled everything in the room. The closed steel door filled Anna with confidence.

Anna sat down in front of the notebook at the furthest end of the table. This gave her the ability to see who was coming into the room and shield her from prying eyes that might want to see what she was doing. She didn't want anyone interrupting her for a few minutes. She needed about thirty minutes all told. She could only hope the tall, stoic guy (Liko?) or her father (pins and needles tingled on the back of her neck; she had to find another word for him) wouldn't miss her or might assume she was playing video games or something. *What a bunch of clueless idiots.*

The room had grimy cinderblock walls and a motor oil smell she knew permeated her wig. She felt comfortable in the dim light and humid interior.

She pressed the Shift key and the blank screen transformed into a login page. What password would he have used? These were Marshall's notebooks. It wouldn't matter if someone set an unbreakable password, Marshall had a memory like a sieve. He would use the unbreakable password once, become root long enough to change the password rule, and enter his own quite weak one. He never worried about it because the computers he used were behind firewalls, which were behind firewalls, which were behind yet more firewalls.

Would he still be using the same password she knew he used all those years ago?

A-N-N-A-B-A-N-A- N-A

The screen changed. She should have felt a sense of belonging. Nothing. He clung to one of the handfuls of nicknames he had given her when she was about five. He finally settled on Squirrel and never looked back. *What an idiot.*

She needed to get back onto the secure IRC channel and look up the history from IRCPlayer.

———

She found what she was looking for. It was a Northrup project and something they had been working with for a while. She wasn't sure what she would find, but she was certain it would be interesting. The software was rather sophisticated, but it didn't seem much more difficult than Flight Simulator.

Except she would be flying a real plane. A jet, in fact.

An F35-C Lightning II. Her eyes widened. Her greatest accomplishment in her previous life paled in comparison to what she would be doing in the next few minutes. She looked over the menu, sidebars, and status displays. She gave the camera in the cockpit a quick move just to convince herself that she had actually connected. She could see some of the other planes parked around her. There was a harbor view off the side of the deck where the jet sat.

Fine. She would get to that in a minute.

HarlequinNinja has entered the room.

IRCPlayer: please tell me you are nowhere near nyc.

HarlequinNinja: i need an address. can you get something for me?

IRCPlayer: i would but you're always dissing me.

HarlequinNinja: get what i want and I'll respect you for a few minutes

IRCPlayer: when you put it that way :p

HarlequinNinja: c'mon. I need something right now

IRCPlayer: ask and ye shall receive

HarlequinNinja: I need a home address

No response. She knew he knew what she wanted.

IRCPlayer: he's got 2 of them. Main or secondary?

Anna thought, *He's got a vacation home, too? Perfect. Two ass whoopings.*

———

Marshall sat in the room where Anna cut herself. He wasn't sure how he was going to make things happen, but he couldn't let her down. She needed him and he was determined to make sure that she would know people who cared for her were there.

A person who cared. Her father who cared.

Guilt was not something he carried well. At some point, what was done was done and moving forward was all he could do. He stood and stretched. Where the hell was Liko? He'd been gone far too long. Marshall wanted to check their timeframe. A trip to Brooklyn was not looking good, but they had to get there somehow. The storm was moving in, and more and more of the roads were closed off. The city was locked down and even if they got past the police, who were risking their lives to keep the rest of the city safe, there was the very real possibility that they could get blown off a bridge into the Long Island Sound or stuck in a flooded area.

He had waited enough. It was time to go. Every passing minute just made the first part of their disastrous trip more disastrous. He had the codes, Liko had the contacts, and HALON was deserted. If there were any personnel there (and there was no way Palma would allow anyone to be in harm's way for an operation of this magnitude; Marshall knew him better than that) he and Liko would move them to safety before doing what he had to do. And he sure as hell wasn't going to enable the failsafe.

He looked at his watch. Anna had been gone for about twenty minutes. Since she was in the makeshift control room, he was sure she was talking with her IRC friends. Or plotting to kill Palma. Both had equal statistical probability.

She had never been on the Internet quite as much before he lost her, but he already knew many of the people with whom she chatted. Since he couldn't be there in person to meet them he did the next best thing: he tapped his daughter's Internet connection.

Her IRC friends were certainly a diverse group. Thankfully, they weren't troublemakers, for the most part, but there was the occasional male who wanted to show off to her that he could get into systems no one else could. Marshall was always sure to document what he saw in case it was ever useful.

He went back into the faux bedroom. There was a notebook there even Liko didn't know about. At least Marshall hoped he didn't. He opened it up and ran a program he had discovered years ago. It would allow him to see what was running on one of his other laptops without the user on the other box noticing. After all the years he'd spent with Monahan and Palma the one thing he knew about was surveillance. And paranoia.

The screen showed the Twirling Donut of Death. Even Linux systems had them, though Marshall was grateful they were a lot sturdier than their Windows brethren.

———

The plane was almost at the target. On the weapons' menu there was a model number. She wondered what it would do. The jet handled well without a pilot, though the chatter from Naval Air Traffic Control was getting on her nerves. She muted the audio.

———

What the hell is that?

Marshall saw the heads-up display and the house directly in his sights. *Whose house is that?*

He saw flames shoot through the roof as the display alerted the pilot of its activation. *Oh my God. WHAT IS SHE DOING?*

———

Anna saw the house imploding as its infrastructure ignited. Ah, natural gas lines. She always wondered what that would look like.

The door burst open and she looked up. Marshall had a look of surprise and shock on his face.

"What are you doing?" He ran over to her as she lowered the screen just enough so he couldn't see what she had just burned to the ground.

"Nothing. Chatting. What are you doing?"

"You just blew up a house," he said.

It was Anna's turn to be surprised. *How did he know? How does he always know?* "No, I didn't."

He was by her side in a flash, grabbed her arms, and lifted her off the chair. "Anna, what have you done?"

"Nothing. There was no one in the house."

He looked into her eyes. *I'll be damned if I'm going to look away.* "Anna, he has two kids."

"So what?"

"They don't have anything to do with this."

"Neither did I. How much did Benson care about me?"

"It wasn't his job to care. It was mine."

"You didn't care either," Anna said.

"Yes, I did. I never left you alone. I always knew where you were and what you were doing."

"You're defending his kids."

"No, I'm defending you. I always had someone there looking after you. I never left you alone."

She shook his hands off her arms. "I was always alone."

She closed the notebook to sever the remote connection to the aircraft. "He's lucky," she said. "I was about to auger the plane into his cellar. And that's just the beginning."

35

EVACUATION PLANS

The men on the ground at Malik Palma's home in Ararat, Virginia secured the perimeter the best they could. It was hard to believe that such a tranquil setting of trees, manicured lawns, and streets without sidewalks had, just minutes before, been a battlefield. The attack on the house was over as quickly as it had started. The jet engines spun down, but not much else was evident.

The two-man security detail notified everyone they could, starting with the DOD Emergency Response Center. Sitting in a sealed room on the George W. Bush aircraft carrier, the men in charge of the test run of the F-35C found that the lock that had kept them out of the control software released on its own. Whoever had taken the place did what they had intended and disappeared.

The software entered back-up mode and the team lead from Northrup changed the password, which disabled all communication ports, making it impossible to fly the equipment remotely. The jet sitting on the lawn in Virginia was now a paperweight. It would need a pilot to come in and fly it back to Northrup where they would take care of re-enabling the remote-control software. The entire exercise had taken approximately thirty-five minutes from start to finish and the protocols appeared to work. While they had lost control of the resource, they were able to shut it down as soon as control was re-established.

The jets circling in Ararat airspace were just a symbolic gesture. The event was over.

In the situation room in the US Mission, General Palma sat in shock. Someone had destroyed one of his homes. The safety of his family confirmed, he tried to make sense of what had transpired. Was this an assassination attempt? Was his family ever at risk or did he, and they, survive due to bad intel?

"The plane is empty, sir," the security officer said on speakerphone.

"I know what happened," he said. "Now tell me what we're doing about it." His molars were in pain. He unclenched his jaw.

Plante spoke before the security officer. "General, four jets were dispatched behind two others that chased it once it left Avenger."

Plante was handling the coordination almost as well as his former assistant. The assistant Palma left for dead out in the woods a few weeks earlier.

Palma thought for a minute. Those pilots were risking their lives to protect him from a vendetta of some sort, or at worst, a lesson being taught to him, or the US, for some real or imagined slight. "Can we leave the jet at its current location?" Palma asked.

"Affirmative, sir. They can't move it even if they wanted to. The hurricane is due to make landfall in the next twelve hours or so and Avenger is already heading south to avoid being in port when it arrives."

This had better not be about HALON. "Do whatever the Navy wants. That plane is their property and I can't help them out there." Was this the Russians? The US had been chasing them away from the coast for years now. This couldn't be some sort of pointless retaliation.

The Chinese? Their way of reminding him who was in control? Didn't make any sense. They were on schedule for the hand-off. Monahan was going to meet them at the facility and everything would be fine as long as they didn't get mixed up with FEMA or any of the other myriad agencies involved in the incoming onslaught.

No, this was too personal. It didn't seem possible that after all this time Marshall would make such a bold move against him, but there was no other explanation. He didn't know what to think. Marshall had to be dead. Anna wasn't smart enough to pull something off like this. If it was an unknown party, there was nothing Palma could do.

"Alert the National Guard in New York. Give them more of the intel we have on Anna Wodehouse," Palma said.

"Understood. But not too much," Plante said.

"No, just enough for them to be successful. Our intel isn't much more in-depth than theirs, but maybe it will help." Maybe if they found her, he could use her as leverage. He wasn't sure how, or for what, but things felt out of place.

"General, I would be hard pressed to think she had anything to do with this."

"I'm sure she didn't. Let's get her off the streets anyway."

———

HALON

Kevin Randerhouk, veteran of multiple tours in Iraq, and a former Detroit police officer, remembered how often he would patrol the streets of Detroit and Iraq and always know when something was off. Perhaps it was a bump on the ground, or a gang around the corner of the abandoned buildings. Both places were the same in his estimation and his sense of the skewed helped him survive more than one surprise in his parallel careers.

That was why he sent his partner, Morgan Strauss, to secure the exits and confirm that the remaining personnel were safe and sound. And out of their way.

The security alarm that had gone off twenty minutes earlier surprised everyone. The first perimeter of the facility appeared to be violated. It definitely wasn't one or more of the thousands of rats in New York City. The sensors could tell the difference between an animal and a person. Given the preparations going on, the odds were high that it was a false alarm. New York had inspectors everywhere making sure that the population was either indoors or outside of the tristate area.

Why would they be near sensors behind keycard-protected doors?

Randerhouk looked over the wall of cameras monitors that constituted his responsibility. Something about the alert felt wrong. He hoped that he was wrong. No, he knew he was wrong because the one thing everyone knew was that their facility was invisible to the world. If anyone had penetrated the perimeter, it had to be someone who knew they were there. It had to be someone who belonged.

The cameras showed empty corridors. Whoever it was had not yet come within range. He had not received word of any special visitors or any escort details. If an escort detail arrived they would be sorely disappointed to know they would not be allowed entry.

The storm was screwing everything up. Word had it that everyone was going to have to stay and ride it out. Not ideal, but not a disaster either. To him and Strauss that meant only one thing: they got to keep an eye on their charges, and ensure no one developed cabin fever. The various support staff and scientists were easy to deal with even if Dr. Jenkins sometimes made their lives difficult. He had had his share of characters through the years, but this crew was a pleasure to deal with. Smart, focused. The kind of people you wanted to protect. What they were doing was both dangerous and useful, and Randerhouk was proud to be there doing what he could.

Then the cameras went off.

Did they just have a perimeter breach?

Randerhouk grabbed his radio. "Yo, Morgan?"

"Yeah?"

"Where are you?"

"Heading toward the main stairwell."

"Watch yourself. Something's up."

No response.

"Yo, Morgue." The hair on the back of his neck stood up. He

slammed his hand down on the one button that would bring everyone to attention.

The air filled with the sound of an alarm they'd only heard during practice. The main stairwell was nearby. He would grab one of the rapid-fire rifles and go after Morgan.

He flipped the communications switch to send his voice to every corner of the facility. "This is not a drill. This is not..." Shots rang out behind him. Someone was shooting out the lock.

The door was solid steel. The doorknob contained an electronic lock that could not be broken. The walls and doorframe were all metal, but holes appeared where there were none seconds before, which told him things had just gotten bad.

The shooter was using armor piercing bullets.

Randerhouk jumped up and ran to the armaments locker. The door swung open and shots rang out as they perforated his body starting from his waist, up along his back, and finally hitting and destroying his neck. He was dead before he struck the ground.

PART IV

———

HUNTING ANNA

36

THE PLAN

Anna could feel the frustration in her neck and in the back of her head. The thought of Marshall scraped away at the inside of her skull. She remembered how much she wanted to kill him, to make him pay (for what? For deserting her? For breaking her heart?), but that felt like so long ago.

Now he was in the other room, the actual garage, and all she could think of was standing next to him so she could screw up whatever he was doing. That feeling of knocking things over, of making a mess, and seeing what he would do overwhelmed her otherwise neutral decision-making powers. PRUDENT RAINBOW was no longer a thing, but something was. Something with a name she didn't know and he refused to tell her.

She sat in the faux bedroom, and felt a degree of focus return to her senses, but the room didn't get any better. It was still dark, dank, and gross. She decided to seek shelter after she blew up Benson's home, and it was all she could do to start the next phase of her nefarious plan. How could she get back at Benson where he lived? Well, she had done that already. Literally. Now she wanted to hit him again before he realized it was her.

This was no better than throwing rocks through someone's window, but it would do for now.

Anna stood, straightened out her bulky gray shirt and jeans, and returned to the other room. The smell of rubber and oil made her throat feel like she was swallowing sand with every breath.

Liko brought her here because there was nowhere else to take her. What did he mean by that? There was a black SUV in the middle of the garage with its rear door wide open. She walked past it on the way to where Marshall and Liko were arguing and she could feel how easy they would be to manipulate.

What kind of a team were they?

Anna didn't bother to listen to anything they were discussing before she said, "That's a stupid plan."

The men stopped bickering. In the smeary yellow light, their skin took on a dark, disgusting pallor.

Marshall was first. "You have no idea what we're doing."

"I don't have to," Anna said. "You're in a garage somewhere in New York arguing about what colors you want for your curtains," she said.

"In fact, we've already picked out the colors," Marshall said. Liko stood like a statue listening to the exchange. "We know where we have to go, we've got the equipment we need, and you're leaving us soon."

"Like I said. Stupid plan." She sauntered over to the back of the SUV. "You know where you're going, but so does Benson."

"Palma. Malik Palma," Marshall said.

"Benson. Jerk-off Benson." The man who destroyed her life with her cooperation. Anna could see that Marshall bit back a retort about her cursing. "If he knows that I'm back hunting him down, he knows you're back trying to stop him. He may be an asshole, but he's not an idiot." She scanned the two men before her. "Not like other people I know."

In the bed of the SUV, there was a stack of equipment under a paint-stained, light gray, canvas tarp. She yanked at the dirty cloth. It covered a stack of guns and flat panels. "What the hell is this?" Anna asked.

Marshall stepped over to her. "Guns. Concussive explosives. Detonator wire."

Seriously? "This is worse than I thought. Call the police, tell them what he's doing, and go home. Do me that favor."

"You don't think I tried?" Marshall asked. "I know you think very little of what I'm trying to do, but I tried to get the FBI involved."

"And?"

"Doesn't matter," Marshall said. He turned away. "Telling the police is a stupid idea even if you don't believe it."

"Tell the police," Anna said.

"Why don't you tell the police? I'm sure they'll believe you right away," he said.

Anna felt her cheeks go hot. "I've dealt with the FBI. They would listen."

"They did." Marshall's face betrayed his distraction. He returned to his spot near Liko, cracking glass shards underfoot. "I got an agent killed."

"Try again," she said.

"We know what we're doing," Marshall said.

For the duration of their exchange, Liko stood silent. She sauntered over to him, a sneer on her face. *Don't think you're getting away easy.*

"This is a stupid plan and you know it. What do you get from this?" she asked Liko.

"I get to see you frustrated and eventually arrested."

Marshall looked at them both and took a step toward her. "No one is getting arrested."

"You're right," Liko said. His attention veered to Anna. "We're all going to die doing this."

Marshall shook his head. "No one dies doing this." He turned to Anna. "Especially you. If we tell the police, we don't know which ones, if any, are on Palma's payroll. They tried to kill you more than once. I don't want to tell you how many times they tried to kill me." He walked back to the rear of the SUV and pulled at the tarp until it covered everything again.

————

The solitary bathroom in the garage was the smelliest bathroom Anna had ever been in. The stink alone was enough to make her run to Canada.

In the corner of the bedroom, by the doorway to the bathroom, she had found the instrument of Marshall's destruction. A landline. If there was one thing she could do to stop those two foolhardy men, it was to make a phone call. The right phone call. She wasn't sure why Marshall hadn't disconnected everything that wasn't a burner phone, but she would be damned if she wasn't going to use his oversight to rain pain down on him. She loved it. He had a lab with enough computers for her to blow up someone's house (and not just anyone's house!), but didn't think far enough ahead to cut any landlines. A phone was as good as a flare, and with a flare she could make herself stand out.

She wanted to use the bathroom but couldn't get herself to sit on the grimy toilet seat. She tried turning the faucet, but the gross, rusty metal repelled her.

————

Anna stepped back into the garage proper.

"So, this is how we are going to work this," Marshall said.

"I can't wait to hear it," she said. *Should I start counting backward from 30?*

The phone rang. *That was quick.*

Both men looked at her.

Liko's eyes were unreadable. To Marshall he said, "You didn't secure the landlines?"

Marshall stared at Anna as he walked over to the nearest phone and answered it.

————

Why is she doing this? Marshall was confused. All he wanted was to get her to safety, but she had to stop being an impediment. At some point, he wouldn't be able to stop Liko from doing something stupid and Marshall was the only one allowed to do stupid things from here on in.

"Hello?" Marshall asked.

"This is 911 dispatch. Someone at this number called for assistance."

37

DIGGING A DEEPER HOLE

As Marshall held the phone, Anna screamed as loudly as she could, "Help me! Help me!" Then she smiled and crossed her arms.

Marshall slammed the phone down then picked it up, listened, and slammed it down again. He looked at her and she felt her stomach sink to her feet. That was the look he had when she was thirteen and had cheated on a test. The school hadn't caught her, but as soon as he'd seen the answers, he knew. To this day she didn't know how he knew, but he did. Somehow, he always knew. The look on his face was identical, except for a few new wrinkles around his eyes.

That look of disappointment.

Her throat hurt and the crocodile smile turned into a frown. Liko moved his hand to the shoulder holster, but dropped it and walked past her to the spot where the handcuffs lay on the floor. He picked them up and tossed them at her, but she let them fall to the floor. *Over my dead body.* He pulled his gun and aimed it at her.

"Stop," Marshall said.

"Put them on," Liko said. "Put them on or I will shoot your right hand first then your left elbow."

Anna held her arms out away from her body. "Do it." She took a step toward him. "Do it."

"Stop!" Marshall stepped in between them. "It's too late, Liko-san." He his voice deepened. "It's too late. Squad cars are on their way. We have to go."

"And what about her?"

Anna's eyes met his.

"She'll do what she wants," he said. "She thinks what she did was clever."

Why is he talking like I'm not here? "Go ahead and shoot me, Liko-san. It's what you want, isn't it?"

The moment was gone. Liko put his gun back in the holster. "No, but it is apparently what you want." He bee lined past her. "And I am not used to humoring spoiled little girls."

Her cheeks felt hot enough to scorch her skin. "I am *not* spoiled."

Marshall picked up some boxes and put them in the SUV. He started to close the hatch when Liko put his hand up to stop him. Liko motioned over to a few other small containers.

Anna's hands felt as numb as the skin on her face. She wasn't the one at fault here. "Let the police take care of this." She took a step forward and stopped. "The police can handle this."

Liko moved the small cases from the workbench to the SUV.

"Liko-san," Marshall said. "Let me show you something before the police get here."

"How much time do you think we have?" Liko asked.

"Enough," Marshall said.

"They traced the call," Liko said.

What Marshall and Liko didn't know was that she had given them her name. The most wanted federal fugitive on the planet was in New York and had given the local police her location. Well, not exactly. She called, told them who she was, then hung up. It was just a matter of time, literally seconds, before they called back. They called faster than she'd expected, but she assumed it was because of the deluge of calls they were getting about the hurricane.

The storm made things harder in some ways and easier in others. This was one of the easy times. Police cars all over the city were looking for her.

Anna blinked. Marshall and Liko leaned over some blueprints, and Anna joined them as Marshall pointed around an area on the paper. Were these the plans to PRUDENT RAINBOW? She didn't know how to read blueprints, but some things were obvious. A room with an entrance into a larger area. Large containment areas. Long corridors that crisscrossed at right angles into other areas. There were doors every few feet.

"What you should be looking for is the main security area," Marshall said.

"I thought that was over there." Liko pointed to an area on another sheet.

"That's one of the satellite rooms. The facility can't be guarded by one detail. There are two on every floor and there are thirty floors."

"So, the main area is on the top floor?" Liko asked.

"Yes, and you just have to take over that one room to set off the emergency fire mechanism."

Anna was confused. Thirty stories? Fire?

"The skeleton crew will run to the evacuation rooms, the halon will go off, sucking the oxygen out of everywhere except the evac rooms, and everything except the people who are there will be dead. You get to escort them out and be the hero."

Anna couldn't take it anymore. "No." She tried to push the blueprints off the table, but Marshall held them fast. "Let the police handle this."

He put up his hand and she stepped back. "Stop. You've done enough."

"Don't you understand that your plan can't work?" she asked. "In a facility that size there are too many people."

"It's a skeleton crew."

"Doesn't matter. You can't control where they are without telling them you're coming and you're not telling them," she said. "Sucking the oxygen out of the place like that, and that's a big place, means they can't leave their hiding places for a long time." Unless they had air ready to be pumped in at a moment's notice. She looked into his eyes. "Did you design the fire response system?"

"No."

"Then how do you know those people are safe?"

"Because I made sure the evac rooms were in place. They're sealed and have fresh air pumped into them 24/7."

"Just call them and tell them to leave," Anna said.

"This is a pointless conversation. They are safe because I know what I'm talking about and you..." Marshall turned when a beep sounded over and over in the computer room where Anna had done her handiwork with Benson's house.

Liko ran to the room, followed by Marshall then Anna. Marshall entered alone.

———

Marshall walked over to Liko who sat at one of the notebooks. The software running on his box was flashing the evacuation message. *How could that be?* Liko accessed the security cameras. Nothing. Nothing. Everything was fine.

The camera facing the door to the security room on the top floor caught the door as it flew open and the guard ran off camera. A man came into the room and fired in his direction.

"Damn it," Marshall said. "They've accelerated their plans or just plain lied."

———

Anna's skull felt crushed by her frustration. The muscles along the sides of her head were sore, giving her another headache. She pushed her hands against her temples, but the pressure didn't let up. *They can't go through with this. I have to stop them.*

She opened the trunk and pulled back the tarp. She didn't know what they were thinking, but they weren't going anywhere with this much firepower. From a stack of black contoured panels, she pulled out a rifle she couldn't identify and gave it a quick once over. She popped the curved magazine out, found that it was packed with large caliber bullets, popped it back in, and walked over to the doorway where Marshall had entered. Without her.

She twirled the leather strap around her wrist and held the rifle up. She pushed the door open and stepped in, aiming the rifle into the middle of the room.

"Anna!" Marshall pushed the barrel of her weapon down so hard that she felt the leather bite into her wrist. "What are you doing?"

"You have to let the police handle this," she said.

"It's too late," he said. "It's too late. HALON's been breached."

38

EXPLOSIVE DISCUSSIONS

Anna heard sirens in the distance. She couldn't tell how close they were, but it was obvious the police had taken her call with a degree of seriousness she hadn't expected.

She opened the door just a crack. The police hadn't arrived yet, but she was sure they would get there before Marshall and Liko could escape. The fury of the sirens grew louder.

"Anna. Get in the car," Marshall said.

The two men had moved into action, ignoring her up to the last minute. Liko was already in the driver's seat. He didn't bother looking toward her.

Marshall slammed his door shut. "Let's go."

"I'm staying," Anna said.

"You can't stay. You know too much now. You'll be killed as soon as they come through the door," Marshall said.

She put her arms out, a look of disbelief on her face. "I don't know anything."

"*They* don't know that. They just know that you were with me and that would be enough."

"He could have killed me a hell of a lot sooner than this."

"Something's gone wrong. The facility's been breached," Marshall said.

"That doesn't tell me anything except you have really good alerts that might be sending you erroneous messages." Facing one of the doors leading to the outside she said to herself, "You've done that before."

———

Marshall turned toward Liko. "Why haven't you opened the garage door?"

Liko held his cell phone up for Marshall's appraisal.

Rain stained the camera lens, but he saw what Liko saw: squad cars were pulling up to the garage. More and more of them. They couldn't open the garage door if they tried. The shooting would start before they had a chance to get the SUV more than a few feet out the door.

"We have to go," Liko said.

"Not without her."

———

Both men jumped out of the car.

"What are you doing?" Anna asked. *Can't make up your darn minds? Was he really going to leave me?*

They ignored her and ran toward the back of the vehicle. The back door opened with a slow mechanical movement that made her anxious. "What are you doing?"

Marshall said, "I think you should be preparing your surrender speech."

Damn it! He's cornered me and I don't realize it yet. "I don't need one." She didn't sound as if she believed her own words.

"Improvisational?" Marshall nodded. "That could work."

Liko slid out one large black panel after another. Marshall grabbed the first one and pushed it against the metal garage door, extending thin metal legs that kept the panel in place. Liko walked past her with his own panel and did the same to the other metal door.

Marshall positioned another panel in the middle of the roll-up door that would have let them drive out to freedom.

"What are those things?"

Marshall stopped in surprise. "You don't know? I would have thought that an ex-con like you would know." Marshall held up the palm of his hand for a second. "Oh, wait a minute. You're not an ex-con. You're a fugitive. Convicted." He pointed toward the street. "Those highly-trained New York City police officers are waiting patiently for you to give yourself up." He checked the panels. "When you give yourself up, those fine examples of manhood are going to shoot you because they don't know what you're liable to do next."

"What am I liable to do next?" Anna looked at the doors. Control was slipping away from her. This was not going as she expected. "What am I about to do now?"

"I don't know, but the holes those concussion explosives are going to make might take down the garage. Liko and I have a way out and you are more than welcome to come with us," Marshall said. "Or you can stay here and hope for the best." He followed Liko, who had just entered one of the remaining rooms that Anna had not yet visited.

Over his shoulder, Marshall said, "If you stay here, you won't feel the brunt of the shockwave. That's what the panels will do on this side. On the other side, the doors are going to go flying into whatever, or whoever, happens to be coming toward it. If they follow procedure, they'll hide behind their squad cars and wait for SWAT to show up. The doors won't hurt anyone but will be part of someone's bad day. If they storm the garage then they work for Palma and you have no chance of making it out alive."

He lobbed Liko's cell to her and she caught it after juggling it in midair for a few seconds.

Marshall walked away.

"You have just a little bit of time to find out which. By the way, we're setting off the panels in about a minute." He stopped and turned back to her again. "I'd get behind something if I were you."

Tears pricked her eyes. He was leaving. He didn't try to get her to go with him at all. She could stay and hide from the explosives, or go with him.

Before the garage collapsed.

———

Marshall closed the door behind him. *Liko would set off those explosives with or without him. She'll be fine if she can get behind something. But she's not that stupid. If I'm right she'll come through that door in the next few seconds. If she doesn't then they'll have her and I'll lose her again.*

I hate being a parent.

———

The lead investigator, using his bullhorn, had just finished calling out to anyone who might be in the garage. He couldn't imagine what the city would be like in twenty-four hours, but right now he was working under the clearest of blue skies. He had lived through city emergencies before. He didn't know what made this fugitive so important, but the feds wanted her and he was going to be the one to bring her in before all hell broke loose and he wouldn't be home for a few days.

He looked around at the dozen or so cars and the officers in positions behind them. Every last one of them had their guns and/or assorted weaponry trained on the doors leading out. They would bring her in and they would make sure that the only person who would be injured would be her if she resisted. This damn storm had everyone on edge.

When the concussion explosives went off, the three doors of various sizes avoided killing anyone because, as Marshall had predicted, the police had stayed where they were supposed to.

The lead investigator's surprise came when the garage collapsed in on itself.

39

THE CALL

"Is she in the building?"

"I don't think so," the officer answered Terrell with just a hint of hesitation, but winked at him anyway. "Police intuition. But if she's in there, we'll find her. It's only been about thirty to forty minutes." He smiled. "Don't worry, Special Agent. We'll find her."

Terrell stood outside the entrance of the American Museum of Natural History. He knew the officer was right. He remembered coming to the museum a handful of times when he was younger, and always wanted to return, but studies, dating, life, always got in the way.

The sandstone-colored steps leading up the imposing doors behind the Teddy Roosevelt statue. His eyes adjusting to the light in the main lobby. The sense of wonder at the ancient skeletons that stood in front of the door as if they were greeters at a big box store. In those days, there was so little, yet so much, to think about. To worry about.

Why was the museum even open? The Sunday before the end of the world, and half the city thought it was a great idea to check out the dinosaurs. If the museum had been closed, Anna would have had one less place to hide and he could have brought her in without much fanfare. He corrected himself. With Anna there always seemed to be fanfare.

If she was half the city girl he thought she was, Anna would know the museum like the back of her hand. She must have had some secret way out that only the initiate knew and was now so far away she would never be found. *Damn, damn, damn.* This didn't feel close to over and he refused to acknowledge the possibility they would catch her today. If there was a connection between Anna Wodehouse and the Secretary of State, there was no telling what kind of danger she was in.

Maybe none.

Maybe too much.

His cell buzzed. The station chief.

Terrell started to walk toward a driveway on the museum grounds. "What's going on, Howard?" Terrell asked.

"That's my question to you. What the hell is going on down there? Word is that MTA didn't stop the train."

Terrell halted in his tracks. "She couldn't have done it. Eyewitnesses say she was just about to fall off."

"How the hell should I know? Maybe someone set off the damn sensor."

Terrell knew the NYC subway trains had speed brakes that could be activated independent of the engineer if the train was going too fast. "Not possible. That was a straightaway. If MTA didn't do it then something fooled the sensors. That would have stopped it on a dime."

"Great. Something else for *The Post*. Are you on point for Wodehouse's capture?"

Wodehouse. Terrell often wondered why a person so intent on pushing away her past still kept her old identity. "This is related to that case you threw me on a week ago."

"Are you kidding me? They might be keeping me out of the loop, but I can tell when you're trying to BS me," Howard said.

"I swear my investigation has been folded into the new case. The Wodehouse girl is connected..."

"To Piercing? One of your money laundering targets?"

"To Piercing, and Monahan, and Palma, and at least one suicide that might have been a murder." He hated saying those things out loud. How much did Howard know? "I still don't have the connection, but she's it somehow," Terrell said.

"Let the professionals handle the round-up."

"I am, Howard, I am." Terrell darted his eyes around. Where the hell was the lead? "Listen, I need you to run interference for me."

"You mean to make sure you don't get fired?" Howard asked.

"Keep our friends out of this for now. I don't need DHS showing up and taking my prisoner."

A few squad cars pulled out of their spots. *Now what?* Terrell knew the cars were pulling out too fast to be returning to their respective precincts.

"You might want to have a chat with the marshals. They always get first dibs. Stay out of their way."

"I need them to stay out of mine," Terrell said.

The squad cars lit up with full lights and sirens and took off north. Something was happening.

"Don't do anything stupid. I'm hearing things, and I'm a little short of bail money this week."

"What are you hearing?" Terrell asked.

"DHS wants her. Bad."

And if DHS wants her it's because CIA wants her because NSA wants her.

"I hear ya, Chief. Play nice." Terrell hung up. An ominous call if ever there was one. He yelled, "Where's the lead investigator?"

Maybe he was wrong. Maybe, if he was lucky, and he was never lucky, Anna was waiting under a desk, hiding.

———

"Someone in a car was allowed to leave the museum?" Terrell couldn't keep the incredulous sound from his question. "And no one stopped him?" He looked at the uniformed pair before him: an older man and a younger woman. Who would he pistol whip first? "This is a full-blown damn manhunt for a federal fugitive."

"We got that," the female officer said. "I also know we couldn't hold him. He had the plates and he had the ID."

"You got a name?" Terrell asked.

"Dianella," she said.

"His name was Dianella?"

Terrell saw her cheeks go red. "No. Um..." She pulled out her ticket pad and didn't look up. "His name was Sum Liko. I think his ID..."

"You think?"

Another pair of squad cars sped by, distracting him with their lights and sirens. How could he hear anything with that ear-piercing noise?

"His ID was from the Chinese embassy."

Terrell jotted down some notes in his cell. *Damn. This is why I needed a partner. The Chinese? With all the money we owe them, and all of the products we buy from them, they're still screwing around with espionage? On-the-street-traitors-involving-dead-drops espionage?*

Don't they prefer cyber-attacks?

———

Terrell was able to get someone from state on the line after about ten minutes of wrangling with various intermediaries, who were either covering for their boss or covering for their boss's boss.

"I know he has diplomatic immunity," Terrell said. "That's not the point. I need to speak with him, off the record. He may have seen something," *or taken someone,* "and I just want to find out. It will be a friendly chat. But it has to happen today. Within the hour preferably."

"You must be new at this," the friendly female voice on the other end of the line replied. "Setting up even a simple meeting like that will take days. I hope you've been reading the news reports."

Days would mean weeks. The storm would be responsible for at least a few days' worth of delays.

"If I get NYPD to find his car and I accidentally happen to run into him, are we going to have a problem?"

"Not with me, Agent Garrison."

Terrell hung up. *I'll run into him alright.*

The swarm of police cars and law enforcement personnel was thinning out. The museum had turned out to be a dead end. She was in the diplomatic vehicle. She was in the car, and frick and frack let her go because they didn't know the art of delay tactics.

Terrell, still outside the museum, had hoped that something would click in his head and he would know what to do next. Monahan and Palma were probably on their way back to their respective homes well outside of New York, and the army of NYPD and US Marshalls would find Anna eventually. He walked a few steps up the stairs and sat down. Why couldn't this be a normal Sunday morning so he could just enjoy a coffee and breakfast sandwich?

His cell buzzed. Who the hell was it this time? Private.

"Garrison."

"Terrell?"

The voice sounded tentative, but he would recognize it anywhere.

"Hey, it's me. Anna."

40

THE LIE

Terrell did his best to look casual. "Where are you?"

"Why? Are you afraid I'm looking at you from my sniper's nest?" Anna asked.

How the hell did I get mixed up in this?

———

Fifteen minutes earlier

Anna looked at the doorway where her father had just exited. *I'll be damned if I'm going to give in to him.* She took in deep breaths. *Okay, I'm cornered. Literally. What do I do now?*

Not my father. I have to stop thinking that.

What's the physics for this? The charges explode.

The doors go out perpendicular to the walls.

The shock wave trails the doors.

She saw two doors, and a garage door. If she stood behind them, debris could crash down from the ceiling and kill her.

If she ran out after the doors blew out, they might shoot her.

If the walls collapsed, and the garage looked like it was well past its shelf life, the ceiling would collapse.

If the ceiling collapsed, it didn't matter what she hid behind. She would be crushed or, if she was lucky, trapped.

She had to get out. Marshall said she had about a minute. He was not the kind of father who lied for kicks, though there was that one time...

She turned and ran toward the door. As she opened it, the charges went off, toppling her into the hallway. *So much for the focused shock wave.* The door slammed shut behind her.

She felt the building tremble. Behind the door she could hear the scrape and scream of metal as the car was crushed. Without a thought, she was up and running down the corridor toward an open door. An open door where he would be waiting. For her.

She wasn't in the mood.

She ran past a metal door to her left. She doubled back, ran in, and found herself in the building the garage must be attached to. If the garage was an extension then it could keel over with no ill effects to the larger structure or its occupants. Anna closed the door behind her, leaned on it for a second, and took off down the corridor. The front entrance had to face somewhere other than where the gauntlet of squad cars was waiting.

———

Anna looked at the cell her father had lobbed at her and put it against her ear. She called the one person she knew she could trust. Mr. Boy Scout himself. She hoped he hadn't tired of her yet.

"Hello?"

"Where are you?" Terrell sounded tense.

To be fair, he had no reason to be happy to hear from her.

"I can't tell you. But I'm doing fine, thank you. How are you?"

"Anna, this is not a joke. You have to come in. This is so much bigger than you know," Terrell said.

"No shit. I almost had a garage collapse on me. I'm pretty certain I know how big this is. The murder of US citizens. False arrest and imprisonment. Secret military bases in large metropolitan areas." Assuming she only knew a fraction of what was going on, there was a lot she didn't know.

"Secret bases?" Terrell asked. "I don't care. We can discuss that over coffee. You have to come in. I can't protect you from what you don't know if you're on the run."

———

"If I come in then I'm a sitting Squirrel, but that doesn't matter. I can get you Arnold Dashman."

"Who?"

This was going to be harder than she thought. How could she negotiate if he didn't know the value of what was being negotiated?

———

Arnold Dashman? That's not possible. "Why Arnold Dashman?"

"Are you kidding? The man who kidnapped me," Anna said. She was approaching the right level of frustration. "Have you not read my file?"

"You don't have him. He's probably dead and you're trying to negotiate with a worthless chip," he said. "Tell me the truth, and I'm serious. Are you working with the Chinese?" He heard a crash and crackling. He called out to her.

"Sorry, but my brain automatically drops whatever I'm holding when I hear something stupid. Are you kidding?"

———

Anna's mind clicked. Did he mean Liko? "Wait." There was a connection she was missing. She didn't know who Liko was or why Marshall was working with him. Had Marshall chosen a new side? "Why do you ask? Do you have a picture of me consorting with a tall, handsome, Asian man? Does that make you jealous?"

"Cut it out. Are you or aren't you?"

Perhaps a bluff? "How do you know about the Chinese?"

"You're a hot item. For some reason, everyone is pulling out all stops to find you. This call is probably being traced."

"I'm on a burner phone, and I'm dumping it as soon as I finish here. You'll find it by a Starbucks."

———

A comedian.

"You have to come in. I don't care if you've found Jimmy Hoffa."

———

Who?

"I want you to arrest my dad, I mean, Arnold Dashman," she said. "He's not my father." All these names were starting to confuse her. Was Arnold Dashman her father's real name? Whatever.

———

She wants me to protect her kidnapper? Of course not. She wants me to protect the only father she's ever known. "Come in. We'll talk about it. If the cops find him, he's dead meat and there's nothing I can do about that. I can do something if you come in."

"What can you do?" Anna asked.

"I can keep him alive. And you."

"Like you did at ADX?"

"I didn't know that was going to happen."

"And yet, there you were," she said.

"It's a long story. I'll tell you all about it," he said, "as soon as you come in."

"No." *What a pain in the ass.*

———

"But I'll help you anyway," Anna said. She was alone and the sense of it surrounded her. It didn't matter if he believed her. She just wanted to stop Marshall and his faithful Indian companion. *Alright, faithful Chinese companion.*

"You do understand that resisting arrest will only make this worse?"

"You'd arrest me?" she asked.

"I can't protect you otherwise."

"Deal's off. You can find out about HALON from somebody else." Silence.

———

Terrell felt his mind stop. *Did she say...?*

"Hello?" the voice on the other end of the call asked. "Hello?"

HALON? Oh my God. He cut the call. If they had a sample of her voice then saying that one word just got her marked for death. They might have traced it already. Would they have a car filled with armed men on their way to her? His one consolation was that he knew they couldn't move fast enough to find her. Damn it! Why didn't she surrender sooner?

The cell rang.

What is wrong with this woman? "Anna," Terrell spoke each word with the deliberation of a parent to a child. "Throw your phone away right now. It's too late to come in. Run. As fast as you can. Go to Canada. Or the Antarctic." He hung up again.

The cell rang.

"Don't hang up!" Anna said. "You've scared the hell out of me. I want to come in."

"I'm going to have to arrest you."

"Please, don't."

"Try me," he said.

"Why does that word scare you? It scared Arnold," she hesitated. "My dad."

"If I said General Palma was being investigated, would that be a clue?"

"Good. HALON is his brain child," she said.

"You have to stop talking. Run."

"Come get me," Anna said.

"It's too late."

"It's never too late."

"Where are you?" Terrell asked.

"I can't tell you."

"Jesus Christ, Anna." Terrell clenched his fist as he spun around looking for a point of stability. He wasn't sure what he would have done if she had been standing in front of him, but he was sure it wouldn't have been good.

"I don't know where I am. I just crossed into Manhattan from the Bronx on some pretty dingy bridge."

Terrell looked up into the sky. "I'll meet you at the Intrepid. Can you get there? And can you bring him along?"

"Who? Arnold?" She said the last word in a high child-like voice like a high school student would when teasing a rival. "He's not with me. You have to go look for him. He was in the Bronx about thirty minutes ago. I can tell you where he was last." She took a breath. "And his traveling companion. They blew up the garage I was in, by the way. Thanks for your concern."

"Intrepid." Terrell hung up.

He put his hand against his face and closed his eyes. Somehow, he had to get to Anna. It was going to take him just as much time to get to her as it would for her to get to him, and there was no guarantee that someone, Palma or Monahan, might have a team ready to take her out.

He shook his head in frustration. How was he going to get out there? He was sure of one thing: to save her he was going to have to arrest her.

41

THE MEETING

The Intrepid Sea, Air & Space Museum

"Where are you?"

Terrell had arrived about fifteen minutes earlier and stood at the west end of 46th Street where it intersected with NY-9A just north of the awning labeled *Intrepid Museum Admission*. The doorway led to an anteroom, which led to a ticket counter, which led into the aircraft carrier. Any further west and he would be in the Hudson River, along with the Essex-class aircraft carrier moored there since 1982. He had never visited the museum, promising himself, as so many New Yorkers do, to do exactly that one day.

That day was here. The vessel was an impressive sight. Anna replied, "Where is everybody? I thought for sure you would bring friends to join us on the tour."

"I'm not arresting you."

"Are we running away together?" she asked.

"You still have to come with me," Terrell said.

"Gladly. If you're not arresting me then what?"

"Where are you?"

"The Mess Deck Café. I'm throwing the cell away now. The Hudson can have it."

————

Terrell, after paying the admission cost (with his credit card, of course. He wanted an unimpeachable audit trail), worked his way to the third deck and entered the café. It looked just like all the old military photos he had tracked down as a teenager: metal pipes, painted bare walls, bench seats. He felt at home dressed in his dark suit and pressed white shirt. The tourists added a measure of chaos to the scene, but he knew that that control was his in the enclosed environment.

Anna sat at a small, round, flimsy, metal table surrounded by three additional chairs that made her look all the more alone. There were two cups on the table. One in front of her, and one in front of the chair to her left. She had both hands surrounding the small cup, blowing into it. If this meeting had been at a Bureau office, Terrell would have had the psychological advantage. Not knowing what Anna had in mind gave her an advantage, but not much.

Anna didn't look up as he walked around the table and dragged a chair across the floor. She wore a blond wig. Her gray top was dusty. Collapsing garages did that. In his estimation, she looked good. She still didn't look up, but her face sagged. Exhaustion did that.

"Good afternoon, Ms. Poole."

She frowned enough for him to notice. "Special Agent," she said. "I guess I deserved that."

"I like what you've done to your hair," he said. He picked up the black coffee and gave it a quick smell. The warmth permeated the inside of his nose. He took a sip. Bitter. "Should I assume this is drugged?"

She finally lifted her head.

"No milk or sugar. Maybe you're trying to hide the taste of the cyanide."

"I only saw you drink coffee once," she said. "That was a long time ago." She pulled her cup along the table. "I'm only using this as a way to keep warm."

"Nice of you to give me a call," he said.

"This is very civilized. I could almost imagine this as a meeting between two people who haven't seen each other in a long time."

"It's been a long time," Terrell said. "At least a few days."

"I thought," she turned her cup of coffee until the seam was on the far side of the cup, "I would be far away by now. When you mentioned Canada, I thought maybe you knew something."

"Canada?" he asked.

"I was told to go to Canada and I would be contacted there. Turns out my..." She pursed her lips. "Marshall." She slid her eyes away from his for a second. "Arnold was just trying to get me out of the country."

"So he's leaving you again," Terrell said.

"Don't put it that way."

"How would you put it?"

"If you arrest him in the next twenty-four hours, preferably in the next few minutes, you'll find him and a Chinese national named Liko heading to a not-so-secret US base called HALON." She wrapped her hands around the cup.

That name again. HALON. "Where is it?"

"I don't know. They wanted me to go with them since I refused to leave the country."

"Come with me," Terrell said.

Anna shook her head. "You have to arrest him."

"You are now a high-profile witness to a high-level counter-intelligence case. The full protection of the United States law enforcement community is at your disposal," Terrell said. "I just have to take you to them."

"Stop being such a white bread thinker. You have to stop them." A fire was starting to burn in her eyes. "HALON's been breached," she said.

His brow furrowed. *This doesn't sound good and I don't even know what it means.* "Breached?"

"Attacked. Infiltrated. I don't know. All I know was the alarms went off and the two of them took off," she said.

Terrell stomach twisted. The control he had was an illusion. "I need to know where. Why do you care?"

"I don't." She put the cup down. "I don't want anyone hurt." She slid her hand across the table toward him, but just enough to seem innocent.

Did she want him to hold her hand? Terrell reached for his cell phone. "Did you blow up General Malik Palma's house?"

Anna's eyes went wide for a moment and she pulled her hand back. "Did someone do something to his house?"

"Anna."

"What a shame." She looked at her coffee cup, eyes wide open. "And by 'what a shame' I mean what a shame he wasn't in it."

This woman was more dangerous than he thought. This was not the same person found seven years ago. An innocent seventeen-year-old wondering what happened to her otherwise ordered world. Through no fault of her own, her entire life was being crushed, shredded. No one was going to be happy with the person who finally came out, including her. Terrell unlocked his phone and started the photo gallery app. He swiped to a picture and expanded it so the item would fill the screen. It was a photo of the stuffed animal that had been mailed to Anna at ADX in all of its ripped-open glory. The one that had been mailed to him for his opinion after the attack on the prison. "What can you tell me about this?"

———

Anna stopped herself from pushing the cell phone off the table. "Why did you do that?" She slid the phone back over to Terrell and crossed her arms.

"What is it?" Terrell asked.

"It's mine," she said, tightening her arms across her chest.

"'It's mine' what?"

"Why do you have it?" Anna asked.

"It's evidence," Terrell said.

"From what?"

"It was mailed to you at ADX."

"But it's all torn up."

"That was prison security. They wanted to make sure there was nothing hidden in it."

"Nothing hidden in it?" Anna yelled and stood up. "Why did you show me that?"

Terrell put his hand out. "Anna, please, sit down." The tourists in the café were looking toward them. "Please."

She grabbed the chair and sat. *Those bastards. They tore up my squirrel.*

She pointed at Terrell's cell. "Were any of the guards who did that hurt during the...you know."

"No."

"Aren't they lucky?" She choked back an invective. "It was a stuffed animal I got almost fifteen years ago." She visibly swallowed. "It was from my dad. A squirrel for his squirrel. His nickname for me."

"Are you going to arrest him?" she asked.

There was a commotion at the door and it seemed like a never-ending stream of bodies entered the café. At first glance, Anna was sure that about 20 people, all uniformed personnel, ran in, but she didn't get a chance to count. A cluster of men headed directly toward them.

Anna yelped as she and Terrell pushed the table forward, spilling their coffees. At least five large men wearing bulletproof vests aimed firearms at them as one of them yelled, "You're under arrest! US Marshals!"

"No!" She looked at Terrell, who had his hands up.

He was genuinely stupefied.

"Don't let them take me."

The other officers behind them were screaming orders to the tourists and escorting them out, but Anna couldn't make out the words.

———

What the hell is going on? "Whoa! Whoa! Whoa! FBI!" Terrell said.

One of the marshals approached Anna with a pair of open handcuffs.

"I'm going to reach into my pocket and show you my identification." Terrell looked at the Marshal with the cuffs. "Don't touch her. She's my witness and under FBI protection." He turned back to the officer, who had a gun trained on him. "I'm going to open my jacket and reach for my ID." He reached down and as he opened his jacket, he let go. *Sigh.* "Okay, nobody go crazy. I'm with the FBI and I have a gun."

"We've got a gun!" Three marshals trained their firearms at him. "Get on your knees! Now!"

"Okay," Terrell said, his voice calm. "Okay." He put his hands behind his head, which opened his jacket enough to display his holster. He looked at Anna and saw the marshal who was about to cuff her now pointed a gun at her instead. "She's unarmed. Don't mess with her. Understand?" He turned to her. "Don't. Do. Anything."

One of the men came over while three others had their Glocks trained on him. The gun no longer in his possession, the marshal reached into Terrell's jacket and pulled out his ID. He read it, scrutinized Terrell's face, closed it, and handed it to him. "Sorry, sir. We received word that a known fugitive was here, but no one told us about the Bureau."

"She's with me," Terrell said.

The officer shook his head. "I'm sorry, sir, but she's with us."

FOR IMMEDIATE RELEASE

U.S. Mission to the United Nations

Media Note: U.S. Mission Host Country Reception Canceled

New York, NY
October 28, 2012

FOR IMMEDIATE RELEASE

Due to the forecast arrival of Hurricane Sandy, the U.S. Mission's Host Country reception scheduled for Monday, October 29, 2012 has been canceled.

42

DISAPPOINTING RESULTS

Sunday, October 28, 2012

At 7:00 pm EST the Metropolitan Transportation Authority shut down all service on the NYC subway system, and the Long Island and Metro-North Railroads. What trains were still on the tracks had departed from their station of origin and would not return until days later. The station booths were empty; the agents sent home. The sun was going down on a locked-down city that experienced sustained thirty-nine mile per hour winds starting that evening.

Hurricane Sandy would touchdown in the morning. The Secretary of State monitored the National Weather Service and was well-aware of how things were developing. Come Tuesday morning things around New York City were going to be different.

Things would be very different.

Plante opened the door to Monahan's office in response to his request. "Sir?"

"Is the car ready?" Monahan asked. He took a last sip of hot coffee.

"Yes, sir."

"Tell them I'll be down in a minute."

Furman Street Fan Plant #5105

The Brooklyn Ventilation Building on Furman Street in Brooklyn was located on a dead-end road encircled by one end of Montague Street. The windowless, tan brick building looked more like a collection of badly stacked boxes than the location of the first above ground point for the N and the R trains after their journey under the East River into Brooklyn.

Construction located behind the building would be unrecognizable in approximately forty-eight hours. The site, like the surrounding area, was abandoned and alone. To the east was the Brooklyn-Queens Expressway with the occasional car driving by. In typical form, the only way to get to the Brooklyn Ventilation Building, also known as Furman Street Fan Plant #5105, was to twist and turn onto Brooklyn streets until you arrived and found you had no better understanding of the route than when you started.

The black SUV turned right onto Montague Street off Furman and circled the building until it was on the side of the building facing the East River. The building had raw fluorescent lights at regular intervals around its perimeter, most of which were lit up. As soon as it made the turn, the SUV's extinguished its lights and crawled until it arrived at the rusted and locked fence that protected the car-width roll-up gate at the rear of the edifice. It parked as close as it could to the construction area to leave the street in front of the building clear. Manhattan, on the opposite shore, took its turn as the brightest light source now that the sun was almost down.

Palma stepped out of the car as soon as his driver came around and opened the door. He was dressed in jeans, black sneakers, a plaid cotton shirt, and a windbreaker.

His driver re-entered the car. Palma stepped over to the window, which the driver lowered. The wind picked up and tousled Palma's hair.

"Are you sure about this, sir?" the driver asked.

"No, but that's never stopped me before." They smiled at each other. "Head back and I'll call when I need you."

Palma had known the driver for many years. This was not the strangest thing Palma had ever asked him to do, but he knew it would be the last. "If the worst happens, we'll be in a secure location. The worst will not happen."

Another SUV turned the corner and pulled in behind them. After turning off his headlights, the driver of that car exited and opened the passenger door, allowing Monahan to emerge. He was also dressed in jeans and sneakers, but the solid gray flannel shirt was the only thing between him and the chilly, windy night air. He exchanged a few words with his driver, they shook hands, and the man returned to his vehicle.

Palma walked over to Monahan and the men shook hands. The smells of the East River swirled around them like the eddies that formed and reformed in the water below. Monahan turned his back to the cars while Palma eyed them until they turned the corner, back onto Furman. Palma reached into his pocket and extracted a garage door opener, which he aimed at the rusted metal fence. The fence swung out and the garage door climbed upward. Both opened in silence.

The beginning of the end. At last. Palma said, "This is the right thing to do. I'll make sure your family is taken care of."

Monahan gave him a sad look and walked up the narrow driveway. "I know. I'm just disappointed you didn't do a better job."

43

COMMAND PERFORMANCE

The call came in as soon as the two SUVs had crossed the Manhattan Bridge into Manhattan.

Denver Marrell, the Diplomatic Security Special Agent assigned to Secretary of State Monahan, was driving the lead vehicle. The cars, having left the Secretary of State and the Director of the NSA at the site of an MTA infrastructure building, had pulled over on Furman Street, a non-trivial distance away from the drop-off. They'd agreed that Marrell would leave first. Adding distance to the two vehicles was just prudent protocol. They had arrived at different times. They should return at different times.

The problem was the worried feeling in the back of Marrell's neck. The kind that involved hair standing on end and overly-tight muscles. His assignment to Monahan has started almost at the beginning of Monahan's tenure. Working for the Secretary of State kept him on his toes, but the daily tedium rarely extended to anything truly exciting. For that Marrell gave thanks. Boring worked for him and his family. So why was his brain screaming for attention? Was it the tail that turned out to be FBI? Was it a collection of little things that seemed out of place, but unexplainable?

Marrell was grateful that in the end it was not his problem to sort out the vagaries of politicians. His job was to keep Monahan safe from everyone, including himself. Police activity was not his problem until it impacted Monahan in some way. So far, it had not.

The car phone rang. It was not to be ignored. Its use was rare, since the security details were given encrypted cell phones that were swapped out every few weeks, but a call coming in on that phone meant a private call to the secretary or a priority message. He pressed Answer on the steering wheel, which automatically turned on the speakers.

"Marrell here."

"Location?"

Protocol: confirm safety. Trackers were on-board both vehicles so security back at state would know where they were at all times. Of course, at the request of the secretary, he had disabled it once they were away from the State Department offices. While a never-ending source of complaints, it was also commonplace.

"Just getting on the FDR," Marrell said.

"Is Secretary Monahan with you?"

"Negative."

"Hold on." The audio went silent then crackled back on. The voice on the other end returned. "Shule?" That was Director Palma's driver. Now they were having a conference call.

"Here."

"Marrell?"

"Here."

"Is there anyone else in the vehicle with you?"

"Negative."

"Negative."

"You are hereby requested to return home", the voice on the speaker said. "I repeat: return home. This is not a drill. The presence of Secretary of State Monahan and Director Palma is required at 799." That was 799 UN Plaza. "Wherever it is that you dropped them off, return and escort back. Return and escort. Understood?"

"Understood."

"Understood." Marrell hung up.

Of course, he had lied about getting on the FDR. He was still fighting his way down Pike Street to get to the FDR, but that didn't matter. He had to turn around and hope for two things: his boss had a cell phone with him, and the cell could get a signal.

Marrell's cell rang. "Marrell."

"It's me." Palma's driver, Jarred Shule. While they didn't know each other well, they had worked together in one of their previous lives. Marrell was with DEA and Shule was Border Patrol. It was a short stint and both men respected each other even as they joked about which was the more dangerous organization to work for. Marrell was sure it was DEA. He proved it by leaving after three years.

"How screwed are we?" Marrell asked. The conversation on their secure phones were not recorded.

"Could be pretty screwed," Shule said. "This happened to me once before. The director needed to return for a security briefing and I had just finished dropping him off somewhere to meet someone. I don't know with who, but that was not the only time."

"The secretary hasn't done this before. If it wasn't because he and the director are such good friends..." Marrell let the statement trail off. This kind of thing was always dangerous. A safe situation turned bad because something unexpected happened. Unexpected meant uncontrollable. He hoped the director was armed. He knew the secretary was not.

"Last time this happened with the director," Shule said, "I went back without him. I don't know what he does or is doing, but you don't want to piss him off. I had a lot of people yelling at me and I almost got fired, but the director made it clear in no uncertain terms that I did the right thing."

"Maybe. You can blame me." Marrell, experienced with the streets of New York, thought of a few different ways to make it back. "I'm turning the hell around."

———

The scratchy fluorescent lights were all that illuminated the Brooklyn Ventilation Building. The two SUVs were parked behind the building so if anything happened, they would be on their own. It was after 8 p.m. and the deserted area looked as empty as it did when they'd first arrived about thirty minutes earlier. The wind gave their cars a brief shake.

"This is a bad idea," Shule said.

Marrell didn't think so.

Both men had their guns in hand and arms extended as they jogged around the perimeter of the building. Marrell didn't want to break into a New York City facility that was already abandoned due to the incoming storm, and cause a firestorm by setting off an alarm that would rain down NYPD on them. They just had to pick up their bosses.

"Does the general have a cell?" Marrell asked.

"Yeah, and I'm not calling him on it."

Marrell felt a chill down his back. The first indicator of an impending cold. He wanted to shake his head at Shule in disbelief but thought better of it. As they returned to the back of the building, Marrell took out his cell and dialed. While a call to the Secretary of State would normally go to his assistant, in this case Cordell Plante, Marrell knew Monahan's direct number. Behind him, the East River sounded choppy.

Nothing. It rang and went to voice mail. He was going to hate himself in the morning. He had to find this guy.

He turned to Shule. "I don't know how these guys got into this building, I don't even know if they're in the building, but we have to get in there."

Shule shook the fence of the automatic gate. "There are doors on either side," he said.

Marrell jogged around the building until he got to a graffiti-covered door. He tried the doorknob. Locked. This was going to make a lot of noise. He aimed his Glock at the knob.

"Wait a minute," Shule said. "What are you doing?"

Marrell wasn't sure what the question was. "I'm going to blow off the lock. The Secretary of State is requested back at the office for who knows what. Not my place to judge, and I don't know where the hell he is."

"Well, wait a minute," Shule said.

Marrell fired off one round into the lock, shook the doorknob, and the door opened.

"Let's go."

44

THE UNDERGROUND

Palma led the way through the ventilation building, down to the ancillary walkway, which led to the staircase, which led to a row of panels, which led to another set of stairs, which led to an old rusted-over doorway that had a panel Palma opened it, revealing a shiny fingerprint reader. He was certain that Monahan had no idea where they were. Palma knew. He was the detail guy.

"This is pre-programmed to accept your right thumbprint," Palma said. "If you have to get back in here, just use this."

Monahan nodded. A man of few words, finally. Palma was certain Monahan would never come through that door more than this once. As good as Monahan was as Secretary of State it was through sheer force of character and charisma. Monahan was a strategist, not a tactician. Stymied as he was by short-term thinking, he would typically look for a victory in the present. Not ten, or twenty, or a hundred years from now. Right now.

Unlike the Chinese. They understood long-term planning and the effect it had on history. It had been Palma's idea to court the Chinese. When they approached Monahan with their desire to have a base for joint operations with the US, Monahan could barely contain himself. But it was Palma who made it all possible and ensured the US would have very little to do with it.

After years of dealing with politics and politicians, he had seen the future of the US, and the present did not paint a good picture.

"Are you going to be alright?" Palma asked.

Monahan made a non-committal grunt, walked through the door, and kept a few paces ahead of him.

Palma found a metal pipe. He picked it up and looked at Monahan as he proceeded down the corridor running parallel to the Montague Tunnel. He placed the pipe onto the floor between the doorway and the door to stop it from closing completely. There would be others coming soon.

"Do you think they'll be happy to see us?" Monahan asked.

"Who? Jenkins and his crew or the new tenants?" Palma asked.

"I'd be good with either right now," Monahan said.

They walked in silence the remainder of the way through the partially lit corridor.

They arrived at an unlocked door that opened onto another stairwell.

"Why aren't we using the elevator?" Monahan asked.

"You don't want to know. We're almost there," Palma said.

———

Palma felt his leg muscles tighten and loosen. They had walked about twenty minutes, each punctuated by Monahan's curses. Palma gave thanks Monahan wasn't his usual talkative self. Things already felt different.

The stairwell, in contrast to the corridor where they walked on level ground, was bright with off-white walls. "Are you alright?" Palma asked.

Monahan stopped and leaned against the stairwell wall. He unbuttoned the top button of his flannel shirt. "I've had better days." He let out a breath. "It figures that if one of us had to pay for this, it wouldn't be you."

"We're all paying in our own ways," Palma said. He froze and scanned the corridor. He didn't see anyone, but he thought he'd heard footsteps.

They exited the stairwell and entered an airlock into a room filled with poured concrete tables and chairs. The room was functional, but antiseptic. Palms had never liked the room and fought Marshall on it, but Marshall made the change and completed it before Palma lodged a veto. Marshall had been in charge of IT infrastructure which quickly turned into facility infrastructure and who knows what else. So much of the facility that Marshall figuratively wanted to destroy was his own doing.

With that, Palma felt at home. No, he *was* home. He had spent so much time in the underground facility that there were nights when he woke up in his own bed in Virginia and wondered where he was. While he loved his children, he loved his work, and at work, he loved what he did.

"Mr. Secretary?" Palma turned to Monahan who collapsed onto one of the concrete benches.

"Who the hell thought these benches were a good idea," Monahan asked.

A story for another day. "We should probably get to the main conference room. This was never meant to be a reception area."

"What the hell is it?" Monahan asked.

"We can wait here a few minutes if you like. We're not in a rush anymore," Palma said.

"Of course not. This is home for at least a few days," Monahan said. "I hope they bought some clothes for me." He scrunched his nose. "This air smells dry. And powdery."

Palma walked to a sink over to one side and pulled a plastic cup from a dispenser sitting on the counter top. The room was as bright as the staircase, but the walls were a darker gray. If the lights went out, a flashlight wouldn't find much to reflect off. Five vending machines filled with free snacks stood on the opposite wall. He forgot who suggested it, probably Jenkins, but Palma made sure everyone knew that he'd arranged for them to be well-fed during their long work hours.

He heard the airlock decompressing.

Palma put down the plastic cup he had just filled with water and walked past Monahan, who sat with a startled look on his face. The door opened and the two people he had never expected to see again entered with their guns at the ready.

Their security detail.

"Agent Shule, what are you doing here?" Palma asked. *Christ Almighty.* Palma's hands started to sweat. His mind awakened to a focus he didn't think he'd need.

Shule holstered his weapon. The other driver, Palma didn't know his name, kept his gun drawn and pointed at the floor.

"Sorry, sir. We got word that you and Secretary Monahan were to report back to 799 and we were not allowed to take no as an answer."

Monahan stood and walked next to Palma. "Good idea to leave the door wedged open."

The door opposite the group slammed open and three men holding QBZ-95 assault rifles entered the room. Palma put up his hands and positioned himself between the two armed groups. "Stop! Everyone stand down!" Palma yelled. *Everyone just has to listen to me.* He imagined the scenarios and their outcomes as feelings, not as conscious thoughts. His chest expanded as he took in and held a deep breath.

Both groups shouted commands to put down their weapons until Palma stood before the three armed Chinese men.

"I order you to put down your weapons!"

The room silenced.

The three Chinese soldiers kept their rifles aimed at the men behind Palma. The man to Palma's right said, "Tell your men to put down their guns. They can leave after that, but they have to drop their weapons."

Marrell looked at Monahan and kept his gun aimed at the potential threat before them. "Sir, what's going on?"

Monahan glared at Shule and Marrell. "Gentlemen, put your weapons down."

"Director?" Shule asked.

"Yes. Holster your weapons."

The two men released their grip and pointed their Glocks at the ceiling as their arms relaxed. They put their guns back in their holsters.

Monahan looked at one of the soldiers who still aimed their rifles at the men, and tilted his head toward the two men to his left. Two of the three soldiers each fired one shot and took down the two men.

"What are you doing?" Palma yelled. He stormed over to Shule's body and unholstered the dead man's Glock. He aimed the gun at the soldiers, and walked over to the two assassins of his men. "Get on your knees. The two of you."

The men aimed their rifles at Palma.

"On your knees. Now!"

Monahan stepped over to Palma. "Stop. This won't bring them back."

"They were good men," Palma said.

"History is littered with the bodies of good men."

"You're right." He lowered the gun. "And sometimes of not-good men." Palma raised his arm and shot Monahan in the head.

45

PRISONER EXCHANGE

Sunday night
October 28, 2012

Anna Wodehouse, a.k.a. Carpenter Poole, was tired.

She lay on the bottom bunk of the 7.5 by 8 foot dark, dirty gray cell in the Manhattan Correctional Center at 150 Park Row in lower Manhattan and realized that all of the theories of the non-existence of free will must be true. Everything had to already have happened with no possibility of change. She was living proof. All her attempts to help, hinder, change, and otherwise affect the things around her were for naught. Somehow, she'd missed the class where the professor had mentioned that not only was the illusion of free will persistent, it was also the ultimate denial of reality.

Benson, Palma, whoever, had won. She was back in prison, the man who raised her was off getting himself killed trying to stop an imagined wrong, and her life was done. Palma had almost killed her twice and now she was a sitting duck.

An orange-suited sitting duck. A sitting Duck a l'Orange.

"Anna?"

The voice was unexpected, but she had been hearing steps in the distance coming toward her, away from her, floating in the air around her. Was she supposed to be angry? Maybe not. Even if she was, she didn't have the energy for it right now.

It was Terrell. *Mr. FBI. Why did he look so good in that suit?* He wasn't alone. An anonymous guard, his face hidden by the shadow cast from his hat, unlocked the cell door.

Anna didn't budge.

"Anna!" Terrell sounded insistent.

She sat up and squinted. This was going to be a waste of time. She looked up at him and felt an ache in her chest and a twitch in her hand. She wanted to hug him and slam him in the jaw at the same time.

"This is not a good time to see me. I haven't spoken to my attorney yet and I'm not wearing my finest blouse," she said.

"Whatever." He came in and crouched down before her. The guard stepped away, leaving them alone. "I've got a deal going with the Attorney General's office. They've seen the evidence against Monahan and Palma. I convinced them that you were an innocent bystander who got caught up in a plan they put together to hide the existence of a project in direct violation of international law and US sovereignty."

Terrell was speaking too fast.

"International law. Sovereignty." Anna looked away. "What strange sounding words. They make my tongue feel weird." She lay back on her bunk. "Make sure you run all of this past my attorney. It'll be useful during the inquest."

Terrell leaned on the bed. His right hand was dangerously close to her right hand. Anna felt the skin around her fingers tingle. In the dim light, she could imagine that he had climbed in through her bedroom window to whisk her away, until her eyes caught the myriad springs and wires of the bed above her.

"What inquest?" he asked.

"Mine." She continued to stare straight up at the bottom of the mattress. She was grateful she didn't have a bunk mate. Too many complications. "You said yourself that they don't know I don't know anything. They're going to come for me. You're going to show up tomorrow or the day after and I'm not going to be here and no one will be able to tell you where I am."

"Stop it. Stop acting like it's all over," Terrell said. "We've got a long road ahead of us."

Anna turned her head toward him. "Do you like me?"

"What?"

She turned back. "Nothing." She folded her hands on her stomach. "Based on everything I've done so far I'm a good candidate for the death penalty."

"No, you're not."

"I killed someone. I broke out of a high-security maximum prison. I blew up the home of a very important official."

"Are you hungry?" Terrell asked.

"For more death and devastation?" *Nice cologne.*

"No, food."

"You got us a reservation at Per Se?"

"Something like that."

"Not right now." She looked down at her legs. "I'm not appropriately dressed."

Terrell reached into his jacket. "You're such a New York girl," he said and handed her an aluminum-wrapped rectangle. "I wasn't sure if you liked pastrami, but."

The smell hit her almost as soon as he opened part of the sandwich. *He brought me a pastrami sandwich. I love pastrami.* "No, thanks."

"It's got spicy yellow mustard and everything. Rye bread."

Lousy bastard. "Maybe later. Leave it on the floor with the roaches. They'll guard it for me."

"Everything's going to be okay." He placed the sandwich on the bed beside her leg and sat on the floor. "No inquest."

"But probably death penalty."

"If the paperwork doesn't come through," he folded his hands across his knees, "maybe the death penalty." His eyes roamed the far corners of her kingdom. "I promise I'll be there to see you off."

Anna took in a deep breath and closed her eyes. On her eighteenth birthday, after she had ruined a small party Aunt Marcie had planned for her, she went up to her room filled with a despair she thought would never end. Even the roots of her hair sent waves of pain into the top of her skull. If it had been a Disney movie, she would have broken out into song or been attacked by the demented step-mother.

Instead she'd burst into tears. Aunt Marcie came up, didn't ask Anna if anything was wrong or if she wanted anything, and just held her. For those few moments, Anna pretended that Ingrid had finally come home. She breathed in Aunt Marcie's perfume, the scent of softener in her clothes, the crisp feel of her blouse. For the first few months, Anna didn't allow either her aunt or uncle to do anything for her around the house. She did her own laundry. Cleaned her room. Cooked her own dinner. But for those few minutes she felt something she had not felt in months. Not belonging, but hope.

As she lay in the bunk next to Terrell she wondered if the warmth she smelled and the warmth she felt in her chest was something she could trust. It still didn't feel like belonging, but she would deal with it.

"You need to go," Anna said.

"Are you going to be okay?"

"No." She chuckled behind a small sob. "But I'll be here waiting for my lawyer to tell me what a great deal I just got."

Terrell stood. Anna couldn't muster the energy to sit up.

"Did you find my father?" she asked.

"Not yet. There's an APB out on him, but the storm is taking precedence right now."

"He's a rather focused kind of guy. If you don't find him soon, you never will."

"You said HALON was breached. What did you mean by that?" Terrell stuck in his hands in his pockets.

"I don't know. I know it scared the hell out of both of them."

———

Monday afternoon
October 29, 2012
5:55 PM

The time for relocation or evacuation is over.
Mayor Michael Bloomberg

The phone call came into the main switchboard of the prison, answered by the lead corrections officer on watch. Personnel was on an as-needed schedule and that meant a full lockdown of MCC. The natives were restless, but that was to be expected. Things were heating up outside. The one thing no one needed was an incident at the facility. The news reports the officer had watched at home showed the impact of the storm on Washington, DC and things were only going to get worse.

The next few days were going to be hell and every phone call was unwelcome. In fact, there had been so many calls from the relatives of the inmates that he was ready to tear the phone out of the wall.

He sat up straight. DHS? Why the hell was the Department of Homeland Security calling in the middle of this mess? He went through protocol and received all the information he needed. This call was for real.

"How soon will your men arrive?" he asked.

"Within the next few hours. Make sure prisoner 21214-327 is available for transport." The officer hated these calls, as seldom as they happened. He was sure that some lawyer was going to ream him out for allowing his client to be escorted off the premise without proper authorization. But when DHS called, and the guys from DOD came by, he didn't have any choice.

Their celebrity prisoner was on her way out.

PART V

———

FRANKENSTORM, OCTOBER 29, 2012

46

MEN IN BLACK

Monday evening, October 29, 2012
8 PM Eastern Standard Time

Hurricane Sandy Makes Landfall in Atlantic City, NJ
Wind speed: 90 MPH

Manhattan Correctional Center (MCC)
Receiving

Receiving at MCC had a skeleton crew of two instead of the usual ten Federal Corrections Officers. Starting at 5 o'clock in the morning almost every morning, the office took care of checking suspects and inmates coming in and out of the federal-side of the facility known as the Tombs. The two officers who drew the short straw for that night had to mind the store while the hurricane blew through. There would be no processing of new prisoners tonight.

However, the corrections officer in charge, Officer Damion Eves, received a call he could not believe. Two men from DHS were on their way up. In the middle of this freaking storm. What kind of assholes were they? There was no way any prisoner was that important. While he didn't know the numbers by heart, he recognized the Bureau of Prisons number immediately. The girl they had brought in Sunday. The one who supposedly escaped Supermax by blowing it up. At least, that was the rumor.

Eves didn't know who the hell she was, but he was sure it wasn't DHS that was going to take care of her. He might have paid her a visit himself if MCC weren't in lockdown. Maybe they would ship her back to the Supermax, or maybe say they were and send her off to Guantanamo where they really knew how to show a girl a good time. Picking her up now had to be their way of making her disappear before anyone noticed. He didn't know any of the officers at the Supermax. He couldn't remember where it was. Montana? South Dakota? It didn't matter. He was sure they were just itching for their turn at that bitch.

He heard the elevator ding. They got past the security desk downstairs, and he would run them through the ringer one last time before handing the fugitive to them for final disposition.

He would send word to get the prisoner ready.

———

The short balding man handed his ID to Eves. Manson Young. The name appeared on the ID as Young, Manson.

Eves chuckled. "You must have gotten teased a lot as a kid."

The man didn't return the smile. "How long before the prisoner is ready for transport?"

"As soon as both your IDs clear she's all yours."

The taller man handed over the card to Eves. Darrick Elder.

Eves chuckled again and, under his breath, said, "Young and Elder. Elder and Young."

"What was that?" the older one said.

"Nothing, sir. I was just commenting on your last names. He looks younger than you, but he's Elder and you're Younger."

"Young." The shorter of the two men looked at his partner and then back at Eves. "Tonight would be good."

"Yes, sir." Eves looked at his screen. The two IDs checked out. These guys were probably spooks. With IDs like theirs they didn't need Bureau of Prison paperwork. The advanced call and the IDs were all they needed. Eves believed in the law, but he also sometimes felt the law was too much. "So, are you taking her back to the Supermax?"

Young looked up at his companion and nodded. "ADX is an all-male prison. She was never at Supermax. She was at Carswell. Anyone who says otherwise doesn't know what they're talking about." Young turned to Eves. "Understood?"

"Yes, sir. Is there anything we need to do?"

"If anyone asks, she was escorted to Danbury. Let's go get her."

"I'm sorry, sir. I already have the sergeant-at-arms dragging her sorry ass down here."

"Call him right now and tell him to leave her there. We have orders to escort her from her cell to our truck." He pulled a long piece of cloth out of his hand. "Since we don't want her making a scene, we would appreciate you putting this on her before she sees us."

"You want me to gag her?" He had never heard of that before.

"You are exemplary at your job, Officer Eves."

"What's going on here?" the prisoner asked. Eves did not have the patience for this tonight. He wanted to close the facility down and go hide out in his office. Even through the solid concrete walls, he could hear the rain picking up.

"I shouldn't be getting moved anywhere. Does Agent Garrison know about this? Someone needs to contact him before this goes any further," she said.

Eves rolled his eyes at the other corrections officer. "Please place your hands in the opening in the door. Failure to do so will result in escalation of force until you comply." He gave her face a quick glance. She was being combative. He was going to have to call in additional officers, who were not in the mood.

"Please," she said. She rubbed the top of her bald skull.

"Please put your hands in the opening in the door."

Nothing.

"Now."

When her hands came through the opening, the other officer looped them into the plastic ties and slid them against her wrist. He then crouched down and looped the leg restraints on her. She could now only walk a few inches at a time. Hopping would be faster and most prisoners resorted to that. All of that in the interest of keeping them too tired to cause a ruckus.

Eves motioned to the officer. "The door, please."

As it swung inward, the prisoner took a step back. "What's that?" she asked.

"Nothing." He spun her around, and before she had a chance to utter another word, he wrapped the gag around her mouth. Tight.

She mumbled something, but it was incomprehensible. If only he could use that at home.

"Let's go." He spun her around again and grabbed her left arm. He pulled her out of the cell and she almost fell because of the leg restraints.

As soon as she saw the two men, she started screaming through the gag. She tried going back into her cell, but Eves held onto her arm. "Don't worry, darlin'. These men are here to escort you to your new venue."

She shook her head over and over. Eves pulled her along to start the long trip back to the front of the prison where he could hand over custody to DHS. It was as if she was trying to tell him something.

Eves was pretty certain she was saying no.

———

Terrell was one of a few dozen FBI agents made available by the Bureau to help keep the locals safe through the worst of the storm. Things were in full motion since Sandy had made landfall about an hour earlier. Command-and-control was in the hands of New York

City with the various jurisdictions taking care of their own piece of the pie. The risk of chaos was great, but Terrell was optimistic. This was New York, after all.

He was in one of the myriad buildings in lower Manhattan waiting for orders so he could assist with something. He didn't know what, but the list was enormous. Just making sure the fuel trucks supplied by Hess would be available to the first responders was a huge undertaking, but all that was under control. If he had to help somewhere, he was sure it was going to be in lower Manhattan because that was where Manhattan was going to be hit the worst.

He had come out of another status meeting when his cell buzzed with a text message. If he wasn't careful, he was liable to spend his night hopping from meeting to meeting.

Prisoner Alert.

Terrell's eyes opened wide. *What the hell?* He read the message three times before he cursed at himself and ran to the elevator. He was walking distance to MCC, but it was a long walk. Would he be able to find someone to drive him there?

An escort detail from the Department of Homeland Security had just picked up Anna and escorted her off premises.

As he waited for the elevator, he dialed the Manhattan Correctional Center. No answer.

47

SLIDING IN THE RAIN

This can't be happening. Oh, please tell me this isn't happening.

Anna's ankles chafed from the leg restraints. The plastic ties were too tight and her wrists hurt when she turned them even a little. She was exhausted. Sleep had not come easily the night before after her conversation with Terrell.

And she didn't get to eat the pastrami sandwich, but that was her own fault. She'd waited too long and when the guard found it, he took it away. Not that it mattered. She didn't like cold pastrami.

Anna and the two men exited the correctional center out the front door on Park Row to buffeting winds. The usual escort stayed inside when they saw the proximity of her transport to the doors. Anna and her two companions were immediately soaked. The two men put their guns away and entered the black SUV parked on the sidewalk in front of the door. One of them opened the rear passenger door for her and practically lifted her in while the other ran in from the other side and slammed the door shut while he could. Anna tried to speak but gave up and just sat back.

"Turn around," he said. "C'mon, turn around."

Anna was seething, but turned her back to him anyway. She heard the wire cutter bite through the plastic and the circulation flow through her hands. She immediately pulled the gag down from her mouth and turned back around.

"I lost you guys at the garage on purpose!" She massaged her wrists. "What is wrong with you?"

"What's wrong with me?" Marshall asked. "What's wrong with you? You were supposed to come out so we could all be in this together." Marshall sat back.

The car drove off the sidewalk onto the flooded street.

"I need you both to be quiet," Liko said. "I can't hear the emergency response band." He started to head downtown. "The city hasn't lost power yet."

"Well, that's a relief," Marshall said. "Now if only they would leave the lights on in the tunnels."

The tunnels? I'm not asking. "Drop me off." How easy for her to go back to feeling powerless. Having other people decide her future. She was done with that. Anna was out of prison (again!) and all she could think about was what she could do to hurt Marshall.

"What? Oh, yeah." Marshall grabbed the back of the driver's seat. "Liko-san, can you find a dark alley somewhere?"

"I'll look for one," he said.

"What do we need a dark alley for?" Anna asked.

"You said you wanted us to drop you off," Marshall said.

"How about here?" Liko asked.

He drove like the ground was dry. Anna felt the tires skid.

"Good," Marshall said. "This is good."

Liko slammed on the brakes and the SUV slid to a halt down a narrow side street. Marshall handed Anna a bag.

"What's this?" she asked.

"Something to tide you over while you walk to wherever it is you want to go."

He wants me to go? "I changed my mind. I don't want to go anywhere."

"That's good, because we weren't going to let you. That's a change of clothes. You can get out of the orange outfit in here or out there in the dark, but you need to get out of that."

"But I'm going to get soaked." Was he purposely trying to humiliate her? What did it matter what she wore?

Wait. Was he angry?

"In here, or out there," Marshall said.

She had never seen him this upset with her.

He focused on the black mat at his feet. "Honey. Squirrel. I know this is a bit much, but," his eyes cut through her, "you have got to get it together. We're going to save New York."

Anna hugged the bag close, huffed at Marshall, and got out. She looked around for a spot where there wasn't water coming down. The darkness hid her from prying eyes, though she noticed that neither man in the vehicle looked her way.

The storm was picking up. Was it possible for it to get worse?

Running didn't seem to be an option.

Anna jumped back into the SUV and slammed the door shut. "I can't believe you."

"I can't believe you," Marshall said. The SUV lurched forward. She noticed him glance at her baldpate. "I thought we were getting along."

"You are in denial." Anna crossed her arms. *Does he still thing I'm ten?* She gritted her teeth. "The only thing we have going is a common enemy."

"We do?"

She pointed at him. "We both have you. You are your own worst enemy. You are my worst enemy."

"Now you're just being angry. It's true. I abandoned you. I'm sorry about that." He clenched his fists. "I'm sorry! But it couldn't be helped. You were better off without me." The rain struck the roof of the SUV in waves even as the car shook from the violent winds. The AC blew cold wind on her face.

"Only an idiot would believe that." She shook her head, sending droplets in every direction. She now wore a light blouse with jeans and a pair of soaked-through waterproof sneakers. The waterproof windbreaker fared no better.

"Or a parent." Marshall sat back. "Liko-san, are we almost there?"

"Not yet. It's hard to see where we're going."

"Well, be careful. We have some time. The subway tunnels won't flood."

Anna's brain went hot. "Are you kidding me? Do you know how much rain is going to come down?"

"You're a meteorology major too?"

"Look out the damn window! In a few minutes, we're going to be standing in over six feet of water."

"Oh my God," Marshall muttered. "The New York City subways pump out millions of gallons of water every day." He leaned forward. "Every day. Millions of gallons. This," he waved his hands in front of him, "is nothing."

"Then why don't we just walk?" she asked.

"Why don't you get rid of that chip off your shoulder?" Marshall asked. "Or better yet, if you really want to go then go. Liko-san and I will do what we have to do."

"You have no idea what you're doing," Anna said.

"How bad can I be? Even you couldn't kill me."

"If I had tried to kill you, I would have."

Marshall smiled. "Well, here's your chance."

"I want to kill you! Don't you get it? You left me and the one thing I want to do is kill you!"

Marshall tried to hold her hand, but she pulled it back.

His chest deflated and his shoulders curved inward. "I know you didn't kill Donnell."

He had that look again. The look that peered into her soul and made her feel like a little girl.

"There are times I wish it had been me on the roof. I would have died instead of him and maybe this could have been over."

What would I have done on that roof if it had been him? The same thing I did that day. Try to find out why he left.

"I can't go with you," Anna said. She wasn't sure if her eyes were tearing or if it was just the water dripping down her face.

"I understand," her father said.

Anna wasn't sure what to say next. "There are other people I have to think about."

Marshall chuckled. "Yeah. Like Bobby Samuels?"

"Bobby Samuels?"

"Yeah. He had a crush on you in high school." He looked up at her and the smile diminished. "I made him go away."

"Bobby Samuels?" *Damn. I liked him.*

"Liko-san? After you drop me off you'll have to take Anna away," Marshall said.

"How far?" Liko asked. The car was shaking and sliding, the dark punctuated by flashes of light from the street lamps.

"Canada."

Liko hit the brakes and the SUV took a few seconds to stop. "You can't do this alone."

"No," Anna said. "You can't do this at all."

"Damn it, Anna." Marshall turned to her. He took a breath and she could see that he was re-wording what he wanted to say. "Squirrel, this is something I have to do. Maybe one day you'll understand, or maybe you won't, but I have to personally stop HALON."

48

DEBUGGING SESSION

"No, you don't," Anna said.

Marshall looked at his little girl and wondered how he could ever explain the responsibility of what he had helped to build. Her eyes told him everything he needed to know. "Yeah, I do."

The SUV rocked back and forth as the winds outside the vehicle did their best to lift the massive hunk of steel and flesh off the ground. It might do better next time.

Liko gazed at him. "Marshall. If I let you go down there alone, there is every chance that you won't make it. One mistake and we're done. With the two of us we've doubled our odds."

None of that mattered. He had to make HALON unusable. By anybody. By everybody. He had exhausted all the possibilities. The government had failed. Law enforcement had failed. He had failed.

But he wasn't giving up.

"I'm talking about this freaking hurricane!" Anna smacked the door with the palm of her hand. "I used to the follow the news more, but everything says a lot of people are going to die tonight. Could we lower the count by three?" She leaned toward Marshall and put her hands down on the seat. "At least by two?"

"I hate to contradict you, but at least two of us are moving forward," Liko said.

Marshall looked over at Liko and felt a tug in the back of his mind.

———

What am I doing? Anna wasn't sure what insane guilt sat on the lap of the man before her, but she neither knew nor cared. She hoped that the guilt of what he had done to her, and all the second-guessing that would torture him for a lifetime, was something he would carry forever. She knew she would.

Yet here she sat: hating him only marginally less than she had after all these years. Here was his chance! Show his daughter how much he missed her! Make up the last seven years! But, no, what was his main concern?

Stop some damn program.

And for reasons she didn't have the time to fathom, she knew that she had to stop Marshall.

"Your face just changed," Marshall said.

"You're being used."

"I am not," Marshall paused, "being used." He widened his eyes and looked away in his signature deep thought look. "No. Palma and Monahan have been as surprised as I've been about this."

Anna shook her head just a little. *What the hell is he talking about?* As the words left her mouth she knew them to be true. "Maybe they're being used too."

"HALON shouldn't have been handed over for another few weeks. Certainly not in the middle of this, no matter how good a cover this is." He felt his eyes betray the movement of the gears in his brain. The SUV shook some more. "Why the rush?" He looked up at Anna. "I haven't been able to figure that out. What are you thinking?"

"What am I thinking?" He was asking for her opinion in the middle of Armageddon? "Are you kidding? What? Do you think this is one of our debugging sessions? I don't know anything." She sat back. "I don't want to know anything."

You can't make decisions from a position of ignorance. Her father's words. *Get out of my head!*

"Then how do you know I'm being used?"

How did she know? She stopped and thought and words came to her that she spoke them. "Because you would never consciously leave me again now that I'm here. Whoever is using you has got you so wound up that you're willing to make the same stupid decision again."

"To leave you. Again." Marshall's eyes unfocused. She could see more gears turning.

"To leave me. Again."

Marshall's own eyes watered as he watched a tear roll down Anna's cheek.

Something hit the driver window of their truck three times. The object hadn't flown into the window. Someone held it.

Amidst the wind and the rain Anna could just make out the uniformed outline of a police officer.

49

SHORT-TERM ACTION HERO

8:30 pm EST

Water from the surge caused by Hurricane Sandy tops the seawall in
Lower Manhattan

"Liko-san, where are we?" Marshall asked.

"Walking distance," Liko answered.

The overhead yellow light flattened out the shadows, making Marshall look like the man from Anna's memories. Only his crow's feet gave away that he was really an old guy.

Three more knocks against the driver's side window. Whoever they were they were yelling, but the sound was drowned out by the roar of nature.

"Prepare to abandon ship." Marshall reached out a hand to Anna. "Stay here. We'll get him away from the car. Drag yourself over to the driver's seat and get the hell out of here."

Another object struck the front passenger side window. Light flashed in the car.

"That's two," Liko said.

"I can count," Marshall said. "Run like hell, Anna. I'll find you." He hugged her before she could react. "Don't lose the necklace."

She made a half-hearted attempt to push him away once he was done. His rough hands held her face for a flash of a second.

He's real.

"They took the necklace when they arrested me." Her stomach knotted, but she wasn't sure why.

Marshall eyes said good-bye. Why were they saying good-bye? "I'll find you. I always have."

"No," she said, "you're not going."

"Don't have time to argue this." Marshall reached for the door handle.

She grabbed the back of his arm. The dark jacket was soaked through. "No." She pulled him back as hard as she could then leveled her face to his. "You don't get it. You're not leaving. I mean...going."

"Anna," Marshall said. He pulled at his sleeve.

Anna tugged him close. "No one kills you but me." Marshall continued staring at her face. She didn't know what her face was saying, but she could feel the heat around her eye sockets. The wetness from her scalp dripped down her face. She felt clammy and she tightened her grip on his sleeve.

Please.

Don't go.

"Liko-san?" Marshall continued looking at Anna.

"Yes."

"Go without me."

Thump, thump, thump!

A light from the back of the SUV shone on the top of Marshall's head. Someone was shining another flashlight into the car.

"That's three," Liko said.

"Everybody out of the car and hands where they can see them," Marshall said. "Let me do the talking."

Anna yanked at his sleeve, but not as hard as before. He locked eyes with her and in his, she saw someone she thought she would never see again.

"It's gonna be all right. Let me do the talking."

Liko and Marshall opened their doors and Anna climbed out after her father. The wind blew the doors hard, and she had to brace herself against the door to keep it from swinging shut on her leg. They all had their hands palms up. Where were the other two cops?

"What the hell are you people doing out here?" The officer by the driver's side door had his hand on his gun, holstered to his hip. Slightly overweight white male.

Okay, so he's being cautious. First weapon.

"Officer, we are so sorry. I have my ID card in my jacket if you'll let me pull it out!" Marshall yelled.

Trash flew all around them and the rain changed direction every few seconds, buffeting them with walls of unavoidable moisture. "We're with ConEd. Well, me and Frank are." He motioned to Liko then to Anna. "This young lady is my daughter."

Did he have to say that? Her thoughts distracted her for a few seconds before she realized her brain was already assessing their chances of getting away.The two other officers struggled to walk around the car. Anna looked at the one coming from behind.

Second weapon.

"What the hell are you doing here with your daughter? And, yeah, I want to see that ID!" the officer yelled over the wind.

He did everything he could to stand straight, but his hand stayed on his gun. The second officer took major strides to walk, and arrived at the first officer's side.

Marshall held up his hand, opened his drenched jacket, and reached into the inside pocket. The officer who was on the passenger side came around and stood to the first officer's left. He had his sidearm in hand.

Third weapon.

They were in place like three dominoes.

Dad, don't move, Anna pled silently.

Marshall extracted a plastic card and held it out for the officer to see. The first officer grabbed it and kept wiping at it with his right hand, which was now not on his gun.

"Why the hell aren't you in a truck?"

Marshall took a step to his left, blocking Anna. "This had better traction." She could hear Marshall's smile. "Besides, we're management."

The officer looked over at Liko who made no attempt to smile. "You know, you don't look like a ConEd worker."

They all heard an explosion in the distance.

And with that Marshall swung his leg under the officer, causing him to fall on top of the other officer to his left causing him to fall on the officer to his left causing all 3 of them to fall to the ground. As the three men tried to maintain their balance on the way down, one struck his head on a fire hydrant, the other on the metal bar of scaffolding that had not been blown down, and the last hit his head on the sidewalk as the wind pushed him down and he pulled his head back to avoid falling.

Anna was speechless.

"And you were about to start a fight in a hurricane with three armed men," Marshall said as he faced her. He nodded at Liko. "Let's go. They didn't hit their heads that hard and the cold water'll wake them up soon enough." He pointed at Anna. "Get in the car and find some high ground. Or maybe get into the Bronx." He stood and almost slipped on the water that was flowing all around them. "Go north, young woman!"

"What was that?" Anna asked, looking up the street.

"The explosion?" He also gazed into the distance. "Probably a power substation. That's going to take down power across a good chunk of the city." He pointed behind her. "Go!"

With that Marshall ran off after Liko who had already taken off down the street.

Anna stood in her dripping clothes and dripping bald head and wet sneakers and wetter feet and thought, *So that's it? This is the end of the rainbow?* She looked at the three men unconscious on the ground, one of whom was starting to stir, and looked at the corner where Marshall and Liko had just turned left.

She jumped in the car. *Time to go.* Her stomach tingled as she reached for the keys. The engine made a grinding sound. *Whoops! Already on.*

She released the emergency brake and threw the car into reverse. The car went back about ten car lengths when she slammed on the brakes, sliding to a stop.

No one kills him but me.

She threw the car into Drive, turned on the windshield wipers, and stopped when she just turned the corner. As she jumped out of the SUV into the shower stall that was Lower Manhattan, she heard gunshots.

50

———————

WHITEHALL STATION

@MTA (via Twitter): We can confirm that there has been water filtration into the New York City Subway tunnels under the East River. We cannot confirm depth.

Visibility down the dark street was getting worse. The streetlights swayed back and forth as the torrent of water flowed in one direction for a few seconds and changed direction a few seconds later. Anna ran in the few-inches-deep water toward the lone slouching figure. He stood next to one of the dozens of large block buildings that gave New York its historical feel, even if the edifice had only been there for a few decades. She kept her head down to try to keep the water out of her eyes.

What am I doing?

"Marshall!" she yelled. She slid while she ran and fell into the cold water, hitting her left shoulder on the street that she couldn't see anymore. The water pushed against her from all directions, but she stood anyway. "Dad!"

Nothing.

Another shot rang out and she saw Marshall give a slight jump. Something else was going on.

"Dad!"

He turned. His hair, straighter and more haphazard than she had ever seen it, lay plastered to his scalp. "What are you doing here?" he asked.

"I heard gunshots." The sound of rain hitting everything made it impossible to do anything but yell.

"Get back in that car."

"What happened?" Anna asked.

"Liko's trying to get the gate opened. No point in standing around waiting for a ricocheting bullet to take me out." He chuckled then lost his smile. He held her hand, squeezed, then let go. "Will you get back to the car? It's dangerous out here."

"You get back in the car. Why is he shooting the lock? Doesn't he have a key? What kind of spies are you?"

"First of all, I'm not a spy," Marshall said. "And neither is Liko-san."

"Marshall! Let's go!" Liko's voice came from the staircase leading down into the Whitehall Street subway station.

"I don't trust him," Anna said.

Marshall gave her a bemused look through the water that poured down both of their faces. "Go. You have to go."

She straightened herself out as much as she could against the rain and wind. "No. I'm not going down there and neither are you."

He shook his head. "You have to stop being such a spoiled brat."

"I am not a spoiled brat!"

"Not only are you a spoiled brat, you're a know-it-all and no one can tell you what to do. Well, let me tell you, young lady, you'd better get back in that car." He pointed up the street to the SUV, its door flying back and forth until the wind slammed it shut.

There wasn't a spot on their bodies that wasn't dripping. Anna motioned towards the ground sending splashes of water off her arm. "You're not going down there."

"If your mother could see how you were speaking to me..."

"Mom would tell you to get your sorry ass into the car and take me home!"

"Well this 'sorry ass', as you put it, has a job to do."

"I could care less! If you don't go, I don't go."

A large pair of hands came between them and pushed them apart. Liko stood between them, not uttering a word, standing at attention. He leveled them each with a stone-cold stare. He pulled out his gun, leaned toward Anna as if he were about to give her a parental scolding, and handed her the weapon.

"Cover us," Liko said. He started to walk down the waterfall that used to be the stairs into the station.

She could swear that he didn't hold onto anything for balance, as though the water was afraid to touch his feet.

Marshall's eyes softened. "Please." He touched her arm. "Go."

She pulled her arm away and looked at the gun Liko had handed her. *Piece of shit.* She lobbed it into the air as far as it could go.

Marshall had grabbed the handrail to the staircase. Water was running down fast enough the she was sure he was going to lose his balance. He was going and so was she. *Why do I hate you so much?*

Was that yelling? She turned and saw two of the police officers they had left behind running at her from almost a block away.

One of the officers shouted for her to stop. The other fell into the water. Anna hoped he didn't get hurt. *What an idiotic thing we're doing. We're putting other people's lives at risk.* She clenched her fist and stood her ground. If she was going to cover them then she would have to hope that they wouldn't shoot an unarmed civilian. Twenty-something white female.

The officer who fell stood up and pulled out his gun.

Maybe she was wrong. She stood her ground. If his gun was soaked then he couldn't fire it, could he? She put her hands up. "Don't shoot!" She started walking toward them to put distance between them and the subway entrance.

The second officer pulled out his gun and pointed it at her. She sent a thought to Marshall: *If they shoot at me, I will haunt you forever.*

"I don't know those guys!" She started to cry. *Will they fall for this?* "Please, you have to help me."

She knelt in the water, covered her face with her hands, and pretended to sob. *Oh, please come closer.* Splashing feet. They were coming over.

"C'mon! We have to get out of here!" The officer closest to her looked behind her. It was obvious he wasn't happy with what he saw. He reached down and held her arm. "C'mon!"

Anna stood. She knocked his gun out of his hand then kicked him between the legs, sending him to the ground. The other officer was still registering surprise when she elbowed him in the chin. He toppled to the floor. Both of their guns were somewhere under water.

"Stop!"

Anna had made it to the staircase when she whipped around and saw one of the officers hold up his gun and aim at her.

She didn't move.

"Don't go down there!"

Anna looked at the stairway leading down, then faced the officer.

There but by the grace of God...

She jumped.

51

FROZEN

OMG! This water is cold!

Anna entered the Whitehall Street subway station grateful that the rain and wind had stopped, but the crashing sound of hundreds of gallons of liquid reverberated all around her. She slid down a few steps on the outside staircase with the slap of wet jeans against her ankles. While her back muscles weren't happy, she'd made it down into the R train station. On a normal day, the train would arrive to take passengers uptown to Queens, or downtown to Brooklyn.

Her penultimate problem: the water that poured into the station was damn cold. The station echoed the invasion of rain and screaming wind until it sounded like the roar of a subway train entering, but never quite stopping, at the platform. Water showered down on her from every section of the ceiling.

Her ultimate problem: the station's main lights were off. The emergency lights created harsh shadows and gave the corridor the appearance of places where the wrong things lived. A tunnel that, in a movie, would be the one place no one should go. Her breath was wet. The water rushed by her feet, making it difficult for her to maintain her balance.

Hypothermia. That's going to be my real problem. But I won't be here that long. "Marshall!" she yelled.

The reecho of the surrounding roar of water rushing into the station masked her voice. She had to be sure he'd heard her. But it felt strange saying his first name. It hadn't bothered her earlier, but for some reason it gave her a sore feeling in the back of her head.

"Dad!" Her feet felt waterlogged, but the adrenaline kept her moving at a fast clip. "Marshall!" She hadn't been gone that long. How far could they have gone?

Why the move into the subway? HALON was sure as hell not down here. Maybe a connection led to one of the buildings above, and they just needed to climb up to the building where HALON existed. That would mean that Benson was hiding the facility in plain sight. *Bastard.* She never liked that as a strategy. It had been done before, and one mistake was all it took for the world to know that the building where they made ice cream and fluffy stuffed animals was really the headquarters for the evil villain bent on world domination.

She heard splashing behind her.

"Stop! Police!" The cop who'd almost shot her had made it down to the station.

She placed herself outside of his line of sight. Her movements were noisy, but the water already created enough of a racket that he wouldn't be sure what was her and what was the mini-Reichenbach Falls.

Or maybe not. He was heading straight for her.

"Stop! You've got to get out. The tunnels are flood..." He snapped back as if something had hit him and fell into the murky lake that was now the Whitehall station.

Anna tried to cover her mouth from the suddenness of his death but pulled her hand back to keep her balance.

Liko came out of the shadows past the turnstiles and holstered his gun. Anna heard splashing to Liko's right.

Marshall appeared. "Why did you shoot him?"

"He was about to shoot her," Liko said and walked into the shadow.

Marshall stood still, looked at Anna, and then at the figure almost submerged in the water. He exhaled several hard breaths while he waved Anna over. She slid beneath the turnstile and stood next to him.

"Are you okay?" he asked over the echoes of the non-stop gushing.

Anna shook her head. She didn't think the officer would shoot. He hadn't even had his gun out, but what if Liko was right? She couldn't shake the feeling that someone who was trying to save her had just died.

"Where's HALON? In the Whitehall train station?" Anna asked.

"In there." Marshall pointed at the end of the platform.

"That leads to the foundation of some building where it's located?" Anna asked. She started to walk in the direction that Liko had gone.

Marshall put his hand on her shoulder for a moment. His palm felt warm against her cold wet skin. It was a moment of comfort. "No." He pointed again into the dark where the tunnel began at the end of the platform. "We're going downtown. It's in the subway tunnel. It's in the Montague Tubes."

————

Marshall gave Anna a headband with a flashlight attached to it and a wristband with the same. Their suit jackets had been jury-rigged to hold bags filled with items small enough that they could store them in the jacket, but not so big that they would stand out. In this case, no one noticed because both he and Liko were so wet that the last thing anyone cared about was what alleged federal agents carried.

Their combined headgear gave them enough light to see by, but she wasn't happy with what she saw. There was debris everywhere. The railroad ties made walking difficult and if they fell, they could potentially break a foot or a leg or just smash their skulls open. But that was nothing compared to Anna's real concern. The water was still rising.

"I thought you said they pumped out millions of gallons of this stuff every day," she said.

The echo had practically stopped now that they were well into the tunnel, but she waited for zombies to come out from around the various hallways and pillars they walked by.

"They must not be pumping today. Maybe something to do with losing power," Marshall said.

His comment got her thinking about something else that used power and should have already killed them: the third rail. With 625 watts flowing through it, the third rail would kill them even if they didn't touch it. The water they were wading through would have been so deadly they would have died instantly. Marshall said it had been turned off the day before, and not to worry about it. However, the emergency lights in the station were about to be a problem. They would only work for a limited time, and Marshall predicted the station was going to be in total darkness in about an hour and a half at most. That meant nothing to them. They had to be in HALON long before that, or they would either die of hypothermia or just drown if the water level climbed high enough.

"You know," Marshall said as he slogged through the thigh-high water, "this tunnel was drilled back in 1920 to connect Manhattan and Brooklyn. You know why?"

Splash, splash, splash.

Anna was getting tired. How long had they been walking? Ten minutes? Fifteen? Five? "I give up." *Splash, splash, splash.* "Why did they dig out this torture chamber?" she asked.

Splash, splash, splash.

"To make it possible for New Yorkers to get to Coney Island."

She loved Coney Island. She hated when they first moved away, and celebrated when they came back when she was twelve years old. She would always remember that. As much as she disliked the city when she was younger, it had changed while she was gone. There was something magical about it and now she hated being away.

The water had been up to her knees a few minutes ago; now it was mid-thigh.

What train was this? She'd read the sign on the way in, but it escaped her. She almost asked Marshall but thought better of it. "I guess it's too late to go back?"

"Anna, as soon as you walked down those stairs it was too late." Marshall went under the water. A few seconds later he popped up and said, "Oh, oh, that was cold."

"Why did you do that?" Anna was incredulous. She didn't remember him being suicidal.

"I spotted some of the HALON beacons. If anyone is in security, they might know we're coming." He started walking again. "The beacons aren't rated for this. I'm pretty sure they can't see us right now, but they will soon."

The air smelled cold. She felt a hard shiver. "How soon?"

"Probably as soon as we get to the entrance."

"There's an entrance? Is it marked 'Do Not Enter. Top Secret Underground Military Base'?"

"Ha, ha, ha," Marshall said as he continued forward. "In fact, there are two entrances and they're both marked 'Do Not Enter. Live Electrical Wires. Authorized Personnel Only.'"

"And if someone were to go in?"

"On a bad day? They would fall ten stories to their death."

52

INTRUDER ALERT

Palma was one level below where he started. Since the top of a building had the highest floor designation, he had entered on the thirtieth floor. His trip down to twenty-nine, by way of the stairs, was him just giving the facility the once over. He knew he had a few days to truly check everything out, even with the new tenants in place, but he wanted to insure there were no loose ends. His new helpers would find the remaining personnel and he would escort them out. He didn't want any more mistakes.

He would take care of Jenkins. Perhaps not as suddenly as Monahan, but Jenkins' role was almost complete.

A man dressed in jeans and a light blue button-down met him halfway down the semi-lit corridor. Even at a head taller Palma looked down on him anyway.

"General," the armed man said, "the men are heading to the designated locations. The remaining personnel should be waiting for them."

"Not a problem, Captain," Palma said.

The corridors on this floor looked like what they were: the connecting hallways of a clean research facility. The floors had off-white laminate on top of a rubber flooring that was on top of a raised floor to allow for the safe placement of wires and conduits. HALON, if maintained, would be in never-ending construction mode, and Palma had taken it as far as he could. It had come together as he had hoped.

"Do you need me to talk to them?"

"My men? No, thank you. But your people don't seem to be around," the man said.

Palma meant if it was time for him to talk with the HALON personnel, but that didn't matter at this point. Water sensors went off, setting off the internal alarms. Palma would make sure the remaining personnel, once rounded up, would pay attention to him. Before Palma sent them home there were things he needed them to do. The storm turned out to be handy after all. Between forcing everyone into predetermined locations, and hiding the arrival of the Chinese, his concern about the storm making things untenable turned out to be unfounded. The only unpredicted event, Monahan's death, briefly threatened to take things into uncharted waters. Palma shrugged it off; they had plenty of properly vented incinerators.

HALON was thirty stories of steel-reinforced concrete with one elevator in and a series of elevators to the various lower floors. There was an emergency staircase up and out, which Palma, Monahan, and the now-dead security detail had taken, and the one elevator back into the subway tunnel, which no one could use until the deceased maintenance worker could be extracted. Palma had decided that the man caught in the gears would be returned to the surface and he would take care of reactivating the compartment once he had moved the body and had the others in place, as well. If the storm was half as strong as the National Weather Service said, their safe sequestration would last for at least a few days.

Palma and his new captain continued their walk down the deserted corridor. He would miss the facility and everything about it when he was gone. Observing the possible, in the proper workplace with the proper set-up, was something he truly enjoyed.

"Have your men gone to the lower floors? There aren't that many locations where they might be and they aren't ghosts," Palma said.

"Understood, General."

"Also, when you find him, bring me Dr. Jenkins. His people need to be kept comfortable so I can escort them out."

"I don't understand, General."

"The remaining scientists are under my protection. I need them brought together for eventual return to the surface."

"I'm sorry, sir." The captain shook his head. "That was not my understanding."

Palma paused and took in a breath before speaking. "What do you mean, Captain?"

"My orders are to find the remaining personnel and terminate. The only personnel allowed to leave alive have already left."

"That is not going to happen." Palma moved closer to the captain. "Before any of your men do anything to my people, they are to come to me for explicit permission. Is that understood?"

"I'm sorry, General, but those are not my orders. I'm afraid you'll need to take it up with others higher in command."

"If I find that any of your men have harmed any of my people, I will shoot them without a second thought."

"And I will be forced to take corrective actions as my men are just as important to me as yours are to you, sir." The captain stood at attention. His QBZ-95 assault rifle, standard issue for Chinese military personnel, was hanging from his right hand. He made no move to raise it.

Is this guy fucking crazy? Palma knew he was at a stale mate, but he wouldn't stand for that at all. Now he would work out how to eliminate these men one at a time without the others knowing, if it came to that. He was nothing if not pragmatic and the people under his protection were under his protection. No one killed his people except him.

The captain's radio came to life.

The words were unintelligible to Palma. He had never learned enough standard Chinese for it to be of any use to him. The captain's face betrayed nothing.

"A proximity alarm has gone off," the captain said. "We should go to the nearest security station."

———

The wireless cameras transmitted high definition video on an encrypted frequency, captured by multiple antennas in the subway tunnel to ensure that at least one of them would return as many of the seventy-five cameras feeds as possible. The bulk of the cameras transmitted video that was accessible to most of the security centers throughout the facility.

Palma flipped through camera feed after camera feed and saw dark tunnel after dark tunnel, all with minimal light. They were going to drown in false alarms.

"This isn't a problem. Has someone seen something?" Palma asked.

"Yes." The captain spoke to the one other man in the security center with them. He leaned forward and entered a camera code into the keyboard in front of Palma. In the visible spectrum, multiple lights floated in the tunnel.

"Can we get any audio?" Palma asked.

"No," the captain said. "The water in the tunnel appears to have impacted some of the electronics, though we're not sure what the root cause is. However," he spoke to the man in Chinese again, "when we look at the feed in the infrared..."

Palma saw the multiple dots of light go from a dark blur into the distinct forms of three people. They were invisible from the waist down as the temperature of the water was disguising their heat signature.

"There are only two ways in. One is disabled so just send two men over to emergency stairwell 1."

Palma stood and walked to the door. He had too much work to do and the people in the tunnel might just be overzealous MTA workers. "If they come down the ten floors to the main door, kill them and dispose of their bodies down on five."

"Should we be concerned?"

Palma shook his head. "No. If they make their way down here, you know what to do."

53

RISING TIDE

The water was up to up to Anna's chest. She saw her father, not much taller and slogging through the water, as he grew more and more tired. If anyone was going to succumb to hypothermia, it would be him. Liko had water a few inches lower than his chest.

"There's something alive down here," Anna said. Would he get the joke?

She saw Marshall smile enough that his cheeks puffed. "Just us," he said.

She cleared her throat. "Do you have a phone?"

Marshall reached into his jacket pocket and lobbed a cell phone at her. She almost dropped it.

"So," Liko said, "While you are a wonderful tour guide about the underbelly of the New York City transportation system, you need to get us into the facility. We're all starting to shiver and we have a lot of work to do when we arrive." Liko gave his head a shake. "We'll need to warm up."

Marshall was canvassing the walls. "I've done this before."

"You have?" Anna asked. *What was he doing when he told me he was at work? I guess he was at work.*

"Alright," Marshall said. "Hold on."

The water covered her shoulder. She hesitated to swim because it would tire her out. She would wait. In the meantime, she looked at the cell. It had five bars. *Seriously?* She took a quick look at the last text message available on the phone.

SAC Garrison.

What was Terrell's number doing in here? Worry about that later. She typed a quick message and hit Send. She had been raising her hands as she typed. The water was coming in faster.

Marshall muttered something. The sound of thousands of gallons of water filled the air hurting their ears as the decibel level increased in the decreasing space between the water and the ceiling. They had to speak up and direct their comments toward whomever they were speaking.

"What?" Anna asked.

"Everything is fine," Marshall said. His shoulder twitched. "Start treading water."

"What are we waiting for?" she asked.

"An elevator."

"How far does that thing need to go?" Anna asked.

"It's not like we could attach a floor indicator."

"It might've helped." The water was at her neck. Time to float.

Both Liko and Marshall were still wearing their full suits. They must have been carrying more than they were willing to admit. She would have dumped any belongings as quickly as she could have.

She felt light-headed. Was that a symptom of hypothermia? The water was cold. She felt the warmth of her body flowing away from her.

She snapped out of it. "Are there cameras here?"

"Of course there are cameras. What kind of security do you think I designed?" Marshall asked.

"They know we're here. They're going to have people with guns at the door," Anna said.

"The cameras are probably not operational and the water should disguise our heat signature."

Was he kidding? That might be true now that they were almost submerged, but that wasn't true for most of their too-damn-long stroll. "Liko?" *Don't be rude!* "Liko-san, is your gun in a plastic bag?"

"No."

"Marshall?"

"I don't like guns," Marshall said.

Anna rolled her eyes. No firepower as they tried a frontal assault on a heavily guarded super-secret base.

The ceiling was getting closer.

"What's going to happen when it gets here? Will the pressure of the water on the door keep it from opening?" Anna asked.

"I don't know. This wasn't one of our scenarios," Marshall said.

He floated along with them, keeping his eyes on the wall. If the elevator was making any sounds, the water disguised it. Anna shivered more and more with each passing second.

"Will both of you float over here?" Marshall said. "When that door opens, we need to get inside as fast as we can."

Liko swam over. "Are we going to have to have to hold our breath the entire way down?"

"Consider it a possibility." Marshall held out his hand to Anna, but she ignored him. They were floating about a foot away from the top of the tunnel.

"Does that thing have any heating?" Anna asked.

"HALON's already too hot," Marshall said. They were all holding their heads above the water. "Get closer to the wall!"

"Dad!" Anna took in one last breath when she felt herself tugged downward. She kept her eyes open in the frigid water and saw a doorway open before her. She swam toward it and headed for the furthest corner of the room. She turned and saw Marshall pressing some buttons on the inside wall and the door closing with the three of them safely inside.

She wasn't sure how long she could hold her breath. Her chest already burned from the exertion of getting into the elevator.

The water was going down! She pushed up and joined the two men swimming above the receding water line, taking lungfuls of air as the water drained out of the bottom of the elevator compartment. In a few seconds, they were in a soaked, but empty, room.

Anna panted, trying to get as much air as she could handle. "What happened?"

"The water drained down the shaft. If we hadn't closed the door, we would have flooded the shaft and possibly the facility."

"That would have solved your problem," Anna said.

"No, that's not my only problem." Marshall and Liko exchanged a glance. "We've got more to do."

There was always more to do. Always one more app, one more load of laundry, one more dish to wash. She felt an unreasonable knot form in her throat as she looked away. They were probably going to die down here, but that didn't matter. Nothing mattered. She hasn't stopped Marshall. Water fell from the ceiling all around them.

"Wait," Anna said. "Next problem. Does the water have a way of exiting the shaft? Is the door where we're heading water-proof?"

"What's the next problem?" Liko asked. He looked back and forth between Marshall and Anna.

"What do you mean?" Marshall asked.

Anna watches as understanding dawned in his eyes. She was tired of the water pouring down on her. She brushed his shoulders off, knowing it wouldn't help at all then noticed her clothes were getting discolored. Her fingers were covered in a thin layer of brownish liquid. Oh, this was gross.

Her eyes opened wide when she peered at the ceiling. Marshall and Liko both looked up in the same direction. Anna screamed and cut the sound coming out of her mouth short as she covered her mouth.

Blood dripped from the ceiling.

54

MESSAGE FROM THE UNDERGROUND

If Terrell's head didn't explode tonight, it was going to be a miracle.

After receiving the prison alert, he commandeered an NYPD SUV and made his way to the Manhattan Correction Center just in time to discover that Anna and two men had left in a black vehicle thirty minutes earlier. They mentioned FCI Danbury as their next stop. *Bullshit! They're on their way to the airport, and they're going to hold Anna in detention until they could get a jet in to fly her out.* Why the hell would they move a recently captured fugitive from one prison to another (regardless that it was for women)? Everyone needed to stay in place. Didn't the mayor just finish telling everyone to stand still? The corrections officer displayed just the right amount of cynicism that Terrell was sure the mayor was right.

The general had lost so many trust points Terrell was very motivated to be the one to send him to prison. What a shame that he had to go through the proper channels. There were so many other FBI cases in which they simply picked up the suspect and did what they had to do. Terrell had never done that, but he understood the sentiment. Sometime a light touch got the job done, but for others the heavy touch was the way to go.

He stood inside MCC, in the dim overhead light, water dripping from his head and his parka, and looked at the parked white and blue squad SUV through the front door, his frustration building. *Where the hell did they take her?* No, he was sure about that part. The question was, where were they right now?

The cameras! There were hundreds of cameras all over Lower Manhattan. There couldn't be that many cars driving in the middle of the hurricane. NYPD would wait for marching orders in case things went south, but for now they would be the first to notice if someone was on the road. Roads closed to everyone but authorized personnel.

He called in to NYPD on the Motorola radio handed out to all the support personnel earlier that evening. He remembered what it was like during Katrina and knew New York would survive this. Sandy had the potential to be so much worse, but the extent of the poverty in New Orleans meant it would take them forever to recover. Unless a nuclear weapon exploded in the middle of the city, New York would recover. There was just too much money here.

Damn it. Where is she?

The officer out front opened the door, and Terrell stepped into the wall of water that stood between him and his vehicle. He ran to the driver's side, jumped in, and started the car.

His phone buzzed. Incoming text message. Then the radio squawked, the phone forgotten.

"Terrell," he said.

"Special Agent, we have news for you."

"That was fast. Do you guys have a time machine?"

"No humor tonight, Agent Garrison. There was an incident over at Broadway and Beaver Street. Three officers attacked at a stopped vehicle. Suspects are two males, one female. An officer gave chase into Whitehall station."

"I thought the stations were all locked up?"

"They are. We'd have more information, but things are getting worse out there. We've got some guys pulling up the video right now."

"What happened to the other two officers?"

"I've gotta go," the voice from the radio said. "They're both being treated at one of the temporary shelters. They saw the third officer give chase into the station. He didn't come out."

"I need someone to meet me over there," Terrell said.

"There's nothing to see."

Looking out his windshield Terrell had to agree even if that wasn't what the caller meant. "I need at least one other officer," Terrell said.

"Special Agent, the two officers who are still alive are in a shelter. The weather is getting worse. You really want to take someone out there?"

"Yes," Terrell said.

"Suit yourself. I'll pass the request along, but you'll do better reaching out to the National Guard."

Terrell put the radio down on the passenger seat. The streetlights glimmered through the tinted windows and the air-conditioning blasted through the vents drying the air and chilling his clothes. He bent his head down and palmed his head with both hands. This was not going to be an easy night. His neck was tight and he grit his teeth. His anxiety rose for about five seconds then he shut it down.

Relax. Unclench the jaw. Take a deep breath.

Broadway and Beaver. Not far. He threw the car into Drive, went about twenty feet, then stopped.

His phone had buzzed earlier. He pulled it out and logged in.

This is Anna. I am in the Montague Tubes.

He dropped the phone into the cup holder and threw the car into Drive again.

The Montague Tubes? The R train from Whitehall stopped at Montague Street in Brooklyn. He had spoken to that woman from the MTA about that.

She's in the tunnel?

Terrell drove up to the station entrance as fast as he could and found himself going slower and slower the closer he got to Broadway. The water was halfway up his wheels and the rain pelted his windshield. He stopped at the station and jumped out, the water up to his calf.

Where the hell is the entrance?

Terrell stumbled as he stepped toward the staircase leading down into the last place the officer was seen.

He could hardly see. Where were the stairs? He didn't use the R train very often so he was unfamiliar with the station logistics. He stepped forward with his right foot and felt where the first step might have been. He lowered himself into the water and in seconds, he was knee-deep.

There was no way into the station without scuba gear. It might as well have been filled with gelatin or concrete. And a flooded subway station meant flooded tunnels.

The tunnel where Anna sent her last message.

55

YOUR WORLD DELIVERED

The water level was getting higher.

The force of the surge knocked Terrell into the water, absorbing his warmth. His parka gained pounds against which he couldn't fight. He pulled himself up as more water pushed against him and knocked him down. He pulled off the unzipped coat and let it fall into the dark water.

The SUV had never seemed so far away.

He pulled the front passenger door open and kept it open through force of will. An unseen hand pushed against the heavy metal, trying to close it against his arm, then his torso and legs. When he was safely in the passenger compartment, the door swung open as if possessed, then slammed shut with enough force to make the car shake. Terrell pulled himself over to the driver's seat and grabbed the radio.

"Dispatch! This is Special Agent Garrison."

"Loud and clear. Where are you?"

"Down at Whitehall. The station is completely underwater and if I stay much longer, I will be, too."

"Affirmative. Are you available?"

Terrell blinked. *Tomorrow.* "Yes."

"Please report to the Fourteenth Street substation. There was an explosion reported and NYPD is looking for confirmation of suspicious activities."

Terrell clutched the radio. "Dispatch, I need to get to the Rail Control Center. I'm on the other side of the island so I suggest you send backup."

"No one else is available for at least another hour, maybe longer. It's you, Special Agent."

He was going to regret this, but he didn't care right now. "Dispatch, take me off rotation. I am heading up to Rail Control. Out." He dropped the radio on the passenger seat and looked down.

Water had found its way into the compartment. Something electrical was bound to fail soon, but he would worry about it then. He threw the car into reverse and drove backward until he got to the Bowling Green subway station of the 6 train. The water level wasn't quite as bad, but he was still driving with his wheels almost submerged. He spun the car around and cut across the sidewalk and the street to the west side. There were no demarcations. The sidewalk and the street all looked the same. He knew when he was leaving one for the other when the SUV would pound down or up.

Where the hell was Rail Control? He pulled out his cell phone and punched the name into his map app. Damn it, all the wrong choices. It was next to a police station. Midtown North? It was as good a guess as he was going to get. He had to go to 54th Street on the west side. Perfect. The street he was heading to would turn into the West Side Highway and with no traffic he could take the lights with impunity. The storm couldn't be as bad further uptown. He turned onto the Battery Park Underpass and headed north.

It had to be better uptown.

The windshield wipers thumped with each swipe and cleared the rain as fast as they could. Visibility was still zero. He was going to hit something, or worse, hit someone. He opened his window, let in the maelstrom, and decided that was a bad idea. It was worse than driving blind.

The one thing he did see was that the streets were underwater.

He needed to go north, but staying on the street would be a good idea. The streetlights were going to be out soon. If one substation exploded then another was on its way. And another. Time was so far against him that he wasn't sure if what he was doing made any sense.

I am in the Montague Tubes.

There was no possible way she could be there. He didn't know much about the tunnel connecting Manhattan with Brooklyn, but he was sure there wasn't cell service that far underground. At least not yet. Anna was somewhere else and this was a wild goose chase. He didn't care if she was yanking his chain or Palma's, but he wasn't biting. At least not without some help.

———

Terrell called AT&T. They'd been helping the NSA for years and would continue to do so as long as their government-sponsored Get-Out-Of-Jail-Free card was in effect. Enough government money was flowing into their coffers and they had plenty of friends on the Hill to keep even the most heinous violator of constitutional rights out of prison.

"I know you can't help me," Terrell said to the man on the other end of the call. "That's why you're going to put the facilities manager on the phone. Right now."

Terrell drove up the West Side Highway, and stopped when he found his cell signal coming in and out. It should have occurred to him sooner that cell towers were going to be going down eventually.

"Cornell Tierney."

"Good evening, Mr. Tierney," Terrell said. After introducing himself, he jumped in. "I need you to triangulate where a cell phone text message came from. And I need it in the next few minutes. Someone's life is on the line, and I know you can do this."

"Once you give me your information, I'll have to verify that you are who you say you are."

"Follow whatever protocol you deem necessary, but get someone working on it right now. She doesn't have the time." *Was she already dead?*

———

Terrell looked at his feet. There was more water in the compartment than before. The engine was going to flood and he'd be stuck until someone could pick him up. He couldn't afford for that to happen. He started up, and took off at a speedy ten miles an hour. Then down to five. He was still in Lower Manhattan. In fact, he hadn't gotten past Rector Street because the Battery Park Underpass had just turned into the West Side Highway. As he was about to go under the Rector Street Pedestrian Bridge he stopped.

It was too deep to go in. He was going to have to backtrack and go around. How the hell was he going to be of any help at this rate? His cell rang again. *Please let it be her.*

"Garrison."

"Special Agent?"

Damn. NYPD.

"We're still trying to piece this all together, but we've managed to get the security footage from Whitehall."

"How good is the feed?"

"You mean resolution? It used to be pretty good, but there was a lot of degradation. We're not sure why. Anyway, what I can tell you is that the officer was shot pursuing a young woman into the station and there were two men with her."

Terrell's face went cold. *I need to see that video.* "Can you send the footage to my phone?"

"No, we can't," the voice on the other end said.

"Are the images good enough for you to text them to me?" Terrell asked.

"I'll give it a shot. Hold on." Terrell heard noise in the background. "Let me call you back. It's going to take me a few minutes."

He tried looking around, but all he could see with any clarity was the water flowing in behind him. He put the car in reverse again and drove backward until he got to the next street back and turned in. The street curved and he was heading northbound again.

His phone buzzed. More text messages. He pulled over again.

Not Anna. An unknown number. Three pictures downloading.

The first one was of a tall man with a gun. He must have shot the police officer. Terrell put him on the top of his new list.

The second picture was of a ghost. Terrell shook his head, not sure what to think. *Marshall Wodehouse. In the flesh.* He was holding onto someone by the arm, but Terrell couldn't make out who it was.

The third picture was a blurry close-up. The technician must have zoomed in to get a better shot. She was soaked to the bone, but he would recognize her if she was covered head to toe in mud.

It was Anna.

PART VI

HALON

56

---

1 POLICE PLAZA

She can't be in the tunnel.

What the hell kind of father was Marshall? Why would he do something so dangerous?

Terrell made his way to 1 Police Plaza where, after he had just taken himself off rotation, he was about to put himself back on. He couldn't think. He needed help and he couldn't think.

If Anna was in the tunnel, she was dead.

The command center was swarming with personnel. Of all the times he had been in this building, and it had been quite a few since he'd joined the Bureau, he could not have felt prouder of the coordination to keep the number of people affected by Sandy to a minimum. Any other day he would have been just another body running around with everyone else collecting whatever information he needed.

At that moment, he felt anxious and hollow. It was time to go to the eighth floor. Maybe they could give him something to work with.

Real Time Crime Center (RTCC)

8th Floor, 1 Police Plaza

"You are so S-O-L, Agent Garrison. I don't know where to begin."

The number of police officers in the Real Time Crime Center was less than Terrell had ever seen before, but more than he would have expected. In fact, he was sure that he recognized some of the people at the keyboards. Afraid of getting caught up in something new, he turned away from them and paid attention to his escort. The black female officer he met at the door took him under her wing and he was grateful. Her name tag read *Clarke*.

The Real Time Crime Center, filled with long gray tables holding up almost-square monitors positioned in various haphazard positions, had about a dozen officers all talking into radios at once, passing information about the state of the city and where needed personnel should go. The smell of sweat told him they had already been locked in the center for too long.

"The one thing I can tell you is if anyone went into that subway station, they had better have come out or they aren't ever coming out." She sat down at a random keyboard and Terrell dragged over a seat. She pulled up some of the security cameras just outside the Whitehall station. There was water everywhere.

His cell rang. "Excuse me, I have to take this." He gave her part of his back. "Garrison."

"This is Cornell Tierney from AT&T. We spoke earlier."

"And?"

"You're either not going to like this or you're not going to believe it," Tierney said.

"I'm good with either."

"The text message came from inside the New York City subway."

Terrell closed his eyes, and smiled.

"Would you like to know where?" Tierney asked.

"Somewhere in the Montague Street tunnel leading to Brooklyn?"

"Actually, less than halfway there from the Manhattan side. How did you know?"

"Mr. Tierney, you have no idea how much you've helped me."

Terrell hung up and turned to Officer Clarke. "What've you got on the Montague Street tunnel?"

———

Terrell found a quiet corner in a quiet room somewhere on one of the lower floors. He had been tempted to haunt the nearest stairwell but decided against that. He couldn't control who might be listening.

"I need to talk to either Secretary of State Monahan or to Director Palma. Either is good," Terrell said.

He couldn't believe his luck. His first call to the State Department and it turned out Monahan was still in New York. Was it possible that Palma had stayed as well? The Deputy Chief of Staff, Cordell Plante, was familiar to Terrell for a number of reasons. Being a federal agent meant that Terrell was always hearing about the various politicians, both elected and appointed, and being part of the State Department meant that the FBI was always aware of the power structure that controlled them.

Terrell also knew that Plante was the main informant in the case against Monahan. Using the secure line meant that whatever Terrell told Plante would only be between them and vice versa.

He hoped for a lot of vice versa.

"As far as I know, Special Agent," Plante said, "both Secretary of State Monahan and General Palma are unaccounted for. Everyone is doing their best to stay calm, but we've got about a dozen of our guys out on the street and a few hundred analysts and intelligence personnel trying to find them. I'm surprised you didn't get called on this. The Bureau has about twenty agents working with NYPD trying to track their last movements."

Terrell remembered hiding from the familiar faces on the eighth floor at the Real Time Crime Center. He should have stayed his usual nosy self. "I apologize. I'll check in with them. Thank you for letting me know. How long have they been missing?"

"I shouldn't be talking with you," Plante said.

"I understand. I'm investigating something that may involve

Secretary of State Monahan. If he's missing then we do need to find him."

"An ancillary investigation is none of my business."

"If I told you the name HALON, would that mean anything to you?" Terrell said.

"Not at all. I'll assume that's the name of a case you're working on," Plante said.

Either Plante didn't know or he was a good liar.

"Where is he, Mr. Plante? I have three people who could really use that information right about now." Terrell asked.

The call was silent. Terrell counted to five before Plante spoke. "This wouldn't be the first time he's vanished without a trace for hours, but he always came back when the detail was told to bring him in. He might be the Secretary of State, but he trusts his security detail. And he trusts me."

Terrell wondered how Plante felt about that.

"Lucky for you."

Terrell knew Plante was right. It was Monahan's trust in Plante that made the investigation possible. "So where is he?" Terrell asked.

"I don't know. We sent a message out a few hours ago and we've heard nothing back. I don't mean that his security detail hasn't found him. We've lost all of them: Secretary of State Monahan, General Palma, and both security details."

57

ALMOST BOTTOM

Terrell, back on the eighth floor, thought his luck had turned. It hadn't. The heat in the building dried him up, but his pants stuck to his legs like a soggy second skin, and his underwear was soaked. He sat in a chair in the corner of the enormous room, bathing in the noise and energy. The good news: Looking at the inbox of his Bureau-supplied cell phone revealed a PDF that had arrived yesterday and somehow escaped his notice. The bad news: After reading it, the document might as well have been blank.

Maybe this is it. Maybe this is as bad as it can get.

If things had gone as bad as he thought then his moment was finally here. He wasn't making any headway in his investigation.

He had waited weeks for the file on PRUDENT RAINBOW to come in, and he hadn't noticed its arrival. Looking over his unread email brought it to the top and he thought for a second that maybe he'd gotten the break he was looking for. He didn't know what to expect, but like so many classified documents it would reveal only as much as he could dig out of it.

In this case, digging revealed nothing. The redacted file was useless. The part he cared about was the most purged: the actual facility location. He didn't need Anna to tell him New York housed the facility. That much he had discovered on his own. Was it in the tunnel where Anna had sent her last message or was that simply the last place where she had been able to send a text? Was this all just a ruse by Monahan or Palma? Something to throw the hounds off the scent? If so, what was the point?

PRUDENT RAINBOW became HALON. The paperwork didn't say that and it never would. Monahan had simply done what intelligence agencies had been doing for time immemorial: interpreting the law to get what they wanted. His goal in getting the PRURAIN paperwork was to find evidence that it even existed. A program of that scope wasn't something you physically tore down and rebuilt. It would get a new paint job and a new sign. Once he proved that, he could get the machine that was the United States government into high gear and do something about it.

What could they do? He would figure it out when he got there. He dialed his cell again.

"Mr. Plante? Please accept my apologies. This is Special Agent Garrison again."

"You do owe me an apology. I'm getting reports that a member of the FBI is trying to divert the search for Secretary Monahan and General Palma."

News travels fast. "Innuendo and rumor. If that were true, I would be trying to focus the search where I think it would do the most good." Terrell paced the corridor. "I don't like calling a source more than once every few days. It could raise flags in phone records, but given the emergency and the missing dignitaries..."

"What do you know?" Plante asked.

"I know that NYPD has tracked their SUVs to the Brooklyn Ventilation Station down by Montague and Furman. They want to send some men down there." Terrell wasn't sure how far he could take his story. He didn't know much more than that. "Should they?"

"What kind of joke is that? Of course, they should send them. Call me when you have more than something that trivial."

"I'm calling to make sure that we aren't putting any more lives in danger. Is there something you'd like to tell me?"

"What are you talking about?"

"I'm talking about PRUDENT RAINBOW. You remember PRUDENT RAINBOW." Terrell stopped pacing. "Don't you?"

Terrell heard Plante exhale. "Yes, I do. I had nothing to do with it, but I was part of the Senate Committee that investigated it."

"Not just part of it. You were part of Secretary Monahan's inner circle and you were the liaison to the committee. You had access to everything."

"I'm afraid you think my role is much more instrumental than it was. Secretary Monahan brought me in to liaise because I knew nothing. I saw only what I needed to see and nothing else."

"Where was PRURAIN located?" Silence. "Seriously, Mr. Plante, you know that the case against Secretary of State Monahan isn't going away. You don't even have immunity."

More silence. "If I tell you, you can't track it back to me."

Terrell waited as the seconds crawled by. He was grateful not to be in the same room with Plante, but he was going to need to see a dentist soon because of how much he gritted his teeth.

"PRUDENT RAINBOW had broken ground years before the investigation and NSA and the Agency had promised to take care of it."

"I guess they did."

"What you're not going to be happy to hear is that I don't know where it's located. If you're telling me it's somewhere in New York, that's news to me. If you think that Monahan and Palma are hiding out there then you might not have a prayer of finding them. There hasn't been any work done at that site in years."

I beg to differ.

———

Desperate times, desperate measures.

Terrell had gone directly to the one person he thought he would never find: the director of the FBI himself, Greg Harlan. Terrell searched office after office and ran into the tall, well-dressed man in the hallway surrounded by an entourage and hangers-on. Harlan sent them all away when Terrell mentioned the Secretary of State.

"I don't care what you've found. We can't spare anyone," Director Harlan said.

"Sir, if I'm right then both Secretary of State Monahan and Director Palma are in danger and we know where they are." Terrell had hoped for this break. Waited for it from the moment Anna appeared in New York.

"I'm not sure how to say this, but the tunnels in New York are all underwater. We have to wait until they are no longer underwater to examine them. We have over twenty agents working on finding them and we're not passing on any leads."

Terrell wasn't used to dealing with the director, but they had discussed sensitive cases before. Harlan always praised his results. "We just have to chase the ones we can chase given the present circumstances. Your lead is a long shot. Before I put anyone in harm's way, you need rock solid proof where they are."

Of course, the praise might have just been so much ass-kissing.

"Sir, please. I just need two or three people," Terrell said.

"To do what? Go swimming?" Harlan motioned around him. "There's a lot going on around here. We're sparing nothing in the search for them even as we're keeping a lid on it, but I can't help you, Terrell. I know you want to do the right thing, but for the next few hours, maybe next few days, there is nothing more anyone can do to make the search for them any easier or go any faster."

58

EMERGENCY EXIT

"Anna," Marshall said, "it's alright."

They all looked at the bloodstained, white-textured ceiling of the elevator.

Then the elevator started to fill with water from the ground up. The cold water engulfed her feet and began the journey up her legs. Anna felt Marshall grab her by the arm and lift her up.

"Take a deep breath!" Marshall yelled as they found themselves submerged once again.

The light in the elevator took on a darker hue. Anna's ears stopped up and her eyes hurt. The elevator came to a stop, but the door didn't open. The pad on the right side of the door behind them had a small, red LED blinking in the top right-hand corner.

They needed an access card.

Marshall took off his jacket and tore the lining. Marshall picked up a plastic card that had fallen out and held it against the pad.

Blink.

Red.

Blink.

Red.

Blink.

Green.

The doors slid open and the water spilled out. Anna pushed herself toward the door and fell out with the seven-foot wave of water. Marshall fell out next.

The floor was harder than she'd expected as she pushed against it to sit up. Were they in some kind of warehouse? *Memories of concrete.* Anna looked at Marshall, and Marshall returned the look. She had seen that look before. His eyes were older, his skin just a touch more wrinkled, but his eyes said *we won this round.* He also looked like a wet dog. They both swiveled their heads toward the direction from which they had poured out and saw Liko standing in the elevator. His hair was so short it might have been dry.

Anna said, "If all you're going to do is show off then you should take that back up." She stood. "By the way, that suit has seen better days."

"And so have you. The Anna I studied was an adept student of Tae Kwon Do. Have you forgotten about balance and grace?" Liko asked.

"Don't let her catch you on a bad day," Marshall said as he stood, too. "She'll show you what she knows about balance and grace." Marshall looked at her. "And leverage." He smiled.

Liko walked out of the elevator and the door closed behind him.

Anna leaned on some drenched boxes. "Where are we?"

Marshall wrung out his jacket and put it back on. "Technically? One hundred feet below the Montague Tubes."

"And?" she asked.

"And?" Marshall shook his arms, sending water droplets everywhere. "Welcome to HALON."

"Why was there blood dripping from the ceiling?"

Liko stepped forward and peered at her. "We killed someone who was on the roof of the compartment," he said.

This was too creepy. She shuddered. "Do you have to look at me like that?"

"I want to know what you think," Liko said.

"I think you're a psycho," she said. She crossed her arms. The shivering started as soon as the initial shock of landing on the floor ended. A massive tremor went through her. "This was a really bad idea."

"I tried to tell you that," Marshall said. He was doing a quick survey of the room.

It was big, but there was an inordinate amount of stuff in it. Boxes, metal shelves overflowing with other boxes, wires, and plastic bags. He spotted a broom and reached for it.

"But, noooo. 'I have to make Dad pay until the day he dies.' Which might be today." He poked hard at metal bubbles hanging from the ceiling. Cameras. He smashed the protective bubbles, then their lens, and pointed them in random directions.

"What are you doing?" Anna asked.

"Nothing. Whatever is in this room might come handy later and I prefer them blind."

"Did we really kill someone?" she asked.

Marshall's eyes again. They said, *It's fine* as he gave her a Mona Lisa smile. "No. I think the elevator might have been out of service, but no one bothered to disable it. Whoever is up there might have been doing maintenance and..."

Liko bent down again to look at Anna. "And then," he tightened both of his hands into fists.

Anna's stomach felt hollow and sandy. "Seriously, you should get some help," she said.

"We might get it sooner than we want." Marshall joined them after dragging over a chair from the far side of the room. "How many men did you count on the security monitor?"

"About ten," Liko answered.

"Okay, let's pretend that's the right answer," Marshall said.

"That is the right answer," Liko said.

"They can't afford to send them all after us," Marshall said. "In fact, they think the elevator isn't working or we would already have been captured and/or shot."

Anna was taken aback. She hadn't thought of that as she threw herself toward the doorway of the elevator. More men with guns.

Wasn't anyone ever going to be happy to see her? "They can't stay stupid for long," she said.

"No. They sent five of their guys to the emergency exit, which is ten stories of staircases leading to a parallel route through the tunnel and out into Brooklyn," Marshall said.

"That's not going to work," Anna said.

Marshall sighed, his shoulders dipped. "Okay, what am I missing?"

"Water. Millions of gallons of it that should have been pumped out of the tunnel, but apparently were not."

"You are very observant," Liko said.

She wanted to make a face at him but didn't want to get familiar. *Oh, screw it.* She made a face at him.

"How else can we get out of here?" Anna asked.

"You mean how else can you get out of here," Marshall said.

"Okay, I'll bite. How else can *I* get out of here?"

"The emergency exit."

"But you just said..."

"The emergency exit and this room are not in direct line of sight. If they don't already know we're here, they will any second now."

———

Main Security Room
30th floor

A light started to flash on the console. The Chinese soldier had been practicing with a version of this console for months. He knew it better than he knew the reasons why he was there.

He punched up the cameras that were signaling for help. They transmitted nothing. That was not possible. He had performed a systems test on the entire video network and with rare exception, everything worked. He decided to radio the men who were waiting by the only other way into the facility.

"Do you see anything?" he asked.

"No."

He could see the five armed men by the open entrance to the staircase. They were going to shoot whoever was unlucky enough to come through that door. In fact, there were cameras in the stairwell and they showed nothing. When they had come into the facility, they'd transmitted video that showed an empty staircase on all forty cameras.

Patience and endurance. The two most important qualities in a soldier. Your enemy would always succumb if you waited long enough.

He flipped to the camera just outside the room where the elevator was located. If he couldn't look inside the room perhaps he could look outside the room.

Water leaked out from under the door.

He radioed back to the men at the emergency exit. "They're in the maintenance room." He punched up the camera and saw the men rush away to their new location.

59

LEVERAGE

"Tell me what I need to know," Anna said. She wiggled her wet toes in the sopping mess of her sneakers. It felt squishy. The room smelled wet, like a moldy basement. Anna felt a low-level whistle, or vibration, in the air.

Marshall came over and she stood away from the stack of crates against which she had been leaning. He started drawing with his index finger in the dirt on top of one of the boxes.

"This is the full size of the floor," he said as he drew a large square. "The floor plan is not a square. In fact, it's an arbitrary polygon."

This is like old times, she thought.

Liko sighed. "Why are you talking to her like that?"

Anna glared at him. "Shut up."

Marshall pursed his lips and turned back to the drawing. "There are lots of right turns, but also lots of cameras. What you have to hope is that they haven't turned on the motion detectors which will have the cameras following you wherever you go. If they have, you're dead."

"They follow me, I'm dead," Anna said. "Got it."

"Just get to the emergency exit. They don't have that many people and they're not going to waste them covering all bases. There are only two ways out and they thought this one was disabled. That means that they're sending at least five guys over here and no one over there." He drew two squares in the larger square. "The corridors are like a Pac-Man game. You can travel up parallel corridors to get to the exit. If they spot you, you're dead."

"They spot me, I'm dead," Anna said. "What's Pac-Man?"

Marshall gripped the sides of the box, sighed, and returned to his dirt sketch. "Right. Here is the safest path to the exit. They've been studying the layout for weeks, maybe months so they know the shortest routes to everywhere. Take the longest route and you'll avoid them."

"What aren't you telling me?" Anna asked.

"What do you mean?" Marshall asked.

"Who are these people?"

"They," Marshall glanced at Liko, "are the Chinese. I think they got tired of looking at us from a distance and decided to move in. We owe them so much money I'm surprised they didn't just call in the loan."

"The loan?"

"That was supposed to be a joke. You know our trillion-dollar debt? The Chinese are one of a select group of countries we owe money to. Lots of money." Marshall gave a slight shake of his head. "This isn't about money."

"That doesn't tell me anything. What is this place? Why are they moving in? Why the hell is Benson helping them?"

"The less you know the better. You have to go," Marshall said.

"I can't help you if I don't know what they hell is going on," Anna said. She leaned towards him. "Do you think they'll kill me any less if I don't know anything? I'm under the Hudson River with a dead man and a stranger! What am I doing here?" Was it too late to kill Marshall anyway?

"Going to the emergency exit and running like hell. Ignorance is bliss," Marshall said.

"Ignorance kept me in the dark for years, and I hated you for it."

"You're a better person for it," Marshall said.

"I am not. Putting us all in danger is a stupid way of proving it."

"Damn it, Anna. You're the only person who can save us. Go get help," her father said.

Liko stepped over, turned her by the shoulders, and pushed her as he said, "Go. Listen to your..."

Before Liko finished his sentence, Anna spun around, clenched the lapels of his jacket, hit him in the legs with hers, and brought him crashing to the ground. "The next time you touch me, it had better be to kill me."

"Like I said," Marshall said over his shoulder as he walked away from them both, "leverage."

———

Marshall heard the door click shut as Anna left the maintenance room. He had given her one of the keycards so she could get the emergency exit door opened. *I am so proud of her. I wish I didn't feel like such a jerk.*

Liko pulled off his jacket, laid it on a box, and unsnapped the lining. There were various items attached to the inside of the jacket, though the Glock was what Marshall hoped for.

"That thing still going to work?" Marshall asked.

Liko open the shaped plastic that encased the weapon. He popped out the magazine, and gave the gun a cursory examination. "Yes, it will be fine." Liko put the gun in his holster. "Why are you wasting so much time sending her away?"

Marshall looked toward the door. "She already called for help. She just doesn't want to tell me." He put his jacket back on. It dripped down the sides of his pants. "If she can hide long enough to get away, maybe she'll live the rest of her life hating me, but she'll still live the rest of her life."

———

Anna ran. She thought she would have felt good about knocking Liko over, but all she felt was guilt.

She didn't like him. There was something off about him, but she was willing to defer to her father. For now. Her paranoia of her father's traveling companion ran deep.

She stopped at every turn and looked around the corner before proceeding, but her heart raced and she dripped with sweat. The white corridors reminded her of her hospital dream. Empty, white, antiseptic, and terrifying. The air was still and thick. Someone always followed her, though she didn't know who. Like a bad horror movie, she never saw them but still saw cutaways of them in her memory.

If they got out of this, she was going to stick Marshall with some really nasty therapy bills.

At one corner, when she finished checking for any stray killers, she looked back. She closed her eyes and tilted her head. *Puddles. Great. Could I be any more obvious?*

The five men stood at the doorway to the maintenance room. Anyone who tried coming out would be shot.

There was water everywhere. The soldier in security decided to make his way over as soon as he saw the water coming from the doorway. There was no need to monitor the room. There was only one way in and one way out.

They had their orders and they knew who was in the room. The American whose name was on the key card was already in the facility, which meant that the number of people it could be was minimal.

The lead took a keycard out of his pocket. He looked at the other four men, nodded his head, and swiped the card.

The lock snapped open with a loud crack. The lead turned the doorknob and ran into the room, closely followed by the team. The lead held his rifle at the ready while the other four took their positions, covering the room in case they were being setup.

Two men stood in the middle of the room. The floor glistened from the water that must have come from the elevator. Had they climbed down the shaft?

The men had their hands extended out to their sides, not over their heads.

One American.

One Chinese.

The lead yelled in Chinese. The American looked over at his companion then back at the men pointing their weapons at him. The lead wasn't happy to use his English. "Silence! Hands on your head!"

Both men swung their hands into position, and the American started to kneel.

"What are you doing?" the lead asked.

The American stopped and stood up. "Sorry, I thought you guys were professional."

60

BREADCRUMBS

"Yo, Abbott," Terrell said to the FBI agent sitting at one of the terminals. "How's it going?" Terrell shook the agent's beefy white hand.

Terrell didn't really know him—they had never gone out for beers or anything—but he recognized him from a brief stint Terrell had spent on a case that Abbott had been on, though Terrell couldn't remember which one.

"How's it going?" Terrell smiled, but not too much. He didn't want to overplay it.

"Hey!" Agent Abbott said. The large man had hair that was too long for his face and a smile that could charm the ladies. His tie was loose and his shirt looked half a size too small.

Terrell was sure Abbott didn't recognize him, but he also knew he would be polite. He was always polite. "Wow, so you survived the case from hell," Abbott said.

Terrell now remembered. It was a boring, open and shut case that involved more people than it was worth due to the nature of the purported victim (a high-ranking member of the Senate Armed Forces Committee and a young woman from Russia) and the alleged crime.

He hated to think what a real divorce would be like.

"Listen." Terrell pulled out the chair next to Abbott so he could sit down and conspire. "I understand you guys are looking for somebody no one is supposed to know about yet."

Abbott's eyes opened just enough to let Terrell know that even other agents weren't allowed to know what was going on.

"Terrell, seriously, I don't know what you're talking about." Abbott hit a couple of keys and the screen went blank. "We're all here to help out during Sandy. What do they have you doing?"

"I took myself off rotation," Terrell said. He leaned in for a moment. "I'm looking for him too." Terrell stood up. "But I don't know anything more than you guys do." He relaxed his jaw. "But if I was looking for two high-ranking government officials in the middle of a hurricane, I mean a kick-ass Frankenstorm," he looked around the room giving his best I-don't-give-a-damn imitation, "I might try looking near the Brooklyn Ventilation Building on Montague Street." He shrugged. "But that's just me." If Anna was where AT&T said she was, and the two men responsible for HALON had disappeared, and Terrell didn't remember seeing any black SUVs except for his own on Whitehall, he assumed there was only one more way into the tunnel.

———

A few minutes later, all hell broke loose on the eighth floor. It started with Abbott calling another agent over and showing him some Brooklyn street cam photos. It ended when FBI Director Harlan walked into the room. With his perfect hair, he should have stayed working in DC as the local police commissioner.

"All agents working on the special project report to the ready room," Harlan said.

Terrell hadn't believed the rumors that Harlan liked to be hands-on in certain cases, but this looked hands-on to him. Terrell followed everyone into one of the few conference rooms that was still available given the massive coordination effort between governmental services.

This is going to be interesting.

It was standing room only in the conference room. Harlan stood before a 60" LCD monitor attached to the wall. In all its blurry glory was a dark photo of an SUV peeking out from behind a building.

"At approximately 9:45 this evening, Special Agent Abbot Werren found the cars we've been looking for. Two black SUVs, DC license plates 2121-4 and 3271-138, assigned to Secretary of State Monahan and NSA Director Palma, were found by traffic cams located to the sides of the MTA Ventilation Building on Montague and Furman in Brooklyn. Having the license plates made a difference, but Agent Werren thought to follow up on a tip he had received and it paid off.

"Now we have a problem."

———

Terrell stood off to the side and watched as five agents left to get into the most secure vehicles they could find and head to the Ventilation Building. Terrell had spoken with Abbott, then they both spoke to Harlan.

———

"Agent Garrison, I know how much you want to be involved in this," Harlan said, "but I need you here. Special Agent Werren, I need to speak with Terrell for a moment."

Abbott walked away, and Terrell knew he was relieved.

"Terrell, this is not a punishment." In his spotless suit, Harlan headed back to the computer area. "Your involvement in the case against Monahan means I need you here because the other agents are out in the field and you know it better than anyone." He stepped in front of Terrell. "I know when I screw up and you just proved I screwed up. Don't let me screw up again." He put out his hand and Terrell shook it.

"But, sir," Terrell said.

"Remember this is all under wraps. That means both Indigo," the case name for the investigation against Monahan, "and this."

————

I am a damn third wheel again.

Terrell pulled out his phone for a peek at a Lower Manhattan map. A lot of it was going to be underwater or close enough to underwater that travel was going to be impossible. The men going to Brooklyn were wasting their time. They could see from the photo that one of the side doors of the ventilation building was open. Someone might have unlocked the door or the door might have been unlocked to begin with, and blown open by the kind of gusts that allowed cows to fly.

This wasn't going to work. Terrell needed something with a bit more firepower. Better enabling technology. He needed to talk to the folks over at the Office of Emergency Management.

When he walked into the main conference room down on the fourth floor, he put himself on his best behavior: he smiled, he shook hands with many of the people, both men and women, who he recognized from the many law enforcement events he preferred to ignore, but attended anyway. Everyone was somber; things were holding together, but there were reports: a multi-story building in Chelsea lost its entire front face. NYU hospital lost power even after they had confirmed the back-up generators worked. Patients had been evacuated.

The tired men and women coordinating the efforts to keep the city safe and calm were holding up as well as the city.

And then Terrell saw the woman of his dreams.

"Cynthia," Terrell said, extending his hand.

The tall, black woman shook it and smiled. "It's good to see you, Terrell. What trouble are you causing?"

He smiled. "None yet, but I need some help."

"You're not going to make me take you to dinner again, are you?"

Terrell's smile widened. *Thank goodness she doesn't hold a grudge.*

"That was about five years ago, and you lost the bet. That was not my fault."

"Said like the experienced con artist that you are." She hugged the clipboard she had been holding in her left hand. "What do you need?"

61

SEARCHING FOR RESCUE

FBI Director Greg Harlan sauntered over to Terrell. "Don't think I don't know what you did. Werren gave you up in a second."

Terrell felt like he and Harlan, surrounded by a mad crush of people, were alone even as the environment around him proved otherwise. The mark of all good listeners. Terrell hoped to be that good one day. Was he now in trouble for being the source of the tip that allowed them to find the SUVs belonging to Palma and Monahan?

"I don't mind giving away the credit if we can save a few lives," Terrell said. Nonetheless, this glad-handing drove him crazy. He'd managed to accomplish quite a bit in the last thirty minutes or so, but he had much more to do. If his luck held up, he might be able to get a search-and-rescue team together, though he had no idea how he was going to do that. Finding them, and then figuring out how to get them into a location where there was nowhere to go, was going to be a challenge.

"I know how much your cases mean to you. I've seen you execute before." Harlan put his hand in his pocket. "Let me know if there's anything else you intend to do before you get anyone into trouble."

"Yes, sir." A thought crossed Terrell's mind. "Any chance I can join the team on their way to Brooklyn?" Why couldn't he get Anna out of his mind?

"Hell, yes," Harlan said. He pointed his chin toward the others around them. "Make all these people proud."

At that Terrell walked down the corridor while Director Harlan marched over to one of the OEM directors who had motioned him over.

With great power comes great ass-kissing.

Terrell wondered how he would be one day if he found himself in that position. Perhaps he would find out. There were plenty of things he wanted to do over the next twenty years.

But first, tonight.

A young man, who looked fresh out of college, waved at him. He wore dark slacks and a knitted sweater over a white shirt. *Yeah, probably from Yale.*

"What's going on?" Terrell asked.

The young man held a cell phone up to his ear and pursed his lips.

"We're not getting any response from the team heading into Brooklyn. I was told you wanted to check in with them and I think the cell towers aren't cooperating."

Communication was disintegrating. It was going to be pointless to send a team to the Ventilation Building because they weren't going to have the equipment to head into the tunnel. If he couldn't coordinate with them anyway, they were going to sit in their cars all night while Anna needed help.

Anna needed his help.

What he needed were resources that knew what to do in a situation like this. Resources with the right tools. He had been planting seeds since he got to 1 PP. Something had to give.

"Keep trying. They're not going to be able to do much anyway."

"Special Agent Garrison!" The director waved him over. "I think I've just found you a new goal."

"You have?" Terrell asked. *I needed a new goal?*

Harlan nodded. "The Chinese Embassy just called. It appears

they've lost some staff in the storm and wanted us to assist in finding them. I think we already have enough people working on your find of the night."

"The Chinese Embassy?" Terrell asked. His eyes opened wide. His chest felt hot and anxiety began a slow creep up his arms. *Are they serious?*

"Yes, I'm sure you remember them. Population over a billion. Manufactures everything we buy. We owe them lots of money."

Terrell wasn't sure he liked where this was going. "But, sir, who are they looking for?"

"They've lost about ten people who were supposed to have returned after an early evening walk. They aren't sure what's going on, but they wanted us to know," Harlan said.

"So, we know. Now what?" Terrell asked.

"Pay them a visit. Find out what's going on. Maybe you'll see a group of ten Asians and give them a ride back."

"Sir, this is not where I should be going."

"Of anyone here, you are the most qualified to talk to them. They've already called State, and State told them to call us."

Great. Now I have to babysit the Chinese? He would find someone to help with this, and coordinate the rescue from his car. He didn't want to disobey the director, but Terrell wasn't in love with his new temporary assignment. Anything that wasn't solving his problem was making it worse.

———

Terrell sat in the dry, black SUV that would normally be used for dignitaries. Unless he kept things under his control, everything was going to go to hell with no possibility of making it back. He pulled out of the covered parking spot in 1 Police Plaza and knew he was doing the wrong thing.

The Chinese were a red herring. Somehow, he had to get out of visiting them or at least wait until he had sent someone out to save Anna.

He put the black police SUV into gear and turned on the flashing lights to identify him from a distance. Where the hell was he? He was going to have to get out of Chinatown first.

His cell buzzed. "Garrison."

"Terrell, this is Cynthia." He had a flash of a memory of her at dinner with him and felt warmer from it. "I think I have something for you."

"You have my attention." He turned on the AC to dry the air and lower the temperature. Unfortunately, the noise from the vents changed the audio characteristics of the phone so he couldn't hear her. He turned the AC off. He hoped he wouldn't freeze in his own clothes.

"First, no one is going to hand you personnel. There's too much going on. The one thing we know is that we'll run out of people long before we run out of things to do."

"Your point? And, by the way, this is not encouraging," Terrell said.

"Follow along, Special Agent. Follow along," Cynthia said. "I was looking over the list of state and federal agencies that have a presence here. Specifically, Lower Manhattan."

Terrell remained silent. He was getting quite a bit of practice on listening today. Maybe someone would finally tell him something he could use.

"There's a group of military personnel at City Hall. I think you should talk to them."

"What makes them any different than everyone else who's already said no?"

"I gave them a call. They said they were waiting for special orders. That means they're not doing anything. You have two rather important people missing. Maybe it's time you paid the cavalry a visit."

62

---

3 > 5

Anna's distance to the emergency exit shrank. She knew she was close because there was a white sign with red lettering pointing to a door that said 'Emergency Exit'.

She smiled. *I am good.* The card reader, a gray plastic pad with rounded corners and a red LED light in the corner, was by the door-knob where she expected it to be. She reached into her pocket to get the keycard and looked up at the dark bubble of plastic protruding from the ceiling. If they were monitoring the halls then her capture would be soon after she entered the stairwell. Worse, there might be someone waiting in the stairwell for her.

She peered around the corner. Empty. The smooth white door to her right was there for the taking. She stepped forward and just as she was about to swipe, a thought flashed. *He's not sending me to get help. He's getting rid of me.*

Anna clutched the card and caught herself before she let out a sound of frustration. The tunnel above them was flooded. There was no way she could leave, which meant that Marshall knew she would hide until she could escape. And how the hell would she know that it was time to escape? She tilted her head back and closed her eyes. *I'm going to kill that man.* She looked down the hallway where she had just been. The men who'd been at the exit were now at the other end capturing Marshall and Liko. *Hello, no.* She felt her eyes focus on her surroundings. Anna's stomach clenched for a second as she chose her new direction.

How could she save them? Or at least keep them from being captured. Marshall said they wouldn't send more than five men.

She could handle that. Well, maybe two at a time.

Maybe one?

She ran down the corridor where she had just come from, slipped on some of the water she'd trailed behind her, and landed on her arms which she tucked in front of her as she fell. She looked down the next hallway. It was empty.

Maybe I need to rethink my strategy.

———

Running was now out of the question, but walking as fast as she could turned out to be useful. Why did Marshall send her down the longest hallway? He was right that she didn't meet anyone along the way, but she couldn't get back fast enough. He knew it was supposed to be a one-way trip.

She hugged the walls again and did her best to look down the corridors without making too much noise. Nothing. Down another corridor.

Stop, breathe, look, go.

Stop, breathe, look, go.

There was the door she had exited. The ground was muddy. She couldn't tell if an army had been there or just Marshall, Liko, and one other person with a gun. Couldn't be just one person with a gun. Marshall or Liko would have taken them out. That's what she would have done and they had a lot more experience with this than she did.

How did a man like her father have any experience with this?

———

"You know, I spent a lot of years commuting to this place," Marshall said.

He had been talking almost non-stop since their capture. Two armed men walked in front of them, a single guard with his rifle pointed at them both from behind, and two more men behind him. An interesting cage.

A loud bang came from behind them. Everyone stopped and the two men behind them ran off around the corner. Liko muttered something in Chinese.

"What did you say?" Marshall asked.

"I said, 'You have a very disobedient little girl.'"

He smiled even as his stomach squeezed. *Why can't you just do what I tell you?*

One of the men went flying toward the wall, bounced off it, and ran back around the corner. Gunfire exploded.

Silence.

Don't call out, Marshall told himself. *Don't. Call. Out.*

The single guard ran toward the intersection. He stopped at the corner and pressed himself against the wall. He yelled out a command to the remaining men who pointed their weapons at Marshall and Liko.

Before the guard turned his head back, Marshall saw an arm reach around the corner, grab the man's weapon, and pull him and the rifle around the corner like a rag doll. Marshall took a step forward and the man behind him pushed his gun barrel into Marshall's shoulder and yelled something unintelligible.

Two guards left.

He and Liko were left. "These guys know English, don't they?" Marshall asked of no one in particular.

"Why?" Liko asked.

Marshall faced the guard. "Kill me."

"What are you doing?" Liko said.

Marshall pushed his chest into the gun barrel. "Kill me." He took a step toward the man. "Kill me." Another step. The man had the wall behind him. "KILL ME!"

Liko snatched the rifle of the man behind him, pointed it away from him, and slammed the rifle butt into the man's chin. The man standing before Marshall aimed his weapon at Liko and said something Marshall didn't understand.

Marshall put his hand over the man's face, pointed the gun upward, and slammed the man's head into the wall. He collapsed without a second movement.

Marshall knelt and felt for a pulse. "They'll live. We need to lock them up."

Liko looked down the corridor where Anna had been.

Marshall could hear his own breathing. "Anna?"

"Dad?" She stuck her head around the corner, took a quick perusal at the scene, and ran over to them.

It was all Marshall could do to keep from grinning ear to ear.

———

Anna pushed Marshall against the wall. "What the hell was that about? How could you send me away? And how could I be stupid enough to believe you?" She sneered. "'You have to save us. Go to the emergency stairwell. They'll never find you.' Yeah, until I climb ten flights of stairs, open a door, and let Niagara Falls in. What is wrong with you? Do you think I'm that stupid?"

Liko leaned in over her shoulder. "It would seem that you are."

She pushed her shoulder into Liko's chest.

"Stop. Both of you," Marshall said. "Thank you for saving us."

Anna glared at him. "I want a gun."

"I don't have one," Marshall said.

Liko reached behind his jacket and pulled out the dry Glock. He grabbed the barrel and extended the grip for her to take. "Sixteen rounds is all you get. Don't waste them."

The magazine stuck out from the grip about two inches. Anna always liked the longer clips. It helped her balance her shots better. "Why are we here?" she asked Marshall.

"Actually, the question is why are we still at this particular spot.

They've seen the destruction we just perpetrated on their guys. There are more people coming and they won't be so easy to fool." Marshall pointed down the hall. "Let's go that way. There's an elevator to one of the lower floors. I think there are some people waiting for us."

Liko jogged away from them.

Anna grabbed Marshall by the shoulder and spun him around. "Don't ever do that again." She felt her eyes water and blinked the feeling away.

"I promise," he said.

"The elevator's over here," Liko said.

63

SKELETON CREW

"Why aren't we locking up those other guys? At least cuff them. And who's waiting for us?" Anna asked as she and Marshall jogged in Liko's direction.

"The people who weren't killed," Marshall said.

"My head is going to explode. Are you ever going to tell me what's going on?" she asked.

"From the looks of it," Marshall said as he and Anna caught up with Liko, "no." Liko extended his hand to Marshall, who gave him a keycard. "Why don't you ask me a question and I'll see if I can answer it."

The display above the elevator doorway read "1".

"Are we really on the thirtieth floor?"

"Yes," Marshall grinned. "You see. You can ask me questions I can answer."

"Who are the people who weren't killed? Don't we fit in that category?" she asked.

The display read "10" and changed quickly.

"I know one of the guys who works here. I told him that something might happen and where he and his people should hide if it did."

Liko raised an eyebrow at Marshall.

"Yes, Liko-san. Someone had to save them." Marshall glanced away and then stared at Liko. "Sorry. I should have told you, but I couldn't wait once we knew the facility was breached."

"As you say here, live how you want to live," Liko said.

Anna was confused. Did her father just call and tell them to hide? "That makes no sense. I mean, it's good that you did that, but how did you do that?"

Again, Marshall looked at Liko before answering. "I sent him a text message."

"What?" Who was this man? This could not be her father. He had never been this altruistic.

The elevator door opened. The compartment was empty. "I sent him a text message. I set up a secure line with him that he thought was from someone else."

"Someone else?" Anna asked as they entered the elevator.

"His brother. He thought he had a secret line out to his brother and really it was my secret line to him." He leaned back against the wall. "Long story."

"What are we doing here?"

"What floor?" Liko asked.

Marshall hesitated. "Seventeen." She saw him reach for her hand and think better of it. "I'm going to need you to protect them. Once we get there you're going to be their last line of defense." The elevator started its descent. "Liko and I will take care of the guards. You have to take care of whoever comes in who isn't us.

"We left the first wave of pain on the floor. When they wake up, they aren't going to be happy.

"I hadn't counted on them showing up so fast," Marshall said.

———

The door opened on the seventeenth floor. The elevator looked empty. Liko stuck his hand over the gap in the door to keep it open and stuck his head out. After looking both ways, he said, "Clear."

The three of them came out with Marshall in the lead. "You know," he whispered, "once you move them you'll be safe too." The seventeenth floor looked more like a hospital ward compared to the thirtieth floor's antiseptic warehouse look. That was something Marshall had done his best to do as well. Make every floor look different than the others. It would keep everyone focused on where they were and what they should be doing.

"I'm not hiding," Anna said.

In the distance, they spied something on the ground. As they got closer they saw that it was a dead body in a lab coat.

The body was in a pool of dried blood. Marshall knelt and felt the man's neck for a pulse. Marshall bowed his head. "He's dead."

"Yeah, didn't see that coming. And they killed him just because?" Anna asked.

Marshall put his palm against his forehead. "He died protecting the others." He rubbed his head. "They could have just held him and traded him or something. This wasn't necessary." Marshall looked over at Liko. "They probably found him after he'd sealed off the room. He knew where they were and I bet they didn't even ask."

Liko was silent.

"The others are here?" Anna asked.

Marshall stood up.

The pieces are in play. I just need to keep everyone calm.

"Help me with this." He walked over to the side of the station where it met the wall. The oversized, curved desk had a faux wood-grain finish but was otherwise empty. No papers, no litter. Marshall popped open three small covers embedded in the wall and opened the latches hidden beneath them. He motioned to Anna, who went to the other side of the station and did the same thing.

"Help me with this," he told her.

He pushed against the station desk, moving it forward. Anna mimicked his movement and the desk slid forward, bringing part of the wall along with it.

That tech must have just closed this when they found him. He knew they would kill him.

Liko pulled the desk from the front. When the wall opened enough to let someone slide in, Marshall motioned to Anna and Liko to step back.

He leaned against the wall to the right of the gap. "It's okay. We know you're in there and we're here to help." There was no sound coming out of room behind the wall. "If you have any weapons, just don't shoot. Is Dr. Jenkins there?"

A voice came from the dark. "Yes, I'm here."

"May we come in?"

Hesitation and then, "Yes."

———

Anna thought Dr. Jenkins was taller than his voice. He was also no better at working with Marshall than she was. Anna, Marshall, and Liko stood with their backs to the light streaming in from the corridor and the others, many still in their lab coats, stood around Jenkins waiting for instructions in the darkened room. There were about a dozen of them.

"Long story, but it's not safe here anymore. You need a new location and you can't leave the facility. The subway tunnel is flooded through and through," Marshall said.

"That's not possible."

"No one is leaving here unless you can hold your breath for twenty minutes and live through hypothermia," Anna said.

"Then we stay here," Jenkins said.

An Indian woman was standing off to his left. "Dr. Jenkins, with all due respect I would rather be moved." Jenkins looked like he was about to object. "This is the gentleman who told us where to hide. I think he knows how to keep us alive."

———

Marshall took Anna to the side as Jenkins and his people discussed their next move. Anna could care less what they decided. She wasn't going to leave Marshall alone anymore. She knew that the only way she was going to get the answers she wanted, no, needed, was to keep him alive long enough to ask.

"Honey, I am going to tell you where you can find five different spots to hole up with these people. With that magazine, you can take everyone out if you need to, but fire judiciously. You get sixteen tries to take out about twelve people."

"I'm not leaving you."

"I need you to do this. This is not a trick. These people need you. I need you to do this. As a personal favor. For your mother. Whatever will make you take these people from here and keep them safe."

Anna had never seen this imploring look in her father's eyes before. He was trying to deal with keeping her safe, and keeping the others safe, and she would have none of it. If Marshall was up to his neck in something, she wanted to be there as well.

"And only you will know where you're going so that neither of us can tell them where you are," Marshall said.

She stepped away from Marshall. "Liko-san. These people are now your concern. Take them some place safe and don't tell either of us where you are going. Would you like my gun?"

64

COMING OUT

Anna held her gun out toward Liko so he could grab the grip, but Marshall put his hand on it and moved the gun down.

"I won't need that," Liko said.

"No, you won't," Marshall said.

For some reason, he didn't take his eyes off Liko. Whatever hidden past they had together, Anna could see the conflict between them clearer than she had before.

Liko turned to Jenkins. "Get your people together. I know this place almost as well as Marshall."

"Yeah, you do. Only you're not taking them," Marshall said.

"Well, I'm not taking them," Anna said. Liko and Marshall didn't move. "Am I?"

"Yes, you are," Marshall said. "Take them to one of the five spots I told you about and stay with them until I get there."

"Okay." Anna felt a hot tingling race up her back.

He didn't tell me any of the 5 spots. Why does this feel like the OK corral?

"The time for that is past," Liko said. "You two are a risk to everything and everyone." He pulled out his gun, but kept it aimed at the floor.

In the partial dark, it was hard for Anna to see everyone, but you could hear a pin drop.

"If I let you take them, do you promise not to harm them?" Marshall asked.

"Wait a minute," Jenkins said.

"You're not in charge." Liko raised his gun and shot a young man who was to Jenkins' left. His face went from surprise to empty as he fell to the ground.

"No one move," Liko said.

Anna flipped her gun so she was now holding it barrel out. As she was about to fire she realized that Liko was already aiming at her.

"Put it down," Liko said.

Damn it! Why didn't I see this? Dad already knew!

"You're going to kill us anyway," Anna said.

"No, I need you, Marshall, and Jenkins. The others should have been evacuated days ago, but they stayed. American work ethic."

Marshall put his hands up. He reached over and put his hand over Anna's gun. He took it from her and aimed it at his own temple. "If you shoot another person, I will shoot myself and whatever it is you thought I was going to do for you will be all over." Without taking his eyes off of Liko he said, "You were right, Anna. I was being used. Liko doesn't want to help me stop HALON. He wants me to help hand it over."

Anna thought of yanking the gun away, but Marshall might pull the trigger by accident.

"Kill another person and I'll kill myself." He took a step toward Liko. "You know how I play."

"Dad," Anna said. "What are you doing?"

"Do we have a deal?"

Liko took a long look at both Marshall and Anna. "Yes."

Anna's hands were trembling. *Please don't do this...*

"Leave these people here. Promise me that nothing will happen to them."

Liko did not move. It looked as if he wasn't breathing. "Agreed. Let's go," Liko said. "Dr. Jenkins, come with us."

"Dad?"

"It's okay, Squirrel." He aimed the gun away from his head and toward the floor. "No one else dies today." He lowered his voice. "At least not until I decide."

Liko said nothing.

Anna's eyes watered, both in anger and frustration. "Don't call me Squirrel."

Marshall moved the gun to his left hand, reached over with his right, and squeezed her hand.

———

Anna and Marshall resealed the room. She couldn't help but look at her father. If he knew he was being used why did he lead Liko here? How stupid could he be?

She thought of the different ways that taking down Liko could turn out. None looked good. It took some doing, but she calmed herself. She knew she thought best under pressure, but not too much pressure. She would continue thinking. Sometimes a good plan took time.

Marshall walked over to Jenkins. "Doctor, I apologize. I thought you would be safer."

Jenkins looked old in the harsh lights of the corridor. The corpse lay on the ground and he'd paid his respects when he'd first come out. He sidestepped the blood, but it couldn't be helped as he walked closer.

Marshall gazed at Jenkin's face. "Did you know him well?"

"He was a lousy lab tech. I wanted to fire him twice and was over-ruled." Jenkins turned toward Liko. "I should have gotten rid of him."

Anna saw Jenkins lead the way with Liko. *If he survives this he's going to need a lot of therapy.* She whispered to Marshall, "Do you know any other hiding places?"

"Why?"

"He's not going to kill Dr. Jenkins." Anna's eyes scrutinized the area around them. "We just have to vanish."

Marshall nodded in agreement.

———

Liko heard silence for a few seconds longer than he expected. "Marshall?"

Jenkins stayed in position.

Liko started to yell, "Marshall!" He pointed his gun at Jenkins. "Go back to where we came from."

"What do you think we'll find?" Jenkins asked.

"Go!" Liko walked behind Jenkins as they retraced their steps. "Marshall! If you don't come out, I'm going to shoot into the room and start killing whoever is unlucky enough to be in my line of sight."

Nothing.

Liko yelled Marshall's name again. He aimed at the wall of the reception desk as Jenkins took a step back and grimaced.

"Don't do it."

Liko pointed the gun at his head.

Jenkins turned his head away as he closed his eyes. "The walls are steel-reinforced concrete. Your bullet won't go through. In fact, it might kill one of us if it ricochets."

"If you move, I will shoot you in the back."

Jenkins straightened up, but only enough to show that he understood.

Liko went to the wall and popped the covers off the latches. The latches were a series of interlocking pieces. How had Marshall unlocked the door? Another of his puzzles?

Liko took a deep breath. Marshall was already one step ahead. In a few minutes, he would be many steps ahead and Liko wouldn't be able to stop him. Liko had to raise the stakes or risk losing HALON before they had even begun.

"Help me get this open."

65

NIGHT MOVES

Terrell found the truck parked out front of City Hall on the Park Row side. The driver rolled down his window as Terrell approached. "I need to talk to your commanding officer," Terrell said.

The cab, separated from the cargo hold by a few inches, held the two parts together with industrial-strength grappling running underneath. An unending stream of water drained from the roof and coated the outside of the container in the truck bed as Sandy shook the vehicle back and forth.

Terrell had already received all the bad news he could bear. The team that had gone to Brooklyn was stuck. They couldn't get as far as Montague and Furman and were going to have to either return, which was fraught with its own level of risk, or stay where they were and pray nothing fell on them.

He hadn't given them much hope, and he was not disappointed.

Standing in front of the truck as he waited for the driver to roll down his window, Terrell knew the night had just started. He didn't think it was possible, but the wind was picking up. *I'm going to get blown away soon.*

The driver opened the door and jumped down. "Identification, sir."

Terrell was a tall man. The driver was a head taller, with hair too short to get in his eyes.

"If I pull out my wallet, it will be the last time I see it ever again. Could we get inside?" Terrell asked. His shoulders, hunched as he tried to cover what little of his chest he could, protected too little of him. Soaked through again, he would probably end up with pneumonia.

"Not without identification." The man didn't appear to notice the wind and rain. He stood frozen solid in front of Terrell.

Terrell reached into his pocket and holding his wallet as close to his chest as he could, he pulled out his FBI ID and held it out to the driver. The card disappeared into an appendage Terrell assumed was his hand and waited while he examined it.

The man handed the card back to Terrell. "Come with me," he said.

The card blew out of Terrell's hand. He sighed and cursed. *I liked that card.* And then he thought, *How am I going to get around?*

Back in the cargo hold, rocking as the storm buffeted it, Terrell sat with a cadre of men who were all dry. They were in uniform and sat along both walls. Ten men sitting up as straight as solid blocks of granite. They looked at him as if he had just gotten out of the shower. He felt that way, as well.

"We've got intel that's told us everything we need. Can you help?" Terrell asked.

"I'm sorry, sir, but our orders are to wait here. If Secretary Monahan and General Palma are missing then people are already looking for them," the commander said.

"I understand, Commander, but the help we need isn't getting here anytime soon and we need you to step up," Terrell said.

"I'm sorry, sir. We take our orders from the Navy and DOD. Any paperwork you had from them would force us to follow you anywhere you wanted. Without it, you're just a visitor who might have to leave at a moment's notice."

The Navy. Who do I know in the Navy?

"Alright, Commander," Terrell said. He reached out and they shook hands again. "You win. Who in the Navy should I talk to? This storm is squeezing every last ounce of patience from me, but I want you on my side, not fighting me." He watched the storm swirl around them. He'd lived through worse.

Well, maybe not worse.

"Commander," Terrell said, "it's like my momma used to say. She used to say, 'Terrell...'"

The Commander interrupted. "Excuse me, sir. When you introduced yourself, you didn't give a name. You just said you were with the Bureau and you had lost your ID card."

"That's right. The welcoming committee out front handed it back to me and it made a hasty escape." He extended his hand out again. "Terrell Garrison, FBI."

The commander smiled at him and shook his hand. "Special Agent Terrell Garrison. If only you'd said so before. We've been waiting for you."

LIVE, IN HIGH-DEFINITION

"Great," Anna whispered. "If we stay here, he gets to find us by taking the place apart. If we leave, they'll shoot us on sight."

Anna followed Marshall into a large crowded storage anteroom that led into a larger warehouse area, or so Marshall had told her.

"This was your idea. I was happy to follow Liko-san back to whoever is running this," Marshall said.

"Not Benson?" Anna asked.

"Probably. But you have to stop calling him Benson. His name is..."

"I don't care what his name is." Anna was still holding the gun and waved it around like a pencil or a baton. "He did this to me because he did this to you. I'm tired of this. I'm holding a gun again. I'm probably going to kill someone again. It's not fair."

Anna paced in the enormous room while Marshall leaned against the wall watching her. She put the gun down on one of metal shelves that lined the flat white walls. "You were supposed to stop me from doing something stupid."

"I tried sending you away," Marshall said.

"You can't stop me from doing something stupid if you're not there." She leaned against the door that led into the room. "I almost killed some guy who looked like you after he was in a car accident, and his daughter was there, and she looked like me when I was little, and his wife," she closed her eyes and covered her face with her hands, "His wife looked like mom." She stood not moving. "She looked like mom." She needed Marshall to come to her. If he hugged her that meant he knew he'd screwed up.

Marshall pushed away from the wall but didn't approach. "I've seen you growing up and it's hurt me beyond my wildest imagination not to be there."

"Don't."

"One day..."

"Stop."

"One day you'll have your own little girl or little boy and the only thing you'll be able to think of is how much they mean to you, and how little value you bring to the relationship. They don't need you."

"I needed you."

"You didn't need me."

"I needed you!"

His eyes watered but not enough to shed a tear. "You did fine without me. The family you were with needed you. I needed you, but not as much as you needed to be without the trouble that chased me everywhere I went." Marshall took a step forward. "I missed my girl. I missed my Squirrel."

Anna's face felt hot from the blood that rushed to her forehead and cheeks. The soreness of her shoulders and chest combined with exhaustion...

Until the air changed. Anna picked up the Glock and pulled the chamber back.

"Are you going to shoot me?" Marshall asked.

She unfocused her gaze and focused on her hearing. "Someone's coming."

————

Three men stepped out from behind one of the many rows of metal shelves. Their rifles were at the ready and they approached Marshall, who now stood at a different location than he and Anna had a few minutes earlier.

He was alone and had his hands up.

"I give up," Marshall said. "Don't shoot." The jacket felt awkward on his torso, but he wanted to make sure they didn't think he was threatening. "Oh," he motioned to their weapons with his head, "QBZ-95 assault rifles. Wait. That's a QBZ-95-1. Nice. Better primer. Non-corrosive. Steel core bullets with copper alloy jackets."

"Be quiet," the tallest of the three men said. "Where is the girl?"

"The girl? She would be insulted to be referred to as a girl." He lowered his arms a little. Days like this he felt his age. He wasn't going to be able to do this for much longer. "She's a young woman. You should remember that. Especially when," he put his arms down, "especially when she kicks your ass."

The three men formed a triangle and pointed outward with the rifles.

Marshall put his arms back up. "Guys, relax. She's not here."

Go. They won't kill me. I'm not so sure about you.

Anna hated when her dad made sense and hated herself even more for listening to him. She could see the men from a distance because she could see across the entire length of the warehouse-sized room. She was lying down on the top shelf of a middle row and aimed her Glock at the middle man who held his rifle up at Marshall. The problem was that the bullet would go through the man's head and hit Marshall in the shoulder or chest. Since there was the very real possibility that she would pierce a main artery, thereby causing him to bleed out, she decided to wait.

The one thing they want, the one person they want, is me, he told her

Why?

I infected their system about a year ago. They still don't know how to get rid of it, but every time they try to use the system my agents crush

another part of it. The only parts I haven't touched have been the genetics, nuclear physics, and artificial intelligence sections.

She wasn't sure what she was lying on top of, but she knew she didn't want to stay there long. It could have been a container for a deadly disease, radioactive materials, or parts of Arnold Schwarzenegger. Whatever was in this warehouse was just the tip of the iceberg.

———

Liko met Marshall just outside the warehouse-sized room. "I don't know how you got in there, but if you don't ask your daughter to come out, I will set fire to the room and wait here while the room fills with smoke."

Marshall, with his hands up as high as his waist, leaned toward Liko. "You know, I would do exactly the same thing. Something smells really bad in there." He touched his index finger to his cheek. "The ventilation system isn't working because the tunnel is filled with water and the smoke would start to fill the floors above this and everyone would die from carbon monoxide poisoning." He crossed his arms. "You're right. You should set fire to it."

———

Marshall knew exactly where they were taking him. He had lived through too many interminable meetings to forget. Everyone stupid and naïve, including him.

Marshall, the three armed guards, and Liko entered a large conference area. A man stood alone with his back to them. Liko pushed Marshall forward.

Marshall said, "You know, you have to like the architecture of a place like this. Solid rebar-reinforced concrete, wood and plaster-board in others, metal walls in others. Refrigeration units, radiation hardened rooms with the appropriate number of sharp right turns..."

The man hit a series of buttons on the console before him. The monitors displayed a video feed of the front of the room. "You could have been one of the chosen ones, Marshall. Instead you decided to play chess and now look at you." The man turned around.

It was Palma. "You destroyed Garth's life, your daughter's life," he waved Liko to bring Marshall closer, "my life. You don't actually care about your life." He pressed a few more buttons. "That turns on the monitors on all the floors." He tilted his head.

Marshall had seen him like this before. When Palma talked about some of the insane ops he had been on. The look of enjoyment was something Marshall couldn't forget.

"This way, Anna, your daughter who isn't really your daughter, will see what I'm about to do to you."

Marshall tired of talking about Anna as if she wasn't his progeny, but he was a patient man. Palma wouldn't kill him, and he wouldn't kill Anna because he knew that hurting her would make Marshall even more recalcitrant then he already was. Palma had to deal. Violence wouldn't work with Marshall and Marshall was grateful for that. If anyone was going to get hurt he didn't want it to be him or Anna.

Marshall's eyes widened as Palma grabbed his lapels, slammed him down on the table, and started punching Marshall's face over and over again.

67

———

RAIN

Anna was in the security room on the seventeenth floor. Ten elevators traversed the length of the building, hundreds of rooms for conferences, meetings, research, isolated work, and sleeping. There were thousands of cameras, each with its own motion sensor.

In the dark room, she entered the master passcode to the underlying software that Marshall had embedded into the system years ago. Palma thought he knew how much Marshall had infected HALON's systems. He hadn't infected the system. He *was* the system. Marshall had written the most invasive rootkit anyone had ever implemented. The Sony rootkit scandal was bad. This was so much worse.

Or better, depending on your perspective.

He could control any system in the facility locally or remotely from a pimped out computing cluster, or from his cell phone. And now the power was hers.

It was time to take some of HALON's senses away.

———

A few minutes later, the single monitor hanging in the corner by the door came on. The sudden burst of light in the otherwise dim room startled her. It was Benson and he was talking to someone. *That has to be Dad.* She would recognize those shoulders and that balding head anywhere. Even in the fake fuzzy photograph of him taken in London that started her journey down the rabbit hole. The photo that came from Benson/Palma as he convinced her that he could bring closure to her confusing life.

Benson grabbed Marshall and slammed him onto the table.

OH MY GOD.

She ran out of the room as the overhead audio came on.

"Anna," the familiar voice said, "glad you're back. If you don't come here in the next five minutes, I won't kill this monster who says he's your father. I'll start carving off the knuckles on his fingers, then his hands, and toes and feet. I will keep him alive until he tells me what I need to know and then I will hunt you down and do the same thing to you.

"So how about if you spare him that indignity and come up to twenty-nine. I'll have someone escort you from the elevator. I know you're on seventeen so I'll give you a little extra time to get here. Rearranging his face was just my way of proving to you I'm serious."

She ran back into the security room. Her heart raced and she blinked uncontrollably.

Damn it! Damn it! Damn it!

Stop.

Breathe.

Think.

She pressed her palms onto the surface of the nearest desk. Her breath was choppy as she slowed down her respiration.

She was in control of a multi-billion-dollar weapon. What could she do to gain an advantage and some time?

———

Marshall sat in a chair leaning forward and wondered if Anna would think to look for some anesthetic to bring with her. As much as she might hate him, he didn't think she hated him that much. At least he hoped not. It took a few seconds for the adrenaline to wear off and for the pain to burn its way down from his skin through his muscles and into his skull.

The pain made him groggy.

The punch was unexpected. Marshall had to admit that he didn't think Palma would get violent with him as too many hits might kill him (Marshall was, after all, not a spring chicken), then Palma would have to take a shovel to the place.

He felt like crap. No, crap felt great. He deserved to get his face punched in. He screwed up. He should have known that Palma was as protective of his people as he was dangerous with his enemies. He wasn't sure which part of his face hurt more, but his cheekbones vied for first place. He felt around his eyes and found swollen tissue. It wasn't until the onslaught was over that he thought about positioning his face so the strikes would hit his cheekbones or forehead.

His nose was broken and blood dripped down his face.

Anna had every right to hate him.

But some anesthetic would be good right about now.

Then it started to rain.

Palma grabbed the handheld mic he had used the first time. "Anna! I know you can hear me. Shut the sprinklers down. Shut them down now or I swear I'll kill him." He swept up a radio from the table and held the talk button. "Send whoever you've got to seventeen. Do not, I repeat, do not kill her. If anyone touches her, they'll answer to me." He lobbed the radio back onto the podium. "That's quite a girl you have. A shame she's not yours."

Marshall lifted his head up. He did his best to look at the ceiling and saw row upon row of sprinklers spraying water streams that became droplets that cooled down on the way to his face and made the hurt less hurtful. He tried to breathe, but his nose was in the way so he sipped some air through his mouth.

———

Palma crouched down in front of Marshall to get in his line of sight. "Whatever you did to the system you have to undo. You've got hours, days, weeks, whatever it takes, to undo the damage you've done. You're not on payroll so consider this a volunteer effort."

———

Anna ran through the corridors away from the security room and back where they had been. Her steps made a flat echo. She spotted the reception desk. *What the hell?*

———

Somewhere on this floor were ten elevators. She'd managed to miss all of them. *Why were they on twenty-nine? Some special room or sacrificial alter located there?*

What an idiot. Did Marshall think she could go up to twenty-nine and control the sprinklers at the same time? It looked like seventeen was mostly for offices or something. If she thought she was running past medical, she would have stopped and gotten Marshall an anesthetic. When she was little, she had struck her face on the sidewalk when she tripped playing with some toy or other. He had taken her inside and put ice on the bruise, which helped make the pain go away, but not the embarrassment. He explained to her how ice numbed the skin and acted as an anesthetic.

Why haven't I forgotten that? She was sure he could use some now if Palma had hit his face that many times. If she hated Palma as Benson he was racking up points as a General.

Her clothes were tight now that they were drying. She needed the jeans to be larger or she couldn't fight as well as she should. She unsnapped the belt and the front button of her pants. She slid to a stop and heard her gun fall behind her. She turned back and grabbed the Glock. She stuck it deep into the back of her pants, hoping it wouldn't go off, and leaned against the wall. She didn't hear anything. She had made enough noise that anyone on their way would have heard her.

She had to look around the corner. As she brought her face into position a guard head-butted her.

68

TRYING TO GET TO 29

Anna didn't fall. She flung herself back around the corner where she leaned back and shook her head. The guard cleared the turn and pointed his gun at her. She struck the barrel of the rifle with her left hand, forcing it away from her face. It went off with a deafening explosion.

She clutched the rifle just above the action and slammed the butt into the guard's face. As his head snapped back she saw another guard behind him. She pushed the first guard into the second, but the second guard stepped out of the way. He also raised his rifle and she threw herself toward his feet, bringing him down to the ground.

The rifle landed on her shoulder so she pushed it away and rolled off the guard. She prepared for his counter-move, but nothing happened after the initial few seconds. He had struck his head against the wall on his way to the floor.

She stood and looked at her conquests. Anna wheezed. *This is idiotic. I can't keep doing this.* She ran down the hallway looking for the elevator. She knew it had to be nearby since they had just taken it.

Her hands were trembling as she swiped the keycard against the proximity pad. It turned green. Sound.

She spun around as another guard came up behind her holding his rifle at point-blank range from her head.

Her eyes opened wide and she put her hands up. "I'm heading to the same place you're going. Wanna share a ride?"

The elevator gave a soft ding and the door opened behind her. She turned her head and said, "See?" She smiled at him.

"Get inside," the guard said.

"I told you we were going to the same place." She pretended to enter the elevator and instead grasped the barrel of the rifle. She pulled it toward her left and then smashed the butt into the guard's face, breaking his nose and snapping his head back.

The strap was still firmly wrapped around his arm so he didn't let go of the rifle, but he was dazed. Anna pulled at the rifle again but couldn't get it off his arm.

As she kicked the side of his face he brought his arm up and deflected her. He released the rifle, still attached to his arm, and jumped at her, pushing her into the elevator.

Get off the floor! She tried standing, but his weight pushed her down. He squeezed her throat and she clapped her hands over his ears until he let go. Anna shoved him against the elevator wall.

The elevator door closed.

She fell back and wheezed a breath. This was a bad time for an asthma attack. They went to their respective corners and the guard threw himself at her again. She palmed him in the face, hurting his already broken nose.

The breath went out of her as he punched her in the stomach. He fell back against the wall while she held her midsection. She had not felt that much pain in a while. She had always managed to avoid getting hit in Tae Kwon Do by blocking and hitting until the clock ran out. Where was a clock when you needed it?

He was going to come at her again. She could see his body tensing. She reached behind her back just as he took the three steps that separated them and she swung the Glock into his head.

The elevator shook for a quick second as he hit the ground.

The elevator came to a halt. Ann pulled the Glock up and waited for the doors to slide open.

I haven't shot anybody yet. I haven't shot anybody yet.

The doors swung open and two men stood with their rifles aimed at her. Anna and the men exchanged looks. One of the men looked down and saw his friend on the ground. They leaned in but were too far for her to do anything.

The door tried to close, but the guard to her left put his foot out to stop it.

Well, I was coming here anyway.

She pulled the gun back and aimed it at the ceiling. Her hands went up in defeat.

———

The sprinklers had stopped.

Anna walked into the conference room on twenty-nine with her head held high. She sure as hell wasn't going to give Benson the satisfaction of thinking she was hurt or afraid. Survival was what she had done all these years and nothing had changed. The five guards he had sent trailed behind her. The two who had found her at the elevator were holding their rifles at her back and the other three were helping each other walk.

Benson/Palma strode over. He was wet, but not as soaked as she and Marshall when they'd first arrived. He was a tall man. "Good to see you again, Anna." His face grew dark as he scanned her face and neck.

He looked at the three men who were battered and bruised. He held out his hand to one of the men standing behind Anna. The guard handed Benson her Glock.

Without looking at it he said, "The Glock 22 is a great weapon. I'm surprised Liko-san let you have it. It's one of my favorite guns and I know it's one of his." He straightened and spoke through his teeth. "I gave orders not to touch her."

He shot the three men one at a time through the head. Anna

blinked involuntarily with each blast. Her shoulders twitched and tightened. *What the hell is wrong with that man?*

"The balance is unbelievable." Liko burst into the room brandishing his own weapon. He surveyed the people and the bodies before directing his attention to Benson.

Benson looked disappointed. "Liko-san, I thought you said your men knew how to follow orders," Benson said.

Liko's eyes were ablaze. "General. Those were my men."

"Under my command," Benson said. "I need better men." He tossed the Glock to Liko, who caught it and juggled it in his hands until he could grab the grip. Benson walked over to Anna. "Please accept my apologies. Those men knew not to touch you. I knew you would put up a fight, but I assumed," he shrugged, "I assumed wrong."

Then he slapped Anna with the back of his hand, sending stars into her vision. Her brain hurt from the sudden snap of her skull.

Benson strode over to the hunched man sitting in the front row. "Alright, Marshall. This is how we're playing it. Anna is the Queen. You are the pawn. You can disable whatever the hell it is you've done to the system and I won't kill this lovely young lady here. If you don't, she can join the other bodies on the ground." Anna's mind stopped processing her environment for a few seconds. Her terrified eyes followed Benson's gaze as it floated to each of their faces, stopping at Marshall. "Does anyone think I'm not serious?"

69

TICKING

Anna's face hurt. It felt like a brick had hit her. She could have used an anesthetic.

She looked over at Marshall and her heart broke again, only this time for him. She wasn't sure what she was thinking, but that man was the only father she had ever known. He'd changed her clothes, taught her how to ride a bike, calculate a quadratic equation, play Zork.

How to feel safe.

It was time to change the game.

"Before you get too attached to your plan for world domination, you should know that the scientists who had been hiding, and for good reason it appears, are all dead," Anna said.

Benson had a look of disbelief. She could see the fire start to burn in his eyes again. "What are you talking about? I need those people."

"Don't look at me," she motioned over to Liko, "Talk to him."

"Liko-san, what is she talking about? You and your men are here at my command. To do what I say."

Anna walked over to Marshall.

"Where are you going?" Benson yelled.

"He can't help you if he's dead," Anna said.

"What is she talking about, Liko-san?" Benson returned to his primary focus.

Liko didn't move. His granite exterior was as solid as ever.

"Did you kill my people?" Benson pushed some of the chairs away from him as if Liko were generating a repellent force. Benson circled him. The Glock was in Liko's hand and his hands were behind his back. Benson took the Glock as he passed behind him. "Tell me she's lying."

"The original plan," Liko said.

"I gave express orders to leave them alone. They were part of a team that knew how some of the most important pieces of this project worked."

Benson was shorter than Liko, but for a few moments Anna couldn't tell.

Benson stuck the Glock under Liko's chin. "They were loyal to this project. They are irreplaceable." He pushed the barrel up and Liko's head tilted up. "Not like you. I needed those people."

Anna pulled a chair from besides Marshall and positioned it in front of him. The seat was well-cushioned. "Hey." She held his hand. "Are you okay?"

He nodded.

She swallowed. How could she have ever hated him? She wanted to wipe the blood off his face, but was afraid of causing him pain. All the years she was alone felt like a day. A day that just didn't matter. "You don't look so good."

"Thanks. I would have told you that you looked fine," Marshall said. His voice was raspy.

"I was never very good with when to lie and when not."

He smiled a small smile. "I always loved that about you." He stood up. "Don't let me fall." He stood on his own two feet. "Excuse me, General."

Benson turned and looked at Marshall and Anna as if he had forgotten they were in the same room with him and Liko.

"Sit down and wait your turn," Benson said.

Marshall shook his head back and forth. "Okay, I'll tell you about the failsafe later." He grabbed the armrest of the chair and started to lower himself back down.

"What about the failsafe?" Benson strode over with Liko in tow.

"I gave my daughter here," he patted her knee, "a code she thought was going to shut down the cameras and give her limited access to the system." He smiled at her.

She saw her father in his swollen eyes. "While it did give her access, it also told the system that there's been an unrecognized breach. You know what kind of breach I mean, don't you? The kind where the facility decides it needs to incinerate the place to keep whatever it is from spreading or causing even worse damage.

"You remember. The nuke you wanted? The one I said was insane and you thought was a great idea? That failsafe."

Benson gripped the Glock and brought it up to his waist. Anna hoped that his anger wouldn't get the better of him. If he shot Marshall, she would kill Benson next. If he threatened her, if he made her a weapon to bludgeon her father...

Anna felt the back of her head flare in pain as Benson yanked her hair back. He pointed the gun at Marshall. "I will only ask this once." He placed the gun closer to Marshall's head. "I will kill Anna if..."

That's it. I have had it! Anna snatched the gun, pointed it at her head, and pulled the trigger. The recoil should have blasted her head, leaving her bloody and dead, but instead the shot missed as Liko grabbed the gun and pointed it up at the ceiling as she fired.

"You will not use me against him!" Anna tried to pull the gun out of Liko's grip, but his strength was considerable. Holding onto his arm, she pulled herself out of the chair and kicked Benson in the chest, throwing him to the ground. Liko restrained her as she tried to jump on Benson. "You will not use me against him!"

Marshall stood and touched her arm. "It's okay. Anna. Anna." She looked at him and felt even worse. "I don't want any of us to die." He glared at Liko. "Well, maybe some of us."

He shuffled over to Benson who was untangling himself from the mass of chairs onto which Anna had kicked him. Marshall didn't extend his hand to help him up.

"I didn't know how any of this was going to go. I'll do whatever you want. Go alone, with just you, or everyone, it doesn't matter. If I can't turn it off in time, we're all dead anyway," Marshall said.

"Disable it or I'm going to shoot you in as many places as I can before you die," Benson said.

"Fair enough." Marshall started to walk toward the doors in the back. "Let's go."

70

APOCALYPSE LATER

The room where the small nuclear weapon was located was in the center of the building. To call it a room was to insult other rooms. It was a sealed cube of concrete that had no opening and no visible marks. The inhabitants of HALON had been working around it for years and no one told what it was.

Eventually it became part of the landscape to the old-timers and something ignored by the newcomers.

The lead sleeve that encased it kept escaping radiation to a minimum. The design of the enclosure was for stealth, not impairment.

A digital circuit board embedded in the concrete would tell the nuke when it should ignite, taking the building and part of the New York City subway system with it. Upon completing its task, a cloud of radiation would eventually make its way to the surface, rendering the tristate area, and the surrounding environs, uninhabitable for decades.

A hardened tungsten alloy conduit encased the cables from the ignition switch through the building from the fifteenth floor down to the first. The conduits, installed over ten years earlier before anyone had decided what the failsafe would be, were but one part of a system that had to be foolproof.

The shielded cables were impervious to external radio waves and static discharge. The insulated conduits protected against changes in temperature and were coated with a non-static and non-magnetic material. When the cables were snaked through from the igniter to the first floor, the conduits were filled with a protective foam to make sure that no mice or corrosive elements could harm the cables.

The thick cables came out of the wall of the Console Room on the first floor. The Console Room, about the size of a comfortable living room, contained only one thing: a Panasonic military-grade server with a translator board and just enough micro-code embedded in the silicon to either activate the nuclear device within a pre-programmed length of time (thirty minutes), activate the device right away, or deactivate it until it was needed again.

———

Benson, Liko, Marshall and Anna all entered the room, once again using Marshall's keycard.

Benson pushed Marshall toward the server. "So that little piece of shit is all that's standing between Liko taking over and a crater in the Hudson?"

"East River," Anna said.

Benson glowered at her as if she had a second head.

"It's technically the East River," she said and added, "Moron." She saw Liko's eyes smile. *Screw you too.* Her anger radiated from her tight chest.

Benson dragged Marshall by the arm to the console. Marshall turned on the monitor. It was dark except for a blinking cursor at the top left-hand corner. Marshall entered some characters. The cursor didn't move by design. If the operator entering the code was with an unauthorized guest, the cursor wouldn't give anything away. That was something Anna had seen at UPenn during one of her late nights working on facial recognition software she didn't get to use.

He pressed Enter.

He typed another sequence of characters.

Enter.

Nothing happened. Marshall shook his head and rubbed his eyes. He hit the backspace key and re-entered the information.

Enter.

The screen changed. White letters on a black background. The screen filled with information: resource status, menus to set timers, safety checks, help screens.

The In-Progress Countdowns item, highlighted, had a clock counting down next to it. Just under two minutes.

Benson took a step back. "Get on with it."

Marshall rubbed his eyes again and grimaced with each motion.

Anna walked over to him. "Anything I can do?" she whispered.

"No, no. Everything is fine," Marshall said. He typed a numeric sequence and at the first character an input box appeared displaying asterisks as he entered the code. He pressed Enter.

INVALID

She heard him sigh and saw him dig the heel of his hand into his forehead. He entered another sequence, going slower this time. She saw him blink.

INVALID

Less than a minute.

"Anna, I'm doing something wrong." They switched positions. "Type in the following characters." He enunciated each number to her. "1-1-3-8-

"3-2-7-

"2-1-2-1-4. Enter."

Anna typed in the first few numbers and couldn't help but read some of the menu items.

F12 - LOCK SCREEN

She pressed F12. The screen vanished.

Marshall stepped to the side, blocking the screen from the others. "What did you do?" he whispered.

She whispered back, "I pressed F12."

"But that locked the screen."

"I know. You wanted to take them down. Now we take them down together." She turned to the group. "Ten, nine, eight..."

Marshall put his hands up. "Everybody stay calm. I accidentally pressed the screen lock and I have to log in again."

"Six," she said.

Benson raised his gun and pointed it at Anna. "What have you done?"

"Five."

"Put the gun down," Marshall said.

"Four."

"It's not going to go off," Marshall said. He stepped in between Anna and Benson.

"Three."

"It was never going to go off," Marshall said.

"Two."

"I disabled it! Years ago," Marshall said.

"One."

Everyone froze. Anna gritted her teeth so hard her jaw hurt.

Marshall was the first to speak, his shoulders hunched. "I couldn't let you install a live nuke under New York. I disabled it. It was never going to work."

Benson aimed the Glock at Marshall. "What?"

"The thermobaric is still active, but I nuked the nuked, so to speak." He bent over the keyboard and logged back into the terminal, which unlocked the screen. The terminal displayed a status of READY and everything else looked normal. "I got myself hired to write the microcode."

"But you didn't exist," Benson said.

"I was good at faking that. I gave them working code. When it was time to burn the chips, I substituted non-working Enable-the-Nuke code. Remotely, of course." Marshall leaned in with his bruised and battered face. "The thermobaric was always the way to go."

"But you've disabled that as well," Benson said.

Anna wasn't sure if he was asking or telling.

"Maybe." Marshall gave his face a gentle swipe. "We'll never find out." He looked up. "Oh, and if you harm my daughter in any way, I still won't fix your system. I will fix it, but leave her alone."

Benson nodded. "I agree." Benson struck Marshall on the side of his face with the Glock.

Marshall fell and Anna launched herself at Benson.

He aimed his gun at her. "Be careful. I might change my mind."

Anna kneeled to help Marshall up. "Why did you do that? It could have all been over."

"Oh, Squirrel, it would have caused what I was trying to stop." He coughed and moaned.

She wasn't sure what to do. "Why did you do it?"

"Lie or disable it? I thought I could scare him enough and then gain his trust again when I stopped it. I guess not."

"I screwed up your plan. I'm an idiot," Anna said.

"Maybe." He gave her a quick hug. "But you're my kind of idiot."

71

BACK PEDALING

Marshall leaned back on the mesh-covered office chair. His face hurt, which debilitated his body, but the rest of him felt fine. Running was pointless, since no one could outrun a bullet and Palma still had plenty of those. He thought about the various scenarios that were available to him, and Anna, and very few of them had good outcomes. The ones that had good outcomes involved Palma spontaneously exploding, or having an unexpected cardiac event. Both Palma and Liko having dual cardiac events. Or perhaps Anna sneaking up on them and pushing them off a cliff.

He sighed. No matter how this turned out, he and Anna were dead. Even if they succeeded.

All along his plan had been to spread enough clues about Palma, Monahan, the return of PRUDENT RAINBOW as HALON, and anything else he could think of so the FBI would have to arrest Palma and Monahan. They would be forced to make inquiries about the secret elevator and staircase leading a hundred feet under the Montague Tubes to a rather large building run by the Chinese, but paid for by the American people.

He could only hope that reality TV had not totally disintegrated the brain cells of the law enforcement community, the Attorney

General of the United States, or the military. He needed them all tonight, and again after it was all over. If there was an after-it-was-all-over, and he and Anna survived.

Was it time for another extreme move?

———

Palma came through the door brandishing the Glock with which he had already shot multiple men and beaten Marshall. Liko was behind him a respectful distance. From the beginning, Liko was an alpha male. While Palma was an alpha as well, Liko was the real thing. He didn't need a gun for anyone to know when he was in a room or to command respect. Palma was a political animal with friends in the good camp, and friends in the bad camp. When Palma needed favors, he went to the good camp. When he wanted to get rid of people, he went to the bad camp.

But there was something about Liko.

Marshall stood up. It was time to shake it up.

"I need to go to medical," Marshall said.

"I need a drink," Palma said.

"I'm pretty certain the office we designed for you is quite stocked in your favorite drinks. What do you want?" Marshall asked.

"Johnny Walker Black."

"I meant why are you here? You make the air toxic." Marshall heard Anna's chair squeak. Squeaking meant fidgeting, and fidgeting meant boredom. Anna didn't do well with boredom. Too much of a penchant for action.

"What was your plan? Why did you come back?" Palma asked.

"I'm flattered that you care." Marshall pretended to read the information at his terminal. "I have a lot of work to do. All unpaid overtime."

"I know you. You've this thought out twenty ways from Sunday," Palma said.

"You should give yourself up," Marshall said. "And that's twelve ways to Sunday."

Palma let out a single loud laugh. The confidence that came from holding a gun. "Seriously. What did you expect to do once you got here?"

Marshall spoke to Liko. "You spent the last few months of your life with me. What did I tell you?" Marshall sat down again. His back was achy. "It's okay. Palma's signed an NDA."

Palma waved him off and said, "Liko-san reported every day on the things you did and said to him. I know the kind of toilet paper you used and how you'd been feeding information to the FBI." He rolled his eyes a little. "That poor FBI guy. Whatever his name was. Bill? Del?" Palma twisted his lips in false consternation. "Had to get rid of him mighty quick. He believed your information. He got in close real quick. I meant to give him some false leads, but one of my guys picked him up and the next thing he knew he was strapped to chair being asked questions he wasn't cleared to hear."

Palma sat down on the edge of the desk to Marshall's left. "After I blew out his knees he was very, very cooperative. Garth was there, you know. He was never as squeamish as you are."

His attention drifted to Anna who sat down again. "Anna, seriously, your father, I don't know why I keep saying that, this guy you lived with most of your life, just never bought into the idea that when something is secret, it's secret. Even if he disagreed with it."

Marshall pursed his lips. *Quite the egomaniac.* "What would you say if I told you that the cavalry was coming?"

"I'd say you have quite an imagination. And you're a lousy bluff," Palma said.

Behind Palma, Liko came to attention. Marshall's curiosity was piqued. Was Liko putting himself into position to fall off the cliff?

"Liko-san, what do I think of poker?" Marshall asked.

"You hate it," Liko said.

"Why?"

"You don't believe in bluffing," Liko said.

"I don't believe in bluffing. Never have, never will.

"The cavalry is coming," Marshall said.

"There's a first time for everything," Palma said. His voice didn't match his words. The sound of doubt creeped in.

"I'm too old for new tricks." Marshall gave his attention to Liko again. "What about you, Liko? What's the protocol for discovery? And I mean like discovery in the next half hour." Marshall tapped his left wrist. Since the broken nose refused to repair itself, he breathed through his mouth. The palms of his hands tingled as his eyes sent waves of pain through his face and down his shoulders.

He jumped when a gun went off.

Anna didn't know what to do. Palma fell to the ground screaming in pain after Liko had shot him in the lower back. She bolted up and stood between Marshall and Liko.

Liko aimed his gun at Anna but didn't fire. "Marshall, I don't have to ask if what you're saying is true. The General knew you longer than I have, yet he doesn't know you." He walked over to where the Glock Palma had been holding fell to the ground.

Palma was crying in pain.

Liko picked up the weapon. "Anna, here's a scenario for you. Let me describe it properly," he said as he strode over to her holding Palma's Glock. "When you had the chance to find and kill your father, you failed."

Anna felt her cheeks grow red and her stomach twist. Hearing what she had planned at the outset, and with Marshall in the room, brought back memories she could never erase: failed exams, forgotten errands, and disappointments she'd brought Marshall.

Who was that Anna?

"When you had the chance to kill yourself, you also failed."

Out of the corner of her eye, she saw Marshall stare at her. She refused to look back. Anna knew she wouldn't survive seeing the hurt in his eyes.

"I did everything I could to convince you to go to Canada. I paid people to follow you. Give you money. Threaten your life. And yet you came here." He stepped forward and she felt a nudge against her belly. It was the grip of Palma's Glock. "You came for revenge. Are you up for that?" He placed the gun in her hand. "Here is your chance."

Palma, on the floor leaning against the leg of a table, looked up at her. "You're a coward. You'll never shoot me."

Anna pointed the gun at Palma. Her finger rested on the barrel, not the trigger. To shoot or not to shoot. A sharp pain formed between her eyes. What she did next would save them or condemn them. *Should I shoot Liko? Do I shoot anyone?*

"Shoot him," Liko said. "You didn't take this long in London."

Her brain was locking up. She had a gun in her hand and she didn't know what to do. Why not shoot Benson?

She turned and aimed the gun at Liko. "No, I won't shoot him."

Liko stood before her as calm as ever. "You really are a coward." That frozen moment was enough for Liko to knock the gun out of her hand. He turned and shot Palma in the head.

Anna was stunned.

His gun aimed at Anna again, Liko said, "I learned a lot from your father these last few months. Including how to enable the real fail-safe." A glance at Marshall. "Yes, I remember what you told me about the thermobaric. This can never be traced back to us, so I'm going to give you what you want.

"Stalemate, Mr. Wodehouse. You win and you lose. HALON will disappear," Liko said.

Liko backed out of the room. "I leave you the Glock so you can decide if you want to wait for the explosive to go off or end it sooner. Either is an honorable way to die.

"Spend your last few moments with each other. Life is ephemeral. Nothing lasts forever." With that, Liko closed the door, the lock snapped into place, and he was gone.

"My life is over," Anna said.

"Don't exaggerate," Marshall said. "Not for another forty-five minutes."

72

SNIPER SHOT

"Well, that didn't go quite according to plan," Marshall said.

Anna stared at him. "I'm glad to hear that. If you had said you'd done it on purpose, you would have freaked me out."

"No, the part about him deciding to set off the thermobaric. That wasn't what I expected him to do. I was hoping he would do something to Palma. The General was out of control. Liko-san was uncomfortable from the moment he arrived here, I'm sure, and convincing him the jig was up was one way to get him to do something. This is an act of war if the Chinese are found out."

"Found out?"

"The Chinese were going to have their own base on US soil," Marshall said. "Long story. Monahan agreed, Palma led," he sighed, "and I implemented. Not one of my better decisions."

"What's a thermobaric? It sounds scary," Anna said.

"Just a non-nuclear equivalent to a nuclear weapon."

"Just." The stale air scratched her throat. "So, this place is still going to blow?"

"Only if we don't stop him." Marshall stood up. He didn't look steady on his feet.

"We're going to stop him?" *Here we go again.*

"Actually, I'm going to stop him. I need you to head up to thirty," Marshall said. He swayed.

How are we going to get away if he's going to need a walker?

"And what am I going to be doing on the thirtieth floor?"

"Waiting for me," Marshall said.

"And why would I do that?"

"Because if the bomb goes off, it won't affect the thirtieth floor. I made sure we had one hardened floor that remaining personnel could go to, and not release radiation that would kill everyone. And not blow a hole in the East River. And not release radioactive particles into the air."

"Who thought a nuke was a good idea?"

Marshall made a face. "I know."

———

Marshall crouched down next to Palma and closed the dead man's eyes. He bowed his head for a moment.

"Why are you mourning him?" Anna asked.

"I'm not mourning him. I'm remembering the man he was. He was highly decorated for the other things he did. Like defend his country."

Anna walked toward the door. "Whatever. Look in his pockets. We're going to need his keycard." She retrieved the gun Liko had knocked out of her hand.

———

Anna opened the door to the large office space. The door opened inward and she crouched down on the floor to look out. *If Liko's going to shoot me at least I'll give him a hard time.* "What floor are we on?"

"Ten," Marshall said.

"And where are we going?"

"Twenty-nine."

"Please tell me there's an elevator nearby."

"There's an elevator nearby."

"Really?" she asked.

"No."

She didn't see anyone so she opened the door and they both stepped out. "How does he know the code for the thermobaric? And why did you think it was such a great idea?" she asked.

"Funny story. Deadly diseases die faster in a fire than in the open air."

"A nuke would have done it too."

"One word: radioactivity."

"There's already nuclear material here and it doesn't like fire very much either."

They both leaned their backs against the wall. Anna peeked around the corner and saw nothing.

"Are there any more of those other guys still around?" she asked.

"I don't know. I lost count of how many the General killed for us."

"He didn't kill them for us."

"Well, we certainly didn't try to stop him." Marshall coughed into his arm. "Liko's not here. The elevator's past that turn. And all the nuclear material is still in cases that will survive the blast."

Anna ran while Marshall hobbled down the corridor until they arrived at their destination. Anna took the keycard from Marshall and swiped a ride. "Can he set it to just go off or is there always a countdown?"

"He can, but he doesn't know how. There will be a countdown, but it won't be long."

The door opened and they stepped in. As the door closed Anna heard running. One of the guards slammed into the door.

"On the floor!" Marshall said.

They both lay as flat as they could as bullets tore through the door and walls of the elevator. The shooting stopped.

"On the rail!" Marshall said.

Anna climbed up on the rail that ran around the walls of the elevator, but Marshall had just gotten one leg up when a new spray of bullets ripped through the bottom of the elevator as it moved up the shaft. He yelled. Bullets popped through his right leg. She jumped down as he leaned against the far wall, holding his right leg up.

"Oh, this isn't good," he said.

"It's fine. You'll be fine." She examined his leg. One bullet grazed his skin, but the other went through his calf.

She ran her fingers from his knees to his ankle. No broken or destroyed bones.

"Is it a clean wound?" he asked.

"Yeah. No fragments."

"Good, that means I can walk on it." He put his right leg down and put some weight on it. He yelped and brought the leg back up. "Alright. Plan B."

———

How much time had gone by? Anna wasn't sure. Liko had been gone longer than she liked.

Anna ran through the corridor and looked around corners when she could, but she had the Glock at the ready. Liko was a better shot, and a better fighter. She had two things on her side. First: she was also trained. Second: she was pissed. He was going to kill them and wipe away all evidence.

She didn't know where the Secretary of State was, but she was sure he would consider himself lucky he'd missed this party when the news came out. She would make sure that headline showed up somewhere. Someone was going to go to prison. This time it wouldn't be her.

She turned the corner, slid to a stop by falling backward on the floor, and flipped herself around the corner as Liko fired at her. "Liko-san, let me by."

"You don't know how to make the most of the moments that are given to you. You could be with your father in these last few minutes," Liko said. "I know you don't believe in the afterlife. The apple doesn't fall far from the tree."

Anna took aim and fired in his direction. Would she have to kill him? "I don't want a few minutes of happiness." Being with him wouldn't bring back all those lost years. "I want a few years to be able to torture him. Let me by."

He fired at her. The bullet ricocheted off the wall in front of her then the wall next to her. *That was close!* Her neck hurt. *Please. I don't want to die now.*

She lay down on the ground and slid to the corner, just enough to spot the Glock.

Deep breath.

"Trust me," he said, "after being with your father all these months I know he is an honorable man. He missed you terribly."

And I don't intend to waste that guilt.

Exhale.

Liko peeked around the corner. Anna fired.

73

MOVING STAIRWELL

The noise in the hall was deafening, but it didn't bother Anna as much as it had a few minutes before. She saw Marshall waiting for her so they could go to the real failsafe room. She hoped the console would work this time. He sat in a wheeled office chair holding his right leg out. His dark pants and shirt were otherwise dry even after they had been re-soaked from the sprinklers, but his right pant leg still stuck to his skin from the blood. He had tightened his belt just below the knee to stop the bleeding, but it looked like it didn't help.

"Liko?" he asked as she ran up to him.

"He kept his honor."

Marshall's face darkened and he turned away for a moment. "Alright, I'm tired of these alarms blaring. My face hurts enough. I don't need my ears in constant pain too."

"Why is everything starting to blow up?" she asked.

"Only the sections that need a preliminary cleaning. The thermobaric might not be perfect."

She felt the floor tremble.

"Yeah, they're kind of extreme," Marshall said.

"So, where is it?"

"It's right here. Swipe the card." He motioned to a keycard proximity pad attached to the wall with no door next to it.

Anna pulled the keycard out of her pocket and swiped it. The wall pulled back about half an inch and slid itself to the left revealing a doorway into a duplicate console room. A chair, desk, and monitor were the only occupants. "Liko would never have found this on his own," she said.

"No, but he had me. I trusted him for a while. I was never completely sure, but at one point he was the only person I could trust."

Anna felt a pang of jealousy. He should have been able to trust her, only she was too busy trying to kill him. She ran into the room and picked up the wired keyboard. "This is a point of failure.

"Oh, yeah? Try yanking it off the desk."

Anna gripped the keyboard as hard as she could and pulled. The cable held and she hurt her hands in the process. "Got it. Gorilla proof."

He wheeled himself to the desk and put the keyboard on his lap. He looked up at the screen and its single blinking cursor. He typed the invisible username and password and the screen lit up with its status display. There were seven minutes left.

Anna leaned over his shoulder. She hoped they would stay alive long enough for her to ask all the questions she had. "Oh, lucky seven." She smiled. "It's your lucky day." She reached over and pressed the alarm button.

A password input field opened. "Seriously? You're already logged in. It thinks someone else is asking to shut off the alarm?"

Marshall entered the password and the alarm stopped. He sighed. "Thank you. Now let's stop this thing." He pressed the main status button, selected the menu for re-setting the countdown, and started to enter his password at the prompt.

She could feel a series of explosions under her feet. This was it. They'd saved New York. Now they had to defend themselves from everybody else.

She put her hand on Marshall's. "Wait."

"What's up?" he asked.

"Wasn't the point of the exercise to shut down this place?"

"We can do that without destroying it," Marshall said.

"Yeah, but we can also do it by destroying it." She gave him a sideways glance. "Right?"

Marshall didn't look sure. The more Anna thought about it the more sure she was about suggesting it. Take down HALON. If it survived, it wouldn't be turned into an amusement park.

"It's got a lot of secrets, Dad. What was your original plan? Kill everyone and walk out?" She sat on the edge of the desk. "Kill everyone and not walk out?" She clutched the armrest of his chair. "I think we get out of here. You said thirty was the place to be."

She pressed F-12 again and locked the screen. Marshall's face registered mild surprise. Anna said, "Time to go. Less than seven minutes."

She grabbed the back of his chair and spun it around like a wheelchair.

"Yes, it is," her father said.

She smiled. The muscles in her face felt as if they hadn't been used in ages.

"You still have your gun?" he asked.

"Why?"

"With the alarm off I can hear people coming. It might be the vibrations of what's going on below us, but I don't think so."

Marshall was right. The concrete flooring vibrated with the thump of feet. It sounded like more than one person.

"Don't get up. I'll cover you."

"You're insane." He stood up and started hobbling. "We don't have time to pretend we have time." He took a step out the door then pulled himself back in as rapid machine gun fire echoed in the hall.

A couple of shots hit the doorway to their left. Anna smelled concrete from the powder puffs from the wall.

She moved Marshall over to the left, crouched down, and looked to her right down the hallway. There were three guards, each hiding behind a corner, some debris that had landed, and one of the labs.

She chose the one around the corner. She got a good look at where his head was.

Marshall stuck his head out and said, "Don't fire at him directly. Hit the wall level with his head, but just before him."

Anna aimed. *Interesting trick.* Since the walls were concrete in this hallway the bullet struck the wall and slid directly toward its target.

One down.

"We need to get out of here," Marshall said over the explosive rounds of gunfire.

"I'm working on it." She wasn't sure how many shots she had left, but she knew she didn't have a full magazine anymore. She had to chase them away. If they stepped out into the hallway, she and Marshall would be down in seconds.

Target number two: the man behind the debris.

She pulled her head back in. The guard in the lab was making it hard for her to get her bearing. "Time check."

"I don't know." He tried looking out but quickly pulled his head back. "Less than five."

"Is there anything in this room that explodes?"

"No." She felt more vibrations through the floor and echoes in the distance. Even if the thermobaric didn't go off, the only thing they could save were the experiments that only the dead understood.

Okay, time to make it seem like they were in trouble.

Anna stuck her head and shoulder out, aimed at the man behind the debris, and shot multiple times at him with an occasional shot toward the lab. She had to cover herself.

Two down.

She heard running. She looked out the doorway and saw the third man escaping. *That's not the kind of luck I want. Why is he running? Doesn't he realize that the place is about to blow?*

"Let's go, Dad." She felt a little woozy.

"Anna."

"What?" He was looking at her arm.

The back of her shirt felt wet. She turned so Marshall could look at it and she looked, too. She was bleeding. "We've got to go," she said. "I have not been shot."

She ran down the hallway in the direction Marshall had told her as he hobbled behind her. Offices exploded in cascading waves of fire, glass, and metal.

There's the door. Their luck was improving.

She swiped the card. The door unlocked and she held it open to wait for Marshall. She let go of the door, which didn't swing shut, and ran back to help him along. "Let's go, old timer. We've only got one story to climb."

She opened the door wide. The staircase hung in a twisted knot.

The stairwell was gone.

74

HOLDING ON

"Time check," Anna said.

"I'd say not more than a couple of minutes." Marshall straightened out and took a closer look at the gaping hole where the stairwell used to be. "It certainly is a long way down."

Anna could hear explosions happening on every floor. The missing floor created a shaft of hot air, smoke, burned flooring, and metal. Flames shot out of various floors, making the smoke thicker.

"I hope you guys were OSHA compliant," Anna said.

"Why?"

"Otherwise the toxic fumes being released by everything will kill us long before we get in there." She looked up at the door one story above them. It was on the wall on their side of the newly created shaft.

"We can climb this!" she said.

"Are you kidding? Your shoulder is wounded, my leg is wounded, and there's no floor."

Anna examined what was left of the floor. "There's enough of an edge that we can get below the door and climb up the rest of the way."

Marshall examined their surroundings for a moment, bowed his head, and then placed a hand over his forehead.

"Don't you dare think about staying behind."

"Anna," he said.

"Let's go! You first." She grabbed his hand, turned him around, and gently pushed him around the doorway to the ledge. She wasn't sure what they would use to climb up, but she would figure that out in about a minute.

Marshall limped along the edge of the remaining floor. When he had moved enough to make way for her, she hugged the wall and started sliding along the edge behind him.

She took a quick look down. *Well, that was stupid.*

"Don't look down," Marshall said. "You're already getting dizzy."

The shaft echoed the destruction happening on all the floors. He was right. The last few minutes had been pure adrenaline and the hot-concrete-wall hugging was burning it fast. Marshall stood under the door. The cracked wall gave her hope they might be able to climb up.

To the locked door.

"How do we open that thing?" she asked.

"You don't. It's unlocked. You don't need the keycard." Hot wind was blowing their hair around. "But you do need to turn the doorknob."

Crap. "How do we do this?" she asked.

"Simple. I'll boost you up."

"The ledge isn't that wide."

"About two feet. Wide enough. Get closer."

She was almost at his position when he motioned her to stop. He cupped his hands together. "There's no time to think. Climb on my hand. I'll push you up and you'll stand on my unwounded shoulders where you should be able to reach the doorknob. Start with your left foot."

No time to think. She stepped on his hand with her left foot. Marshall leaned into the wall as she gained altitude then put her right foot on his shoulder.

"Use the wall for balance but don't push against it too hard," he ordered.

She straightened herself out as he pushed her up.

She placed her other foot on his shoulder and felt him sag. "Dad?"

"Keep going!"

She reached for the doorknob. It was just out of her grasp.

"Don't point your feet. You'll push me off."

Her heart was in her throat. How to reach up without pushing them both off the ledge? Her arm felt shorter than normal. "I can't reach it."

She heard him say to himself, "Okay." He reached up and stuck his hands under her feet.

He pushed up hard, and she went up another few inches.

She turned the doorknob. The door swung open.

She fell in as his hands fell back. "Dad!" Sliding on the floor, she spun herself around, and reached down. "Give me your hand."

"Close the door!"

"No way! Give me your hand."

"Anna, you have to let me go," Marshall said. "There is no way you're going to be able to pull me up." He looked down.

"Dad! Don't do this. We've only got another few seconds and you have to get up here. Either you give me your hand or I keep this door open and we both go."

She heard him curse under his breath. "Great. You're as stubborn as your mother." He spoke to the wall. "I failed you. Don't let me fail you again."

"I swear I am going to climb down there and push you off myself if you don't get up here." She could feel her center of gravity was off. "Wait a second."

She ran into the room and looked for anything that could hoist him up. She found a spool of bright orange electrical extension cord. She pulled out about twelve feet worth, ran to the open doorway, and dropped the makeshift rope to her father. He wrapped it around his hand and she, in turn, wrapped her end around her hand, and started to pull. When Marshall was high enough to reach over the edge of the door, she saw his hand, which made her pull even more.

Up he went. First, his head and shoulders. He was halfway in the room when she let go of the orange cable and grabbed his hands. She pulled him in the rest of the way and with his good foot he slammed the door shut and stood.

"We have to go," he said. He put his arm around her shoulder and led her to the other end of the room where there was another door. "Swipe it!"

When the thick door opened, Marshall almost threw her inside. After stumbling in himself, he swung it shut and the proximity pad went red.

The building shook for about twenty seconds with a two-minute aftershock. Every floor, each made of steel-reinforced concrete, after being scorched clean, fell in pieces on top of each other, for all twenty-nine stories.

The only external sign that an underground explosion had taken place was a giant plume of water that extended hundreds of feet into the air as the pressure release shaft exploded outward into the East River.

75

LETTING GO

Here I am, sitting on the bare concrete floor of a multi-billion dollar secret project and they couldn't even heat it right.

Anna shivered and couldn't stop. She thought she smelled smoke and burnt material, but that was such a long time ago she was sure she imagined it.

HALON had stopped trembling a few minutes earlier.

Marshall sat in another wheeled office chair and tried to make small talk, but even he grew silent. He straightened his back, but he couldn't stop from slumping. He squirmed to fix his posture, but nothing worked. Anna thought he should just embrace the slump.

She hurt. Having been shot in the left shoulder, she put all her strength into her right to drag Marshall over the threshold. She didn't realize how much effort and exertion it cost her until it was all over.

It was all over. They did it. They shut down HALON.

That bastard Benson was dead.

Now they were going to die because they couldn't go back the way they came. In the midst of all their crises, Hurricane Sandy had been something to worry about later, maybe never.

It had been a long night. Marshall motioned her over. "Stand up and let me take a look at your shoulder."

Every muscle decided to scream in pain as Anna did her best to stand. Her back stuck to the wall. She was still losing blood out of her shoulder. The wound wasn't enough to kill her right away, but time wasn't on her side.

Marshall sighed. "That is not good."

"Oh, oh." She couldn't get any words out. Until she stood she hadn't taken a good look at Marshall. There was a small puddle of blood on the floor. "Stand up, stand up." She held her hands out and he gripped them while he stood on his left leg.

She didn't see anything until she turned him around. Blood covered the right side of his shirt. "What happened?"

"I don't know," he said. "Must have been some shrapnel or something." He pushed the chair over. "I'm hot. I want to lie down on the floor. Give me your gun. Let's sleep in shifts in case one of those guys is still around and we need to pop him off."

Anna chuckled. "'Pop him off?'"

Marshall smiled. "Yeah. Pop him off."

She thought she'd heard something earlier, but thought better of it.

———

The floor felt cool. Anna had joined him on the ground as they both looked up at the ceiling and made small talk. Marshall was singing part of a John Denver song. She remembered he was a fan. "Poems, and Prayers, and Promises."

"Dad? You know," she took in a breath, "in that song he talks about passing a pipe around. I don't think they were smoking tobacco."

Marshall coughed. Droplets of blood flew through the air. He wheezed as he breathed in. Anna kept her voice steady.

"You're missing the point of the song," he said. "It's about what life is really about and how easy it is to think it's about anything except the people you love."

"Am I your daughter?" She had to ask. This might be her only chance.

"Wanna run a blood test? I think there's plenty around for you to use."

She looked around the locked room. Blood on the floor. Blood on the wall where she had been leaning. It looked like the scene of a murder. It would be soon.

Two murders. Benson was going to get them after all.

Breathe in. Silence.

"Dad? Tell me about Mom." She felt cold. Breathe in. Breathe out.

"Your mom. You are as beautiful as she was. And as smart." Wheeze. "I'm a moron compared to her."

"I missed you so much."

"I missed you too, Squirrel." Something smashed against the door. Marshall let out a groan. "Don't worry." He reached across the floor for a gun. "I think there's still a few rounds left."

His breathing was getting shallow. The room was fuzzy. Was she passing out? She shook her head and breathed in as deeply as she could, stopping when the pain in her ribs became more than she could handle. A shallow breath. She needed more so she started panting.

"Squirrel?"

"I'm okay. I'm okay."

Smash! SMASH!

"Am I holding the gun up? I can't feel my arm," he said.

She pulled herself over. His arm was still on the ground just holding onto the grip.

"You're good. Hold it like that."

"Okay. Okay." He reached up with his left arm and hugged her for a few seconds. His left arm dropped to the ground after that. He laughed. "This is like the last scene in Butch Cassidy. Only it's not the Mexicans coming."

"Dad?" She wasn't sure if she could say it. "Dad..."

"I love you, Squirrel."

"I love you, Dad."

The room was becoming a collection of lights and outlines. She blinked, but her vision didn't improve. She shook him.

"Dad. So, this is it. We're all going to die."

They both laughed softly. She leaned back and her head found his arm. Her neck was uncomfortable, but only just. Anna's perception was getting softer and softer like her vision. "I wonder if Arthur Dent or Ford Prefect will come and save us before the Vogons blow up the planet." Silence. "Dad?" She shook him with all the energy she could muster and just managed a soft pull. "Dad? Don't leave me again. Please."

The door burst open to a sea of dark figures yelling and covering the light as she blacked out.

———

Blurred visions.

Nothing.

Movement in the dark.

Nothing.

Warmth on her hands? Pressure? She saw something and forgot it. She thought about being underground. Constrained. Caskets. Roots breaking into the box. She was detached.

The sound of gunfire. She smiled. *We got them.*

We got them.

Nothing.

PART VII

THE END OF THE RAINBOW

PRESS RELEASES

Tuesday, October 30, 2012

The Morning News

"...and news following Hurricane Sandy continues to pour in. The devastation is setting new records as the toll so far has reached billions of dollars in damage to the tristate area and the loss of approximately 45 lives..."

"In addition to the tragic loss of life due to the superstorm comes the tragic news that Secretary of State George Monahan and NSA Director Malik Palma may be among those who have lost their lives. In a statement filed by the State Department, both Secretary of State Monahan and Director Palma had decided to make an unscheduled trip to the Office of Emergency Management located at Cadman Plaza East in Downtown Brooklyn to offer additional help from their respective departments. Both of their vehicles were swept away in a freak flash flood that landed their vehicles in the East River where they, and their security details, may have been overwhelmed by the storm. Unsubstantiated eyewitness reports say the vehicles sank under the waves within seconds. There do not appear to be any survivors. No word on the recovery of their bodies, but a contingent of Navy Seals stationed near the Brooklyn Bridge have been dispatched to find any possible survivors..."

"In other news, the Army Corp of Engineers is expected to announce that in additional to the extensive damage done to the shorelines of New York, New Jersey, and Connecticut, the Montague Tubes, the tunnel that runs between Manhattan and Brooklyn, will be closed, possibly for over a year, while repairs are performed to fix the extensive damage sustained by the worst flooding to ever hit the subway system in its entire history. The N and the R trains will not be running during that time, but the MTA will have alternate routes and buses available to handle the crush of riders sure to be affected by the closing..."

———

Fifteen Months Later

MTA Press Release
September 15, 2014

GOVERNOR CUOMO ANNOUNCES EARLY COMPLETION OF SUPERSTORM SANDY RECOVERY WORK IN MONTAGUE SUBWAY TUNNEL

R Train Service between Brooklyn and Manhattan Restored Ahead of Schedule and Under Budget

"Governor Andrew M. Cuomo joined Metropolitan Transportation Authority leaders and elected officials from New York City to mark the restoration of normal R Subway service between Brooklyn and Manhattan. This announcement follows the successful rebuilding of the Montague Tube subway tunnel that was inundated with salt water during Superstorm Sandy...

"The $250 million project was completed ahead of schedule and under budget, during an unprecedented full shutdown of the

Montague Tube subway tunnel under the East River. An estimated 27 million gallons of water poured into a 4,000-foot stretch of the tunnel during Sandy, which corroded every element of subway infrastructure from electronic signal equipment to tunnel lighting to the steel rails themselves...

"MTA Chairman and CEO Thomas F. Prendergast said, "New York's transit network suffered more damage during Sandy than anyone at the MTA has ever seen in our lifetimes. The effort required to rebuild the Montague Tube was nothing short of heroic..."

76

OPEN BACK

Wednesday, October 31, 2012
Two Days after the Destruction of HALON

New York Presbyterian/Lower Manhattan Hospital

Anna Wodehouse knew she was alive because she couldn't open her eyes. The light coming from wherever-she-was was bright enough to penetrate her eyelids and make the skin over her eyeballs look gray-ish. She tried to stretch and just managed to bend her back enough to feel the starchy sheets on her bed.

My bed? No. Where was she?

She fought her eyelids this time and got them open just enough to feel blinded. She moved her stiff right hand and covered her face with her arm. Instantaneous: a hospital.

Her eyes popped open from the rush that exploded in her head. She blinked and blinked and blinked. She tried to sit up, but her muscles complained about the abuse. She tried to slide up, but the back of her hands hurt and she couldn't quite balance herself. She bent her arm and found tape covering the inside of her elbow. She looked to her right and found an intravenous needle stuck in the crook of her arm feeding her fluids.

"Hello?" she asked no one in particular.

Her room, made up of three chairs, a lot of monitoring equipment, a TV hanging from the wall, and a white board that said: "Your nurse: Silvia Velez" scrawled in black marker, was rather spartan. A police officer walked in. *Where's Dad?*

Whoa. Aren't you a big one.

"Where am I?" she asked.

The officer raised his eyebrows and tilted his head as he keyed the radio on his left shoulder.

She heard him say, "She's awake."

"Yes, I am." Her throat hurt. Had they intubated her? Gross. Some future doctor was going to think she was bulimic.

Wait. She was alive?

She frowned as the stale air, mixed with disinfectant and sweat, entered her nostrils, awakening olfactory senses that nauseated her. *This is terrible. I died and ended up in a landfill.* The high-pitch whine of the fluorescent lights and the monitoring equipment made her shake her head. Where was her dad?

Her brain turned up the volume. WHERE WAS HER DAD?

She started screaming. "Dad!"

The officer turned around, gave her a look of terror, and ran out.

"Dad! DAD!" She pulled at the tape holding the various tubes and needles. She knew it would hurt, but she was now a woman on a mission. Out came the first few needles starting with the one in the back on her hand.

She yelped and slid down the bed to get around the guardrails. Was she feeling dizzy? Nah. Everything was fine.

People ran in. Nurses. She put her hands up. "Stop! I won't put up a fight."

The three nurses froze in place and looked at her with eyes open wide. "Where is my father?"

All three of them glanced over at the police officer who had returned to the room. He gave them an almost imperceptible shake of his head. But Anna caught it.

"We can't tell you," the youngest nurse said. He didn't look old enough to drive.

The oldest nurse, a Hispanic woman old enough to have multiple grandchildren said, "Idiota." She nodded at the officer. "Ask him."

Anna stared at him.

"Get back into bed, young lady. Everything will be fine," the officer said.

She started screaming as loud as she could. When her chest hurt, she stopped and put her hand on her breastbone. She looked at Great-Grandmother Nurse who motioned for her to keep going.

She took a deep breath and screamed again.

"Will you guys do something?" the officer asked.

The three nurses grabbed her arms and forced her back onto the bed.

"No!" she yelled. "Let me go!" She thought she heard steps in the hallway when a man ran in with his gun drawn.

It was Terrell.

Anna stopped her banshee imitation. She smiled and the name slid out of her mouth. "Terrell!" She sat up and felt her shoulders relax. "Hi." A familiar face! Just what she needed. "You'll take me to my dad, won't you?"

"I shouldn't," he said as he holstered his gun. "But I will."

———

"I didn't know you were a screamer," Terrell said.

The nurses had procured a wheelchair for Anna and helped her into it when she almost fell sitting down.

"It's amazing how much more attention you get if you leverage female stereotypes."

"You're telling me," Terrell said. "I always knew you were a schemer."

They turned into a room down the nondescript hallway. And

there he was. Five other people were in the room, but they were just background noise.

Marshall looked tired, but he was alive. He was here. It wasn't something that happened in a fantasy or a dream.

He was back.

She smiled at him and he smiled back. "Hi, Squirrel."

"Hi, Dad."

"Careful. Your face is going to crack," Marshall said.

"Yours too."

———

"I need to think about it," Marshall said.

The white- haired man picked up a sheaf of paper that was on the mobile table over Marshall's bed.

"I'm an old man and you're taking advantage of me."

Anna listened to most of the conversation, but she zoned out every so often. This was the conversation she thought they would never have because they weren't going to survive long enough.

Anna said, "So you're offering us protection from a foreign power who shall remain nameless?"

"Yes," the white-haired man said.

Earlier, Marshall had introduced him as being from the State Department.

"What about protection from the Americans?" she asked. She could tell she embarrassed him. "And what about money? And a job? And a place to live? And anonymity? And, while you're at it, what happened at Area 51?"

"All of that is laid out in the paperwork, Ms. Wodehouse."

"Where's our lawyer? Neither of us is a lawyer," she said.

The white-haired man looked at Marshall as if they had spoken about this prior. The next man up was younger, with a crooked nose and a tie to match. He ignored Anna.

"Mr. Wodehouse, you know this is the best deal you're going to get. You and your daughter will be taken care of."

"Yeah, that's what they told me the first time," Marshall said.

They exchanged a few more words and Marshall's reluctant entourage marched out of the room. The white-haired man stopped when he got to Anna. "You may not know this, but your father is a great lawyer."

She was taken aback. Marshall, pretending to ignore her, gazed up at the ceiling and pretended to whistle.

"And," the white-haired man said as he walked out, "we're not going to tell you about Area 51."

With everyone, except for Terrell, out of the room Marshall said, "You're not the only one with a double major."

Anna shook her head. "That's technically a graduate degree."

Terrell walked over to the foot of Marshall's bed. "You had the Navy Seals on call."

"No, I didn't," Marshall said.

"They were waiting for me," Terrell said.

"Weren't we lucky?" Marshall asked.

"They were waiting. For me," Terrell said.

"I don't have that kind of pull," Marshall said.

"There was one team at City Hall, another on the Brooklyn side of the Brooklyn Bridge, and another at the 14th Street Pier."

"I had nothing to do with it," Marshall said. His eyes gleamed.

"Did you think you were invading Panama? How many FBI agents did you pull into this?"

Marshall's face went dark. "Only one other."

Terrell straightened up. "Del Kirby?"

Marshall didn't answer. Terrell tapped the footboard and bowed his head. He reached up and rubbed his eyes. "The paperwork said that Palma was responsible for the Seals."

"It's amazing what paper can say. Who knew he was such a forward thinker," Marshall said.

"What happened to him?"

"He was lost in the East River from what I heard. Maybe one day we can talk about all this over a few drinks." He slid down the bed and positioned one of the two pillows behind his head. "Maybe we'll just have the drinks."

Marshall asked, "Were you close?"

"Yes," Terrell said.

"You have my sympathies," Marshall said. "He was a good man."

Every muscle of Anna's body went into high alert when she stood up and hugged Terrell. As he hugged her back she said, "Watch those hands. This has an open back."

77

THE END

Wednesday evening

Outside Beekman Street, three police officers and one FBI agent ran toward Marshall and Anna as they sat in their wheelchairs on the sidewalk outside the hospital. It was a cold November evening and Anna was glad to have Terrell's suit jacket over her hospital gown. They wouldn't be discharged for another few days, but Marshall, growing bored, had shown her how to exit the building and not be seen by security.

Her father, biological or not, was a strange man.

She still struggled with forgiving him. Her life had been tortuous as she dealt with her abandonment, but she was grateful to have that choice to struggle with.

When the four agents of the law arrived and found Anna and Marshall sitting in their respective wheelchairs talking, they split up into two groups of two and stood on opposite sides of them at a respectful distance.

"They won't get in trouble, will they?" Anna asked. The wind picked up so she hugged herself for warmth.

"Nah. I won't mention it if you won't," Marshall said.

"I think you should take the deal."

"I don't want to," he said.

She knew he did. He was just being contrary to hear her opinion.

"Can I add a few things?"

"Like what? Tickets to the Smithsonian when no one else is there?"

"No. I have a friend who's in jail for helping me find you," Anna said.

"CrapIsKing?"

Damn! How does he do that? "Yes, CrapIsKing. He helped me put together a lot of the pieces. Including," she lowered her voice, "PRU-DENT RAINBOW." She looked around with her eyebrows furrowed. "Cue the spooky music."

"He's just another smart-alecky kid." Marshall shivered and pulled his sweater closed. "Like you." He smiled with his eyes. "I don't like him."

"You don't have to like him. You're not the only one with special friends." Would Anna have to give up the few friends she had even if they lived in the shadows of places like the dark web? In her world friends were hard to come by.

"I like that other guy. Agent Garrison. Special Agent. Garrison."

"Me too." *I'm going to miss him.*

———

The white-haired man was back. This time Marshall signed the papers and the man left after shaking hands with him and Anna. She didn't trust him, but at least she could always sue the government if things went wrong and not worry about him showing up and shooting her.

"So, there you go," Marshall said.

He spent most of his days in bed. It was going to be months of medical attention and physical therapy before he could do the things he used to.

"We are now part of WitSec," Anna said. She wasn't sure if the feeling in the pit of her stomach was anxiety or nausea. What kind of life would they have in Witness Protection? "And we've been pardoned," she said. Of course, Anna knew what she was being pardoned for, but what had her father done? Oh, yeah, he destroyed a multi-billion dollar government facility.

"Well, a secret pardon," he said.

"And we have a place to live."

"In a secret location," he said.

"No one will know what a pain in the ass you are," she said.

"I guess I should be grateful for small favors."

"CrapIsKing is free," Anna said.

"Also a secret pardon."

"And everything about HALON and those assholes is even more secret than before."

She'd been angry when told that the case against Monahan and Palma was shelved indefinitely. In seventy-five years there might be a Freedom of Information Act request for the files, but case files had been known to disappear before.

"We're under NDA now. Don't tell; don't ask," Marshall said. "We can go our own way."

Non-disclosure agreements were all the range in the private sector. This deal had one all its own.

———

Six months later, with the appropriate paperwork filed and all the proper arrangements made, and Marshall was feeling well enough to stand on his own, he and Anna arrived in their new home in an undisclosed location somewhere in the United States.

Four weeks later, when their case officer came for their first status check, she found their door unlocked and a note on their dining room table.

The note read: *Everything is fine. We'll be in touch.*

EPILOGUE

THE ACCIDENT

September 1991

Marshall Wodehouse couldn't stop blinking.

He was in a hospital with no memory of how he got there. The lights in his room were off and he could hear the sounds of heart monitors beeping, and buckets filled with water being rolled around on the floor just outside. The smell of ether was strong. Through the curtain surrounding the bed, he could see a New York State Trooper flirting with one of the nurses. Maybe she was a doctor.

The sounds were hushed. It was late.

He lifted his head and the room started to spin. His hands were cold. He pushed down on his elbows and lifted himself up a few inches. What he thought was a bed was a gurney. What he thought was a hospital room was a section of the ER.

The throbbing in his head was getting worse. "Nurse," he called out in a whisper that he hoped would be a shout. "Hello?" Why was there no clock on the wall? How was he supposed to know what time it was?

Marshall knew he was late for something, but he didn't know

what. He pushed his fist into his forehead. *Think, think, think.* Where was he supposed to be?

He let his head fall back on the gurney. He took in a deep breath. *Ingrid isn't here. That means she doesn't know what's happened. I don't know what's happened.*

The young woman he had seen earlier pulled back the curtain, just enough to step in, and pulled the curtain closed again.

"Hi. I'm Doctor Carver. I just want to ask you a few questions."

"What happened?" Marshall asked.

"You were in a car accident. Do you remember any of it?"

A car accident? "No. Was anyone hurt? Was anyone with me?"

"Can you tell me your name?"

"Arnold Dashman." He had stopped carrying real identification years earlier. Everything in his wallet read Arnold Dashman.

If you wanted real privacy, he would tell anyone at the Agency willing to listen, *you have to do more than just protect your identity. You have to create a new one.* Privacy was one of the few things on which he and Malik Palma agreed. That and paranoia.

Palma. Oh, no. Palma was doing something he wasn't supposed to, but Marshall couldn't remember what it was. Was it PRUDENT RAINBOW?

It was PRUDENT RAINBOW. Palma had already killed someone over it.

"Are you alright, Mr. Dashman?" Dr. Carver asked. "You just lost all color in your face."

He lay back down. "I'm fine."

"Mr. Dashman, I have terrible, terrible news," she said.

———

Marshall's bones hurt. He had looked under his shirt and found a rash on his skin from the seat belt that had held him in place. It had saved his life. It hadn't saved Ingrid. Maybe one day he would remember the accident and see her just before anything happened.

He'd reach out to her and tell her that he couldn't live without her. But he would have to. Live without her.

After the doctor had left he had turned on the gurney and cried to himself. He didn't want anyone to hear him or think for even a second that he wouldn't be able to care for the rest of his family. He and Ingrid didn't believe in baby sitters so Marshall also deduced one other thing. His daughter Anna was in the car with them and the doctor didn't mention her. Marshall was so overcome by the news of Ingrid's death that he couldn't speak, but his daughter's two-year-old face was the first thing he thought of when he had sobbed out all the tears he could spare for the one woman he had loved more than anyone, and anything, in the world.

He had to find Anna.

———

"Tired?" the state trooper asked. "You look distracted."

"One of the accident victims. He's got retrograde amnesia. He doesn't remember anything from the last few years. At least three years," Dr. Carver said. "He's lost everything."

"I'm sure his memory will come back."

"No, I mean, he lost his family. I just told him that he's lost his wife."

"That's terrible."

"He was in that three-car pile-up. I couldn't bring myself to tell him about his daughter," Dr. Carver said.

"How old?"

"Five."

"If you want, I'll tell him later," the trooper said.

———

Even traumatized, Marshall knew what he had to do. While he felt beaten up, he otherwise looked normal. They hadn't torn up his street clothes. He walked out of a side door, wedged it open just a crack, and walked back in through the ER entrance. The receptionist greeted him.

"Excuse me." He tried to appear lucid, but anxious. "Is this where the ambulance brought the car accident victims?"

"Yes," the young woman behind the plastic window said. "Do you have a family member involved?"

"I think so."

"What's the last name?"

"Dashman."

"Please accept my apologies. Let me get the nurse on duty."

"Wait," he called her back. "There was a little girl in the car with them. Where would she be?"

"She's probably still in the ER unless she was injured, in which case she might be in surgery or pediatrics." When the young woman stepped away, Marshall returned to the ER by the side entrance.

She's here. I can't lose her.

He would let Ingrid consume him later. He had to focus on Anna.

For now, luck was with him. Somewhere in the ER was his little girl. She was going to be afraid and he needed to find her. Fast. He grabbed a lab coat and a stray stethoscope, and walked up to a woman he hoped was a nurse. "Excuse me," he said and shook her hand. "I was called in for the little girl. The one in the car accident. Which bay is she in?"

"I'm not sure. I only started my shift a few minutes ago. Let me find out."

She left and he stayed behind. No use having someone like Dr. Carver see him wandering the halls.

The nurse returned within a few seconds. "I've found her, but there was already someone in to see her. Are you sure...?"

Marshall looked down at the frail little body. *We have to get out of here. If Palma knows that I was the informant to the Congressional Committee then we need to go hide. He's capable of anything.*

He picked her up after examining her, cut off the hospital wristband with her identifying information, and prepared to make good his next disappearing act.

The wristband fell to the floor unread.

———

A single security camera caught them on the way out, but he knew that by the time anyone noticed, he and Anna would be gone to places unknown. He carried her out and made a beeline to the back of the hospital. He would hotwire a car. Preferably one parked as far away from all the others.

He would drive as far as he could go, and steal another, and then another, then take a cab to some out-of-the-way hotel and disappear for a while. Until he could decide what to do. Until he could remember what happened.

Anna woke up. She sleepy eyes glanced briefly at him. She put her head back down on his shoulder, and fell asleep again. He smelled her hair. Ingrid must have changed her shampoo. He didn't recognize the scent. He must have really hit his head to forget the scent of Anna's shampoo.

If he was going to get this car going, he was going to have to put her down. He took her into the shadows and lay her down on the cool grass. Her eyes opened and she sat up the way two-year-olds sit up. He didn't remember seeing that outfit before, but he was sure it was hers. It had Ingrid's flare. A small gray trench coat over pink leggings.

He broke open the driver's side window and started working the ignition. After a minute or so he heard crying.

"Mommy," she said. She pointed to the ground where she had been pulling at the grass.

There was a baby bird on the ground. It had fallen out of its nest just after he'd placed her on the grass. Marshall picked it up and held it up to her. She began to pet it when it stopped moving. He took the little body, whose life ended before it had begun, and placed it at the base of the tree.

Anna held her arms out to Marshall and he picked her up.

"Don't worry, little girl. Everything's okay." He gave her a soft kiss on the cheek. He looked at her and felt his chest fill with pride and love.

He could imagine her growing up, always happy. He would always be there for her. One day, he knew, she was going to make a difference at something no one else would be able to. Was it just parental pride? He didn't think so, but he couldn't help himself in any case.

He pushed back some of her hair, looked into her two-year-old eyes, and whispered, "I love you, baby girl. You're going to be great."

FREE DOWNLOAD!

Get a free ebook copy of Part Two of the *Kidnapping Anna Trilogy, Kidnapping Anna: ADX Florence*, and a selection of short stories, after downloading the *A. B. Alvarez Reader* by going to https://www. abalvarez.com/free-book-en/!

CONNECT WITH A. B. ALVAREZ

Follow me on Bookbub:
https://www.bookbub.com/authors/a-b-alvarez

Follow me on Goodreads: https://www.goodreads.com/abalvarez

Read my blog: https://www.abalvarez.com/bonus-content

Visit the Brushed Steel Books web site:
https://www.brushedsteelbooks.com

OTHER BOOKS BY A.B. ALVAREZ

Please visit your favorite ebook retailer to discover other books by A.B. Alvarez:

The Kidnapping Anna Trilogy

Book One: Kidnapping Anna

Book Two: Kidnapping Anna: ADX Florence

Book Three: Kidnapping Anna: The Montague Tubes

Short Stories

Hilt

Destiny

Changing Gears

Embracing Shattered Glass

Fortuna's Head

Matador

ABOUT THE AUTHOR

A.B. Alvarez lives in New York. He doesn't have any cats, dogs, ferrets, or other pets. He does, however, have a daughter whom he did not kidnap.

ACKNOWLEDGMENTS

I wouldn't have made it to the end of Anna's adventures without the help of so many people to whom I must say thanks.

Thanks to my cover focus group: Jessica Lassiter, Lisa Serrano, Melissa Serrano, Cristina Valcarcel, Lindley Valcarcel, Luis Valcarcel, Silvia Velez, Bill Velez, Cathy Velez, Victoria Velez, Elizabeth Velez, Alicia Velez, Casey, and Marina.

Many thanks to my two incredible siblings: Silvia Velez, and Luis Valcarcel.

The incredible cover is due to the hard work of Cathi Stevenson from Book Cover Express, and the wonderful edits to Samantha Stroh Bailey. Thanks, as well, to Glen M. Edelstein from Hudson Valley Book Design for additional visual design on the excerpts.

A big hug and thanks to my daughter Lindley. You are an inspiration to me every day.

Again I must say: the wonderful parts of the book are so because the folks around me stopped me from screwing it up. The mistakes are when, once again, I didn't listen.

New York City and its residences were not harmed in any way in the writing of this book.

A.B. Alvarez
New York City, 2017